graveyard
of memories

ALSO BY BARRY EISLER

NOVELS

A Clean Kill in Tokyo (previously published as *Rain Fall*)
A Lonely Resurrection (previously published as *Hard Rain*)
Winner Take All (previously published as *Rain Storm*)
Redemption Games (previously published as *Killing Rain*)
Extremis (previously published as *The Last Assassin*)
The Killer Ascendant (previously published as *Requiem for an Assassin*)
Fault Line
Inside Out
The Detachment

SHORT WORKS

The Lost Coast
Paris Is a Bitch
The Khmer Kill
London Twist

ESSAYS

*The Ass Is a Poor Receptacle for the Head: Why Democrats Suck at
Communication, and How They Could Improve*
Be the Monkey: A Conversation about the New World of Publishing
(with J. A. Konrath)

graveyard of memories

A JOHN RAIN NOVEL

Barry Eisler

THOMAS & MERCER

Text copyright © 2014 Barry Eisler
All rights reserved.

Published by Thomas & Mercer, Seattle

www.apub.com

Amazon, the Amazon logo, and Thomas & Mercer are trademarks of Amazon.com, Inc., or its affiliates.

ISBN-13: 9781477818169
ISBN-10: 1477818162

Cover design by Jeroen ten Berge

Library of Congress Control Number: 2013917641

Printed in the United States of America

For the memory of Michael Hastings,
and in solidarity with Barrett Brown

Life can only be understood backward;
but it must be lived forward.

—Kierkegaard

chapter
one

If there's one lesson I learned early on during the decades I've spent in this business, it's that of all the qualities that distinguish a hard target from everyone else, among the most important is self-control. Yes, you have to be able to think like the opposition, which enables you to spot the ambush. And yes, you have to be able to take immediate, violent action in case—*oops*—your ability to spot the ambush fails. And yes, sentiment is a weakness. But fundamental to the rest is self-control. Because if you're not in control of yourself, someone else is, most likely an enemy, and in my business, an enemy isn't someone who wants the promotion you're after, or who covets your corner office, or who wants to beat you on the tennis court or golf course or display a better car in his driveway. In my business, an enemy is someone determined to end your life, and probably with the means to bring it about.

But there's another lesson, too, one that took longer to learn and that, in the end, is even more important. You have to live with what you've done. Not the killing as such. If you couldn't do that, you wouldn't have gotten into the business in the first place. You wouldn't have been able to. No, I'm talking about the consequences of killing—to your conscience, your relationships, your future, your life. If you knew at the outset what you understood at the end, would you make the same choices, take the same risks, accept the same sacrifices? No. No one would. You can't appreciate the weight of that burden until after you've assumed it. You can't comprehend what it really means.

But in Tokyo in 1972, I didn't know any of that. I was going on guts, instinct, and youthful reflexes. The real hard target skills came later. And acquiring them almost killed me.

I was a CIA bagman at the time, part of a cash-for-contracts program that got exposed in 1975. Google *"Lockheed bribery scandals"* and you can find out all about it. Well, not *all* about it. A lot more would have come out if I hadn't been on cleanup detail. You have to remember, the history the powers-that-be feed you always excludes what they managed to bury. Or whom.

My case officer was a guy named Sean McGraw, a cantankerous Korean War vet and old Asia hand. Christians in Action had some Japanese politicians on the payroll, an army acquaintance had told me, handing me McGraw's number, and they needed someone with an Asian face and local language skills to handle the cash. I had just returned to the States from Vietnam, having left the military under a cloud, the origins of which I was able to understand only years later. My mother, the American half of the marriage, had just died; I had no brothers or sisters; and America felt even less like a home than it had when my mother had taken me there at eight years old, after my father had been killed in the street riots that rocked Tokyo in the summer of 1960. Japan hardly felt like a home, either, but what other prospects did I have? Whether it was fate, or circumstance, or just bad luck, a lead to the secret world represented my path of least resistance.

The mechanics of the job were simple enough. Once a week or so, I would pick up a cheap shoulder bag from McGraw. Sometimes the handoff would be on a train; sometimes at a *tachigui*—eating while standing—street stall; sometimes, the symbolism not lost even on my younger self, in a public urinal. I would then exchange the full bag I was carrying for an empty one carried by a flunky from the other side, a plump and incongruously garrulous middle-aged Japanese guy named Miyamoto, who fancied floral-patterned ties that were flamboyantly wide and loud even by the tragic sartorial standards of the day. Two cutouts, so a lot of protection for the principals. Initially, I wasn't even sure who the principals were. I was mildly curious—I was barely twenty years old, after all, and didn't yet understand that the corollary to the expression "knowledge is power" is "knowledge can be dangerous"—but I had no real way of finding out. I'd looked inside the bag enough times to know it always contained fifty thousand dollars in cash. But the choice of currency offered no clues to the money's provenance, or to its destination. The yen was laughably weak; the euro had barely been conceived in Brussels, let alone born; and though Nixon had recently taken America off the gold standard, the greenback was still the world's reserve currency, accepted with no questions asked from New York to Riyadh to Timbuktu.

I was naïve, but I wasn't stupid. I knew anyone with working arms and legs could be a bagman. So I understood I wasn't being paid just to carry a bag. I was being paid to take a fall. If it came to that. The trick for me was to make sure it wouldn't. And that's where I screwed up.

I had just completed the exchange with Miyamoto in Ueno Park, part of Shitamachi, old Tokyo, the stalwart remnants of the city that had survived both the Great Kantō quake of 1923 and the American firebombs of some twenty years later. Even back then, the city was immense—the population over eleven million at night, with another two million swelling the streets and trains and office buildings during the day; forests of blinking neon in the entertainment quarters of Ikebukuro and Shibuya and Shinjuku; soot-covered, multilevel elevated highways dissecting neighborhoods and darkening sidewalks; everywhere a cacophony of truck engines and commerce and construction work. The war, barely a generation distant, still clung to the country's consciousness like a nightmare from which its people had only recently awakened, and the city's energy was not yet so much about pursuing prosperity as it was about putting distance between the hope and progress of today and the horrors and loss of the recent past.

I was wandering among the street stalls along Ameyoko, short for Ameya-Yokochō, Candy Alley, so named because the area's earliest commercial establishments had been *ameya*, or candy stores. That the moniker continued to work as shorthand for America Alley after the war, when the street had become an important black market for American goods, was mere serendipity. Either way, its stalls, most of them squeezed between narrow buildings to one side and the monstrous bulk of the elevated JR train tracks to the other, offered everything from spices and dried food and fresh fish, to clothes and hardware and sporting goods, to all manner of electronics—most of it cheap, all of it attracting crowds from morning to night.

It was a typical summer afternoon in Tokyo, which is to say oppressively hot, humid, and polluted, and the air was heavy with the smells of yakitori and *takoyaki* and the other street delicacies of Ameyoko. Hawkers held their hands to either side of their mouths and cried out, *Hai, dozo! Hai, irasshai!* this way and that over the sounds of nearby truck traffic and the occasional passing train, gesturing to shoppers being carried along by the slow-moving pedestrian river, entreating prospects, handing out samples, reeling in customers from the endless, shifting flow. I bought a cup of iced watermelon juice from a rheumy-eyed *oyaji* who looked like he'd been manning his fruit stall from the time the city had been called Edo. He took my ten yen with a wordless, toothless smile, and I moved off, sipping gratefully, sweat trickling down my back under the slight pressure of the empty shoulder bag I'd taken from Miyamoto, the late afternoon heat seemingly magnified rather than alleviated by the awnings draped haphazardly over either side of the alley.

I had no particular purpose in being there that day; I had simply wandered over after the handoff to Miyamoto, and was killing time before heading to the Kodokan to train in judo. I was new to the sport, but I liked it. It built on the wrestling skills I had acquired in high school, adding throws to takedowns, and armlocks and strangles to pins. I trained for several hours every day, the demands of my job being light and the hours flexible, and in only three months I'd gotten as good as any new *shodan* in the training hall. They wouldn't let me formally test for black belt until I'd been there for a year, though, and the restriction, which I found stupid and unfair, only spurred me to train harder so I could defeat more of my "superiors" and prove to them just how wrong they really were.

It's funny to consider how important things like that felt to me then. Proving people wrong. Fighting stupidity. Wanting formal recognition. It took me a long time to learn that proving people wrong is purposeless, fighting stupidity is futile, and formal recognition prevents people from underestimating you—and thereby from ceding to you surprise and other tactical advantages.

I turned left under the elevated tracks just as a JR train went by overhead, its roar rattling shop windows and obliterating the din of the crowd. Seconds later, it was gone. The crowd was thinner here, *pachinko* parlors and ramen shops and other such indoor attractions more prevalent than stalls. I passed a cutlery shop and slowed to examine the offerings displayed in its window.

Someone slammed into my shoulder hard enough to spill what was left of my watermelon juice. I looked up. A *chinpira*, low-level yakuza punk or wannabe, was glaring at me, the rolled-up sleeves of his black tee shirt showing off a weightlifter's muscles. "*Oi*," he growled, "*koryaa, doko mite aruitonen, kono bokega!*" Hey asshole, watch where you're going!

5

If the same thing were to happen today, I would apologize regardless of who was at fault, while taking a step back, blading my body slightly to offer a reduced target profile, and raising my hands palms-forward in a gesture ostensibly placating, but in fact tactically sound. I would convey with my tone, my posture, and my attitude that the aggressor was in fact fortunate I was being reasonable, while at the same time offering him no challenge, no insult, and no hostility, nothing but apparent respect and an opportunity to move on with no loss of face. I would do all this while simultaneously being intensely aware of what was happening at the periphery of the action, and never assuming the aggressor was alone. If he turned out to be too stupid to take the hint, I would act suddenly and decisively—no warnings, no posturing, no gradual escalation. And I would leave the scene the moment the threat was neutralized, keeping my head down and avoiding the eyes of potential witnesses.

But that would be today. Back then, I was fresh from combat, poisoned by testosterone, and filled with inchoate resentment at the world. After what I'd seen and done and survived, I didn't have to take shit from anyone, least of all some street punk who thought he could woof me into submission.

So rather than doing anything sensible, I took a step toward him and said, "*Urusei na, omae koso kiotsukero yo!*" Loosely translated, Go fuck yourself, asshole!

The *chinpira*'s eyes narrowed and his nostrils flared. "*Oi!*" he bellowed. I thought he was yelling at me, but then I saw movement beyond him at the entrance to the *pachinko* parlor—two buddies, similarly attired, similarly bulky, and now looking at me with malevolent intent.

Three against one, and each of them bigger than I was. The first guy raised his right arm and began to jab a finger in my chest. Apparently thinking this was going to be just a fight, or better yet, a simple beat-down. But I had already clicked into combat mode.

My muscle memory was built on wrestling then, not yet judo. I parried the incoming right arm with my left, caught him under the triceps with my right hand, swept his arm through and past, and simultaneously scooted behind him—a circle drag, a setup I had favored on the mat in high school. He tried to spin, but I trapped his right arm against his side, my hands circling his waist, following his movement so that we were facing his buddies, who were now moving in from only a few meters away.

What I did next was all stupid reflex. I dropped my hips, got my weight under him, and exploded up and arched back in a suplay, another wrestling move that had served me well in teenage competition. The *chinpira*'s body rocketed over me like the last car on an off-the-tracks roller coaster, one arm still secured to his side, the other flailing crazily. I saw the world sail past in my peripheral vision, the ground looming, and then there was a shock up my arms as the back of the *chinpira*'s head smashed into the pavement. I heard his skull split from the impact, followed an instant later by another *crack*—his knees hitting the ground as his legs continued to accelerate over and past his ruined cranium.

I rolled to my side and scrambled to my feet just as the other two reached me. I might have been able to escape, but stun-and-run wasn't yet part of my close-combat toolkit. My default was continuous offense. So I closed with the guy to my right, a tough-looking punk as ugly as a gargoyle, absorbing a punch to the cheek on the way in and going for his eyes. The other guy grabbed at me, got ahold of the shoulder bag, and hauled me back with it. I turned toward him, slipped an arm between the strap and my body, and bent forward. The bag came free and he stumbled away. The gargoyle jumped on my back. I tried to roll him but lost my balance. We both went down, but I twisted en route and managed to plant an elbow in his side so he took most of the impact. I scrambled on top of him, not yet experienced enough to know the importance of getting clear when there are or could be multiple attackers, grabbed his head, and sank my thumbs into his eye sockets. He screamed and thrashed and I bellowed back, an engine of destruction, gripping tighter, trying to force my thumbs through his eyes and into his brain. Then his buddy was back, throwing punches—I was lucky he didn't have a knife, or even a pipe—and I released the gargoyle and trained my attention on the more immediate problem. Whatever he saw in my expression, he decided he wanted no part of it. He turned and sprinted away. I almost went after him, the combat switch much easier to flick on than off, but somehow got hold of myself. I glanced around. A cluster of people had gathered in a circle around us, ominously quiet amid the background noise of Ueno. The first *chinpira* was lying still; the second was writhing on the ground, clutching his face and screaming. *Shit.* Instinctively I looked down and shouldered through the onlookers.

I circled back to the crowds of Ameyoko, drifted along for a few minutes while discreetly checking my back, then made my way to Okachimachi Station, where I caught a JR train. My heart was racing and my hands were shaking and I felt like I must look guilty of something. But none of the afternoon train riders, mostly uniformed schoolchildren and a few pensioners sweating in their shirt-sleeves, seemed to take any particular notice of me.

I got off at Tokyo Station and made my way to the street. It didn't even occur to me that someone might be trying to follow me and I was lucky no one was; I was just putting distance between myself and the incident. Once outside, I started to think.

How badly had I screwed up? I wasn't sure. I realized I hadn't handled the whole thing well. I wasn't a civilian; I couldn't afford to take civilian risks or indulge civilian impulses. I'd already done the exchange when the whole thing happened, yes, but I was still part of something covert, and I had to accept the discipline that came with that. I couldn't be discreet "when it counted." I had to remember, I had to know, that it *always* counted.

All right, a good lesson. But what had it cost me to learn it? Maybe . . . not too much. With luck, the one I took down with the suplay would be all right. But even if I'd killed him—and I knew from the sound his skull had made when it smashed into the pavement that I might have—how could anyone connect it with me? It was a random encounter in a random place. Even if the police were interested in investigating the death of some street hood, and they probably wouldn't be, witnesses wouldn't be much help. The only thing they got from me was the bag, which was presumably as anonymous and widespread a model as the Agency had been able to procure. Maybe my fingerprints were on it. But would the punk who fled with it share it with the police? More likely he had already ditched it. And even if he did share it with the police, and even if they could get a print, would they be able to match the print to me? No. They wouldn't. I was all right.

But the bag. Something about it was nagging at me. And then I realized.

There were three bags, all identical. The procedure was, I would pick up a full bag from McGraw and hand him an empty. I would then repeat the operation in reverse with Miyamoto. Someone always had an empty bag to exchange for a full one. So I had to have a bag for my next exchange with McGraw.

All right. Not such a big deal. I could just tell McGraw I had lost the empty bag.

But no, that wouldn't work. If I'd been careless enough to lose the bag while it was empty, I might be careless enough to lose it when it was full. I didn't want to seem like a screw-up, even though—or actually, because—right then the description felt pretty damn accurate. I liked the job and I needed the money. What else was I going to do? In those days, there was no contractor industry for spec op veterans. I'd just been run out of the military and knew there was some kind of cloud hanging over my head. By luck, I'd landed a plum job, one of the few of them, and I didn't want to risk it.

All right, then, I could just buy a new bag. No one would know the difference.

I suddenly realized I couldn't recall quite what the bag looked like. It was black, and made of leather . . . or was it vinyl? I hadn't really taken that close a look. It was about two inches wide, it had a zipper top . . . a brass zipper. Or brass color, anyway.

Shit. I headed back into the station and checked in several stores. There were numerous models like the one we used for the exchange, but I didn't see one I was sure was an exact fit.

I went out again, frustrated and angry at myself. I'd learned in the jungle to pay obsessive attention to my environment. Sounds and smells. Shapes and shadows. A broken branch, a displacement in the elephant grass. Birdsong, or its absence. It all meant something, and often what it meant was the difference between living and dying. And you had to learn to see the patterns in advance because when a silent foe is trying to kill you, you don't ordinarily get a second chance.

I suddenly understood this was all equally true in urban environments, and that I'd just been too stupid to realize it. Cities had their own rhythms, their own patterns, their own details that counted. I had to learn to pay attention. I had to educate myself.

All right, another good lesson. But what to do about the situation at hand?

I saw only two choices. I could buy a bag and, if McGraw noticed a discrepancy, just tell him it was the bag Miyamoto gave me—and then hope he didn't have a good way to check with Miyamoto. I could even buy three bags and swap them in one at a time until all the bags we were using were once again identical.

But if McGraw noticed anything amiss, I'd look like worse than a screw-up. I'd look dishonest, too. They might cut me loose for screwing up. But if they caught me lying to try to conceal it, I didn't know what would happen. What I did know was, getting cut loose might be the least of it.

That left only one real choice. Get in touch with McGraw and come clean. It wasn't such a big deal, was it? I hadn't really done anything wrong. At least, nothing I'd have to own up to. I mean, what were they going to do, kill me?

chapter
two

I contacted McGraw, who told me to meet him that night at a bar called Kamiya in Asakusa, one of the oldest districts in the city. I was curious about the choice of venue. Asakusa was in eastern Tokyo, and, apart from the Sensō-ji Temple complex and some related tourist attractions, presented a somewhat out-of-the-way district for foreigners and anyone else who favored the more cosmopolitan airs of the city's west.

After the evening's training at the Kodokan, I rode east on my motorcycle, a 1972 Suzuki GT380J in Roman Red and Egret White I couldn't afford but had gone ahead and bought anyway. I loved that bike, loved everything about it—the way it cornered, the growl of the engine, even the temperamental gear shifts. I called it Thanatos. Heavy-handed in retrospect, but it felt appropriate after what I'd done during the war.

It was near dark as I rode past Asakusa Station, the western sky holding some last lines of pink, the wind a welcome counterpoint to the heat still radiating from the pavement. I looked around, not sure exactly where the place was, and immediately saw a dense-looking concrete building, at the top of which KAMIYA BAR was emblazoned in impossible-to-miss red neon.

I parked the bike, crossed the street, and headed into a bright, spacious room with a half-dozen large communal tables and seating for maybe seventy-five people. Most of the vinyl-covered wooden chairs were taken, and the clientele seemed exclusively composed of blue-collar *edokko*, the salt-of-the-earth sons and daughters of old Tokyo, mostly middle-aged and older. The moist air seemed composed of equal parts oxygen, cigarette smoke, and the smell of draft beer, and the walls and low ceiling reverberated with laughter and boisterous conversation.

It took me a minute to spot McGraw. He was sitting with his back to the wall at a smaller table in a kind of alcove to my left, the one location in the otherwise open room that offered a modicum of privacy. He was the only non-Japanese in the place—a tall, meaty Scots-Irish, mid-forties, auburn hair going to gray. Not exactly inconspicuous in Tokyo, especially back then, when there were fewer foreigners, and I assumed he chose the out-of-the-way local place to lower the chances of anyone who mattered observing us together. He was already looking at me when I saw him, and waved me over.

I took the chair across from him. Even then, I wasn't comfortable sitting with my back to anything but a wall, but he hadn't left me a choice.

"Been here long?" I asked.

He shrugged. "Don't like to keep people waiting."

McGraw struck me as someone who would keep the pope waiting without particularly giving a shit, and I wondered about his response. I noticed wet ring marks on the wooden tabletop—too many and too thick to have been made by the nearly empty single glass set before him now. Had he been here long enough to drink several beers? I sensed he had. And was immediately pleased that I had noticed the revealing detail. It was exactly the kind of thing I knew I needed to improve at—and maybe I was already doing so. But why arrive so early? Getting the tactical seat, I decided. And ambush prevention generally. If someone is setting up for you, you preempt him. The same principle for the city as for the jungle.

Unless, of course, you're the one doing the setup. That would require an early arrival, too. But I was confident McGraw's tactics were primarily defensive, not offensive. I hadn't yet developed the paranoia, or call it wisdom, of experience.

"Beer?" he said.

"Sure."

He signaled the waitress for two, then looked at me. "What happened to your face? Looks worse than usual."

I'd learned to ignore McGraw's gibes—or at least to try to—by reminding myself it didn't matter if he liked me as long I got paid. The substantive part of his question was about my left eye, which was partially closed from one of the punches thrown in Ueno, the area around it purplish and swollen. Not quite a classic black eye, but in the neighborhood. I could have passed it off as a judo injury, but there was no point in lying—I was here to tell him the truth. Mostly.

"I got jumped in Ueno today," I said. "After the exchange. That's why I called."

This was the first time I had contacted him to set up a meeting. Ordinarily, it was the other way around. We used payphones and a preset code to keep our connection secure.

He studied my face, frowning. "What do you mean, 'jumped'?"

I told him what had happened. He listened carefully, asking for a detail here, a clarification there. The waitress brought our beers, but I didn't touch mine, wanting to get the story out first. From his patient demeanor and probing questions, I sensed McGraw would be a good interrogator, and I was glad I wasn't trying to lie. Though I was downplaying the way I'd gotten in the *chinpira*'s face.

When I was done, he looked away for a moment, drumming his fingers on the table as though contemplating something. "You're sure this was a coincidence?" he said.

"What do you mean?"

"When I hand it over to you, that bag has a lot of cash in it. Don't tell me you've never peeked."

Better to neither confirm nor deny. I said, "It happened after the exchange."

He looked at me for a long moment as though wondering how I could be so dumb. "Maybe these three geniuses didn't know you'd made an exchange. The bags are identical, remember?"

I hadn't thought of that. I said nothing.

He took a swallow of beer. "You're being as discreet for the exchanges with Miyamoto as I am for the exchanges with you, right? Turn a corner, stand next to him on a train, nice and casual, bam and you're done, right?"

I decided his characterization was close enough for government work. "Right."

"Then maybe they were following you, they missed your discreet exchange, so they thought you still had the original bag. You said the third guy ran off with it."

"He did, but . . . it felt like he was just grabbing at me to pull me off his friend."

"Why'd he run off with it, then?"

I had trouble articulating it, but I tried. "In fights . . . people repeat things. Whether it's working or not. When they grab something, they hold on. They don't think to drop it. Even if it's useless to them. That's what this felt like to me." Although, I had to admit to myself, it could also have been what McGraw was describing.

He nodded slowly, looking at me as though he could see right through me. "You do a good SDR after the exchange?"

SDR was Agency-speak for Surveillance Detection Run. A route designed to force any surveillance to either reveal itself or lose you.

"Of course," I said automatically.

But the truth was, I hadn't. I'd done the exchange with Miyamoto, and yet not only did I not do anything afterward to make sure I hadn't been picked up by anyone who might have been following Miyamoto, I didn't even leave the scene. I didn't game out whatever vulnerabilities the exchange might have created; I took no steps to mitigate; I just assumed I was done for the day and could wander among the Ueno street stalls as clueless and carefree as a civilian. It was sloppy, it was stupid, and it was nothing I was going to admit to McGraw. I'd learned my lesson. He didn't need to know how.

He took a long swallow of beer and belched. "Tell me again . . . what did you say to this guy?"

I shrugged. "It was all in Japanese."

"Translate for me."

"More or less, 'You're being annoying and you should watch where you're going yourself.'"

He laughed. "That's the literal translation?"

I took a sip of beer. "Pretty much."

"Son, don't bullshit a bullshitter. I'm not asking what you said, I want to know what it meant."

The first time he'd called me "son," I made the mistake of telling him to knock it off. Maybe it was just what he called everyone younger than, say, forty, but I didn't like it. In response, naturally, he'd made a habit of it. As I had made a habit of suppressing the urge to punch him in the throat in response.

"Maybe . . . 'Go fuck yourself, asshole,'" I said quietly, imagining I was saying it to McGraw.

He laughed again. "You do realize that 'Go fuck yourself, asshole' does not constitute de-escalation, right?"

"Yeah."

"Then why'd you do it?"

"I wasn't thinking."

"Is it going to happen again?"

I didn't like being talked to like I was a stupid child, even if in fact I had behaved like one. But I needed the damn job. And getting irritated at him now, I realized, would be the most elegant demonstration possible that it *would* happen again, or at least that it was likely. What I needed to demonstrate was the opposite.

"No," I said evenly. "It was stupid mistake, I shouldn't have let it happen, it won't happen again."

He nodded and took a swallow of beer. "Look, I don't want to make too big a deal of it. It sounds like no harm, no foul. Though we better hope you didn't kill that one guy, and that there's not a serious investigation if you did. But I can monitor all that. The more important thing is whether I can trust you. You have a little bit of a reputation, did you know that?"

I looked at him, tamping down the anger. First, talking to me like an adult chastising a child. And now, bringing up this shit. I reminded myself again that he might have been testing me—trying to get a reaction, or to determine whether I had sufficient self-control to prevent one.

I sipped my beer, deliberately casual. "I know there are people who might want you to think that, sure."

He smiled, seemingly pleased at the response. "Yes, there are. But why?"

I started to answer, then stopped myself. I didn't have to answer his questions; he was just making me *feel* like I had to. Probably deliberately. I had the sudden and uncomfortable sense that as deadly as I had proven myself in combat, in other contexts I was naïve. And part of my naïveté lay in my assumption that the people I was dealing with were no more cunning or sophisticated than I was. A mistake I never would have made in the jungle.

So instead of answering, I said, "Why don't you tell me?"

This time, he didn't smile. "Don't be coy with me. Your Agency contact with SOG. William Holtzer. You had a problem with him and you broke his nose. Don't tell me it didn't happen—two army officers saw the whole thing and filed a report. And don't tell me the guy was an asshole and deserved it. I'm sure he was and I'm sure he did. That's not the point, any more than it was the point with these punks you fucked up, or maybe even killed, earlier today."

I'd had enough of his condescension. Who did he think he was talking to? I imagined myself grabbing him by the hair, dragging him out of his chair, putting fear into him and maybe leaving some bruises to make sure the lesson took. But I willed the image away, knowing if I didn't, it would come to the surface.

He looked at me. "So what *is* the point, son? Why are we having this conversation?"

It's a test. Don't let it be personal. Don't let him push your buttons.

It wasn't easy, but I managed. I said, "The point is, I have to use better judgment and better self-control." I paused and looked at him. "Even when I'm dealing with assholes."

He threw back his head and laughed. "Yes. That is the point, exactly." He extended his glass. Reluctantly, I picked up mine. We toasted and drank.

He set down his empty glass heavily and wiped his mouth with the back of a hand. "Well, the good news is, from what you've told me, it sounds like it was just one of those things. I'll monitor the police reaction to make sure and let you know."

I nodded. "Thanks. And . . . I guess we'll need a new bag."

He stood and threw some yen on the table. "I'll get you a new bag, hotshot. But don't lose another one."

chapter
three

The following night, I trained at the Kodokan as usual. I was in a good mood. There had been no word from McGraw that day, which I took to mean I was probably safe. Whatever had happened to the guy I'd dropped, however much the police might be looking into it, none of it was being connected with me.

The *daidōjō*, where free practice was held, was massive—four tournament-size mats, high ceilings, stands for spectators, room for a hundred or more *randori* sparring matches. There was no air-conditioning, and in the summer the great hall was thick with the smell of decades of sweat and exertion. The *kangeiko*—ten consecutive days of hard training in the winter—was held early in the morning, when the air in the *daidōjō* was cold enough to fog the breath, and the tatami were as forgiving as cement. The summer equivalent was held in the afternoon, when Tokyo's scorching days were at their hottest. Making things harder as a way of fostering *gaman*—perseverance, endurance, fortitude—was a Japanese fetish, and I loved it. I rotated through a variety of partners, my *gi* soaked with sweat, the hall around me alive with grunts and shouts and the impact of bodies hitting the tatami.

I was taking a break on the sidelines when a tough-looking black belt—about my age and height, though at least ten kilos heavier—nodded his head at me and gestured to the mat where he was standing. He had thick lips, eyes too small for his face, and patches of dark stubble on his cheeks. There was something about him I instantly disliked. Maybe it was the curt way he'd gestured, as though he was summoning me and I was bound to obey. I wondered what he wanted. It was a rare black belt who would invite a white belt to spar with him—most likely it would be boring, and what glory was there in beating a beginner anyway? I looked back for a long moment, thinking of him as Pig Eyes and doing nothing to prevent the thought from surfacing in my expression, then walked over. He offered the faintest of bows and started circling to my right.

We came to grips, and I attacked with what at the time were my favorite combinations—*kouchi-gari* to *ouchi-gari* to *osoto-gari*; *ouchi-gari* to *uchi-mata*; *tai-otoshi* to a sneaky little standing strangle and back to *tai-otoshi*. I couldn't make any of it work. He was strong, and that was part of the problem, but it was more than that. I sensed he was using his greater experience to anticipate my combinations, and was subtly adjusting his stance and his grip to shut down my throws in the instant before I launched them. Occasionally, he would chuckle derisively at my futile efforts. I started to get angry, and therefore sloppy.

We circled counterclockwise, each of us right foot forward. I shot my right arm out, looking for a high grip, but Pig Eyes intercepted me, snaking his left arm inside mine and reaching around for a sleeve grip just above my elbow. I didn't like the grip he had taken and tried to jerk back, and as soon as I did, he punched his right hand forward, grabbed me high around the collar, and exploded into the air off his left foot. His right leg smashed down between my shoulder and neck as his head dropped back, and before I even knew what he was doing, his weight had dragged me down and I was crouching over him, my right arm and head trapped between his scissored legs, his back against the tatami as he looked up at me, bridging his hips, his ugly face twisting into a smile. I strained backward, my line of sight passing the stands as I did so, and I saw one of the guys who had jumped me in Ueno, the one who'd run off with the bag, leaning over the railing, watching us intently. He was smiling, too.

Before I could process any of it, Pig Eyes was pulling my right arm across his body and yanking me forward and down with his legs. I felt his left leg slide forward to figure-four his right ankle—*sankaku-jime*, a triangle strangle. My neck felt like it was caught in a vise, which effectively it was. I tried pulling his right knee down and circling counterclockwise to ease the pressure, but the strangle was too tight. I heard a dull roar in my ears like the crash of waves on the beach, and knew my brain wasn't getting oxygen—in seconds, I would pass out. I tapped his shoulder with my free hand, the traditional judo signal of surrender.

Many judo techniques, especially joint locks, are so dangerous that judoka develop a conditioned reflex to the feel of a tap, instantly releasing a submitting opponent rather than risk breaking an arm or separating a shoulder. The reflex can be so strong that judoka interested in judo for combat applications, and not just for sport, should take measures to guard against its accidental triggering in a real-world setting.

But not only did Pig Eyes not release his strangle in response to my tap, he actually tightened it, smiling while he did so.

Fear shot through me. I couldn't speak, but I tapped again with my free hand, harder this time. Pig Eyes looked at me, his smile intent, sadistic, and in that instant, understanding shot through me. The nature of the connection with the guy in the stands, how they'd found me, how they planned to get away after leaving me on the tatami . . . none of it mattered then and I gave it not one second's consideration. What mattered was that he was there to kill me, and that suddenly I was fighting for my life.

Which meant he was now fighting for his life, too. The difference was, he didn't know it. I did.

I stepped back with my left leg, creating precious space between our bodies, the world going gray at the edges now, the roaring in my ears the only thing I could hear. I groped with my left hand for his testicles. He understood at once and shifted right and left, but he had to trade mobility for the tightness of the strangle, and he could dodge only so much. I got hold of his package through the pants of his *gi*, but he bucked out of my grasp. The grayness crept in closer, the edges of my vision now speckled in black. Again I acquired my target and again he shook free. The gray was all I could see now, eclipsing everything, the roar in my ears fading, muffled, muted. With one last effort, I shot my hand forward and this time crowded my body in behind it, jacking him up onto his shoulders, raising his crotch higher. I felt the contours of a single testicle between my shaking fingertips. I put all my weight on him, pinning him in place. The world was melting and I felt myself dissolving into nothing, nothing . . . nothing but a small bulge that was somehow caught between my fingers, and the need, the final, desperate distress call sent by a dying brain, to crush that bulge into pulp.

And suddenly I could hear again, the echoing sounds of the great hall, and points of light crept into my vision, and I could feel something, a man under me, struggling, coughing, gagging as though on the verge of being sick. Through my confusion and vertigo, I managed to keep my weight on him, staying with him as he tried to twist away from me, taking his back, wrapping my legs around his, riding him, rolling him so that we were both facing the ceiling, buying myself time to return to my senses.

Seconds passed, and I remembered where I was and what had happened. I realized the precision squeeze I'd applied to one of his testicles had caused him more damage than I'd incurred from the moments I'd gone without oxygen. He was still flailing and retching, unable to prevent me from sliding my right hand under his chin, all the way across and around his throat, until my thumb was under his left ear, the knuckle over his carotid. I got my left arm under his left, took hold of his left lapel, and fed it into my right hand. Despite his debilitation, he recognized I was going for *okuri-eri-jime*—he tried to turtle his head in, and managed to get a hand to his own lapel to contest my grip. But too late. I crossed my left hand over and took hold of his right lapel, dragged it down, and ratcheted my right arm back, turning the collar of his *gi* into a guillotine. Soundlessly, he thrashed left, then right, but he was secure within my legs and there was nowhere for him to go. I arched back and cranked on his collar so hard I might have decapitated him. In extremis, he started frantically tapping my thigh, as though I was going to release him after what he'd tried to do to me. He clawed at my hands for a moment and then began to convulse. I realized he was vomiting, but with the strangle, the vomit couldn't pass. He was choking on it.

I looked up into the stands. Pig Eyes's buddy was there, gripping the railing, his face frozen in shock. I smiled at him, the smile no more than a grimace from the exertion I was putting into the strangle. He was watching his friend die in my hands and I was glad. I wanted him to see what I would be coming to do to him.

Then his paralysis broke, and he turned and ran. I saw no resolution in his expression or his posture, only panic, and I understood he wasn't coming to the aid of his friend, only trying to save himself. I had to choose—finish Pig Eyes, or pursue the one I sensed was the principal?

And suddenly I realized it was no choice at all. I couldn't kill this guy, not right in the great hall of the Kodokan in front of two hundred witnesses. Of course I'd be able to claim it was an accident, but a successful prosecution wasn't even my main concern. It was the investigation itself, the inevitable attention, that I couldn't afford. I'd seen dozens of people choked out on the tatami, two concussions, and one horrifically broken leg. Judo is a contact sport and accidents happen. But a death? That would be headline news.

Hating that I had to do it, I released the strangle and shoved Pig Eyes off me. His back heaved and a remarkable quantity of pressurized puke shot from his mouth and nose. I supposed that meant he would live. I scrambled to my feet and ran for the stairs. The great hall tilted in my vision and I threw an arm out to balance myself, still unsteady from the effects of lack of oxygen. People were watching me, maybe wondering if I was going to be sick and trying to get clear of the tatami before doing so. I blasted through the exit doors and took the stairs to the stands three at a time, one hand on the bannister because I didn't trust my balance yet. I yanked open the doors, but the *chinpira* was gone. There were two sets of stairs—he must have taken the other.

Maybe there was still a chance. I turned and bolted down the stairs, bursting into the lobby at the bottom and looking wildly right and left. No one, just the wrinkled *oba-san* behind the concession stand. "Did someone just run out of here?" I said. "From down the steps?"

She didn't answer, instead simply raising her eyebrows and tilting her head toward the main doors. I dashed out to the sidewalk and looked left and right. A few passersby, mostly salaryman types in suits heading home after a long day at the office, glancing in curiosity at a sweating judoka standing barefoot and wild-eyed on the sidewalk. There was no sign of the *chinpira*.

Damn. But maybe I could learn something from the other guy. I headed back inside and raced up the stairs. I paused outside the doors to the *daidōjō,* and saw a small crowd gathered around Pig Eyes. They were helping him to his feet, while giving wide berth to the area on the tatami newly decorated with his vomit. This wasn't going to work. I had to go.

I headed down to the locker room, quickly changed into my street clothes, and packed up my gear. No time to shower. I didn't want to answer any questions and I didn't want to linger another minute now that these people, whoever they were, knew they could find me here. I had to go. I didn't realize it at that moment—and couldn't have comprehended it, even if I had—but I was about to begin a decade of life as a fugitive.

chapter
four

Irode Thanatos to Nishi Nippori, the northeast of the city. Nishi Nippori was boring, blue collar, and unremarkable in every way—the kind of place no one who didn't live there ever bothered to visit. I had taken an apartment there because it was about the cheapest place I could find that still offered a station on the Yamanote loop line. Between the train and Thanatos, there was nowhere in the city center I couldn't reach in under a half hour. Something in a slightly more upscale neighborhood wouldn't have offended me, and better proximity to the Kodokan would have been nice. But even back then, there was something that made me want to stand aloof from the society around me. The war was a significant part of it, but not all. I'd been told in a hundred ways while growing up in Tokyo that I wasn't welcome, that I didn't really belong. Maybe keeping the city at a distance was my way of saying, *Fine, I don't want you, either.*

Feeling a little paranoid, I circled the block before arriving at my building, a squat wooden structure surrounded by weeds and skeletal bushes. It offered a view, to use that term loosely, of the Yamanote train tracks below, which were in the process of being expanded to handle Tokyo's ever-burgeoning population. I parked Thanatos in front and looked down. The tableau, bleached to harsh white by overhead klieg lights, was a forbidding mass of concrete blocks, giant transformers, and steel rails. Beyond it all, more gray buildings and a sky the color of ashes against the neon glow of the city beneath.

I realized it was lucky I'd taken this place, and not something on the main street among the various shops and restaurants surrounding the station. The decision had been driven entirely by the better rent—everything closer to the station had been more expensive—but now I saw there were tactical advantages here, too. If anyone knew where I lived—and after the Kodokan anything might be possible—it would be much easier for them to ambush me amid the tumult surrounding the train station. Here, they'd have no concealment. I'd have to remember that next time I chose a place.

I went inside, climbed the stairs to the third floor, and unlocked the door of the six-mat room. Tatami mats are a standard unit of measurement in Japan, and six of them come to about nine feet by twelve. I pushed the door open wide, and flipped on the light switch before going inside. I couldn't imagine anyone would be waiting for me, but not long ago I couldn't have imagined anyone tracking me to the Kodokan, either. The room was hot, still, and empty—just a futon in one corner, a desk and chair in another, and a bureau in a third. A kitchen that was really no more than a stove; a bathroom as spacious as what you get on a commercial airliner; a tiny *genkan* with a worn cabinet for storing shoes. More a bivouac than an apartment, but at the moment I wasn't sorry I didn't have much to my name. I hurriedly packed a bag: some clothes; my passport; a toothbrush. A handful of mementos from my childhood—letters from my parents, a few fading photographs, that kind of thing. Tokens and talismans of the past. I don't know why I grabbed anything that wasn't strictly practical. Maybe a desire to prevent anyone who searched the place later from uncovering something personal. Maybe a superstitious sense that the past was a kind of anchor that would keep me from drifting over a horizon I was still afraid to cross.

I headed out, pausing on each riser on the way down to check the stairs below me, sweat trickling down my back. I was used to moving with extreme care in the jungle—*pause, look, listen, move; pause, look, listen, move*—and there was something incongruous about doing the same thing now on a wooden stairwell. I told myself the precautions were temporary. The war in Vietnam didn't last forever; this one wouldn't, either.

Outside, I slung the bag across my neck and shoulder, got on Thanatos, and started up the engine. I paused to gaze once more at the industrial wasteland below me. It was ugly, and I had always ignored it before. But suddenly it felt like some comforting thing that was about to be torn away from me. I knew I couldn't come back until I figured out what the hell was going on. And, whatever it was, resolved it. But when would that be? And how?

I rode off, Thanatos's engine whining, wanting only to put some distance between myself and the apartment or anywhere else someone might lay an ambush. It started to rain but I didn't care; I was soaked with sweat already. The city went by me in a wet, gray blur, windshield wipers and umbrellas and dripping overpasses and eaves, droplets fine as mist suspended in Thanatos's headlight.

Away from the apartment, I started to relax a little and think. My gut told me the run-in with the three *chinpira* in Ueno had been a coincidence. If they were still after me, it was likely follow-up—revenge for the outcome of the initial encounter. But then how had they known where to find me?

I considered. They'd seen how confidently and crisply I'd dropped the lead guy with that suplay. Maybe they hadn't recognized the move specifically, but I was clearly some kind of grappler, and one whose skills were pretty sharp. If you were looking for a grappler in Tokyo, where would you start? It wouldn't be a sure thing, of course, but with nothing more to go on, you might want to check out judo dojos. And the one you'd probably begin with, because it's the biggest and best known, would be the Kodokan.

I chewed on that, and couldn't find anything wrong with it. Yeah, it made sense. A little imagination, a little diligence, and a little luck, and there I was. They'd probably been thinking it would be a long shot. They must have been thrilled when the bet paid out. Well, it hadn't paid out quite the way they'd been hoping. But damn, it had been a near thing. That guy in the *daidōjō* had been intent to kill me—I had seen it in his pig eyes. So who were these people? They had enough time and manpower to start casing judo dojos in Tokyo on a long-shot bet. They were motivated enough by revenge to invest that time and manpower. And they had at least one guy on the payroll who was willing to kill someone, in a public venue in front of two hundred witnesses, just because they told him to.

The only thing that made sense was, the three in Ueno hadn't been just punks. They were more connected than I'd guessed. Maybe one or more of them was a made member of one of the yakuza clans. Maybe I'd pissed off the wrong people.

The really wrong ones.

I nodded as I bombed along on Thanatos, pleased with myself for coming up with what felt like the right explanation. It was only later that I came to learn how dangerous it is to allow yourself to be seduced by that first attractive theory. If you don't keep testing for alternatives, you might wind up satisfying yourself with, and proceeding on, what's no more than a partial truth. And a partial truth, I would understand soon enough, can be more dangerous than a lie.

If the problem was yakuza, what would be the solution? McGraw might be helpful. At a minimum, he would have access to information I didn't. But if he knew I had this much heat on me, I didn't know what he might do. Probably just cut me loose. Damn it, I didn't want to take that chance. Better to just sit tight and wait to hear from him—he'd said he would be in touch as soon as he learned anything about what had happened in Ueno.

But shit, if I waited to tell him about the latest problem, he'd conclude—correctly—that I was holding out on him. He wouldn't like it.

It wasn't an easy decision, but I decided not to call him. Better to seek forgiveness than ask permission. I'd give him another day, anyway, and give myself a night to sleep on it.

Sleep. Where the hell was that going to happen? A hotel, I supposed. But not one of the big ones—I couldn't afford the rates, for one thing, and didn't want to deal with a front desk or other forms of scrutiny, for another.

I looked up at a passing road sign and saw I was heading toward Uguisudani—Nightingale Valley, though if nightingales had ever been prevalent there, they had long since departed for more salubrious climes. The area was known, even notorious, for streetwalkers, many of them of the "mature" variety, and for its profusion of love hotels. These were smaller establishments catering, as the nomenclature implies, to amorous couples looking for a place they could use for an hour or at most a night. Love hotels were numerous, they were discreet, and they were everywhere. Tens of thousands of people rotated through them every day, sometimes every hour. Finding someone hopping from one to another one night at a time would be a shell game not even the yakuza could win.

I parked Thanatos in a lot overflowing with bicycles and motor scooters, and walked along the road paralleling the train tracks. The night was still warm and it had stopped raining, but my clothes were wet, and I was cold to the point of shivering. I picked up a bento dinner from a vendor, and turned in to a labyrinth of twisting alleys lit in the gaudiest neon, the signs advertising places with names like *Pussy Cat* and *Aladdin's Cave* and *Casanova*, some with plaster cupid statues in front of them, others with illuminated fountains, each more garish than the next. Hookers dressed to cater to every fantasy—demure schoolgirl, brazen slut, leather-clad dominatrix—trawled the area, sizing me up, trying for eye contact, forgetting me the moment they failed to achieve it.

I ducked down a particularly narrow alley, and was rewarded with a place called Hotel Apex. Devoid of cupids, fountains, or even neon, it was obviously a no-frills place serving the lower end of the market. Just what I was looking for. I ducked inside the privacy wall and went through the front door. Inside was a tiny lobby—not much more than a vestibule—with a reception window to the left and an elevator the width of a coffin straight ahead. I stepped over to the reception window, and was surprised to see a very pretty girl sitting on the other side of the glass. I had been expecting an *obasan*—the standard receptionist in this type of establishment being an old woman.

The girl glanced up at me, her expression neutral. It looked like she had been reading something, though I couldn't see what. There was a tape recorder on the desk to her left, playing some kind of jazz. I loved Bill Evans—I'd first heard *Sunday at the Village Vanguard* when I was sixteen—but didn't know much beyond that, and didn't recognize what she was listening to.

"Rest or stay?" she asked, meaning did I want a room by the hour, or for the whole night. Her tone indicated supreme lack of interest, and pretty as she was, there was something tough in her demeanor, though I couldn't put my finger on what. She had long hair, at the moment pulled into a ponytail. Her skin was beautiful, I couldn't help but notice, and—in contrast to that of the professional girls outside—unembellished by makeup. Nor was she dressed to impress: a navy sweatshirt with *New York City* stitched across the front in faded gray letters; no earrings; no adornments. I wouldn't say I was particularly subtle or sophisticated at the time, but I got the message she was trying to convey: *I'm not trying to look good for you, so leave me the fuck alone.*

"Uh, a stay, I guess," I said.

She looked at me for a moment, probably wondering how someone could be so dumb that he wandered into a love hotel not knowing if he wanted a room for an hour or for the whole night. The fact that I was alone wasn't itself remarkable—plenty of men checked in to love hotels by themselves and then phoned for take-out. But they probably had a clue about how long they wanted the room.

Still, all she said was, "Four thousand yen."

I fished the money out of a pocket and pushed it through a hole in the glass. She scooped it into a drawer and slid a key in the other direction. "Three-oh-two," she said. "Left as you come out of the elevator."

I took the key and thanked her. She nodded and looked down again, to whatever I guessed she was reading in her lap. I wanted to say something more, but couldn't think of what, or even why. If she noticed my hesitation, she gave no sign.

After a moment, I turned and went to the elevator. I didn't want to think about my situation, or what I was going to do about it. All I cared about right then was the thought of the hottest bath I could stand, then my bento dinner, then sleep. I'd worry about tomorrow once it arrived.

chapter
five

I headed out early the next morning, wanting to get to a public
phone and see if there was news from McGraw. I took the stairs,
not liking that coffin-sized elevator, and as I reached the bottom, I
heard a man's voice, slurred and aggressive, shouting in Japanese.
"I already told you, I just want a rest!"

I opened the stairwell door and emerged into the tiny lobby. A
Japanese man in a rumpled suit and holding a cheap battered briefcase was standing in front of the reception window. I could smell
the sake from ten feet away. A salaryman, I guessed, who'd stayed
out too late and now just wanted a place to sleep it off for a few
hours before going back to the office.

"I understand, sir," came a soft female voice from the other side
of the glass. "A rest is two thousand yen."

I recognized the voice. The same girl who'd checked me in the
night before.

"I told you, I only have a thousand. I'll get you the rest later,
when the banks are open. When the banks are open I'll even give
you an extra thousand for your trouble. All right?" He shoved a
crumbled bill under the glass.

The girl pushed the bill back. "I'm sorry, sir. Full payment in
advance. No exceptions. Company policy."

"Fuck your policy!" the man shouted.

On a whim, I dug a thousand-yen note out of my pocket and

walked over to the window. I put the bill down in front of the glass. "I'll pay the difference," I said.

The girl looked at me like I was crazy. The money just sat there.

The guy turned to me. "Who the fuck are you?"

"The bank, apparently."

He glanced at the thousand-yen note, then back to me, his eyes narrowing. "Why would you pay for me?"

I glanced at the girl and shrugged. "A thousand yen seems like not very much to get you to leave her alone."

He leered at me. "What are you expecting, you pay for the room, you're going to follow me up there so I can suck your dick? That what you're thinking?"

All he was looking for, I should have recognized, was the opportunity to save a modicum of face. That, or it was some weird kind of projection or trial balloon, and he was hoping I really did want him to suck my dick. Either way, all I had to do at that point was calmly say something like, *Do you want the money or not?* It was clear he would have taken it.

But I was still young, and stupid, and prone to take things personally. I said, "I'm expecting you to take the money, while it's still on the counter. It'll be a lot easier to retrieve from there than it will be after I shove it up your ass."

His eyes widened and he flushed. His mouth twitched, but whatever he saw in my eyes got the twitching under control before it turned into words. He pushed the note under the glass. The girl took it and slid him a key. He picked it up and headed toward the elevator. As he got inside, he spat, "*Baka yaro!*" Asshole!

When he was gone, I turned to the girl. She was dressed as she had been when I'd arrived—obviously, she'd been there through the night. I was struck again by how pretty she was, and by how deliberately she seemed to be doing nothing to accentuate it. "You okay?" I said.

"Why would I not be okay?"

I was surprised. I realized I was expecting something more along the lines of a thank-you.

"I don't know . . . I just wanted to make sure. That guy was pretty belligerent."

"You don't think I deal with assholes like that about five times a week on average?"

"I don't know."

"Well, I do. Without anyone's help."

"I . . . guess I don't know much about hotels," I stammered.

"Yeah, well this one's not known for its high-class clientele. You want that, try the Imperial."

Why was I arguing? I had more important things on my mind. I shook it off and said, "I didn't mean to suggest you couldn't handle it yourself. I'm glad you're okay."

I moved off, out the exit door, past the privacy wall, into the narrow street. I was about to turn the corner when I heard the door open behind me. A voice called out, "Hey."

I turned. It was her. But it took me a second to process—what was she doing sitting?

No, not sitting. She was in a wheelchair.

She pushed the wheels to propel herself forward a few feet, closer to where I stood. Then she stopped and regarded me.

"Thank you," she said. But before I could overcome my surprise and come up with something in response, she had spun around and disappeared inside.

chapter
six

I checked in with the answering service I used. There were two messages. One from McGraw: I should meet him that night at a place called Taihō Chinese Cuisine in Minami Azabu. Okay, that was good. I didn't have to worry about the pros and cons of what he might make of my not calling him about what had happened at the Kodokan. I could hear what he said, and play the rest by ear.

The other message was from a good friend, maybe my only friend, who I'd been avoiding since getting mixed up with McGraw. His name was Tatsuhiko Ishikura—Tatsu—and we'd known each other in Vietnam, where the Keisatsucho, Japan's National Police Force, had seconded him to learn counterterror strategies. We'd gotten close there, being the only two Japanese speakers for thousands of miles, and had seen each other a few times since I'd arrived back in Tokyo. He was a good man—smarter than the people he worked for; stout as a bulldog and twice as tenacious; and funny as hell when he'd had too much sake and was venting about his "superiors." I missed him. With my mother gone, my father no more than the increasingly remote memory of a child, and no siblings or other close relatives, I felt worse than orphaned. I felt marooned, unmoored, capable of anything because no one knew me anymore, no one was watching. I needed a connection to someone, or something—even at twenty I understood that. But Tatsu was a cop, and working for McGraw and hanging out with a cop just didn't strike me as a particularly tenable set of simultaneous relationships. I felt sad about it, but there wasn't much to be done. If I didn't call back, maybe he'd stop trying. And that would probably be for the best.

I spent the day reading in a variety of parks and coffee shops, feeling like a homeless man. I was used to having time on my hands, but this was different. It was knowing I shouldn't go to the usual places. My apartment was out, obviously, and so was training at the Kodokan. Even the Tokyo Metropolitan Library, where I'd whiled away many an afternoon with a book, felt suddenly dangerous and uncertain. All I could do was drift from place to place on Thanatos, my bag slung across my back, feeling disconnected, in between, a *rōnin*—a masterless samurai, literally "a floater on the waves"—with nothing to look forward to but a single scheduled meeting, and nothing to do but wait.

I arrived in Minami Azabu on Thanatos at seven, and found a small storefront with a plain, unpretentious sign advertising TAIHŌ CHUUKA RYŌRI, a few pink, vinyl-covered stools and a wraparound counter just visible below the *noren* curtains hung across the frontage. I ducked under the curtains, and was struck by the tangy smell of fried rice and pork and spices. A man in a black tee shirt and jeans and white apron, who I understood immediately by his demeanor was the *maastaa*, or master, stood behind the counter, studiously attending to the stove before him, the sounds of frying meat loud even amid the conversation of the small restaurant's dozen or so patrons. A woman alongside him who I sensed was his wife looked up and greeted me with a smiling *"Irasshaimase."*

I returned her greeting with a nod and glanced to my right—the one blind spot from where I was standing—and was unsurprised to see McGraw. Once again, he was the only white face in evidence; once again, he had a beer in front of him that I sensed wasn't his first. He was watching me as though wondering how long it would be before I finally noticed him.

I stepped over to his table and sat. He glanced at the bag I was carrying, but didn't comment, instead saying only, "You hungry?"

I hadn't been, but the delicious smell of the cooking had already changed that. "I could eat."

He called out to the woman behind the counter in passable Japanese that we would have two orders of *gyoza*, two of fried rice, and two Asahi beers. He seemed entirely at home. I wondered how he found these places, and whether he favored them more operationally or more for the food. Maybe both.

A pretty girl appeared from the back carrying a tray laden with beer. She looked like the woman behind the counter—the daughter, then, a family operation. She placed two bottles and a glass for me on the table, collected McGraw's empty, and went on to service other customers. McGraw picked up the fresh bottle and tended to his own glass. In Japan, failing to at least offer to fill your companion's glass is markedly rude. Maybe he didn't know, but I doubted that. Nor did he offer to toast, instead immediately taking a long swallow. Whatever. I followed suit, resisting the urge to say anything, reminding myself of my theory that McGraw used silence to draw people out.

He glanced down at my glass, from which I had taken only a small sip. "You might want to finish that," he said, his voice loud enough for me to hear but not loud enough to carry over the hubbub of conversation around us. "And maybe another, before I brief you."

Was that supposed to rattle me? It did, but I wasn't going to show it. "Up to you," I said.

"All right. Don't say I didn't offer." He took another swallow. "I have bad news. And worse news."

"Aren't you supposed to ask me which I want first?" I was proud of my apparent sangfroid. In fact, I was getting increasingly worried.

"You think this is funny?"

"I don't know. You haven't told me what it is yet."

He looked at me for a long moment, so much disgust in his expression I sensed he was actually relishing what he was about to tell me. "That kid you tuned up in Ueno," he said. "You killed him."

"Is that the bad news, or the worse news?"

"That's the bad news. The worse news is, he was the nephew of Hideki Fukumoto. Name ring a bell?"

"Should it?"

"If you know anything about the yakuza, it should. Fukumoto is the head of the Gokumatsu-gumi. The biggest yakuza syndicate in Tokyo, and therefore the biggest in Japan. You get it now? You fucked up. You killed a yakuza prince. A punk, sure, but a prince. And the two who got away? One was a nobody, relatively speaking. He's in the hospital, where they're not sure if he'll recover his vision. What did you do, stick your thumbs in his eyes?"

"Something like that."

"Something like that. Jesus. Well, the other was the dead nephew's cousin. You know what that makes him?"

"Fukumoto's son, I'm guessing."

"Well, listen to Albert Einstein here. I guess you're not as dumb as you act. And the best part is, the two cousins were close. Close as brothers. You want to know Fukumoto Junior's nickname?"

"I don't know. Do I?"

"Mad Dog. So you, genius, just killed the cousin of a yakuza named Mad Dog. Proud of yourself?"

I didn't say anything. I was suddenly scared, and I felt like McGraw could see right through my bravado.

The waitress returned with our food. But I had no appetite. I picked up a *gyoza* with my chopsticks, dipped it in sauce, and chewed it, barely noticing the taste. "What does this mean?"

"Mean? It means you need to get your candy ass out of Japan. And not come back, ever."

I shook my head. "I can't just . . ."

I stopped. I didn't even know what I was trying to say. What was it I couldn't do? Go back to the States, which felt like an alien planet when I'd briefly returned after the war? Admit I wasn't reliable even to carry a bribery bag for a bunch of corrupt politicians and businessmen? Accept that I'd lost my temper, and fucked up, and blown everything?

McGraw must have seen my distress. Uncharacteristically, his face softened. "I'm sorry, son. You're no good to me now. You're too hot. Word is, they already have a contract out on you."

"Yeah, I got that feeling. They already made a run at me at the Kodokan."

"What?"

I wasn't sure why he was so surprised. What did he think a yakuza contract entailed? I told him what had happened.

"Well, it's good you didn't kill the guy," he said, when I was done. "Bad enough you have the yakuza on your ass, you don't need the police, too. Now look, I'll make sure you get a ticket home. But that's all I can do."

I don't have a home, I thought. No, not thought. Realized. What the hell was I going to do?

He inhaled several *gyoza*, then tucked into the fried rice. I forced down a few more bites, thinking hard, looking for a way out.

After a few minutes, I said, "What if I don't want to go?"

He took an enormous swallow of beer and belched. "You stick around, the Agency will put out a burn notice on you. They don't want the attention, you understand? Or worse, they'll drop a dime. Not to the police. To Fukumoto, or to Mad Dog, or to whoever. A lot of people would be happy to have guys like that in their debt."

"Why don't you?"

He looked at me, his skin puffy, gin blossoms under his eyes and across his nose. But somehow, for an instant, I could see the formidable young man he must have once been.

"Because I'm not gutless. Because I believe in karma. Because if you get your shit together and learn to control your temper, you have your whole life ahead of you, and I don't want to be the one who cuts it short."

We sat in silence again, eating, McGraw with gusto, I with considerably less enthusiasm. My mind was racing, rebelling. Things had been okay. After some of the places I'd been, okay was worth a lot. And now this. It was a mistake. It didn't have to happen. I didn't want to go.

Something came to me. A long shot, but I didn't see a lot of options. "Who's my problem here?" I asked.

McGraw looked at me suspiciously. He chewed and swallowed. "What do you mean?"

"I mean, who's motivated to come after me?"

"I told you, Fukumoto and his son."

"Because I killed Fukumoto's nephew. The son's cousin."

"Is that so hard to understand?"

"But you said the nephew was a punk. A prince, but a punk. What did you mean by that?"

McGraw waved a hand dismissively. "The kid had a reputation. Trouble with the police. Multiple fuck-ups. High profile, low profits. He and Mad Dog were peas in a pod, and equally close."

"So this . . . problem I have. It's being driven just by, what, family honor?"

"'Just' family honor? Do you know anything at all about the yakuza? You think a guy named Mad Dog is going to turn the other cheek when someone kills the cousin who was like a brother to him? And Fukumoto Senior can't let this go. He'd look weak. He'd lose face. His enemies would move in. If he wants to prevent all that—and I promise you, he does—he needs to kill you, simple as that."

"Right, he has enemies. People who don't give a shit about the nephew. People who would celebrate if something were to happen to Fukumoto himself."

McGraw stared at me for a moment. Then he chuckled. The chuckle migrated to a laugh. The laugh became a guffaw. The guffaw went on and on. He looked at me, wiping tears from his eyes. A few times he tried to speak, but was unable. I watched him. I was tempted to make him stop laughing. More than tempted. And I could have. I could have made it so he never laughed again. But I needed him. Maybe I was learning to control my temper. If so, he had no idea how lucky he was.

Finally, his fit subsided. "Oh come on, son. I know you SOG guys are tough. But what are you going to do, take on the entire Japanese mafia?"

"From what you've told me, I don't have a problem with the entire Japanese mafia. Just with Fukumoto. And his Mad Dog son."

McGraw was watching me. He wasn't laughing anymore. "You're serious."

I said nothing.

"No," he said. "I can't authorize this. It's—"

"Who said anything about authorization? We're just . . . this is all just hypothetical."

He snorted. "Hypothetically, where would you get your intel? Their locations, movements, that kind of thing."

"Who could say? Maybe I could hear a rumor. An anonymous tip."

"Yeah? What would be in it for the informant?"

I looked at him. "That would depend on what the informant wanted."

He rubbed his chin. I thought he looked intrigued. Certainly he seemed to be considering something.

He went back to the fried rice. After a few moments, he said, "You need intel on two people. What if the informant gave you intel on three?"

I didn't even pause. "Then I'd take care of all three."

He nodded. "That might make it worthwhile."

"It would also have to make us even. The informant and me, I mean. Hypothetically."

It amazes me now, that something like that once struck me as tough negotiating.

"I'm sure it would," he said.

I didn't even pause. "All right. Who's the third?"

He looked at me for a long moment. "You sure you're up for this, son? Have you really thought it through?"

"Have you?"

"I just did. But you'd be the one taking all the risk. You really want that?"

"Who's the third?"

He shrugged. After a pause, he said, "Hypothetically? The third would be Kakuei Ozawa."

The name was vaguely familiar, but I couldn't place it. "Kakuei Ozawa . . ."

"The LDP *sōmukaicho*."

"The Liberal Democratic Party LDP?" This was the political party that had been running Japan since the war. And presumably, the primary beneficiary of the American largesse I delivered regularly in a briefcase to Miyamoto.

"The same."

"And . . . the *sōmukaicho*, you mean the chairman of the Executive Council."

"I do, yes."

"You're talking about the second most powerful politician in Japan."

"Third, actually, or even fourth. The secretary-general and the chairman of the Policy Affairs Research Council have more clout, at least on paper. But the *sōmukaicho* has the most influence over the day-to-day dispensation of patronage. More even than the prime minister himself."

"And you want me to waste this guy."

McGraw winced at my directness. "You want my help with your problem? Help me with mine."

"All I need from you is intel. You're asking me to pull the trigger. On an extremely high-profile target."

"I didn't know you SOG guys were so squeamish."

"If that's what you call my preference for not spending the rest of my life in a Japanese prison, then fine, I'm squeamish."

"You only go to prison if you're caught."

I didn't much care for how smoothly it glided out of his mouth. "What's that, the official CIA slogan?"

"No, our official slogan is, 'And you shall know the truth, and the truth shall make you free.' John 8:32."

"Odd choice of slogan for people who lie for a living."

"Sometimes, son, we're defined by our paradoxes."

"And sometimes by our bullshit."

He laughed. "Sometimes they're one and the same."

"Anyway. I'm not doing it."

He shrugged. "Up to you, hotshot. Nobody's holding a gun to your head."

I nodded, wondering whether that was true, strictly speaking.

He polished off the last of the fried rice and slid back his chair. "Well, good luck with everything. I'm sure it'll all work out."

"Wait a minute. What about . . . the intel. On Fukumoto. And his son."

"I thought you didn't want that."

"That's . . . you know I want it. I told you I did."

"And I told you what it would cost. You said you didn't want to pay. That's fine. Just capitalism at work."

"It's not capitalism. You're trying to gouge me."

"Call it what you want. Either way, it's what the market will bear. Or not."

I didn't answer. I was looking for a way out, and didn't see one.

He looked at me, as though wondering where he found the patience. Then he pulled his chair in again and leaned forward. "Let me explain something to you, son. We're not partners. We're not friends. We're not brothers-in-arms. This is a business relationship. You provide some benefit, and you represent a cost. Well, now your own damned stupidity has increased the cost you represent, by turning you into a shit magnet for the yakuza. You want me to keep you on the payroll anyway? Fine. Tell me what's in it for me. How are you going to increase the benefit you provide to offset the increased cost? Tell me. I'm listening."

I said nothing.

"All right then, I think I understand. You want me to keep you around, at increased risk to my own operation, and you want me to provide you with classified intelligence files to help you commit what the Japanese judicial system would surely call murder, and you expect me to do that . . . what, out of the goodness of my heart?"

Again I said nothing. Inside, I was smoldering. Half at the situation, half at the brutally direct way he'd just characterized it. He had me, had me so tight he didn't even have to pretend otherwise. I hated it. I hated that I had no choice.

"All right," I said. "You win."

He chuckled. "Don't think of it that way, son. This is business, remember? We're both coming out ahead."

I blew out a long breath, trying to shake off the humiliation. "What did Ozawa do?"

McGraw frowned. "What do you mean?"

"Why do you want him dead?"

"Listen, son, don't forget your pay grade. You don't need to know why. All you need to know is who. That's all."

Maybe I sensed this new thing he wanted gave me leverage I hadn't had earlier. Maybe I just couldn't tamp down the anger anymore regardless. I said, "Like hell I do. You want to keep me in the dark about a bunch of cash in a briefcase? Fine, I don't give a shit. You ask me to grease the fucking Executive Council chairman of the LDP? I want to know what I'm getting into."

He smiled slightly, as though impressed by my gumption. "All right. Suppose the U.S. government supported elements of the Japanese government. In exchange for the continuation of policies the U.S. government finds desirable. Maintenance of the mutual security and cooperation treaty. Keeping the Seventh Fleet at Yokosuka. The Marines on Okinawa. Purchase of aircraft from U.S. defense contractors. That kind of thing."

"The U.S. government bribes Japanese politicians?"

"Capitalism at work, son, how many times do I have to tell you? Each side has something the other needs."

"You mean, one has policies to sell and the other has cash to pay."

"Like I said, you're not as dumb as you act. Keep this up and you might start to understand the way the world really works."

I wondered for a moment if McGraw's insults might really be intended as terms of endearment. I thought it would be helpful if I could look at it that way. Otherwise, at some point I might lose my temper, as he liked to put it.

"So what's the problem with Ozawa? He's asking too much?"

"He's giving out too little. He seems to have developed the idea that the program is a private annuity. It isn't. And the people he's freezing out are beginning to squawk. As in, 'If we don't get dealt in properly, we go to the press.' They'll nuke the financial gatekeepers and the whole program along with it. We need someone who'll spread the wealth more equitably. Someone with a diplomat's touch, not a selfish entitled prick like Ozawa. Got the picture now?"

"I think so. How do I get to him?"

"I'll get you his particulars. He's no hard target. Should be a piece of cake for a SOG hard case like you. How it happens is your call. Within certain parameters."

"Which are?"

There was a pause, then, "Make it look natural."

"How am I going to do that?"

"What, now you're asking me to micromanage you? You'll figure something out. What we don't want is for the LDP Executive Council chairman to eat a bullet, not unless the coroner would prove it came from his own gun and by his own hand. He's not the prime minister, not even close, but a straight-up assassination of a prominent political figure would bring down way more heat than anyone is willing to accept. Do this well, and you'll be in a position to call in a lot of favors. But don't fuck it up. You'll find yourself in a very uncomfortable position if you do."

"Give me the information on the two yakuza first."

He laughed. "Do you know something called the 'call-girl principle,' son?"

"Not exactly."

"It means the value of services rendered plummets immediately after the rendering. Right now, you need me, so you like my price, or at least you're willing to pay it. Once I give you the two yakuza, all you'll want to know is what I've done for you lately."

"If I do Ozawa first, how do I know you'll follow through with the information I need?"

"If I don't, will you kill me?"

I looked at him, and a strange chill settled inside me. "I think I'd have to, yeah."

He laughed. "I told you. You're not as dumb as you act."

chapter
seven

B ack on Thanatos, bombing through night Tokyo, I was roiled
with conflicting emotions. Relief that I had a potential solution to my yakuza problem. Fear at how extreme and unlikely the
solution was. Anxiety at the implications of what I had just agreed
to do—those I could imagine, and even more, those I was probably
missing. But for now, there was nothing I could do but wait for
McGraw's intel and continue to avoid places like the Kodokan,
where Mad Dog and his friends would be looking for me.

I shoved it all aside and thought about the girl at the hotel,
instead. I liked how unruffled she'd been in the face of that drunken
guy's bullshit. And how tough she'd been with me after. And the
wheelchair . . . why? Something congenital? An accident? The reason
the sight of it had surprised me so much was that she had struck me
as so competent, confident, in control. I realized these weren't qualities I associated with someone needing a wheelchair, and that my
unconscious expectations were simply assumptions based primarily
on foolish prejudice, itself likely the product of a lack of thought
and experience. Was it weird I found her attractive? I decided I didn't
care. I didn't even know if she could have sex. But . . . I wondered.
Anyway, thinking about her was much more enjoyable than ponder-
ing the guerrilla war I was about to wage against mobsters determined to kill me.

I knew I shouldn't go back to the same hotel, especially not
twice in a row. But I told myself there would be no harm. It wasn't

like the girl knew my name, or even the first thing about me. There
was no way anybody could trace me there. One night, two nights,
it wasn't going to make any difference. I needed a place to stay. And
someplace familiar wouldn't be the worst thing.

It didn't take long to get back to Uguisudani, park the bike,
and run the gauntlet of streetwalkers again. As I walked through
the front entrance of the hotel, I was suddenly gripped by doubt.
Maybe I was being stupid. Maybe she would think I was a creep for
coming back. Maybe she wouldn't even be there.

But she was. A different sweatshirt this time—gray, and no
lettering. Other than that, she looked just the same. Just as good.

She glanced up and saw me. There was a pause, then she said,
"I didn't expect to see you back here." There was a slight emphasis
on the "you." Other than that, her tone was as neutral as her
expression.

She was listening to jazz again. I wondered who, and why she
seemed to like it so much.

"Yeah, well, the Imperial was full."

I thought that was reasonably funny, but she acknowledged it
with only the barest hint of a smile. "Let me guess. A stay?"

"How'd you know?"

"Intuition."

Her expression was still so neutral, I had no idea what she was
thinking. I said, "What are you . . . doing here? This job, I mean."

"What are you talking about?"

"I mean . . . you're young. You know, mostly it's an *oba-san*."

"You stay at love hotels often?"

I felt myself blush. "No. Everyone knows that."

She shrugged. "If you say so."

Man, I was really striking out. "So really, why?"

"The interesting people I meet."

The robot-neutral affect was killing me. Laughing to conceal my embarrassment at what I thought was a dismissal, I pulled out a five-thousand-yen note and slid it under the glass. "I guess it would work for that."

She slid the bill into a drawer and came out with a thousand-yen note. She held it, not yet pushing it under the glass, and looked at me as though trying to decide something. "A job where I can sit is good. One where I can sit and study is even better."

I grabbed onto the reprieve. "What are you studying?"

"English."

"Why?"

"Why not?" This time her tone wasn't neutral. It was vaguely irritated.

Jesus, I couldn't seem to say anything right. "I mean, what do you want to do with it?"

I thought I detected something in her eyes—amusement, maybe? As though I was a well-meaning pet that was maybe just cute enough to deserve a little patience. But overall, other than the fact that she was talking, there was no evidence that she was the least bit interested in me. It was disconcerting.

"You might have noticed, I need a job that requires a lot of sitting. If I speak English, maybe I can get something a little better than this one."

"I don't know. I speak English, and it hasn't helped me get the job I want."

"What job do you want?"

"I don't know. Maybe that's part of the problem."

That glimmer of amusement flashed in her eyes again, then was gone. "Do you really speak English?"

I nodded. "I'm half American." I didn't know why I said it. It wasn't something I ordinarily shared with Japanese.

She scrutinized my face, searching, I knew, for the mongrel in it. "Now that you mention it, I think I can see it. Your mother was Japanese?"

I shook my head. "Father."

"Where did you grow up?"

"Both places."

"You're lucky. America's where I want to go."

"Why?"

She looked around. "Because I hate it here."

Given my own love-hate relationship with the country, I wasn't sure how to respond. So I just nodded.

She looked at me. "You don't?"

"It's complicated."

"Were they hard on you?" She didn't need to be more specific than that. She was talking about the *ijimekko*—school bullies.

"Sometimes." A monumental understatement.

She held my gaze for a moment, then slid the thousand-yen-note under the glass, followed by a room key. I took both, feeling I was being dismissed, trying to think of something I could use to engage her further, coming up with nothing.

Finally, in a fit of creativity, I said, "I'm Jun." Jun was my given name, bastardized to John in English.

She nodded as though this was possibly the least interesting thing she'd ever heard.

"What's your name?" I said, going double or nothing.

She looked at me for a long beat. I imagined I knew what a microbe felt like under a microscope.

"Why would you want to know my name?" she said.

"I don't know. So I have something to call you, I guess. Wait, now you're going to ask why I would need to call you something, right?"

She raised her eyebrows and nodded slowly as though impressed by what a quick study I was.

"I don't know," I said, flailing but plunging ahead regardless. "In case I'm back here. If I come back, it could be the third time I talk to you. I feel like the third time I talk to someone, I should know her name. I'm not sure why. It just feels . . . like I should." I realized I was babbling and couldn't seem to find the off switch.

"I'm not familiar with that custom."

Jesus. "Yeah, well, I guess that's because I just made it up."

She smiled at that, I thought half out of good humor, half out of pity. "Well, Jun, if you come back again and we talk for a third time, maybe I'll tell you my name then."

I tried to think of something witty to say and couldn't. So I just nodded and took the key, then headed for the elevator. I hoped she would think my wordless exit was confident and cool. But I was pretty sure she knew better.

chapter
eight

I went out early the next morning, the same time as the day before. I wanted to catch the girl again before the shift change.

She watched me wordlessly as I slid the key under the glass. "Don't you ever get any sleep?" I asked, casting about for something to start a conversation.

She shrugged. "Sometimes I nod off. It's usually pretty quiet after three or four."

"Well," I said, screwing up my courage, "this makes three times."

She looked at me, saying nothing.

"So . . . you know, the custom. I thought you'd tell me your name."

"Doesn't feel like three times to me. I've been up all night."

"Hmm, I think that's a technicality."

"Just trying to respect your custom."

Was she trying not to smile? I couldn't tell. "You're really not going to tell me your name?"

"How old are you?"

The question caught me off guard. "Why?"

"Are you sensitive about your age?"

"What? No. I'm twenty." That was true. By about a week.

She raised her eyebrows. "Are you lying to me?"

"No, why would I lie?"

"Because you look like a kid."

I felt myself blush, doubtless reinforcing the impression. "People have always said that about me. I think it's because I have small ears."

"What?"

"It's true. Small ears make you look younger. Because your ears grow by about one one-hundredth of an inch per year. That's why old people have big ears. I read it in a magazine." I turned my head. The crew cut I'd worn in the military had grown out, but my hair was still short enough for her to see.

She took a long look, then laughed. "I think you might be right."

It was the first time I'd heard her laugh. I liked the fact of it as much as the sound. Before I could think of some way to keep the conversational ball in the air, she said, "Actually, I can't figure out how old you are. I was thinking pretty young. But with that drunken guy yesterday, you looked . . ."

She trailed off. I waited, wondering what she thinking. Finally, she said, "I don't know. Serious, I guess. Even scary. Not like a kid."

At that point in my life, girls were still a mystery, and trying to navigate the unfamiliar terrain of conversation with an attractive woman made me feel anxious and awkward. But violence . . . violence I knew. I supposed it stood to reason that I would come across as ungainly in romance, and confident, even imposing, in a confrontation. I could see where the contrast might have confused her. But it wasn't something I wanted to explain. Instead, I said, "How about you?"

"What about me?"

"How old are you?"

"Twenty-five."

"That's a good age."

She frowned. "Good for what?"

"I don't know. Just sounds . . . good." I imagined a fighter jet burning into the tarmac and exploding in flames.

She shook her head and laughed again. "Why aren't you in school?"

"You mean college?"

"Assuming you graduated from high school."

I hadn't, in fact, having skipped out during my junior year to lie about my age and join the army. But I didn't expect she would find any of that particularly impressive.

"I don't know. I guess I haven't gotten around to it."

The truth was more complicated than that. At the time, life in Tokyo's universities was dominated by various radical student factions, some complaining about Japan's complicity in America's war in Vietnam; others about how the American military was going to remain on Okinawa even after returning the island to Japan; and still others agitating for socialism, communism, real disarmament, discontinuation of construction at the new airport in Narita, and other such things. Several Tokyo universities had been paralyzed by student occupations and pitched battles with police—armed battles featuring tear gas, rocks, and staves. There had been rampages, bombings, arson, hundreds of arrests. I didn't see any real difference between the students and the Japanese Red Army, which was busy hijacking airplanes and taking hostages in pursuit of paradise on earth. At best, they all struck me as pampered narcissists and dangerously misguided dreamers. Maybe they meant well, but to me it all felt like the same undifferentiated mob that had meant well during the riots that killed my father. I'd seen how the world really worked, and had paid for the privilege. I had nothing in common with any of them. I would make my own way.

"How about you?" I said. "Did you . . . are you in college?"

She frowned, but with a hint of amusement. "Don't you have anything better to do than hang around here talking to me?"

"Not really. I mean, yes, but . . ."

She looked at me with an expression that could probably best be described as "charitable."

"Do you like jazz?" I asked, flailing.

"What gave you that idea?"

"Well, you're always listening to it on that tape recorder."

"I was being sarcastic."

I realized I should have quit while I was ahead. "Okay," I said, "I guess I should go."

"Okay."

"Maybe I'll see you later."

"Maybe."

"Bye."

She gave me a tiny wave, half friendly, half dismissal, from behind the glass.

I headed south on Thanatos for a while, going nowhere in particular, nursing my wounded dignity. Then I shrugged it off and started to focus. I stopped at a payphone and called my answering service, hoping I'd have some word from McGraw. Instead, the woman on the morning shift told me, "You have a message from a Miyamoto-san. He asks that you call him back."

Miyamoto? I wondered why he was contacting me. We'd had coffee together a few times—Miyamoto was talkative for a courier, and though I recognized social contact would at best be frowned upon by the people we worked for, I was too green to know I should rebuff him. He was friendly and inquisitive, unabashed about asking questions that were uncharacteristically direct for a Japanese: how was it to grow up in both countries, what was life like in the American army, had it been uncomfortable for me to fight in a western war against Asians, things like that. I liked that he took an interest, and that his questions were tinged with sympathy rather than judgment. He himself had fought with the Imperial Army in the Philippines, and though he claimed not to have distinguished himself, I sensed he was being modest. All soldiers are liars: either they exaggerate, or they downplay. I'd asked him what the hell he was doing carrying a bag at his age. He'd laughed and told me that as a younger man he'd foolishly made an enemy, and that this enemy, as chance would have it, had risen to prominence among the people with whom Miyamoto worked. The menial job was supposed to be an ongoing humiliation, but Miyamoto professed not to care. He loved Tokyo, he said, loved watching it change, the seasons along with the skyline. And the walking was good for him. Life was strange, and if it was his karma to be a courier for someone else's cash, why should he complain?

I considered. The call might have been routine—a cancellation, change of venue, some logistical thing like that. Or maybe he just felt like exchanging pleasantries over coffee again with his fellow bagman. But given everything else going on, I couldn't help feeling suspicious.

I made my way to another payphone and dialed. "*Hai, Miyamoto desu,*" the voice on the other end said. Yes, this is Miyamoto.

"It's Rain," I said in Japanese.

"Ah. Thank you for getting back to me so quickly."

"What's going on?"

There was a pause. "I would prefer if we could speak in person. Perhaps . . . coffee?"

A few days earlier, I would have met him without another thought. But now, I wasn't sure. Playing for time, I said, "Where? When?"

"Wherever you would like. Now, if that's convenient."

That he was willing to leave the location to me was mildly reassuring. Still, what did I really know about this guy? He might be yakuza himself, and maybe he was contacting me for this "meeting" on behalf of Fukumoto & Sons, Inc.

But I realized also that I had no good way to avoid him. Not if I wanted to keep my job. Once a week or so, he and I had to meet to exchange our bags. Which meant that, if Miyamoto were part of a setup, they could ambush me pretty much anytime I went to see him.

Which was itself mildly reassuring. Why go to the trouble of calling a meeting now, when there would be one in due course soon enough? Why take a chance on alerting me with something out of the ordinary?

Besides, he might have useful information. Maybe I was rationalizing, but on balance I thought the risks were worth it.

"I can meet now," I said, trying to think of the safest place possible just in case. "Where are you?"

"Shinjuku."

"I can probably be there in twenty minutes. Let me call you again and I'll tell you where."

"All right. That's fine. Thank you."

He sounded uncertain. Maybe he was bewildered by why I wouldn't name the place until later. That was also mildly reassuring—if he'd been too smooth about my reticence, I would have assumed he had reason to expect I might be nervous. As it was, so far he just seemed oblivious.

Still, I wasn't going to take any chances.

I rode Thanatos to Shinbashi, a business district in the southeast of the city. I called Miyamoto again from a payphone just outside the JR station. "Sorry," I told him. "I don't think I can make it to Shinjuku. How soon can you meet me in Shinbashi?"

"Shinbashi? Well, I could be there in a half hour."

"You know that row of banks—Taiyō and the Bank of Tokyo and Fuji? On Sotobori-dōri, with the view of the Kasumigaseki Building?"

"Yes."

"I'll meet you in the lobby of the Taiyō Bank in thirty minutes."

He hung up without objecting to my unusual suggestion of a meeting place. Maybe he thought I had something to take care of at the bank and was killing two birds with one stone. I didn't really think he was trying to set me up, and being so cautious felt a bit unreal to me. In the jungle, it had become second nature, but just as it had been at my apartment, here all the environmental cues were different. This was the city. Glass and concrete and lights; suits and cars and restaurants. Not the jungle. Not a war.

And then I thought of Pig Eyes at the Kodokan. The way his face had twisted into a smile as he tightened that strangle.

Tokyo *was* a jungle. Hell, the *world* was a jungle. And I damn well needed to remember it before someone else decided to remind me.

I walked the short distance to Taiyō Bank, these days known as Sumitomo Mitsui. There were six lanes of traffic across Sotobori-dōri and the area was bustling, but the uninterrupted clusters of buildings on either side of the street were all still low, no more than ten stories each and usually fewer, the sky wide overhead, the overall feel that of a medium-sized older city rather than a modern metropolis. But the Kasumigaseki Building, dominating the skyline to the west, made it impossible to miss that Tokyo was growing now, and growing almost impossibly fast. At thirty stories, the otherwise unremarkable structure had been Japan's tallest building when it was completed four years earlier, but it had held that title for only two years, the Tokyo World Trade Center surpassing it in 1970. Then the World Trade Center itself had quickly been eclipsed, by the Keio Plaza Hotel in 1971. Two more skyscrapers—the Shinjuku Sumitomo Building and the Shinjuku Mitsui Building—were already under way, each set to take its brief turn as the new titleholder upon completion, and on and on and on. And for every one of these record breakers, there were scores of other monoliths sprouting freakishly skyward all over the city. At that moment, Tokyo felt to me like a city still clinging to the vestiges of its childhood, and inexorably losing its grip. The city I remembered was receding rapidly, driven off by forces it couldn't understand, heading to oblivion, to be replaced by what I didn't know.

I had selected the bank for our meeting because I figured the street's heavy financial presence, with its concomitant guards and related security measures, would dissuade anyone who might have been planning anything untoward. But I decided not to wait inside. That's where I was expected, and I thought I'd do better to watch the entrance from a discreet distance, to make sure Miyamoto came alone. So I browsed among the storefronts at the opposite side of the street, lurking under the shadows of awnings to make myself less visible and to evade the murderous midmorning sun.

Miyamoto showed right on time, strolling down Sotobori-dōri from the direction of the station. Probably he'd taken the Yamanote from Shinjuku. I watched him enter the bank, then spent a few moments scanning the sidewalk in his wake. He seemed to be alone, but I couldn't be sure.

I strolled over and reached the entrance just as he emerged. "Ah," he said. "I thought you would have beaten me here."

"No, I just arrived. Do you mind if we take a cab somewhere? And then maybe just walk?"

"A cab? But I thought . . . but all right, if you prefer."

He seemed disconcerted and possibly a little nervous, but not unduly so. If this was a setup, I figured he'd be more on edge. Still, no sense taking chances.

We took a cab to Hamarikyu Teien, a centuries-old garden a mile or so to the southeast that was once the property of shoguns and emperors but that more recently had been opened to the public. Between the cab and a walk in the garden, I was confident anyone tagging along with Miyamoto would have to reveal himself.

The grounds were nearly empty, and we strolled along one of the paths in silence for a few minutes, clinging to the shadows of the trees to one side, avoiding the monotonous, leaden heat of the sun, the only sounds those of our feet crunching the gravel and the raucous cries of crows in the trees. Today, the garden is surrounded almost entirely by modern high-rises and has something of a fishbowl feel, but back then it was an unsullied oasis of green knolls and clusters of trees dense as broccoli stalks and ponds graced by gently sloping wooden bridges, with no hint of the metropolis around it beyond the occasional distant rumble of a train. As we moved along, I had several opportunities to glance behind us. No one had followed us in.

"I had forgotten how lovely Hamarikyu can be," Miyamoto said, dabbing at his perspiring brow with a handkerchief as we walked. "Why have we not been using it for our exchanges?"

His ordinarily earthy Japanese diction was markedly formal today. I wondered why. "Well, it's not too late."

He chuckled. "That is true."

I waited for him to go on, thinking of the way McGraw seemed to use silence to elicit information. But nothing came of it.

We came to the wisteria-covered trellis at the end of the Otsutai Bridge. A discreet wooden sign announced that waiting at the other end, on stilts at the center of the large pond, was the Nakajima Teahouse, serving potent green *matcha* and offering enviable views of the surrounding garden since 1707. I said, "Maybe a cup of tea?"

"By all means, yes. It would be good to sit. And to get out of this sun."

I couldn't disagree with any of that. And it would be good to have near panoramic views of the garden, too, in case I had missed anyone behind us when we first entered. I wondered if my caution was excessive. I decided I didn't care. There seemed little to be lost from it, and much that might be gained. And besides, it was only temporary.

We crossed the wooden bridge, the slight breeze over the water a godsend, and came to a tiny island of rock and thick shrubs, occupied almost in its entirety by the single-story, green-roofed teahouse. We removed our shoes at the entrance and followed a kimonoed hostess to a corner overlooking the pond, where we sat on the tatami and ordered the *matcha* Nakajima was known for. We were the only patrons, and the still space, redolent of cedar and old tatami, felt solemn to me, imbued with the ghostly presence of generations of previous patrons who had sat and chatted here as we did now, all of them long since dead. The waitress brought our tea on a small lacquer tray, set it before us, bowed, and left us to talk.

I picked up the earthen cup and went to take a sip. "Not like that," Miyamoto said. "Let it cool a little. Give yourself a moment to appreciate the aroma, the feel of the bowl in your hands."

I was a little surprised and didn't respond, though nor did I drink any tea. Miyamoto flushed. "I'm sorry," he said. "This is why my children prefer to avoid me. Only . . . it seems a shame, not to pause to appreciate the small things. So often they're more important than what we think are the big ones."

Somehow, being corrected by Miyamoto didn't sting. "It's fine," I said. "Do you know a lot about tea?"

He shook his head quickly as though embarrassed. "Very little."

I sensed he was being modest. "You've done *sadō*, I think," I said, referring to the Japanese tea ceremony—literally, "the way of tea."

"Perhaps I was exposed to it somewhat, when I was younger. But still it's really not right for me to suggest to others how they should comport themselves."

"No, I don't mind," I said, setting my bowl down. "Show me the way you would do it."

He beamed. "All right, since you ask. What's important is not much more than what I said. The purpose is to appreciate, to pay careful attention . . . to be mindful. Not to overlook what seems small but that is in fact significant. The rest is commentary, no?"

The word he used for "mindful" was *nen*, which typically means "sense" or "feeling." If he hadn't offered the additional context, I wouldn't have quite understood his meaning. I nodded and followed his lead, holding the bowl, appreciating the aroma, savoring the taste. At first I was just being polite, but after a few moments, I started to wonder if he might have a point. I knew there were tradecraft things I'd been missing. Why wouldn't there be everyday things, as well? What would it cost to become more heedful of those things . . . and would the practice of becoming more heedful of one naturally cause me to become more heedful of the other? I thought this *nen* was an attitude worth cultivating. Not just to appreciate the things that make life worth living. But to be attuned to the things that can keep you alive.

When we were halfway through the tea, and he still hadn't mentioned why he had contacted me, I thought it was time to nudge him. "So," I said, "what's on your mind?"

He nodded emphatically as though he'd almost forgotten and was grateful for my reminding him. "Ah, an embarrassing situation," he said, setting down his cup. "Although I have an opportunity to resolve it."

"All right."

"The . . . funds we exchange. They are provided to various grateful recipients according to a formula designed and implemented by people far worthier than I."

"Okay."

"And, it seems, one of these recipients is less grateful than would be proper. He has made unfortunate threats about revealing the existence of this . . . assistance program that so many other people understand and value. As a gesture of goodwill, those other people attempted to propitiate him."

"And that didn't work."

"It did for a while, it seems. But having gotten his way seems also to have encouraged him. He is making threats again."

"That's regrettable," I said, mirroring his formal style, thinking that would make him more comfortable.

"Indeed. But I'm sure it will be dealt with. In fact, that's precisely what I have been given the opportunity to arrange."

I said nothing.

"What would be helpful, and most appreciated, is if someone could make this troublesome problem go away. For ten thousand U.S. dollars, and with no questions asked."

Well, his diction might have been the soul of refinement, but the message was blunt enough. And not entirely surprising, given the conversation that led up to it.

I wondered if it was just a coincidence. Or karma. Or something about my demeanor that was suddenly making everyone swoon for my apparent potential as a contract killer.

"Forgive my directness," I said, "but this is a pretty . . . sensitive thing we're talking about. Why did they put you in charge of it? I thought you were carrying a bag because you're on someone's shit list."

"Oh, I most certainly am. This is like the new Clint Eastwood movie, *Dirty Harry*. 'Every dirty job that comes along.' That's me."

"They're having you take care of this so you can take a fall after?"

"Only if something unforeseen were to occur. I would of course prefer that such a thing not come to pass. That's why I hope to rely on you. I know you. I feel I can trust you. And . . . from our conversations, I think you have the kind of experience I think would be relevant."

I didn't pause to consider whether those earlier, seemingly innocent conversations over coffee had in fact been more akin to job
interviews. Nor did I wonder if we ever recognize the forks in the
road we sometimes come to. They're not common in life, and they're
never marked. Certainly, I didn't recognize this one. Or maybe I
just didn't want to.

"I'm honored you would consider me for something this
important," I said. "But my experience was all in war. In a dozen
ways, as you know, that's different."

"Yes, but—"

"But that's only part of it. More important, this just isn't the
kind of job I want. I don't know what's next for me, but . . . it's not
going to be that."

"Perhaps it doesn't have to really be a 'next.' You could think
of it as a one-time-only opportunity. With a generous cash bonus
attached, of course."

"Yes, it is generous, and perhaps if I were a little bolder, I'd be
tempted. Have you considered trying to solve this problem . . .
yourself?"

He nodded. "I have. But strangely enough, such self-reliance
would be frowned upon. The powers-that-be wish to put distance
between themselves and the outcome. They would be uncomfortable if the same person were to receive their instructions and carry
out the act."

I shrugged. "Don't tell them it was you."

And in that instant, an idea blossomed in my mind, as complete and profound as an archetypal Zen satori. Call it enlighten-
ment. Call it insight into one's own nature.

Call it an awakening.

"That notion has also tempted me. But I'm afraid the consequences of being caught in such a deception would be . . . very dire.
I wish I were bolder. But I'm not."

"I understand. I'm not, either. I'm really very sorry."

Miyamoto nodded. He clearly had pushed as hard as he felt he could, and looked crestfallen that his efforts had come to nothing.

"There's really no one else you can go to with this?" I asked.

He smiled wanly. "My superiors will have alternatives, I'm sure. To be honest, despite the risks, I was glad the opportunity came to me first. I know they were using me as a disposable intermediary—I'm accustomed to that. But if I could have made it happen, it might have impressed certain people. I'm . . . embarrassed to admit this could even be a consideration. I wouldn't mention it, but you asked and it would be rude of me to be dishonest in response."

"I understand."

I sighed as though I was about to concede something and said, "What if I could put you in touch with someone who could help you? Would that be useful?"

He looked at me, his eyes bright with hope. "Could you?"

I shrugged. "I might know some people who I don't think would object to this kind of work. And who have the kind of experience you would find relevant. If you'd like, I could make an inquiry or two. If there's interest, I'd pass on your phone number. But beyond that, I wouldn't be involved. I'm sorry."

"No, please don't apologize. This would be very helpful and I'd be most in your debt. I would even insist on paying you a finder's fee for your important contribution."

"That is very kind of you," I said, my style again as formal as his, "but no, I would merely be offering an introduction of two people who I think might want to know each other better. It would be unthinkably rude for me to accept any kind of compensation for such a small favor as that."

Miyamoto smiled, understanding now that when I said I didn't want to be involved, I meant it. "Then I will accept this gracious favor as one generously bestowed by a valued friend. But only upon one condition."

"Yes?"

"That my friend should know I will now be in his debt, and that I hope one day he will be kind enough to allow me to do him a kindness in return."

chapter
nine

I left Miyamoto at Hamarikyu and walked back to Shinbashi to pick up Thanatos. I wondered if I'd been crazy to offer to introduce him to someone who could help him with his "embarrassing situation." But I sensed it was the right way to go about it. At least in general—the details still eluded me. I had to figure them out, and I knew I'd better get it right the first time. I doubted there would be any second chances.

I stopped at a payphone and checked with the answering service. McGraw had left a message: he wanted to meet at Zōshigaya Cemetery that afternoon. The message left me feeling equal parts relief and trepidation. I hoped there was no hidden message involved with his choice of venue. Maybe he was just being funny.

I ate a lunch of ramen near the station, then rode Thanatos northwest toward Zōshigaya. I knew the cemetery well—a serene stretch of green in Tōshima Ward, it had been a favorite of my mother's, especially during cherry blossom season when, lovely as it was, it was less popular than some of the city's other premier *hanami* locations, and therefore less crowded. She had taken me there many times when I was small, usually on the Arakawa-sen, which today is the city's sole surviving public tram line. Even back then, the trams were dying out, being buried by train tracks as fast as the city's wooden houses were being torn down and replaced by ferroconcrete.

I was still early for the meeting, so on a whim I parked Thanatos outside Waseda Station and boarded the Arakawa line, which would take me to Zōshigaya. A pastel-yellow train was already waiting at the terminal—a pretty fancy description for an open-air, street-level platform adjacent to the sidewalk—so I walked on, paid the fare, and moved past a dozen other passengers toward the back of the single-car carrier, really no larger than a bus. A young mother was holding her small son's hand by one of the windows. The child was asking, *Why aren't we going?* and the woman was smiling and explaining that of course we had to wait for the other passengers but that soon we would be off. I looked away, surprised by a feeling of overwhelming sadness. Some of my earliest memories were of my own mother taking me for a ride on the *chin-chin densha*, the ding-ding train, so named for the distinct double bell the driver sounds when pulling out of a station, and when the train started forward and the bell rang, I felt my eyes grow moist. My mother had succumbed to cancer just over a year earlier, while I was away at war. Her absence was still an acute ache in my life, and being back here on the train sharpened it. It wasn't just the sound of the bell—everything around me suddenly reminded me of what now was lost. The serene and sedate neighborhoods rolling slowly by; the tracks half overgrown with grass; the gentle swaying of the train and the *chunk-chunk, chunk-chunk* of the wheels passing over the ties. The *chin-chin densha* was still here, steady and stalwart, and I was glad for that. But I was riding it alone now, a *rōnin*, a revenant returned from some faraway place, my past and everyone part of it sundered, irretrievable, accessible to me now only as painful and haunted memories, some still sharp, some increasingly indistinct.

The train continued along at its leisurely pace, *chunk-chunk, chunk-chunk*, settling into stations along the way, waiting for passengers to board and depart, easing forward again with its musical *chin-chin*. I was the only passenger to get off at Zōshigaya. I waited until the train had pulled away, then walked across the tracks. Across from me, on the other side of a sleepy, narrow street, was the cemetery. But for a profusion of markers sprouting up from the moss-covered earth, it might have been a small forest planted in the midst of the city around it.

I entered along the northwest path, then stopped. Insects buzzed around me and there was a slight rustling of tree leaves. Other than that, everything was completely still. And yet, something didn't feel right. This was where McGraw had told me to meet him, but I realized there was no reason I had to approach from this angle, which is what he would have been expecting. I could as easily have approached through the cemetery from the opposite direction, or from any direction at all.

I shook off the feeling, thinking it must have been the sudden splash of green, the sound of unseen insects, that was triggering combat reflexes shaped in the jungle. McGraw had no reason to set me up. I was just being paranoid. Still, no downside to coming in along a less obvious route. I started to back up, but then saw McGraw, strolling along one of the east–west paths to my right, a map in one hand and a camera in the other. He looked like nothing more than a foreign tourist on an outing. Which I supposed was exactly the point. He nodded his head at me and walked over. Yeah, I was being paranoid. All right.

I had to admit, I was impressed by the choice of venue. I didn't think many foreigners living in Tokyo even knew about Zōshigaya. It was about as off the beaten track as you could reasonably get inside the Yamanote.

"You know your way around Tokyo pretty well," I said, as he approached.

He stopped in front of me and mopped his ruddy brow with a handkerchief. "Son, I'd have to be a piss-poor case officer not to know the local terrain well enough to exploit it."

Christ, he was an ornery prick. "I just meant you're not from around here. I don't think many foreigners know Zōshigaya."

He glanced at the bag I was carrying. "And you do?"

I thought of my mother. "I grew up here, remember?" I didn't see the need to share any details beyond that.

"Yeah, I guess you did."

I looked at the camera. "So if someone stops you, you're, what, taking pictures?"

"Are you going to teach me about cover for action now, son? You think the map and the camera are all I've got? I've been using the camera, it's not just a prop. So yes, if anyone asks, I'm making a pilgrimage to the graves of some of the famous people buried here. Lafcadio Hearn in particular. I've got the photos to back it up. From here and from some of the other cemeteries in Tokyo—Aoyama, Yanaka, you name it. The cemeteries of Tokyo are a hobby of mine, in fact, you get it? You want a cover to work, you have to live it."

I didn't respond. I couldn't deny, he was good at what he did.

"You satisfied?" he said. "You want me to run the same kind of test on you? Let me guess, you just came out here for the fresh air, is that it? You better hope that's enough on the day someone really probes your cover. Christ, I wish you'd shape up. I don't think you know what tradecraft even is."

I felt my anger kicking in. "Yeah? Why don't you teach me?"

"What do you call what I just did?"

I stood there, stung and smoldering. He was right. What I would have called it was an insult, but it was also, undeniably, a lesson. It was up to me which part to focus on.

I shrugged it off. "Where's the information?"

"Not here. I'm not giving it to you directly."

"Why not?"

"Because I'm not going to get caught handing over classified U.S. government information that could be used to prove I conspired to commit a murder. Call it my 'don't spend your retirement in jail' plan."

"I guess that's a good reason."

"It is. I'm glad one of us knows what tradecraft is."

I shrugged that one off, too. "Where do I retrieve it?"

"You know Shibuya Lion?"

"I know Shibuya, but I don't know a lion."

"It's a coffee shop to the right of Dogenzaka as you walk up from the JR station. Been there for about twenty years. Longer, if you include the previous incarnation, which was destroyed during the war but rebuilt to the same design. You can find it in the yellow pages. Go to the second floor, and sit in the fourth booth from the front alongside the windows."

"What if that booth is taken?"

"Then you'll sit somewhere else and wait until it's open. But it probably won't be taken."

"Okay."

"You'll find an envelope taped to the bottom of the seat. Do I need to tell you to read it, memorize it, and then fucking burn it?"

"I guess you just did."

"I'll say this for you, son. You may not be fast, but you're not ineducable, either."

"I'm glad to know there's hope."

He laughed. "I wouldn't go that far. Let's see how things turn out with Ozawa."

chapter
ten

Imade my way to Shibuya, and from there to the place McGraw
had described. It was at the top of a hill snaking off Dogenzaka,
the main artery leading from the station, an incongruous little
building with arched doors and windows, a red and blue tiled roof,
and a makeshift garden of potted plants lined up at its base. I parked
Thanatos, scoped the area on foot, and, finding nothing out of
place, went inside.

What I discovered surprised me: a space more akin to a cathe-
dral than to a coffee shop. The ceiling was low in back but open to
a soaring second floor at the opposite end; the walls were lined with
red velvet booths that might have been pews; and at the front,
elevated on a pulpit and rising all the way to the second floor, stood
a pair of massive and ancient-looking wooden speakers from which
issued an organ piece I recognized from the classical music my
father had favored—Bach's Tocatta and Fugue in D Minor. The
sudden organ music would have been unsettling in its own right,
but combined with the overall decor, it was downright spooky. I
wondered for a moment if fate weren't having some fun with me
just then, first with the reminders of my parents, and then with the
graveyards and churchlike buildings—all portents, perhaps, of a
direction I was traveling that was less a thoroughfare and more a
one-way street.

There were some flyers by the door—a local yakitori place;
some sort of live theater; a guy named Terumasa Hino playing

trumpet at a jazz club called Taro in Shinjuku. I guessed the various establishments in question paid Lion a fee for the privilege of advertising there, hoping coffee aficionados would also be attuned to yakitori and live theater and jazz.

I stepped inside and looked around. The light was low, mostly what was seeping through the opaque glass along one wall, but also provided by a few dim wall sconces and a glass chandelier up front. The air was redolent of decades of coffee and tobacco. Most strikingly of all, there was no conversation—the dozen or so customers, men and women of varying ages and attire, each sat silently, some reading, some sleeping, some swaying in slow rapture in time with the music. Other than the dramatic notes of Bach's organ piece, the room was utterly silent. I had the impression that whatever dust had collected here on the curves of the dark wooden pillars and among the stacks of hundreds of albums had lain undisturbed for decades.

I made my way across the back and up a steep, creaky set of wooden stairs, pausing at the top to look around. The atmosphere and decor were much the same on high as they were below, with another half-dozen customers silently enjoying their respite and reverie. Most were occupying the center booths, perhaps because they favored the acoustics in the middle of the room. I realized McGraw must have been aware of this tendency among the clientele, and chosen for the dead drop a booth less likely to be occupied. I didn't like him, but I had to acknowledge once again that he was a good case officer.

I sat in the booth McGraw had described, and waited a moment. An unsmiling waitress wearing an apron over her jeans came over and silently placed a laminated menu the size of a post card on the small wooden table in front of me. The paper inside the laminate was yellowed and stained, and I realized that Lion's scant offerings— essentially coffee, tea, and milk, hot and cold—had probably

remained unchanged since more or less the beginning of time. I
pointed to the entry for coffee. The waitress nodded, collected the
menu, and moved off. As she did so, I noticed that the varnish on
the table was so worn the wood was practically bare. I looked
around and saw a similar effect everywhere else—the floor, the seat
backs, even the wood around the window hasps—and I felt a sudden and surprising surge of affection for the place. In a dozen small
ways, Lion indicated it didn't give a damn how or how fast Tokyo
might be changing outside. It didn't give a damn about Tokyo,
period. This place had found the right way of doing things, and it
would keep on doing them without regard to fad or fashion.

The waitress returned in less than three minutes, carefully
arranged before me a small white cup of exceptionally dark coffee,
an even smaller bowl of sugar, and cream in a silver cup the size of
a thimble. The bill went next to it all, for whenever I was ready, and
then the waitress was gone, once again without a word. Her reticence didn't feel unfriendly, though; it was more like there was an
understanding here, a mutual comprehension, alongside which
words would be superfluous and perhaps even rude.

I reached under the seat and touched paper taped exactly where
McGraw had said it would be. But I felt no particular hurry about
retrieving and opening it. Instead, I closed my eyes, listened to the
music, and began sipping the coffee. It was ungodly strong but also
delicious, and I realized someone had employed a lot of care to
impart that much richness without bitterness or anything else creeping in to overpower the flavor. I had been expecting just a routine
cup of coffee, and was struck by the notion that even in an everyday
thing like coffee preparation, there was a way of doing things right,
with care and maybe even devotion. Maybe this was part of what
Miyamoto had been trying to describe as we had taken our tea at
Nakajima. I wasn't unfamiliar with what it meant to be ruthlessly
squared away—ask any combat veteran about the care that goes

into planning, training, weapons maintenance, and everything else on which your life might hang in the balance in the field—but this was different. Lion spoke of devotion brought to bear on small things, everyday things, things that otherwise might have seemed inconsequential or have been overlooked entirely, and like the confidence that characterized the place, I sensed this kind of everyday devotion was also something to which a person might want to aspire.

I pulled loose the envelope, opened it, and removed a file. There was a lot of good information: home and work addresses; known cronies and habits; a half-dozen photos; a brief bio. Married, two grown children. No known vices. He'd been a captain in the Imperial Army. Received a commendation for valor, and a leg wound in Manchuria. But that had been a while back. The man I saw in the photos was now sixty-something, thin and sallow-faced, probably from a lifetime of tobacco. His warrior days were behind him. Along with, soon enough, everything else.

I immediately understood the value of the extra photos McGraw had enclosed. A single shot can be misleading. Seeing the subject from multiple angles, on the other hand, at various times, in different clothes, and in varied surroundings, made a positive ID in person much easier and more certain. You really wouldn't want to drop some clueless civilian because of an accidental likeness to a single low-resolution surveillance photo.

Looking at the photos was weird. Not because it made me feel queasy. Rather, because it didn't. I was examining the face of a man I was going to kill, and I was as emotionally involved as if I were doing a crossword puzzle. I wondered about that. Was it because after all that time in the jungle, I had become inured to killing? Was it because no one knew me anymore, no one was watching, I had no one to account to?

What about God?

I laughed at that. My mother had tried to raise me as a Catholic, but war had deracinated whatever meager plantings her efforts had achieved. No God ever would have stood silent spectator to what I saw in Vietnam. To what I did there. Either there was no God, or there was and he didn't give a damn.

And besides, was the absence of feeling really so strange? Ozawa was part of a corrupt system. You take part in a system like that, you have to realize grievances aren't going to get aired in court, or worked out in group therapy, or solved with mediation. This guy knew the risks, and he took them. It wasn't my fault the risk/reward ratio wasn't going to offer the outcome he'd been hoping for.

It was a rationalization, of course. Even back then, I knew that. Maybe I needed the rationalization, like a shot of booze to get up my courage. The strange thing was, even knowing it was a rationalization didn't make it less effective.

People talk about morality. Sometimes I think there's just what you can do, and what you can't.

Well, I could. And I was going to.

chapter
eleven

Before leaving Lion, I memorized the Ozawa file, then walked outside and burned it as McGraw had instructed. I briefly considered saving it as leverage in case anything went wrong, but decided there was no point. There was nothing on any of the pages to tie them to McGraw, or to anyone else. I'd come to appreciate how careful McGraw was, and imagined he would have handled everything so as to ensure he left no fingerprints, literal or figurative. The person the file could connect to Ozawa, though, was me. Better to just get rid of it.

I took a long and aimless ride on Thanatos, setting Ozawa aside temporarily and thinking about how to communicate with Miyamoto, instead—mapping out the logistics, creating a coherent cover story, pressure-checking all of it. When I had a plan in place, I parked the bike in Shibuya and rode the Ginza line. It didn't take me long to find what I wanted—Gaienmae Station would work well enough. I walked up and down the platform, decided how I wanted to handle things, then got back on the train.

When I reemerged in Shibuya, it was late afternoon. There was still time to start my recon on Ozawa. The path to solving my yakuza problem went through him, and I wanted to get started.

According to McGraw's file, Ozawa lived in Kita-Senju, a neighborhood way out in the northeast on the other side of the Sumida River. I'd actually never been there, never having had a reason to go. Well, I did now. I stopped at a gas stand to fill up

Thanatos, then headed over, not sure what I would find, hoping it would be something I could use. Killing a guy was one thing. Making it look natural . . . I didn't know how the hell I was going to pull off something like that.

Kita-Senju turned out to be a quiet, unpretentious neighborhood consisting primarily of modest single-family houses interspersed with mom-and-pop shops, doubtless run by couples living over the store. Off the main thoroughfares, the streets were barely wide enough for Thanatos, their narrowness accentuated by the tendency of residents to line the few inches of curb in front of their houses with a variety of potted plants, and to park bicycles in front of those. The houses were of wood or ferroconcrete, some even of corrugated iron, most of them small and clustered closely together, but all well maintained. I liked the neighborhood. There was nothing fancy about it, certainly, but it felt real.

I found Ozawa's street and turned onto it, slowing as I came to his house. Unlike the other houses I'd seen, it was built partly of brick—unpretentious, but denoting a certain level of importance and success. Two stories, with just a little bit of land in front and to either side; surrounded by a short metal fence; a concrete parking space behind a sliding gate to one side. The parking space was currently occupied by a shiny Toyota sedan. McGraw's file claimed the household possessed only one car, and that Ozawa himself was provided a driver by virtue of his position as LDP *sōmukaicho*. I took this to mean the wife was home. Ozawa probably was not—a guy like that would rarely be home before dinner, and in fact probably not until well after, when his business socializing was done.

I drove on, feeling discouraged. The house itself seemed to offer few possibilities. I imagined I could get inside while the wife was out, but what then? And what if I was mistaken and the wife was home, or there was a parent or in-law around for that matter? These days, it's less common for Japanese extended families to all live under the same roof, but back then it was the norm. I pictured myself intercepting Ozawa as he got in or out of his chauffeured car. Sure, I could do it, but it would be about the least natural-looking outcome imaginable.

I circled the block and came to a large building with an elaborate, authentic Japanese roof, several dozen bicycles lined up before it at the curb. A Buddhist temple? I wondered how long it had been there—from the style and grandeur of those graceful, tiled curves, probably since at least the turn of the century. The word for "roof" in Japanese is *yane*—literally "house root," implying the importance of the roof as the basis for everything else. Whoever had designed this structure had taken that philosophy seriously, and I felt an odd sense of respect for and even connection with the architect, unknown to me and probably long since gone.

I came closer. A blue *noren* curtain with the name Daikoku-yu was stretched across the entrance, the three kanji meaning Great Black Hot Waters, and there were several dozen shoes placed in cubbies inside a small vestibule. Interesting. Whatever purpose it might have served originally, the place was obviously now a *sentō*—a public bath. Though they've been gradually disappearing since the war, back then the *sentō*—literally, "hot water for a penny"—served a vital function, fostering both a sense of community and good hygiene, and Tokyo still had several thousand, ranging from tiny no-frills neighborhood places to grand ones like this.

I thought about Ozawa's house again. It was impressive, but it looked fifty years old at least. Newer places were being built with their own baths, but there was a decent chance the Ozawa residence wouldn't have one. If that were the case, I imagined Ozawa would visit the neighborhood *sentō* regularly, perhaps every night. Or even if the home had its own bath, it would be a shame to live so close to a *sentō* as spectacular as this one and not make use of it. In fact, the more I thought about it, the more I realized that of course

Ozawa would be a frequent visitor. Japanese politicians always mixed with their constituents. They had to show their humble origins, demonstrate they were of the *shomin*, the common folk. And though Ozawa's house was better than average, a guy in his position easily could have afforded more. That he chose to scale back was another reason to expect I might find him at the *sentō*. After all, it wouldn't do to be living aloof in that better-than-average home and to never engage in a little old-school *hadaka-no-tsukiai*—naked bonding—with the hoi polloi. My gut told me the *sentō* was the opportunity I needed, either the place itself or somewhere between it and his house. I just had to find the right way.

I parked Thanatos and wandered the neighborhood on foot. There were two routes Ozawa might use—one along the neighborhood's little *shōtengai*, or shopping street; the other something of a shortcut along several much narrower roads. No way to know which he'd prefer, or whether he would consistently use one or the other. And even if I could know, neither potential route offered a way I could loiter inconspicuously. I decided to try the *sentō* itself.

I walked inside, placing my shoes in one of the cubbies at the entrance. The interior was old but well kept: sturdy-looking pillars ascending to a lovely, carved wooden ceiling; leather couches for anyone who wanted to relax before or after a bath; good lighting and immaculate lacquered floors. I walked over to the *mama-san*, who was seated behind a desk between the women's entrance to one side and the men's to the other, and along with the entrance fee paid for soap, shampoo, a towel, and a washcloth. No question the place would be popular in the neighborhood, but the fact that they were selling toiletries and renting towels suggested they also attracted visitors from farther away—maybe because of the grand old structure itself; maybe because in addition to the *sentō*, they offered an *onsen* or *rotenburo*, natural spring or outdoor bath. Certainly the *mama-san* evinced no surprise at the sight of an unfamiliar face—another good sign.

I walked into the men's changing area, undressed, and put my clothes and bag in a locker secured with a charmingly inadequate lock. Then I went through the sliding-glass doors and into the men's bathing area. Instantly I was enveloped by steam and heat and the floral smell of soap. High on one wall was the requisite mural of Mount Fuji, practically a national law. There was a lot of light—not just from fixtures, but from a pair of large windows along the high ceiling and a skylight overhead. About twenty men of all ages were seated on short stools before the spigots lining the walls, some shaving, some scrubbing, some dowsing themselves with hot water from wooden buckets. One man was helping a little boy into the tub, and for a moment I was struck by a memory of my own father, introducing me to the neighborhood *sentō* when I was no longer young enough to be bathed in the kitchen sink. I remembered that day clearly, the steam and the soap and the sight of all those unselfconsciously naked people. It had felt like a rite of passage, and my parents had been sure to mark it as such, with my mother fussing afterward about how grown-up I was now, and even my ordinarily distant father, perhaps pressed by some memories of his own, smiling with uncharacteristic sentiment, and for the second time that day I sagged under the paradoxical weight of memories of people and things that no longer were.

I shook off the feeling and walked to the back, where the tubs were located. There were four of them, forming an L along two walls: the main tub, with a cold plunge pool next to it, comprising the long end of the L; and two mineral baths, with signs advertising their benefits for muscle aches and a variety of skin conditions, forming the short end. The main bath was at the base of the L, between the cold pool and the mineral tubs, and was easily twice the size of the other three combined.

I went through another sliding door and found myself in an enclosed outdoor garden with another tub at the center, this one done in natural stone in keeping with the setting. A *ronteburo*, unusual for a *sentō*, and, as I'd suspected, probably part of the appeal for people from outside the neighborhood. For the moment, the *ronteburo* was empty, but overall, the place was pretty crowded. So while a steady flow of strangers would allow me to spend some time here to reconnoiter, the same crowds would pose a significant challenge when it came time to act. But one thing at a time.

I went back inside. Japanese bathing etiquette always involves extensive, even elaborate soaping and scrubbing and rinsing before entering the tub, but I went at it even beyond the already strict requirements, wanting to extend my stay as long as I could without becoming conspicuous. While I painstakingly went over every inch of my body with the soapy washcloth, I considered. I thought there was at least a decent chance I could acquire Ozawa here. If so, it wouldn't be hard to head out shortly before he did, and come up from behind as he headed home. But how was I going to make something like that look natural? I considered a judo strangle, but immediately rejected it. My strangles were pretty good, but I knew I had nowhere near the finesse to put in a fatal one and leave no visible damage to the throat.

I scrubbed a second time, then sluiced the water off myself with a bucket, refilling the bucket with increasingly scalding water each time. My father had taught me the trick to easing into the molten waters of the *sentō* that very first time he'd taken me, and I'd never forgotten. You can't wash with tepid water and then get right into the bath, he'd explained—the trick is to increase the temperature of the wash water until you can barely stand it. At that point, your body is acclimated, and you can get right into the bath. I did as he had taught me, and when I was done, my skin sunburn-red, I stood, walked over, and eased into the steaming waters of the large hot bath.

Within minutes, my muscles had been reduced to jelly by the pulverizing heat. As the tension flowed out of my body, I felt the anxiety about how to handle Ozawa dissipating from my mind. I've always loved the *sentō*, and this one was beautiful. I forgot about Ozawa for the moment and let myself be mindful, as Miyamoto had advised with regard to the drinking of tea. This was an old and noble building, used for a ritual that went back millennia, and I was here and I was connected to all of it, and that was good. That was enough.

A wrinkled *oyaji* walked slowly over, gripped the railing with fingers gnarled from arthritis, and eased himself into one of the mineral baths. I figured the minerals must help with the arthritis. I thought if I were lucky, I might get that old someday. But I didn't really expect it. I watched as a few clusters of people arrived and departed. No Ozawa.

When I had soaked for as long as I could stand and was about to hit the plunge pool to cool down, a man came in. I squinted through the steam. Ozawa? He'd been clothed in all the file photos, obviously, and it was throwing me to try to make the match with him naked. But there—the limp from that war injury. He came closer, pulled up a stool, and sat in front of one of the spigots. His back was to me but I could see him clearly in the mirror he was facing. It was him.

I hit the plunge pool, the shock of cold finishing off what the sight of Ozawa had already done to my reverie. Then I sat on the side for a few moments, cooling down, watching unobtrusively. A few people greeted Ozawa, and he exchanged brief pleasantries here and there, but this area was for serious bathing. Most real conversation would take place on the couches in the waiting area outside.

When he was done washing, Ozawa stood with some effort and headed over to the baths. The limp was quite pronounced. I watched as, eschewing the main bath, he eased himself into the available mineral tub. I supposed that, like the arthritic *oyaji*, Ozawa found the superheated mineral water eased the discomfort of his wartime injury.

I paused, that phrase *mineral water* repeating itself in my mind for no good reason. Unlike the other two baths, the mineral baths were one-person affairs, each not much more than a large tub. They were enclosed. They were small. And of course, they were filled with minerals. Salt, mostly. So salt water.

Salt water, which is especially conductive of electricity.

I was suddenly excited, and had to concentrate on maintaining my casual posture. Could I do this? Would it work?

The *oyaji* pulled himself up and went to rinse off. I got back into the hot bath. This time, I barely felt it. I waited and watched unobtrusively. After about ten minutes, Ozawa leaned forward, gripped the faucet of the tub, and pulled himself out.

The way he'd gripped that faucet . . . was that a habit? Things were more primitive in those days, ergonomics not yet a science, and the baths at Daikoku-yu were devoid of railings and handholds and steps. For anyone physically challenged—like the *oyaji*, like Ozawa—the most natural handhold to use when it was time to leave the bath was the faucet.

The metal faucet. The *grounded* metal faucet.

I got out of the bath again, letting one hand dip unobtrusively into the mineral bath on the way. I tasted a finger. Salty, as I had hoped. In the corner of the room, immediately to the left of the mineral-water baths and sharing a common wall with them, there was a door marked SERVICE. To its left, along the adjoining wall, was a spigot and stool—the last washing station along a row of ten. If I could get that station, I'd be not much more than an arm's length from the closer of the two mineral baths. Unless someone was at the station right next to me, I thought I might have the necessary freedom of movement to carry out what I was beginning to see in my imagination.

The problem was, I saw no electrical outlets. This wasn't completely surprising. Electrical codes were a lot less stringent in those days, and items such as ground fault circuit interrupters were not at all widespread. It would be dangerous to have an outlet in close proximity to the baths—it might encourage an idiot to use a radio, or a hair dryer, or whatever—something electrical that could accidentally wind up in the water. But there would be an outlet somewhere, and I had a feeling that service closet would be the place. I'd have to check a fuse box, too, of course, and ensure one way or another that any overcurrent protection would be inadequate. But that was a distinctly minor challenge. The main thing was, if I did things right, there would be no marks, no evidence, no signs of foul play. Just a man who, whether from the heat or from exhaustion or from some other nebulous thing, had lost consciousness and slipped peacefully beneath the water. An arrhythmia, maybe. Maybe an embolism. Maybe the random act of a cruel and capricious God. No way to know, really, and so there would be no investigation, only sympathy and sadness and speculation, and even these, I expected, would be short-lived.

The most immediate thing I needed was a way to look the place over, set things up, and do a dry run. It wouldn't do to drop something in the tub only to have—*oops*—a circuit breaker kick in and kill all the lights. I had to come back, when everyone else was gone.

I rinsed off, dried myself, changed in the locker room, and headed out. Ozawa was already gone. That was all right. The way he'd made a beeline for that mineral tub, I knew he was a regular. He'd be back. And I'd be ready for him.

I headed out, pausing while I knelt and tied my shoes to examine the lock on the front door. It didn't look like much—this was a bathhouse, not a bank, after all—but it didn't look like the toy locks they had on the clothes lockers, either. I could force the door, I was sure, but that would be noticed. I realized I didn't know anything about picking locks. And that I was going to have to learn. Fast.

I inhaled a bowl of *tachigui* ramen and a beer near the station, plus about a liter of water to replace what I'd lost in the *sentō*. It had been a long day, and on top of being tired, I felt half drugged from the excessive time I'd spent soaking in the boiling tub while waiting for Ozawa. But I really wanted to get started on my crash course in lock-picking. I wondered where I might find someone to teach me. It would have to be someone skilled, obviously, while also not unduly concerned about bonding requirements and the other such niceties governing the lock-smithing trade. Which implied . . . someone who Japanese society didn't fully accept, and who held himself apart from that society in turn. As I did. My mind immediately flashed on Shin Ōkubo, Tokyo's Koreatown. Yes, that felt right.

I didn't feel like riding all the way across Tokyo yet again that day. But what difference would it make? Shin Ōkubo had plenty of love hotels; nearby Shinjuku, even more. I could try to find the right person and then just spend the night in the area. It wasn't as though I had a fixed address to return to.

I shook my head ruefully. The problem wasn't riding all the way back to the western side of the city. The problem was, where I really wanted to spend the night was here, in the east. Specifically, in Uguisudani. I wanted to go back to the Hotel Apex and see the girl who worked there again. Which was idiotic, given the amount I already had on my plate, but still.

Well, I supposed I could just head over, look for the kind of guy I needed, then head back. It wasn't really so far, and rush hour was already long since done, so it wasn't as though I was going to hit traffic, neither on the way out nor especially coming back. Sure, I was on the run and mixed up in murder, but what did any of that have to do with maybe getting to know a girl a little better?

I was still young, of course. I didn't yet understand just how dangerous a rationalization could be.

chapter twelve

I bombed west on Thanatos, cruising along one of the elevated highways, the lights blurring past me, the cooling evening air glorious after the pummeling heat of the *sentō*. It took me less than a half hour to reach JR Shin Ōkubo Station, where I parked and started strolling east, along Ōkubo-dōri, the main thoroughfare. Once away from the blinding lights and giddy electronic music of the *pachinko* parlors surrounding the station, it didn't just feel like I was in a different section of Tokyo—it felt like I was in a different city entirely. The buildings lining the street were ramshackle, with an insane variety of tiny storefront restaurants serving *bolgogi* and *ogokbap* and every kind of kimchi, all of it advertised by laminated photographs with Korean and Japanese captions and by hawkers calling out in a mix of both languages to passersby from the sidewalk. The street itself felt narrow relative to the density of stores and restaurants, offering only one lane in each direction, and the crowded sidewalks would have been dim if there hadn't been so much indirect light spilling out of the densely clustered shops. There were karaoke joints and massage parlors; counterfeit handbag and perfume purveyors; all-night discount stores selling everything imaginable and all for under a hundred yen. I passed through air pockets perfumed by grilled meat, spiced vegetables, sweet pastries; tobacco and beer and sweat. But the kind of person I was looking for wouldn't have a shop on the main street. The rents would be too high there, and his trade wouldn't require the *shōtengai* foot traffic.

His customers would know where he was located, and they would come to him.

A kilometer or so from the station, the crowds began to thin. As packed restaurants gave way to shuttered shops, the sidewalks grew dimmer; the streets, quieter; the atmosphere, for my purposes, more promising.

I turned onto a narrow street lit only by a stand of vending machines. The buildings on either side were mostly of wood, dried and darkened by decades of heat and humidity, their corrugated awnings jagged and torn, exposed bolts bleeding rust. A mad profusion of wires and pipes clung to the facades like the tentacles of some exotic alien parasite, garbage piled in plastic bags beneath the tangled tapestry. All the stores seemed closed. But there were a few dim lights glowing amid the overall gloom ahead, and I moved toward them.

The first place I reached was a tiny bar, filled with eight laughing customers. The second was a Korean noodle place, similarly small, similarly filled. The third was a shop advertising itself in Japanese—and presumably also in Korean, which I couldn't read— as *Spaaki*, which in English would be Sparky. I thought perhaps this was a play on the English phrase *spare key*, and indeed the large image of a key on the bottom of the sign suggested I might have found the place I was looking for.

There was an old, emaciated man sitting at a table inside, a desk light on a swivel arm shining down before him and casting his face in shadow. His tee shirt sagged, and the white headband knotted around his temples and thick glasses perched on his nose made his head look too large for his body. A smoldering cigarette stub dangled from his lips like a growth. Several cooking knives were assembled in a row in front of him, and he was honing one of them with long, precise strokes across a grinding stone. There were clusters of electronics piled up all around—toasters, fans, a vacuum cleaner. This looked like my guy—a *benriya*, more recently known as a *nandemoya*, literally a "Mr. Anything," a local jack-of-all-trades who residents could come to with any household thing they needed help with.

I knocked on the glass. The man looked up from the knife he was sharpening and squinted. "Closed," he said, in Korean-accented Japanese, around his cigarette. "Come back tomorrow."

The man was obviously *zainichi*, as I had hoped. Ethnic Korean, marooned in Japan after the Korean War, welcome in neither country, and belonging to neither. Beholden to neither.

"I can't wait until tomorrow," I said, pulling a ten-thousand-yen note from my wallet and pressing it up against the glass. "Are you sure you can't help me now?"

He looked at me over the tops of his spectacles for a moment, then set down the knife he was working on and stubbed out the cigarette. He didn't look dangerous, but still I was glad he had laid down the weapon. It implied a certain baseline trust without which there wasn't much hope he'd be willing to help me.

He walked over and stopped on the other side of the door. "What's the emergency?"

"I need to learn how locks work."

He squinted. "You're locked out?"

"No. I just want to learn."

The squint deepened. "You want to be an apprentice? I don't need one."

"Not an apprentice. I want you to teach me."

"You sure you're not just locked out? It would be faster for me to let you in than to teach you to do it yourself."

"I told you, I'm not locked out. I don't know anything about locks. I want to learn. I'll pay you."

He looked at the ten-thousand-yen note, an encouraging hint of greed in his eyes. "Sure, I could teach you. But I'm not cheap, you know."

I realized I should have held up a smaller bill. But too late now.

"All right, teach me."

"Come back tomorrow."

"No. Now."

"Are you crazy?"

"Do I seem crazy?"

He grunted. "Crazy people don't always seem crazy."

I realized I had no answer for that. Instead of even trying, I knelt and slid the bill under the door. I stood. "I want to start learning now."

He stooped to retrieve the note, then straightened, silently examining it for a moment. He pulled a rag from his pocket and blew his nose so loudly the building practically shook. Then he cleared his throat, put the bill and the rag back in his pocket, glanced behind me, and, doubtless against his better judgment, opened the door.

"Is it all right if I come in?" I asked, not wanting to alarm him by entering too suddenly or without his explicit permission.

He squinted, which I guessed was his default expression for incomprehension. "How am I going to teach you if you stand out there?"

Fair point. I stepped inside and he locked the door behind me. Then without another word, he cleared the knives he had been sharpening and began pulling a variety of detached door locks from various drawers and shelves, placing each on the table in a row before retrieving yet another.

"How'd you know it was door locks?" I said.

He glanced at me. "Are you a bicycle thief?"

"No."

"Car thief?"

"No."

"Safe cracker?"

"No."

"Then it's door locks."

The guy was shrewder than he looked. I realized I had given too much credence to the scrawny body and the obvious age, and had underestimated him. Watching him set up what would be our makeshift classroom, I wondered whether there would be some value to that. Getting people to underestimate you. Not letting them see what was under the hood. Preventing them from seeing it coming. I thought of the Japanese expression *Nō aru taka wa, tsume o kakusu*. The hawk with talent hides its talons. It had always been just that for me, an expression. But for the first time, I felt an inkling of what it might really imply.

He finished assembling what he was going to use for the lesson and blew his nose again. My ears rang from it and I hoped it wasn't a habit of his. Though I sensed it was.

"I don't have another chair," he said, shoving the rag back into his pocket. "Why don't you sit?"

"No, no, that's fine. I'm happy to stand. You go ahead."

He nodded and sat on the other side of the table. I realized a second late that he knew I was going to demur, but this way he got credit for being courteous and the more tangible benefit of the use of the chair, too. I was beginning to think he was a clever old bastard. Which didn't bother me a bit. I certainly didn't want a fool for a teacher.

"We'll start with the basics," he said, pulling out a set of lock-picking tools from a drawer and adjusting the swivel light to his satisfaction. "The most common type of door lock is a pin tumbler. All the locks on this table are examples."

I looked at the locks he had assembled. "How long will it take?"

He set one of the locks in a vise. "To understand the mechanism? Five minutes. To learn to pick a pin tumbler lock slowly, in good conditions? An hour. To learn to open different locks fast, with different tools, in different circumstances? A long time. When you can open a lock in the dark and wearing gloves, you'll know you're good."

"Why would I ever want to do something like that?"

The guy laughed. He knew exactly why I might want to do something like that. But luckily, he didn't care.

I looked around the shop, suddenly fascinated. "How'd you learn how to do this? Locks, I mean. And fixing things."

He looked at me, perhaps pleased that I was seeing something more than just the facade. "I hold things in my hands," he said. "I ask them how they work, and I listen to what they say. And then I take them apart, and put them back together. I've been doing it since I was a little boy."

I looked at him, trying to imagine him as a little boy. Yes, I thought I almost could. It was like suddenly seeing him . . . more completely. Three dimensions instead of just two.

"Can anyone do it?"

He shrugged. "I don't know. Not many people do. They'd rather come to me. No one has ever asked me to teach him before."

The comment made me feel strange. Sad for the old man, but also mildly awed. A lifetime of learning, and he was about to share it with me for only ten thousand yen. That just a moment earlier I'd been irritated at myself for not driving a harder bargain made me feel vaguely ashamed.

The time went by quickly. Sometimes he would offer a suggestion—slow it down, easy on the torsion wrench, start with a different pin—but for the most part he watched me in silence, apart from periodic ear-splitting nose blows. At the end of an hour, I was reliably, if somewhat slowly, opening the various locks he had set out in front of me. It actually wasn't that hard—mostly a question of understanding the mechanism, and of patience and deliberation. After I had defeated each of the locks twice, he nodded. "You have a good touch," he said. "I think if you practice, you can understand the way things work."

I resolved that I would. And not just locks. Other things. Everything. As he said, it was just a question of practice. And mindfulness, of course.

I bowed, long and low to show my respect, then straightened. "I have a good teacher," I said. In Japan, complimenting a teacher would be considered rude—where would the student get the idea that he's in a position to opine on the quality of his superiors?—but it felt like the right thing to say to someone who'd never been a teacher before. And besides, he wasn't Japanese.

He returned the bow. "There's not much more I can teach you. About pin tumbler locks, anyway."

I smiled, taking this to mean it was either time for me to go, or to pay more money. "If I come back sometime, will you teach me other kinds of locks?"

He squinted and rubbed the back of his neck. "It's difficult, being so busy."

Busy? I thought. It looked to me like he didn't have anything more to do than sit here all day, tinkering with the appliances people brought him to fix and the knives to sharpen, maybe periodically rousing himself to let into a house someone who'd forgotten a key.

Then I realized. He was just haggling. It was the way this particular thing worked.

"Really?" I said. "Even on the same terms? Ten thousand yen an hour?"

He blew out a long breath as though he was about to make the most difficult concession in the history of negotiating. And maybe he was—because he must have known he could milk me for more than that. But he didn't. Instead, he just said, "Well, I suppose I could make some time. You're a good student."

I stood to go. "Oh, one more thing. Can I buy a set of those lock picks from you? To practice with."

He squinted. "You're not a licensed locksmith. It would be illegal."

I wondered what he would produce if I asked to see *his* license. But I realized that by "illegal," he merely meant, "expensive."

"How about another ten thousand yen?" I said.

He rubbed the back of his neck again and looked pained.

"Twenty thousand?" I said.

The old guy must really have taken a shine to me, because he didn't squeeze me for more than that. I thanked him sincerely for his time and expertise, and told him I would see him again. Then, armed and dangerous with my new skills and new tools, I made my way back to Thanatos. It had been a long and eventful day, and I was looking forward to a good night's sleep at the hotel in Uguisu-dani. And to seeing the girl, of course. It would be the third time we met, so hopefully she would finally tell me her name.

chapter
thirteen

The girl was there when I walked in. If she was surprised to see me, she gave no sign of it. She gave no sign of anything, in fact.

I walked over to the window. "Hey," I said, demonstrating my creativity.

"Hey," she said back. Somehow it sounded better coming from her.

"Well, I'm back."

"I can see that."

She looked good in her usual way. Ponytail, sweatshirt, no makeup.

"I mean it's our third meeting."

She wrinkled her brow. "Can I ask you something?"

"I guess so."

"Why do you keep coming here?"

I couldn't very well admit that it was because I wanted to see her, and I couldn't think of anything else, so I said nothing.

"I mean, the first time, I had no idea. I just figured you needed a place to spend the night for some reason. You're a little younger and less corporate-looking than most of the clientele, but I figured, I don't know, maybe your girlfriend threw you out."

I didn't say anything, and she went on. "The second night I told myself the same thing. But now I'm thinking, either you're in some kind of trouble and trying to hide from it, or this is about me. Or both."

Jesus, I thought. I'd been focusing so much on my own needs, my own outlook, that I hadn't considered what things must have looked like from her perspective. That failure to consider the view from the other side was stupid. Here, the penalty was nothing more than embarrassment. In another context, the penalty could be considerably worse.

"It's a little bit of both," I said, not knowing how I could coherently suggest otherwise.

"What kind of trouble are you in?"

I was a little disappointed she was more interested in that side of the story. "Nothing I can't handle."

She laughed. "How many people do you think have been in over their heads, and said that right before they drowned?"

I didn't have an answer for that. I said, "Are you going to tell me your name?"

"Why do you want to know my name so much?"

"I don't know. I keep thinking of you as 'the girl at the hotel.' It just seems demeaning."

I was trying for funny, but she didn't laugh. Instead, her lips parted and her eyes narrowed and she looked at me for a long time, like she was *really* looking at me, like she was trying to figure something out.

Then the look was gone, replaced by a frown. "To which of us?"

"Well, I meant to you. But I guess to both."

Another long moment went by. I thought she wasn't going to tell me, and that I should probably give up. But then she sighed and said, "Sayaka."

I liked it. It suited her. Without thinking, I said, "Hi, Sayaka."

I immediately regretted it, thinking she would make fun of me for saying something so lame. But instead, she said, "Welcome back, Jun. Just don't expect any mints on the pillow, okay?"

I couldn't tell if it was just a joke, or if she was letting me know I wouldn't be waking up next to her. Or both.

"Do you work here every night?" I asked.

"I have a day off now and then. Do you stay here every night?"

I shrugged. "Like you said, I'm in a little bit of a jam. I need a place to stay while I figure it all out. It's not a girlfriend, though."

I realized that was actually a stupid thing to add. It would have been just fine if she figured my taste for stays at love hotels had to do with a domestic problem. I didn't need her speculating, or asking, beyond that.

"Well," she said, "I hope it's nothing too serious."

"I've seen worse," I said, which was true. I'd been chased by a North Vietnamese battalion in Cambodia. So far, at least, I'd take the yakuza any day.

"So . . . a stay?"

"Yeah, as usual." I pushed the bills under the glass, and she slid a key in the other direction.

"You know," I said, "I think I'm going to have this whole thing straightened out pretty soon. At which point, I won't be coming by anymore. But I thought . . . I found this great coffee place today, in Shibuya. You ever feel like a cup of coffee?"

She flushed, and for a moment, a look of consternation crossed her face. Then she said, "It's nice of you, Jun, but . . . no."

Damn. I'd really thought she was going to say yes. "Are you sure?"

She nodded. "I'm sure."

I should have just taken the hint. But it seemed like she was interested, somehow. I didn't get it. Without thinking, I said, "Why? It's just coffee. I know I'm a little younger, but . . ."

There was an awkward pause. "It's . . . hard for me to get around. Shibuya's a little far."

I felt like an idiot. "Shit, I'm sorry. I didn't even think of that."

She smiled at that. "I know you didn't."

"Well, how about if I could find a place closer by?"

She laughed. "Maybe."

"I'll try. I don't know. It would be good to see you someplace besides this hotel."

She looked at me. "I really don't know what to make of you, Jun."

"Is that a good thing or a bad thing?"

"I haven't decided yet."

I grinned, feeling a little more confident. "Well, I like that you're thinking about it."

"Yeah. I'll let you know how it all turns out."

chapter
fourteen

Tired as I was, I was also pretty keyed up from all the day's events, and maybe especially from the conversation with Sayaka at the end of it. Sayaka. I liked her name. Liked it a lot. And liked that she had told me.

I fell asleep so late that I actually slept past eight. When I left, she was gone, replaced by a stone-faced *oba-san* who took my key with all the animation of a vending machine.

The first order of business was Miyamoto. I had never spoken to him other than in Japanese, but he'd told me he dealt with Americans from time to time, so I assumed his English would be at least serviceable. Well, we were going to find out. I practiced disguising my voice, slowing it down, lowering it, making it raspier, older sounding, sharpening my inflection and changing my vowels as though English was other than my native tongue. When I felt I was ready, I went to a payphone and called him.

"*Miyamoto desu.*" This is Miyamoto.

"Hello," I said. "We have a mutual friend who told me you have a problem I might be able to help with. Let's not say his name." I spoke slowly and precisely to make sure he understood me.

There was a pause while he took it in. Maybe he hadn't been expecting I would put him in touch with someone so quickly. "Yes, yes that's right. He spoke with you?"

"He did. I'm prepared to help you with your problem. I know

you don't know me, but I hope our mutual friend's introduction will be evidence that you can trust me."

"All right."

"Do you want my help?"

There was a pause. "Yes."

"Then here's what I need you to do. Take all the information I'll require—name, work address, home address, photographs, and any other information you have that could reasonably be useful to me under the circumstances. Put it all in an envelope, along with half the fee that you offered our friend. The currency should be American dollars."

I thought he might object to paying a total stranger half up front, but he didn't. "All right," he said. "But where shall we—"

"I don't want to meet you. I don't want you to know anything about me beyond the sound of my voice. It's better that way for both of us." Actually, even if I were really the third party I was pretending to be, not meeting would have been better only for me, but I thought it was more polite to suggest my concern was broader than just that.

"But then how can I get you the envelope?"

I'd asked myself the same question. Answering it was why I'd been riding the Ginza line the day before. "You know Gaienmae Station, on the Ginza line?"

"Of course."

"Go in through the Number Three entrance. Walk onto the side of the platform where Shibuya-bound trains arrive. As you walk down the platform, on your left you'll see two sets of benches, each consisting of five chairs for a total of ten. Do you understand so far?"

"Yes."

"Tape the envelope to the back of the first chair you pass, the one right in the corner. Do it by eight o'clock tonight, and I'll retrieve it at some point afterward. When the job is done, we'll do the same thing with the remaining payment."

"But . . . that's a lot of money, to just leave there in the station."

"When you see the spot, you'll understand it's sufficiently secure. It won't remain there long, I assure you. But understand one other thing, too."

"Yes?"

"It should be obvious to you why it's best if we make our connection as minimal as possible. And equally obvious that, for my own security, I don't want anyone to see my face. I expect you to respect my wish for privacy. So, as I approach the platform—maybe on train, maybe on foot, maybe on one side, maybe the other—if I see anyone I think is there to make me—to identify me, that is—you will never hear from me again. Do we have an agreement?"

There was a pause. "We do."

"Repeat my instructions, so we can be sure there are no misunderstandings."

He did. When he was done, I said, "Good. The package will be in place by eight o'clock tonight?"

"It will be in place."

I hung up, thinking that's what an experienced contract killer would do at that point, and went to get some breakfast. The metabolism of a twenty-year-old isn't something that can be ignored for long. Once I'd fueled up, I rode Thanatos to Akihabara, Tokyo's electronics mecca. I visited a variety of stores, and bought five items: an iron, a curling iron, an extension cord, a roll of electrical tape, and a volt-ohm milliammeter, or VOM, a device for measuring electrical current. I was no electrical expert, though I did gradually and painstakingly acquire such expertise later, in no small part by "listening" to things, as the old *nandemoya* had described it, but I knew the basics. The danger from shocks isn't voltage as such, but rather amperage. That is, other things being equal, it's not the overall power that's most directly the danger, but instead how quickly that power moves through your body. This is why even relatively low-voltage systems like home wiring can be fatal. The current is moving fast. As long as resistance is low—the way it is when, say, your skin is wet—a low-voltage shock can be enough to cause ventricular fibrillation and immediate unconsciousness, followed rapidly, absent intervention, by death.

I made one last purchase at a drugstore—mineral salts, advertised as offering relief from arthritis and a variety of skin problems, and therefore presumably something similar to what the proprietors of Daikoku-yu put in the water of their own special soaking tubs. Then I took my purchases back to a dilapidated love hotel in Ueno, all molded ferroconcrete and plastic cupids, where I paid for a rest in a deluxe room with an *ofuro*—a bath.

As soon as I was in the room with the door locked behind me, I turned on the bathwater, keeping it piping hot to replicate the conditions at Daikoku-yu as closely as possible. I closed my eyes, and imagined the mineral baths at Daikoku-yu. From what I knew, I thought if the electricity were introduced between Ozawa and the drain or faucet—either of which would function as a ground— much of it would bypass Ozawa. But if Ozawa were between the source of the electricity and the drain or faucet, it would have to go through him.

When the tub was full, I shut off the water, lay the VOM on the adjacent, closed toilet, ran one of the electrical leads into the water, and taped the other to the faucet. There was no outlet within reach of the tub, and I was glad I'd thought to pick up an extension cord along with the other items. I plugged the curling iron into the extension cord and the extension cord into a wall socket in the bedroom. Then I went back to the bathroom, wrapped a towel around the curling iron, and pitched it into the bath.

Nothing seemed to happen, and I realized I was half expecting something dramatic—sparks, hissing, arcs of lightning. I smiled, thinking I had seen too many movies. I yanked the plug from the outlet and checked the VOM. The needle had moved to 35 milliamps—a severe shock, no doubt, but would it be enough to be fatal? I repeated the operation, this time with the iron, and was rewarded with a reading of 76 milliamps.

Next, I dumped in the bath salts and stirred them around until they were dissolved, then repeated my experiment. The amperage more than doubled because of the better conductivity of the salt water—72 milliamps for the curling iron, and a whopping 160 milliamps for the iron. I assumed the iron was producing the more impressive results because of its larger heating element.

Whatever kind of overcurrent protection the hotel had—and given its parlous state, "whatever kind" might easily have meant "none"—160 milliamps in the bath hadn't been enough to trip it. With a little luck, things at Daikoku-yu would be similarly lax. And if Ozawa's way of grabbing the faucet to pull himself up was a habit, and if I could time things right, I could deliver the shock into the water and from there right through his chest and out through his arm, which would be attached to a metal pipe that would offer the path of least resistance, and therefore the most attractive route for the jolt I planned to deliver.

I had a sudden moment of doubt. Yes, the salt water was a better conductor, but electricity seeks the path of least resistance. What if, relative to the salt water, Ozawa's body was more resistant than it would be relative to fresh water, and therefore pulled in less electricity?

I decided I'd have to take the chance. If he wasn't in one of the small tubs—both of which were filled with mineral water—none of this was going to work no matter what. There was too much water in the main bath; there would be other people in it; and I wouldn't have unobtrusive access in any event. Regardless of salinity, I thought if I got the iron in the water in the right spot, and if Ozawa's hand were on the faucet at the right moment, his body would conduct enough of the electricity to stop his heart.

I left the hotel and headed over to the Tokyo Metropolitan Library, where I spent several hours perusing a series of old medical and engineering tomes on the effects of electricity on the body. It seemed there was a sweet spot for inducing a ventricular fibrillation: between 100 and 200 milliamps. Lower than a hundred, and although the muscles in the vicinity of the shock might seize up, the heart itself wouldn't be sufficiently affected. And shocks over 200 milliamps seemed to induce the heart itself to seize, protecting it from arrhythmia, while also involving the risk of burns. But those numbers were about conductivity in the water or at contact with the skin. They didn't account for the possibility of funneling the shock directly through someone's chest. On balance, I decided the curling iron would be the better alternative. High enough amperage to induce an arrhythmia; not so high that it might cause marks on the skin or prevent an arrhythmia entirely. Also, the curling iron was significantly smaller and less obtrusive than the clothes iron.

When I was done at the library, I stopped at several hardware stores and picked up a variety of door locks. Then I went to a discount store and bought a baseball cap, a pair of sunglasses, a cloth surgical mask, and a heavy wool jacket that would add the appearance of twenty pounds to my build. Hell, yes, it would look like a disguise, for anyone inclined to pay attention to such things, but this was long before 9/11 and the birth of the national surveillance state. If someone wanted to ride the Tokyo subway looking like a movie star hiding from paparazzi while sweating off a few pounds in an unseasonable jacket, no one was going to give him a hard time about it.

At eleven o'clock that night, about an hour before the trains stopped for the evening, I got on an Asakusa-bound Ginza-line train at Shibuya Station. I boarded a car at the front and stood on the left, the side with a view of the opposite platform. As we pulled into Gaienmae Station and slowed to a stop, I got a complete view of the Shibuya-bound platform. There were a handful of late-night office workers waiting for a train, but no one who rubbed me the wrong way. I noted each of them carefully. If anyone I saw now was still standing on the platform when I returned, I would know I had a problem.

At Aoyama-itchōme, one stop farther down the line, I got off and waited for a train in the other direction. I didn't have to wait long: even off peak, Ginza-line trains ran every three minutes. I got on, this time near the back. As we approached Gaienmae Station, I pulled the surgical mask up over my nose and mouth. Japan is a remarkably considerate society, and it was common for people suffering from head colds to wear the cloth masks to reduce the spread of germs. Happily, the masks have other uses, too. Between the hat, the sunglasses, the mask, and the coat, I was confident even someone who knew me as well as Miyamoto did wouldn't recognize me. And if someone managed to snap a photo, that would be useless to them, too.

The train eased to a stop. I got off quickly and started walking down the platform toward the Number Three exit. Everyone I could see who had been waiting on the platform got on the train. The twenty or so people who got off started heading toward various exits. Everything looked copacetic.

I continued along the platform. The train started pulling away. No one lingered. When the train was gone, I checked the platform on the other side of the tracks. There were a dozen or so people there, but I had seen none of them when I had passed through a few minutes earlier.

I came to the benches I had described to Miyamoto. I sat on the last of them and looked around. No one was within view on my side of the tracks. On the other side, two salarymen were walking down the platform, neckties loosened, laughing about something or other. They didn't even glance my way. This was the moment. I reached around to the back of the chair and felt an envelope. I gripped one side and pulled. There was the sound of adhesive giving way, and then it was in my hand, two inches thick and wrapped in heavy tape. I shoved it into my bag and headed out. I passed several people and a station guard on the way, but if any of them wondered why Halloween seemed to have come early to Tokyo, none gave any sign. I left the station and, when I was satisfied I wasn't being followed, found a public restroom and checked the contents of the envelope. The money was all there—five thousand dollars, a fortune to me at the time. And there was a file on a guy named Mori, which I'd review later. I called Miyamoto and, disguising my voice again, told him I'd picked up the package and that I'd be in touch soon.

I got on Thanatos and headed to Ueno, where I checked into a cheap business hotel. I wanted to see Sayaka, of course, but it wouldn't do to have her see me coming and going in the middle of the night. I didn't want to have to explain myself, and I didn't want her to be more concerned or suspicious than she already was about what kind of trouble I might be in. Weirdly, I wondered if she would think of me. Probably I was being stupid. Probably she wouldn't even notice that I had spent the night somewhere else. If something didn't go right, if I got spotted by Mad Dog or one of the other yakuza trying to collect on the contract, she might wonder about me once or twice, and then probably never think of me again.

And nor, I realized, would anyone else. Unmoored, on the run, in a dim room in a grubby business hotel, and I had to realize something like that. I wondered how I had reached this point.

I didn't have an answer.

chapter
fifteen

While I waited for the hour to grow sufficiently late, I reviewed the file on Mori. For whatever reason, I'd been expecting an older guy, but Mori was only thirty-five. He cut a handsome figure, favoring Italian suits and slicking his hair back like a movie star, and had a reputation as a ladies' man. He'd been promoted unusually fast within MITI, the Ministry of International Trade and Industry, these days known as METI, the Ministry of Economy, Trade, and Industry. But apparently not fast enough. The impression I got from reading the file was of a guy impressed with himself and disdainful of his superiors, a guy who didn't want to wait in line for the power and prestige he felt he deserved. I didn't blame him for threatening his bosses as a way to get what he wanted. But I didn't blame the people who'd decided he should take early retirement, either.

Apparently, he was a karaoke enthusiast, his singing talents nearly those of a professional. He liked to entertain business and political associates at a hostess bar called Higashi West, in Akasaka, one of Tokyo's high-end entertainment districts. *Higashi* is the Japanese word for "east," so the club's name meant East West, presumably a reference to the composition of its hostesses, many of whom were from Europe. A decade or so later, gaijin hostesses would be a common theme in Tokyo, but at the time having them on staff was still noteworthy. Many Japanese men were both fascinated and intimidated by foreign women, and apparently Mori believed that mixing with them was a sign of his taste, confidence, and sophistication. Maybe he had a point. I didn't know—at that age, all women were fundamentally a mystery to me, regardless of where they came from.

I thought about how I would handle him. A gun would be the most obvious choice, but where was I going to get one in severely gun-controlled Japan? McGraw might be able to procure something, I supposed, but being the careful man he obviously was, he probably wouldn't do it. Too loud. Too much ballistics evidence. Too much possibility it could be traced back to him.

A knife would be the next thing the average person would think of. But a knife involved potential drawbacks, too. I knew from unpleasant combat experience that except in the movies, people rarely die quickly or quietly when they're killed with a knife. A single well-placed stab to, say, the femoral artery might work—just hit it and keep walking—but if you miss your mark, then all you've accomplished for the enormous risk you just took is to alert the target that he's a marked man. If you want to be sure, you have to stab the target repeatedly and then sit on him while he screams and thrashes and bleeds and dies. You can try to avoid a long and noisy drama by cutting through the trachea and carotid, of course, as I was taught to do in the military, but it takes a hell of a lot of luck with a cut like that not to get a Mount Vesuvius of blood all over you. Not an easy thing to wear inconspicuously in crowded Tokyo. And it's not just the appearance of being covered in blood that's a problem. That much blood smells, and people know what the smell is even if they've never smelled it before.

But the ladies' man part of the file . . . that was interesting. I thought I could make that fit with something other than a knife or a gun. After all, a guy who slept around indiscriminately might have a lot of enemies. If I did it right, I could create something that to the police would seem personal, not professional. There was already a narrative . . . maybe if I created a few facts consistent with that narrative, it would distract investigators from coming up with an alternative—and in this case more accurate—theory.

Was my analysis cold-blooded? I supposed it was. But with sufficient exposure, you get acclimated to anything, killing included. If you've never had that exposure, survived those conditions, lived in those environments, I imagine a clinical approach to killing seems like a horror. But after what I'd seen—and done—in the jungle, it just felt sensible. Even normal. There was a problem I needed to solve, and I wanted to solve it in the safest, most efficient way I could. I thought that was all that mattered.

I shelved my thinking about the Mori hit—Ozawa was the more immediate problem, and that meant I needed to practice with the picks on the door locks I'd bought earlier. Not having a vise to clamp them in, I used a drawer, which I pressed closed with a knee while I worked. This made the job considerably more difficult, but that was good. As the *nandemoya* had said, from here on it was a matter of practice.

At three in the morning, about as late as it could get before it started getting early again, I rode Thanatos into Kita-Senju, nothing in my bag but the curling iron, the VOM, and the extension cord; nothing in my pockets but a wad of cash and my new lock picks. I parked the bike near the station and walked from there. The last trains had stopped running hours earlier, and the last taxis had delivered the last late salaryman not long after that. The air was cool and moist and utterly still. Other than a lone cat assessing me silently from between two refuse containers, I saw not a living soul.

I approached Daikoku-yu indirectly, first circling it, listening intently, hearing nothing. The front was lit as fully as it had been the evening before, when it had been open for business. I hadn't counted on that. But unlikely that anyone would be watching from one of the few houses with a view of the entrance. I ducked beneath the *noren* curtains, slid my lock picks to the back of one of the shoe cubbies, and waited inside the vestibule. If the worst happened and the police showed up now, at least I wouldn't have any burglar tools in my possession. If I'd been caught lurking outside a bank, doubtless it would be another matter, but I thought the idea of breaking into a *sentō* would be sufficiently absurd that even if the police did show up, they would probably let me go rather than have to deal with the paperwork.

Of course, if that were to happen, I would still have to figure out how to get to Ozawa. I needed this to work.

After ten uneventful minutes, I felt it was safe to proceed. I knocked on the door and waited. Nothing. I knocked again, louder this time. Unlikely as hell anyone was in there, but better to blurt out some bullshit about having left my wallet earlier that day than to be caught red-handed working the lock. Still nothing. Okay. I retrieved the picks and got to work. There was more light than I could reasonably have hoped for—an uncomfortable amount, in fact, despite the partial privacy afforded by the vestibule and the *noren*—so at least I didn't have to work entirely by feel, which was a skill I wouldn't acquire until much later. Between the *oyaji*'s quality instruction, the time I'd spent practicing afterward, and, to be fair, the low quality of the lock itself, it took only a minute to get inside. I kept my shoes on, violating Japan's stringent customs about such matters, but if things went sideways, I sure as hell wasn't going to have to hoof it back to Thanatos barefoot. The lights were off inside, but there was enough indirect light coming from the windows and skylight in the bathing area for me to get by. I used a shirtsleeve to wipe down the doorknob and other surfaces I'd touched, then retrieved a towel from a hamper and cleaned my soles carefully, less out of respect for custom than to be certain I wouldn't leave any dirt on the immaculate floors, which would certainly be noticed.

I padded silently into the bathing area, the spacious room ghostly now, light from outside shimmering off the still waters of the *ofuro*. I heard water rhythmically dripping from somewhere and the faint hum of a fan, but other than that, the room was silent.

I walked over and checked the door I had noticed the day before, the one next to the mineral-water baths. I was pleased to find it locked. Pleased, because if they kept it locked it wouldn't occur to them that someone might have gotten inside. And it might also suggest that they didn't access the room often themselves. Otherwise, having to lock and unlock it would have been more of a hassle than it was worth.

I opened the lock so quickly that for a moment, I was afraid I'd broken it. But no, it was simply old and the tumblers were just unusually forgiving. The room was windowless and dark. Shit, I should have brought a flashlight. I closed the door and flipped on the light switch. A dangling incandescent bulb came on overhead, revealing a tiny room, not much more than a closet, really. The walls were lined with shelves on which were set various tools—a hammer, a saw, a power drill. There were buckets of tile grout and cans of paint. The tools, I noted, were rusty, the paint cans collecting dust. There was nothing of an everyday nature: no cleaning supplies, no neat stacks of towels. It smelled slightly musty, too, as though the door hadn't been opened in some time. As I had hoped, this room was used to store things that didn't need accessing very often. The everyday stuff, apparently, was kept somewhere else. Good.

I knelt, scanning under the shadows cast by the shelves. There was an outlet on the wall adjacent to the mineral-water baths. I smiled.

I was going to plug in the extension cord I'd brought, but then thought of that electric drill I'd just noticed. And sure enough, on one of the higher shelves, I found a heavy-duty extension cord. I was about to pull it down when I remembered I had to be careful about touching things. Damn it. I should have brought gloves as well as a flashlight. All right, I was learning. Afterward, I'd review everything to figure out what I could have done better, and then implement it all going forward—what the military called an after-action report. For now, I'd have to improvise.

There were some old rags alongside the paint cans, and I used them to retrieve the extension cord and plug it in. I was about to connect the curling iron when something occurred to me—was there any chance the outlet would be governed by the light switch? Unlikely in a storage room, where no one would plug a lamp into an outlet, but still I didn't want to take the chance. I connected the curling iron and flipped off the light. Within seconds, the iron began to get hot. Okay, the outlet was live, and with or without the light. I flipped the switch back on, went out to the mineral-water bath, and hooked up the VOM, putting the leads in near the drain. I came back, grabbed the iron, took a deep breath, and tossed it into the far end of the tub.

I waited a moment. No flickering lights, no electrical shorts, nothing. Excellent. Not a perfect experiment because during business hours they might be running some appliances that were off now, but another amp or so of draw on a system that was already handling, say, a washing machine and air conditioner would represent a trivial amount of extra load. The iron itself, I noted, white and with a white cord, wasn't particularly noticeable against the background color of the bath. Of course, it would be easier to see during the day. But I thought I might have a way around that.

I unplugged the iron and fished it out, then checked the VOM. Fifty-eight milliamps—much higher than I'd gotten at the hotel, I supposed due to a higher concentration of salts than what I'd managed to duplicate in my practice session. The materials I'd read at the library claimed 100 milliamps was the lower end of the fatality range. But that was for point of entry. What really mattered was what happened in the chest cavity, and there, 6 milliamps was considered fatal. If I put nearly 60 milliamps into the water at the same moment Ozawa grounded himself by gripping the faucet, I was reasonably confident that a sufficient portion of the electricity would travel straight through his heart.

I left the extension cord plugged in and turned off the light with a knuckle. I pulled the female end of the cord across the threshold and carefully closed the door over it. There was a good-sized gap at the bottom of the door, and I was able to wedge the female end in the crack just under the hinges. I shoved it back an inch or so with the toe of my shoe, then stood examining it for a moment. It was practically invisible, and I didn't think it would be any more noticeable during the day, either. Who pays any attention to the crack at the bottom of a storage room door, the same door that's been there day in and day out for years if not decades?

I locked the door, wiped it down with my shirtsleeve, and left the building, repeating the process on the way. I walked quickly back to the station, giddy from adrenaline. I was going to do this. I was going to make it work. I didn't consider anything more than that, didn't even pause to consider the potential cost of what I was buying.

chapter
sixteen

I woke up the next morning and the first thing I thought was, *Today I'm going to kill a man.*

It was a strange thought. Every morning I woke up during the war was a day I might kill someone. But in the war, I had never known whom. And anyway, of course I was supposed to kill someone, even a lot of people—after all, it was a war. As Patton said, the point was to make some other dumb bastard die for his country. This was different. This was specific. And it wasn't sanctioned. But did that make it worse? Killing someone specific was worse than killing someone generic? Killing someone for my own reasons was worse than killing someone for reasons I was told by some politician?

It might have been another rationalization. But I couldn't argue with the logic, either. And in the end, I was going to do it anyway.

I bought more locks that day, and killed time practicing on them. Each, I discovered, was a little bit different, varyingly tough or vulnerable, loose or tight, easy to work by feel or unyielding. But there could only be so many types, and I imagined there would be broad principles. With enough practice, I'd learn by feel what type I was up against and defeat it more easily.

The hours ticked by excruciatingly slowly. I saw on the news that President Nixon had announced the last U.S. ground troops had been withdrawn from Vietnam. He didn't mention Cambodia. Nobody questioned him about it. I supposed they preferred to be lied to. Anyway, it didn't matter. Any idiot knew the war was lost.

I was glad I'd gotten out, that I could accept it was over. Earlier in the year, a Japanese Imperial Army sergeant, Shōichi Yokoi, had been discovered in the jungles of Guam. He thought the war was still on, and that he was still fighting it. *Hazukashinagara, kaette mairimashita*, he had famously said upon arriving back in Japan. Though ashamed, I have returned. I was glad I wasn't like him. Any fighting I did from now on would be for myself.

Late in the afternoon, I set out on Thanatos for Kita-Senju. I wore a shirt, pants, and shoes. Nothing else—no socks, not even any underwear. My bag was slung over my shoulder, but I'd stowed my personal effects and the money Miyamoto had left me under the mattress at the hotel. Not the most creative place in the world, but I didn't have to worry about maid service until the next morning, and I was reasonably confident it would all be safe there. I had already burned the file on Mori. The hotel room key I taped to the back of a toilet in the train station. I was traveling as light and sterile as I could under the circumstances.

I parked two blocks from Daikoku-yu, in the direction of the train station. If I had to tear ass out of there, I wanted a little head start to gain some distance before firing up the bike. I used a coin to unscrew the license plate. I doubted anyone would notice the absence on a parked bike. Anyway, I was less worried about that than about anyone remembering the plate number later.

I meandered the area in a slow loop. By overshooting Ozawa's house on one end to the limit of my vision and doing the same with Daikoku-yu on the other, I managed to stretch out each lap to a good twenty minutes, giving people fewer opportunities to wonder who was strolling in their neighborhood and why. Now that I knew he limped, I was betting Ozawa would consistently use the shortcut to the *sentō* rather than the main road, which made anticipating him easier. I hoped I wouldn't have to do this day in and day out. Even with the various steps to reduce my profile, strolling this way wasn't exactly inconspicuous, and though I doubted anyone would pay much heed on any given day, over time the behavior would start to attract scrutiny.

After two hours, a dark sedan with curtained windows turned onto Ozawa's street. It had to be him—I couldn't imagine another person with a car and driver in this neighborhood. All right, he was home. Now I just had to hope it was his habit to visit the *sentō* every evening. I used the moment to duck into an alley off the path I'd been following and urinate. I had deliberately dehydrated myself, knowing I wouldn't have many such opportunities while waiting for him, but now that I'd seen him I was nervous, and I knew from combat experience that dehydration or no, it wouldn't be long before I would need a toilet.

As it turned out, he kept me waiting only for an hour, probably enough time to eat dinner or at least to exchange pleasantries with his wife, maybe his in-laws. It was just growing dark and I was on the heading-back-toward-Daikoku-yu portion of my loop when I saw him approaching, limping slowly along in a bathrobe and slippers, a small plastic bucket and towel in one hand. I turned into an alley so he wouldn't have a chance to make out my face, and waited three minutes. Then I headed in, opening up the laces of my shoes wide so I could pull them on in a hurry if necessary, and placing them in a waist-level cubby where I wouldn't have to stoop to retrieve them.

This time, I had brought my own toiletries and towels from the hotel, and only had to pay the entrance fee. It was the same *mama-san*, though she didn't seem to remember me. Of course, if this went well, it wouldn't matter either way.

I used the toilet, then placed my clothes carefully in a locker, closing it but not engaging the lock. If things went badly but I had any time at all, I would want to pull my clothes on as quickly as possible, probably while trying to talk my way out of whatever had gone wrong. With nothing but pants, a shirt, and a bag, I wouldn't need much time.

I rolled a towel around the curling iron, leaving the plug accessible at one end of the roll, and another around the toiletries, then went in through the sliding-glass doors. The steam and heat wrapped themselves around me, but I barely noticed. I was intent on Ozawa. He was seated in front of one of the spigots, lathering up with a soapy washcloth. There were ten people in the main bath and another ten soaping up or rinsing off. Both mineral baths were empty. The last spigot in the row, the one next to the mineral baths, was empty. I walked over and sat in front of it. I glanced around. No one was paying me any attention at all. Bathhouse etiquette—with all the naked bodies in a *sentō*, people tend to be conscientious about not staring, and the habit was working to my advantage now. The head of the extension cord was still barely visible where I had jammed it under the storage room door. Okay.

I put the towel with the curling iron rolled up tightly inside it against the bottom of the storage room door. To anyone who might have glanced over, I would look like someone just trying to keep a towel dry by placing it out of the way while he washed. I attached the plug to the extension cord, sat on the stool, and started soaping up. After a minute, I leaned over and touched the towel, confirming that the iron was beginning to heat. No reason to expect otherwise after the dry run I'd done earlier, but combat teaches you not to assume. I knew from having handled it earlier that if I left it too long, it would start to scorch the towel. But I didn't think I'd need even that long.

I finished washing quickly, left my toiletries and the second towel in front of the spigot to mark it as being in use, and made it to the mineral baths ahead of Ozawa. I needed him to use the outer of the two, so I eased into it now. If someone else were to use the other in short order, I'd still be able to vacate this one so Ozawa could get in. And if, as he approached, the other one were empty, I would switch. Odd behavior, certainly, but I doubted he would say anything about it. He'd just wonder absently why someone would do something like that, and avail himself of the open bath.

It turned out to be a good plan. A minute after I'd entered the tub, an old-timer eased himself into the one next to me. "Hot enough for you?" he said, turning to me and smiling with an almost comically perfect set of dentures. I nodded bruskly and turned away. I didn't care if he concluded I was rude; I just didn't want to interact with anyone more than I had to, or to do anything else that would make me at all memorable.

But he didn't take the hint. "You from around here?" he said, sliding down lower until the water was at his chin.

"No, not really." I used an Osaka accent, thinking if anyone did describe me, it would be better if they described the wrong thing. Ozawa was done soaping up; now he was rinsing himself with the bucket he had brought.

"Sure, I can tell you're not. Kansai, is it?"

Kansai is western Honshu, the main island of Japan, where Osaka is located. I nodded. Ozawa stood and stretched.

"So? What brings you here?"

"The waters," I said, thinking of *Casablanca*.

He laughed, and I wondered if he had caught the reference. "I mean, what brings you to Tokyo?"

Ozawa glanced over at us, then headed to the *rotenburo*, the outdoor tub. *Fuck*.

Had he been planning to use the mineral baths, but then changed his mind when he saw they were occupied? Would he skip them entirely tonight? Damn it, I'd been so close, and now I wasn't sure.

"What?" I said to the old man, realizing he had said something but not having processed what.

"I said, what do you do in Tokyo?"

"Ah. I work for Matsushita." This was what Panasonic was called back then.

"You don't say! I worked at Matsushita. I'm retired now, but my son-in-law is there. What do you do?"

Jesus, I thought, feeling I was losing control of the situation, *what are the fucking chances of this?*

"Uh, air-conditioning." *And if you tell me your son-in-law is in air-conditioning, too, I'm going to drop that curling iron in your tub.*

Instead, he said, "I was in lighting. So is my son-in-law."

"Yeah? That's great."

"Well, it's a living. Long hours, though. No time for anything but work. He's gained twenty pounds since he started there. Not like you."

"What do you mean?"

"You look like an athlete. Lucky to have time to exercise."

Enough. "Whew," I said, pulling myself out. "That's as much as I can take. Good talking with you."

He laughed. "Easier at my age. Less to lose."

I glanced at the towel as I got out. Still there, just a rolled-up towel someone had placed at the foot of the storage room door.

I dunked myself in the plunge pool and waited. The old man got out and went to one of the spigots to rinse himself. Both mineral baths were empty. I thought about repeating what I had done before, but I was afraid of a similar outcome. I decided this time to just wait.

After a few minutes, Ozawa came back inside. He glanced over at the mineral baths, and seeing them empty, started to head over. I got out of the tub and realized I had overestimated how long it would take him to reach the baths—he was going to beat me there, and he had walked past the outer tub and was about to get in the inner one. *Shit.*

"Uh, listen," I said, reaching him just in time. "It's none of my business, but I don't think you want to use this one. I couldn't help notice . . . the old guy who just came out, he seemed to have had a little accident on the way, if you know what I mean. I don't want to make a big deal of it or embarrass him. I'll tell the *mama-san* so she can take care of it discreetly."

Ozawa's eyes widened and he glanced at the tub, perhaps to check whether the accident in question had been of the *shoben* or *daiben* variety—in English, number one or number two. There was nothing to see, but still, who would want to soak in urine?

He thanked me and got into the outer tub. My heart was pounding. I glanced around. No one was paying either of us any attention at all. Ozawa eased back against the wall, sliding all the way down into the steaming water.

I sat in front of the spigot I had been using earlier, and inspiration suddenly took hold of me. I leaned over and grabbed the towel with the iron wrapped inside it, letting a sufficient length of cord pay out as I straightened on the stool. Then I turned toward Ozawa and, holding the rolled-up towel at the edge of the bath and glancing into the water, said, "Oh my, it looks like he had an accident in this one, too. I think that's a turd behind you."

He sat up abruptly and looked over his shoulder. "What?"

Come on, come on . . . "No, not there. The other side. Behind you."

He looked the other way, and then, seeing nothing, scooted forward and grabbed the faucet to pull himself out. The instant his fingers curled around the metal, I released the rolled-up iron into the water just behind him.

For an instant, it seemed nothing had happened. Ozawa wasn't moving, wasn't reacting at all, and I wondered whether something had gone wrong. But then I saw he was shaking slightly, almost vibrating, his hand frozen fast to the metal faucet. His mouth was contorted into an odd rictus of effort, and a barely perceptible half groan, half squeal was issuing from between his twitching lips. If he'd been sitting on a toilet instead of reclining in a tub, he would have looked like nothing more than a man straining to achieve a difficult bowel movement.

I watched in horrified fascination. He seemed to be looking straight ahead, but I sensed he could no longer see. I glanced around. No one was looking. I didn't know if he'd received a lethal jolt, but the longer I waited, the greater the risk of discovery. I grabbed the cord, pulled the plug out of the socket, and hauled the iron out of the water.

Instantly Ozawa's body relaxed. His hand drifted from the faucet, his lips parted, and a long, sibilant sigh escaped from his mouth. His eyes rolled upward, and he eased back into the water like a man lying down to sleep. His shoulders went under, then the back of his head, and then, his eyes now trained in the direction of the ceiling, his face.

I squeezed the excess water out of the towel, and used the bottle of body soap I had brought to shove the protruding end of the extension cord back under the door. If anyone looked inside the storage room, it would still be odd to find the cord plugged in, but not as odd as finding it plugged in and jammed under the door. Either way, I doubted the proprietors would go out of their way in sharing any suspicions they might have. Confirmation of an electrocution would be bad for business, and knowing this would help them decide that any suspicions were far-fetched and not worth sharing.

I heard someone say, "*Daijōbu?*" Is he all right? I glanced over. One of the men in the main tub was standing and pointing at Ozawa. But his question was to the people around him, not to me specifically. I wrapped the second towel around my toiletries and the wet towel with the iron inside it and stood, looking around as though unsure of what the man was talking about. Another man hauled himself dripping and streaming from the main bath and started heading over, his focus on Ozawa. I took a step back as though uncertain and wanting to give him room. Another man ran forward from one of the spigots.

I kept moving, wanting to put as much distance as I could between myself and where everyone would soon be focusing their attention. By the time I had reached the sliding-glass doors, they had pulled Ozawa into a sitting position and several more people had converged on the scene. Ozawa's skin was blue and his head lolled on his neck. If he wasn't already dead, he was at least deeply unconscious.

I headed straight to my locker, shoved everything into my bag, and pulled on my pants and shirt. No one emerged from the bathing area. I imagined by now they had hauled Ozawa out of the bath. These days, with the prevalence of portable defibrillators, he might have had a chance. But from what I'd just seen, even if anyone in there knew CPR, it wasn't going to be enough.

I went out to the vestibule, forcing myself to walk slowly, the way people inevitably do after boiling themselves in the *sentō*. I slipped into my shoes and headed at a steady but not attention-getting pace back to Thanatos. I fired up the bike and rode off, the wind cool against my wet skin.

I dropped the curling iron into the polluted waters of the Sumida River. The towels and toiletries I threw in anonymous trash bins. Only when I was back inside the Yamanote did I permit myself a moment of exultation. I had done it. Later, I would go through what had gone well and what I might have done better. There would be lessons to be learned. But for now, I had done it.

I pulled into the shadows of a deserted parking lot and let the shakes work their way through me. So many things could have gone wrong, but they hadn't. Logistical problems, electrical problems, witness problems. But in the end, it had all been okay.

It's so easy to miss the forest when you're focusing on all those trees.

chapter
seventeen

I called McGraw. I didn't know where he was at that hour, but an embassy staffer put me through to him.

"It's done," I told him.

There was a pause. "It looks the way it needs to look?"

"You'll read about it in the paper tomorrow, I'm sure."

"I'll look forward to that."

"You owe me two more files."

"If I read in the paper what you just told me I'll be reading, they're yours. Meet me tomorrow morning. You know the Nakagin Capsule Tower?"

I'd read about the tower. Completed that year, it had caused a lot of excitement in Japan as an example of a movement called metabolism, which claimed to be a new approach to building and habitation, fusing architectural concepts with those of biological growth. Each of the Nakagin's residential units was individually attached, upgradeable, and replaceable—supposedly the future of human urban living. Today, only a few of the one hundred forty capsules are still inhabited. The rest are used for storage or office space, or have been abandoned entirely, and the building itself feels like a ghost, a monument to an ideal that was promised but that never came to be, its exterior dark with rot and rust, its once bright circular windows dull as cataract-covered eyes, an Ozymandias of a structure standing mute and helpless and alone while the city fathers who blessed the building's birth now dither over plans to bury it.

"Yeah. I know it."

"In front, ten o'clock."

I didn't like him telling me what to do. "You better have those fucking files," I said, and hung up.

I got back on Thanatos and headed off, thinking about where I should stay that night. I felt like Sayaka would take one look at me and know what I'd just done, or at least know I'd done something. But that was ridiculous. There was no mark of Cain. Or, if there was, I was already wearing it. In spite of everything that was going on, I wanted to see her. No, not in spite of . . . because of it. I didn't have anything else right then. I didn't want to lie awake alone in another anonymous room, with nothing for company but my own thoughts and nothing to look forward to but another set of files and another set of kills. I wanted something outside all that. I wanted something to look forward to. I wanted her.

I rode Thanatos to Uguisudani, parking near the station as usual and walking to the hotel. Sayaka looked up when I came in and smiled. I couldn't help noticing the newness of both those behaviors. Ordinarily, she'd hear the door and pause before looking up from her textbooks, obviously caring more about studying than she did about who might be coming in for a room. And she'd never smiled when she saw me.

"I wondered whether you were going to come back tonight," she said, as I walked up to the glass.

I smiled back. "It's my home away from home."

"Yeah? Well, you weren't here last night."

"Were you worried about me?"

She rolled her eyes theatrically. "Don't get cocky."

In fact, I didn't feel cocky, though I was glad she seemed to be showing some interest. I just didn't want her to ask anything more about where I'd been.

"Anyway," I said, "here I am."

"I guess this means you haven't sorted out that jam yet?"

"I'm . . . getting closer."

She looked at me. "You okay?"

I should have deflected it. Instead, I said, "What do you mean?"

"I don't know. You look . . . different. Tired or something."

"Well, I am a little tired."

There was an awkward moment of silence. She said, "So . . . a stay?"

"Yeah. The usual."

I gave her the money and took the key. I was about to turn and go when she said, "In case I don't see you in the morning—tomorrow's my day off. Well, night off."

Impulsively I said, "Yeah? You want to do something?"

She laughed. "You are feeling cocky."

"I'm serious. How about dinner?"

Her laugh faded, and she looked at me with a directness and honesty I found half moving, and half intimidating. "Look," she said. "I can't get around well."

"I don't care."

She nodded. "I know you don't, and I won't deny that's something I like about you. But if you think you know what it's like to go out with me, you don't."

I was mildly giddy at her protests. They all struck me as practical, and practical concerns could always be addressed, right?

"Why don't we find out?" I said.

She was still looking at me so directly. "Because, Jun, finding out for you might be embarrassing for me."

I realized what she was telling me wasn't easy for her. That tough facade she always presented . . . it was a kind of armor. And she was removing some of it now. It was exciting, encouraging. And it also made me feel strangely honored, and in her debt. She was trusting me, and I had to show her I was worthy of that. Had to *be* worthy of it.

"I really don't think there's anything about you that should ever be embarrassing," I said. "At least not to me."

She smiled. "That's sweet."

"I mean it."

"I know. Thanks."

I shook my head. "Don't thank me. Just let me take you to dinner."

She laughed. "Okay."

"Okay, great! I'll find a place that's . . . ground floor. You know, no stairs. What kind of food do you like?"

"I like everything."

"Sushi?"

"I think sushi's included in 'everything,' yeah."

"Okay, I'll find a place. Where do you live?"

She shook her head as though in amazement that I could be so dense. "Close by."

"Oh. Right. Of course. Well, how about if we meet in front of JR Uguisudani Station? North entrance? Seven o'clock?"

She nodded. "Okay."

I couldn't help grinning. She rolled her eyes again and went back to her studying, the armor firmly back in place.

Except that I'd seen underneath it. A little.

I took the longest, hottest shower I could stand, then soaked in an equally scalding bath until the water began to cool. It relaxed my body, but my mind wouldn't follow suit. I was excited about dinner with Sayaka and I tried to focus on that, tried to use it to eclipse everything else. But I couldn't. Not entirely.

I felt . . . bad. Not as bad as I supposed I should. But maybe my mother's efforts at Catholic indoctrination hadn't been quite as futile as I'd told myself. I felt like I'd crossed some line tonight, done something I would need to account for, expurgate, confess. But I'd also felt the same way after my first combat kill. It had passed then, and I imagined it would now.

What was different, I thought, was that up until now, everything had been sanctioned by war. Well, the *chinpira* in Ueno hadn't been war, but it had been self-defense, and that's close enough. Even the civilians—and there had been civilians, and I would carry that with me forever—it had all been under the rubric of war; it had all been hot-blooded. I had been a soldier, my presence in battle sanctioned even if some of what I'd done had crossed a line, even if some of what happened had slipped out of my control. No, *because* some of it had slipped out of my control. As opposed to now, when I was being fully deliberate. That was the difference, and I felt like understanding it was important.

What was strange, and unsettling, was that none of it felt remotely as awful as it should have. I should have been wracked by conscience, tormented by guilt, appalled that I had done something enormous, irrevocable. I should have been gripped by what that poet said—"The awful daring of a moment's surrender / Which an age of prudence can never retract." I should have known I had crossed a bridge too far, and arrived in a land offering no hope of return passage.

Instead, mostly it felt like just another step, an incremental movement along a path I'd been traveling for years.

chapter
eighteen

I headed out at just before six the next morning. Sayaka was doz-
ing when I emerged from the stairs, but woke from the sound
of the door.

"Sorry," I said, walking over to the window. Jazz issued softly
from her cassette deck. "Didn't mean to wake you."

"It's okay. You're up early."

"Places to go, people to meet."

She looked at me. "Problems to solve."

I shook my head. "It's really nothing. Almost done."

"Whatever you say."

"So . . . see you tonight?"

She nodded and smiled a little ruefully. I wondered if she was
having second thoughts. I almost said something that would let her
off the hook, but then I thought maybe she would take it the wrong
way and think I was the one having second thoughts. Better to just
let it go.

I enjoyed a breakfast of fatty tuna and rice at a stall in Tskuji,
adjacent to the massive wholesale fish market of the same name,
then walked to the nearby Nakagin Tower. I was early, but McGraw
was already waiting. He had his camera with him and I supposed
if anyone asked, he was here to capture the Tower Of The Future
in the bright morning light. He nodded when he saw me and
walked over.

130

"Nice work," he said by way of greeting. "I read about it in the paper this morning."

I didn't respond. I didn't need his assessment. I knew the work was good. Though I also felt I'd been luckier than I deserved.

"You know," he went, on, "if you hadn't called me last night and I'd just heard about this, I'd have thought it was a coincidence."

"If you'd told me it was a coincidence and you didn't owe me for it, it wouldn't have gone over well."

He mopped his brow with a handkerchief. "How'd you do it? The paper says it was some sort of heart attack in a bathhouse."

"Maybe it was."

"You did something to electrocute him, didn't you?"

"How would I do something like that?"

"That's what I'm asking you."

"What do you care? It's done. Now give me what you owe me. The files on the yakuza."

"I'm saying, if you've got a knack for this kind of thing, you could make a hell of a living. Being a bagman is bullshit. You know what certain people would pay to have problem individuals die of natural causes?"

"I don't want to do this for a living. I just want to go on living. Now where are the fucking files?"

If he made anything of my newfound irritability and assertiveness, he didn't comment. He shrugged and said, "Café de l'Ambre."

"What is that?"

"A coffee shop in Ginza. Eight-chōme, ten-fifteen. Not far from Shinbashi Station. How'd you like Lion?"

"I liked it fine."

"You'll like this, too. Sit at the counter, seat second farthest from the entrance. The file's under the seat. Oh, and try the Number Three blend. It's the house specialty."

"What is it with you and coffee shops?"

He chuckled. "Tokyo has some of the best coffee around, son, and I've been all over the world. If I have to spend time somewhere for a dead drop, I might as well enjoy myself. You only live once. Remember that."

I didn't like all the hoops he made me jump through to get these files, but I told myself not to look at it that way. It was just good tradecraft. I hadn't wanted to meet face-to-face with Miyamoto, had I? McGraw was just being careful, not playing games.

"Just one thing," he said. "At the moment, there's only one file—on Fukumoto Senior."

I looked at him, thinking, *If you fucking try to cheat me, McGraw . . .*

"Relax," he said. "I'll get you the one on Mad Dog. We don't have much that's actionable on these two, and putting together the basics on the father seemed like the priority. He's the one in charge. Meaning in charge of having you hunted down and killed. I would have had them both ready, but I never thought you'd manage Ozawa so fast. At least now you have something to work with while I assemble what you need on the son."

I nodded slowly, not liking it, but not finding a further reason to protest, either. I realized that if McGraw tried to screw me, I would kill him. I would have to, like I'd told him earlier. I already had the yakuza after me. Adding the CIA seemed like not so much.

"Relax," he said again, probably reading my thoughts from my expression. "I'll get you the other file."

I considered telling him what would happen if he didn't, but recognized that doing so would have been childish, the product of ego. Worse, because he already knew what would happen, verbalizing it could only serve to dilute the strength of the threat. Because why would anyone waste breath describing what was already axiomatic?

I didn't realize it right away, but that was a big moment in my development. Self-awareness leading to self-control. I had a long way to go, but you have to start somewhere.

It took me a little while to find the coffee shop—it was small and the signage was modest, just an illuminated placard over the window reading CAFÉ DE L'AMBRE. COFFEE ONLY. For some reason, I liked that. It was so confident, so assertive. Almost a fuck-off to anyone inclined to order a muffin or macchiato.

I stepped into the air-conditioned coolness of a small, unpretentious shop. A middle-aged woman behind an old-fashioned cash register to my left asked, "How many?" I told her it was just me, and she came around and escorted me the eight feet or so to the counter. To my right were six tables for two people each, a bench against the back wall, chairs facing it; to my left, an L-shaped counter with ten stools, the farthest two forming the short end of the L. The tables were full, but there were a few seats open at the counter, including the second farthest from the entrance, just around the bend on the short end of the L, the one McGraw had used for the dead drop.

I sat and looked around. Everything was old, dark wood: the walls, the ceiling, the counter itself. Old-school didn't even begin to describe it. Behind the counter was an ancient balance-beam scale, a hand-cranked grinder, and an icebox—an actual wooden icebox, not a refrigerator. The air was suffused with the delicious smell of coffee.

There was a small black-and-white television playing atop the icebox. The LDP had named Ozawa's replacement—a surprisingly young-looking guy named Gai Kawasaki. I wondered how he'd managed to leapfrog all the septuagenarians who must have been in line ahead of him. Maybe McGraw had done something to help—a quid pro quo for Kawasaki promising to be a better team player than Ozawa. A reporter put a microphone in his face, and

Kawasaki spoke smoothly and reassuringly of Ozawa's legacy, how no one could hope to fill the great man's shoes but that Kawasaki would humbly try for the sake of the party and the nation, etc.

I immediately sensed the thoughtfulness behind McGraw's tradecraft: people who sat at the counter would mostly be alone. The farthest seat, at the end of the counter, would be naturally attractive to anyone who didn't want to sit between two people. If there were other open seats, it would be a little odd to take one adjacent to one already occupied. Meaning that statistically, that second-farthest seat was likely to be available just a little more often than the others. McGraw might have used the booth behind one of the tables, but people who came with a companion were more likely to linger, and if the dead drop were occupied, there might be a substantial wait. At the counter, seats would open more quickly. Of course, there were no guarantees, but McGraw's way made it more likely things would go more smoothly. Focusing on the details, gaming things out . . . it all offered only an advantage. Again, not something I was unfamiliar with in a combat context. But I could see the importance of adapting the concept for urban environments. McGraw was an asshole, but that didn't mean there was nothing I could learn from him.

I sat and waited while the *maastaa* prepared a cup of coffee. He was a rugged-looking man of about sixty in shirtsleeves and a sweater vest, with a full head of steel-gray hair and solemn eyes behind a large pair of glasses. There was no coffeepot to pour from; instead, the Café de l'Ambre method seemed to be the preparation of a single cup at a time. I watched as he poured ground beans into a cloth filter held in a wire, placed the filter over a copper pot, then slowly poured water over the coffee from a boiling kettle, his arm moving the filter in a slight circle as he did so, his head cocked to the side so he could better observe the steaming water trickling into the ground beans, the flow starting at the center, then working its way out, then back in again. After a moment, he set down the kettle, waited while the last of the boiling water flowed through the coffee, briefly heated the pot over an open flame, poured it into a china cup, and placed the cup in a waiting saucer in front of the customer. Then he made his way down the counter to me.

I bowed my head in greeting. "*Omakase de onegai-shimasu.*" I'll have whatever you recommend. McGraw might know coffee, but I doubted he knew it as well as this guy.

He nodded. "Strong? Mild?"

"Please, I know little about coffee but am trying to learn. Whatever the master himself believes I would enjoy."

He considered me for a moment, then nodded and placed a saucer in front of me. He turned to the shelves behind him, considering among the various glass jars stored there. After a moment, he selected one and prepared my coffee as he had the cup before it, this time first grinding the beans in the hand crank. He set the cup in the saucer and said, "This is a 1952 Brazilian Bourbon. Rare and delicate. A bit more expensive, but if it isn't to your taste, I'll only charge you for a regular cup."

"I didn't know there were aged coffees. I thought fresh was better."

He gave a quiet *harrumph*. "It's like wine. You wouldn't lay down a Beaujolais, but drinking a Premier Cru Bordeaux right away would be infanticide. The right coffee can become quite special with age. Subtler, more complex. But you have to know what to look for in the beans."

At the time, I didn't know the first thing about wine, so I decided to take his word for it. I picked up the cup and held it for a moment, feeling the warmth in my hands, letting the aroma drift upward, remembering to be mindful. It smelled delicious—strong but balanced, assertive but not overpowering. I moved the cup closer and was rewarded with a different spectrum of fragrances: toffee, maybe, or caramel. I closed my eyes and took a small sip. It was delicious: rich but with no bitterness, with hints of the toffee the aroma had promised.

I nodded my gratitude, thinking any words I might offer would be superfluous. The *maastaa* nodded back, clearly pleased. "You say you know little of coffee. Perhaps you know more than you think."

"I'm really just trying to learn."

He bowed. "*Sekiguchi desu.*" I'm Sekiguchi.

I bowed my head in return. "*Yamada desu.*" I thought it best not to use my real name. Yamada was the Japanese equivalent of Smith or Jones.

"Come back some time, Yamada-san. It will be my pleasure to teach coffee to one who appreciates it so much."

I bowed my head at the compliment. Sekiguchi moved off to attend to another customer, and I enjoyed the cup he had prepared me. It really was outstanding. I was amazed to think of the swill I'd been drinking when there were places like this in Tokyo.

After a few minutes, I looked around. People were talking, or reading, or silently contemplating the subtleties of whatever it was they were drinking. No one was paying me any attention. I reached under the seat, felt the envelope taped in position, pulled it free, and pocketed it. Unsurprisingly, McGraw had taped it dead center, presumably to minimize the chance that someone momentarily gripping the edge of the seat might feel something with his fingertips. I finished my coffee, thanked Sekiguchi and assured him I would see him again, and headed out into the wet Ginza heat.

I rode to nearby Hibiya Park, where I sat at a bench in the shade of some trees and opened the file. Fukumoto lived in Denenchofu, an upscale, leafy suburb of single-family houses in the southwest of the city, outside the Yamanote. The headquarters of the Gokumatsu-gumi was in Shinjuku, and presumably he would spend substantial time there, but attacking a yakuza stronghold seemed like a fairly bad idea and I didn't even consider it. The Gokumatsu-gumi controlled Shinjuku's prostitution, ran most of the city's *pachinko* parlors through an affiliated Korean gang, and managed various nightclub interests. Beyond that was loan sharking, extortion, strikebreaking, and drug trafficking. Fukumoto had personal investments in several hostess bars throughout the city. But trying to get to him at one of the clubs sounded like a shell game to me, with a low probability of success.

I grimaced. It was an analyst's file, not an operator's. McGraw was fucking me.

Then I took a deep breath. Maybe there was another way of looking at it. Presumably, McGraw had wanted Ozawa dead for some time, and the Ozawa file had been a reflection of that desire. But no one had planned a hit on Fukumoto. McGraw was playing catch-up. He hadn't had time to put together something more focused.

All right. At least I had a home address. I could do a drive-by. Nothing for the development of appropriate tactics like seeing the actual terrain.

I stashed my bag in a locker in Tokyo Station, then rode to Denenchofu. I found Fukumoto's house easily enough—it was the most impressive in an already wealthy neighborhood. The style was slick and contemporary, and Fukumoto had obviously chosen it not just for its looks, but also for its security. Situated on a corner lot, it was a three-story structure surrounded by a high metal wall, with the front entrance protected by an exterior gate and a dog run around the side similarly secured. There was a two-car garage with a vertical door—closed, unsurprisingly. I considered how I might get inside. The wall looked easy enough to climb, but I had to assume there were additional precautions on the other side. It would be a shame to pirouette perfectly over, only to land in a den of

Rottweilers. I might have a shot outside the house, while Fukumoto was coming or going, but I doubted it—that garage door looked designed to get him in and out of the structure without ever having to expose himself. This was obviously no soft target like Ozawa, but rather a guy who knew he had serious enemies, who understood that his house was a potential vulnerability where he would need to be extra careful.

I circled the block, looking for possibilities, seeing none. I rode through the neighborhood. It was extremely quiet—not even any children in the streets, though I imagined that would change soon, as schools got out. The area's torpor wasn't going to make things easier for me—I saw nowhere I could conceal myself outside the house, whether to gather intelligence for later, or to find a way in now. Which, I supposed, was part of the reason Fukumoto would have chosen this neighborhood.

I decided I could afford one more drive past the house. But no more than that today, in case anyone was watching. As I turned onto the street facing the garage door, I saw a car nosing its way out. *Son of a bitch.* I was already going slowly and I dropped back even further on the throttle. But just as I was getting my hopes up that I was actually going to be able to follow Fukumoto, the rest of the car revealed itself. A yellow Porsche 911 Targa, the roof removed, with a Japanese woman alone at the wheel. She had on a pair of oversized sunglasses that did little to conceal her beauty. She paused at the edge of the street to check for traffic, saw me, and waited. Without thinking, I pulled over and waved for her to go. She smiled, looking even more confident and gorgeous as she did so; reached up to the visor and touched something; and pulled out. I heard the mechanical sound of a motor engaging and realized she had pressed an automatic garage door unit, and that the sound I heard was of the door closing. Damn, if I gunned it, I thought I might be able to scoot inside just before the door reached the ground. But the woman had paused at the corner to check for traffic. Too great a likelihood she would hear Thanatos's engine and see me in the rearview.

She made a left, and as soon as she was gone I gunned the bike forward, but too late. The door was already too low for me to have time to get off the bike and slide under it. I leaned down and saw a shiny chrome bumper and a single pair of wheels, and then it was gone, the door connecting solidly with the ground. *The hell with it*, I thought. If I couldn't improvise one way, I'd improvise another.

I pulled forward and glanced left. She was at the end of the street, her left turning signal blinking. I eased out and headed in her direction, hanging well back.

I followed her onto the main road, speculating. Her looks, the car . . . obviously, this wasn't the cleaning woman. And she was far too young to be Fukumoto's wife, given that he had an adult son. So what was she doing at Fukumoto's house in the middle of the day?

What the hell do you think?

But why his house? Why the middle of the afternoon?

Who could say? Maybe Fukumoto's wife was out then, having her hair done or at a weekly coffee klatch or whatever. Maybe for discretion, Fukumoto preferred to meet just before school got out, when the fewest people would be around. Maybe he'd just been horny and picked up the phone. I knew she was no call girl, though—there was that expensive car, for one thing, which felt like a gift from a rich patron. And the fact that inside her car was an opener to Fukumoto's garage. Not something he would give to a casual acquaintance. No, my gut told me the woman in the Porsche was Fukumoto's mistress.

But I cared about all that only secondarily. What mattered to me most right then was that if I could get to her car, I could get to that garage door opener. And if I could get to the garage door opener, I could get to Fukumoto.

I followed her to Daikanyama, northeast of Denenchofu and just west of the Yamanote, hanging back, keeping plenty of traffic between us. A yellow Porsche wasn't exactly hard to keep in view, even from a distance. She parked on the street and went into one of the clothes boutiques Daikanyama was known for.

These days, I would never have plunged ahead with so little preparation. Hell, I never would have plunged ahead with so little thought. But back then, I was young, and impulsive, and stupid. I didn't know how much you could manage luck, and why it's critical to at least try.

Instead, the sum of my analysis was more or less, *Never going to be a better chance than this one.*

I parked Thanatos a little ways off. I strolled along the sidewalk, pausing to look at the Porsche as though admiring it. It was a new model, and in fact sported one of the *jikōshiki* license plates the authorities had started offering just a couple years earlier—essentially a numerical vanity plate, green by day, glow-in-the-dark by night. This one had been issued by Shinagawa, number 1972. I guessed the idea was to proclaim the car's model year to anyone who cared.

I looked around—lots of people, no one paying me any particular attention. I snatched the garage door opener off the visor, walked back to Thanatos, and buzzed off. I could be back in Denenchofu in no time. I doubted Fukumoto would be expecting company so soon after his mistress had departed. With luck, he might even be enjoying a little postcoital nap.

So far, it had all gone smoothly, the timing and the circumstances all lining up right. I should have realized it had all been just a little too easy. But I didn't.

chapter
nineteen

I stopped at a pharmacy and bought a few medical supplies, including latex gloves. I didn't need anything but the gloves, but I thought it would be lower profile to look as though I was preparing for surgery rather than for crime. Would it matter? Probably not, but I saw no downside to obscuring the centrality of the gloves. I was learning.

I also went to a discount store and bought several items for the kind of light disguise I'd used when I retrieved the file from Miyamoto, this time deciding on a dark nylon windbreaker instead of a wool one. I also bought a cheap kitchen knife in a plastic sheath. A gun would have been better than a knife, but I had no way of acquiring one, and I didn't want to go in without some kind of weapon at hand. I wasn't worried about how I would take care of Fukumoto—other things being equal, I was confident I could use an improvised blunt object or even my hands for that. The problem was, I didn't know what kind of opposition I might encounter, and I didn't want to be holding nothing when I encountered it.

Before parking Thanatos at the station, I removed the license plate and hid it under a vending machine. Then I slipped on the windbreaker and the rest of my light disguise, and walked the kilometer or so to Fukumoto's house, nothing on my person but the latex gloves and knife in my pocket and the garage door opener in my hand.

I took a quick walk past the front of the house. Everything looked the same as it had when I'd been here just forty-five minutes earlier. A hit of adrenaline radiated out from my gut. I went down the side street. All clear. I breathed slowly in and out, willing myself to stay calm, stay relaxed.

I hit the remote-control button and watched the door slowly ascend. I saw the car I had glimpsed earlier—a Mercedes, this one a full-sized sedan, black. The other space was empty, some oil and transmission fluid stains in the concrete. Obviously, there were ordinarily two cars parked here, and one of them was out now. My chances of finding Fukumoto alone would never be better. I stepped inside and hit the button again, and while the door descended, I pulled the gloves on, moved up to the wall alongside the door to the house, and got out the knife. I didn't know where Fukumoto would be inside, or whether he would hear the garage door. But if he came out to investigate, I wanted to be ready.

The garage door closed, and I was suddenly enveloped in darkness. My eyes were used to the bright light outside, and it would take a few minutes for my night vision to kick in. Shit, I hadn't thought of that. Well, nothing to do but wait. My heart was thudding and I concentrated on breathing slowly, in and out, managing my nervousness the way I had in combat.

There was actually a decent amount of light seeping in along the seams of the garage door, and it didn't take long before I could make things out. Besides the Mercedes, there wasn't much. Car wax and other cleaning products on a shelf. Weights, piled up in a corner and looking as though they hadn't been used in years. Some tools hanging on the wall—screwdrivers, a saw, pliers. A nice-sized claw hammer.

I darted over to the wall, grabbed the hammer, and returned to my position alongside the door. Keeping the knife and the hammer in one hand, I tried the knob with the other, slowly and gently. I was expecting it to be locked, and was prepared to pick it. But I was pleasantly surprised when it turned.

I inhaled and exhaled deeply, then pulled the door open a crack. Snuck a quick peek, then jerked my head away. Fragments of a kitchen. Other than that, nothing. I looked again. No one was there. I opened the door a fraction wider and snuck another quick peek. Again, no one.

I dropped down and opened the door wide, scanning, ready to slam the door and fall back if anyone opened fire. Nothing but a large eat-in kitchen, neat, clean, and empty.

I stuck my head inside for an instant and pulled back. The quick peek revealed a doorway to the left and another straight ahead. A dining room and living room, I guessed.

I stuck my head in a third time, and this time held the position, *listening*. I thought I heard voices, but from far off and I couldn't make out what they were saying. People? A radio or television, maybe?

I eased the door closed, crept across the kitchen, and stopped alongside the doorway to what I guessed was the living room. Again, I paused to listen intently. I could hear the voices slightly better from here. They were male, and I was pretty sure they were live, not television or radio, but I still couldn't make out what they were saying.

I snuck a peek. A staircase to the right; an empty corridor and an open door at the end of it. The voices were coming from there.

I crept down the corridor, my back to one wall, scanning in all directions, planning contingencies, mapping escape routes. There was probably a science to securing a house and I promised myself I would learn it, but in the meantime skills honed in the jungle were translating reasonably well. The carpet was plush and my footsteps were silent. I could hear the voices more clearly now—two of them. It sounded like a management meeting, something about putting a new guy in charge of collections. But I barely processed the words—it was the tone I was keyed on, and the tone I overheard was even, involved, engaged. They were paying attention to each other and their conversation, not to anything outside the room. I held the knife in my left hand and the hammer in my right. I took a step, stopped, listened. Repeat. And again.

When I was ten feet away, one of those steps caused a floorboard to squeak. Loudly.

I froze. The conversation I'd been overhearing stopped. Dead silence. Not another word, not even a "What was that?" or a mild "Did you hear something?"

The decision happened instantaneously, automatically. If there had been anything other than silence, I might have paused to wait them out, to see if there would be an opportunity to get a little closer and gain additional surprise. But that absolute silence—it felt like certainty, like preparation, like hard men reaching for weapons. It felt like if I didn't move now, I'd cede all the initiative. The only question was attack, or fall back.

I chose attack.

Juiced on adrenaline, I sprinted forward and burst into the room, bellowing a wild *kiyai*. A drawing room of some kind, and four men, all in suits. Two seated on either side of a coffee table at the far end of the room, two in chairs closer to me. One of the two at the far end I recognized from the file photo as Fukumoto. The other was a similar age and looked like management. The third and fourth looked like security—younger, punch-permed, their jackets tight over muscular physiques. And Muscle One and Muscle Two were already coming to their feet, as I had imagined, and reaching under their jackets.

There's a reason battle cries are as old as war. Whether Comanche, or rebel yell, or banzai, or whatever, an atavistic primate roar can be tremendously intimidating and disorienting to the enemy.

So yelling again like a madman, I launched the hammer at Muscle One, the one to my left. He was spooked by my sudden appearance and my screaming, and too focused on trying to access his weapon even to flinch. The hammer sailed into his face with a tremendous crack of metal on bone. I was already turning and charging at Muscle Two. His eyes were bulging in a sign of near panic and he was back-pedaling directly away from me. About a decade later, a guy named Dennis Tueller in Utah would show that inside twenty-one feet against a knife, trying to get a gun out is typically a losing bet, especially if you're backing straight up rather than getting off the line. This guy wouldn't be around for the study. He did manage to get out his pistol, but I slapped my free hand over the muzzle and turned it away, at the same instant plunging the knife into his belly. He shrieked and jerked back and I stabbed him again. And again. He gave up the gun and tried to turn away. I was all the way back in the war now, charging an ambush, a demon, a berserker, a fucking killing machine. Muscle Two collapsed and fetaled up. I pointed the gun at his head and tried to pull the trigger. *What the fuck?* I looked—a Browning Hi Power, cocked and locked. No wonder Muscle Two hadn't gotten off a shot, even to the side. I thumbed the safety down and shot him in the head. I strode over to Muscle One. He was splayed on his back, blood flowing from a gash in his forehead. I fired directly into the gash.

Fukumoto and the other guy were on their feet now, but there was no way out of the room except through me, and neither wanted to charge me first. I advanced into the room, the gun up, my teeth clenched, snarling like a werewolf.

Fukumoto raised his hands and screamed, *"Nande temae?"* What do you want? I shot him in the face and he went down. The other guy braced to try to run past me, but I was already swiveling. The first shot hit him in the neck. He spun away and fell. I moved forward and shot him in the back of his head. I went back to Fukumoto and put another round in his head, too, then did the same for Muscle One and Muscle Two. I paused, panting. The room stank of gun smoke and blood. And shit—someone had lost control of his bowels. For an instant, I didn't know where I was, the carnage and the smell all dragging me back to the jungle, but my eyes telling me I was in somebody's goddamn drawing room.

I focused on my breathing, slowing it down, cuing my heart rate to do the same. I tried to think. Was there anything I needed to do? Any evidence I was leaving behind, anything I could manipulate to fool the police and the mob?

Nothing came to me. It was all too unfamiliar, too confusing. I couldn't transition from combat to crime scene. All I could think to do was get the fuck out before reinforcements showed up.

I wanted to keep the gun, but I realized I couldn't. It might be useful, but no way was I going to carry around the murder weapon. I tossed it onto Muscle Two's corpse.

But wait, Muscle One had one, too. At least, it looked like he'd been going for one.

I knelt and opened Muscle One's jacket. There it was, another Hi Power, in his waistband. I searched through his pants. No spare magazine. Guess he wasn't expecting a drawn-out gun battle. I checked the load. The magazine was full—thirteen rounds. Wait, would Muscle Two have a spare? I thought probably not. Besides, he was lying in an enormous pool of blood and I didn't want it creating shoe prints through the house. But shit, I could have taken the magazine from Muscle Two's gun—it would still have five rounds in it. Instead, I'd tossed it onto his corpse, which was now surrounded by a moat of blood. *Drag a couch over, lean down, and retrieve it?* No, not worth the time. One gun would have to do.

I glanced around the room one more time. Had I missed anything? *Wait, the knife, the knife.* I'd paid cash but still, better not to leave it. I'd dropped it after taking the gun from Muscle One . . .

where? I looked around frantically. *There.* I picked it up, wiped it on his pants leg, and slid it into the sheath. *Wait, goddamn it, the hammer, too.* Maybe better not to leave it. What would be the theory behind someone attacking four armed yakuza with a hammer? I couldn't articulate why at that moment, but I thought the hammer should go back where it belonged. I picked it up. Shit, it had a good amount of blood on it. I hurried to the kitchen, grabbed a few paper towels, and cleaned it off. *What about you?* I glanced down at the windbreaker. Yeah, there was some blood on it, but most of it wiped off easily, and the dark color took care of the rest. I pocketed the towels and headed back into the garage. I replaced the hammer on the shelf. *Okay, good to go.*

I took two deep breaths, and was about to hit the garage door opener when the door engaged and started to rise of its own accord. For a split instant, all I could think was, *What the fuck?* And then I realized, *Someone's here.* I dashed around to the front of the Mercedes and squeezed down below the bumper, my back against the wall, the Browning in my hand.

The door kept going up. I snuck a peek under the car. I saw the wheels of another car, paused in the short driveway while the door ascended. As soon as it was fully open, the car eased forward into the open space. I scrunched down lower. The car stopped, the motor died, and the driver-side door opened. I saw a pair of sensible pumps and two thick ankles in stockings. The wife? Probably. Kill her, or let her go? *Safer to kill her.* But I hesitated. The door closed. The ankles appeared on the far side of the garage, crossed behind the Mercedes, and moved to the interior garage door. *Now or never.* But I hesitated again. I heard the sound of a key sliding into a lock, the key turning, a pause, a little under-the-breath *hmmph*, the key turning again, the interior door opening. The exterior door started to close—she must have pressed a button. I heard the interior door close. The second it did, I sprang out, dashed forward between the cars, and rolled under the door just in time. I got to my feet, peeled off and pocketed the gloves, and walked as quickly as reasonably possible toward the station. If I was lucky, she would pause in the kitchen, go upstairs, do some chores or whatever before finding what I'd left behind. If I was unlucky, she would head straight to that drawing room and immediately call the police, or more yakuza, or both. I might have only a few minutes.

I made it back to Thanatos, retrieved and secured the license plate, and roared off. I crossed the Tama River and followed it south for a few kilometers, tossing the knife in along the way and leaving the gloves, windbreaker, and other disguise items buried in various trash bins. Then I went back to Daikanyama, hoping I might find the girl's Porsche still there so I could replace the garage door opener. But, unsurprisingly, she was gone. I cruised around the streets for about a half hour, hoping she might have just driven the car to another boutique—it was hot enough that she might have done so to avoid the walk—but I saw no sign of the car. A bit of a shame. It would have been good for the police to have no idea how someone had gained access to the house. With no signs of forced entry, they might have formed a working theory of "someone the victims knew," something like that. As it was, I was reasonably optimistic they would reflexively classify the whole thing as a yakuza hit, and that the yakuza would do the same. If a bunch of mobsters wanted to start killing each other in retaliation, that was fine with me. I preferred them trying to kill each other rather than coming after me.

And then I realized . . . would the girl say anything to the police when she discovered the garage door opener was missing? "Hi, I was his mistress, I couldn't help notice the garage door opener he gave me went missing from my car on the day of the murders." I seriously doubted she would come forward. And even if she did, so what? Maybe she was being tailed by the yakuza team that had carried out the hit. Maybe they had intel about her relationship, and the plan all along was to get the garage door opener and use it to gain entry to the residence. It didn't matter how it all played out, as long as none of it could lead back to me. And I didn't see how it could.

I stopped in a park to think a little more. *You okay?* I asked myself.

What? Never better.

In the movies, they always make sure the hero kills only in self-defense, typically in the instant before the bad guy gets the drop on him. Even in that film Miyamoto had mentioned, *Dirty Harry*, Clint Eastwood blows away a guy who had kidnapped, tortured, and killed a teenage girl only when the guy goes for a gun.

To me, that's all bullshit. More than anything else, killing is about survival. About doing everything you can to deceive, and cheat, and stack the odds in your own favor. You don't wait for the other guy to go for his gun; you shoot him before he has a chance. If he has his back to you, that's even better. If you can call in an air strike, that's better still. You don't just do everything you possibly can to prevent a fight from being fair—preventing the fight from being fair is the entire point. Do you want the enemy to have as good a chance of killing you as you have of killing him? Or do you want to make sure he gets no chance at all? As far as I'm concerned, the people who think a fair fight is desirable can go ahead and die in one. I wanted to live, and that meant hitting the yakuza hard, and unexpectedly, and never, ever giving up even the smallest advantage.

Still, you just killed four more people. Five in three days.

Is that supposed to bother me?

Shouldn't it?

I didn't have an answer for that. Other than:

It doesn't.

Because sometimes there's just what you can do, and what you can't.

chapter
twenty

I called McGraw from a payphone. "It's done," I told him. "What's the status on the last file?"

"Done . . . you mean, done, done?"

"What the hell do you think I mean?"

"It was fast, is what I mean. I'm surprised, that's all. Impressed."

"What's the status on the last file?"

"Just about completed. I'm sorry it's not quite ready yet. I have to tell you, I never dreamed you'd be able to act on these files faster than I'd be able to prepare them."

"When can I get it?"

"Tomorrow, I think. Meet me at noon in front of the Benzaiten shrine. You know it?"

"There are a few. Shiba Kōen, Ueno Kōen, Inokashira Kōen. Which one do you want?"

There was a pause. "I didn't realize there were so many."

"Popular goddess, apparently."

"Well, I meant the one at Inokashira. I'll see you there." He hung up.

I blew out a long breath, closed my eyes, and shifted mental gears. I realized I hadn't done anything about finding a good place to take Sayaka for dinner. Outside the love hotel district, I didn't know Uguisudani at all. In fact, I didn't know much of anything. Food was mostly functional for me, and more than ramen or a rice bowl was a rarity. What would she like? What would be special for her?

Well, she listens to jazz all the time. Maybe something with jazz? I thought of the flyers I'd seen at Lion in Shibuya. Shit, why hadn't I thought of it right away?

I couldn't remember the name of the performer . . . a guy who played a horn, that was all. But the club . . . the club was called Taro. In Shinjuku.

Shinjuku. All the way across town from Uguisudani. She said she couldn't go far. It wasn't going to work.

Yeah, but what if there were a way? A live jazz concert . . . that would be pretty special. Had she ever even been to one? I knew I hadn't.

I found the club in the Tokyo yellow pages. It was in Kabukichō, one of the more salacious parts of Shinjuku. Not so much during the day, but it could get pretty tawdry as sunlight gave way to neon and the nocturnal clientele began to arrive in force, released from the maw of the corporate machine, animated by sake, emboldened by night. Still, one of Tokyo's charms is the complete lack of zoning, official or otherwise, and just as you might find a foundry next to an *izakaya* next to a chicken coop next to a house, so too will you find citizens and sinners walking side by side through even the dimmest ventricles of Kabukichō's neon heart of darkness.

The only problem was that Kabukichō was infested with yakuza. Next to places like the Kodokan, where I might be anticipated, it was probably the last place I should be going. But still, there couldn't have been more than a handful of yakuza who had any idea what I even looked like, and it wasn't like they'd be on the lookout for me in Kabukichō. Nor was I planning on visiting any of their clubs. I decided I was being paranoid. Later in life, anytime I found myself thinking, *You're being paranoid,* I'd pat myself on the back. But back then, I looked at it as more a bug than a feature.

I rode out to the club to reconnoiter. It was in the basement of a mixed office-entertainment building at the edge of Kabukichō. I looked down—a steep, narrow flight of stairs. Shit, this wasn't going to work.

Well, I'd come this far. I headed down. There were some flyers by the entrance. Terumasa Hino, right, that was the horn guy's name. Nine o'clock that night. I folded one up and pocketed it.

The door was open and I went inside. The place was tiny—room for maybe twenty people, and that's if they were crammed in tight. Everything was black: walls, ceiling, floor. There was a labyrinth of pipes and vents overhead, and clusters of mismatched tables and chairs throughout. A mirrored bar and a half-dozen stools to one side. A petite Japanese woman was setting up the stage. She didn't notice me when I came in, and I watched for a moment in awe of her speed and energy—connecting cables, adjusting lights, moving equipment. After a moment, I said, "Excuse me, I'm sorry to interrupt . . ."

She paused and looked up. "Yes?"

"I, uh, I have a friend who's a jazz enthusiast. A huge Terumasa Hino fan, in fact." That last part wasn't necessarily true, but I didn't know that it was necessarily untrue, either.

"Yes?"

"And I'd really like to find a way to take her to tonight's performance. I think it would mean a lot to her."

"You should. Just get here early. Hino-san is popular."

"This is the thing. She's in a wheelchair."

The woman said nothing.

"I don't know how to make it happen, but if you could help, it would make someone really happy. I could pay you, that's not the problem."

"Pay me for what?"

"I don't know. Making sure there's room for her chair or something."

"You don't have to pay me for that. But how are you going to get her down the stairs?"

"I don't know. I'm just trying to figure out one thing at a time."

"Well, could you carry her?"

"If she'd let me, I guess. Sure."

"Then maybe you could carry her down the stairs and I could follow with the wheelchair. I think they fold up, right? Does hers?"

"I actually don't know. I can check."

She glanced at her watch. "I'll make sure we have space. What's your name?"

"Jun."

"I'm Kyoko Seki."

"Seiki-san . . . I don't know what to say. Thank you."

She nodded. "I have to get back to work. Just get here by eight-thirty."

"I will. I'm just . . . thank you."

I headed back up the stairs. There were a dozen things I still didn't know, a dozen things that could make it all fall apart, but still . . . I thought maybe I could do this.

But how was I going to get her out here? Thanatos was out of the question. And I didn't have a car. I could rent one, but I was going to need something specialized. A passenger van, something like that.

I went to a phone booth and found a place that had a Honda step van. I had to go all the way out to Haneda Airport to get it, but I didn't mind. It was an awkward-looking little vehicle—a van, yes, but too high and too thin, as though someone had squashed its sides together and its mass had nowhere to travel but up, and with ridiculously diminutive tires that made it look a bit like the automotive equivalent of a dachshund. But the back door opened at the top and the bottom, creating a good-sized cargo-loading space, and the floor was close to the ground. And it had air-conditioning . . . that alone might be worth the price of admission. If Sayaka was game, I thought it would work. I pushed Thanatos in back, drove to Ueno, and found a construction site, where I liberated a couple of two-by-sixes. I might have been able to lift her into the van, but it would be easier with a ramp. Then I found another business hotel, where I pulled Thanatos out of the Honda and parked it. I checked in, showered, changed, and drove to Uguisudani. Along the way, I was more nervous than I'd been outside Fukumoto's house that very afternoon. It already seemed like a long time ago.

chapter
twenty-one

I parked the van illegally near the Uguisudani Station entrance.
If a cop came, I'd need to move, but if possible, I didn't want
Sayaka to have to go too far. I stayed inside, keeping the engine
running and the air conditioning going, until I saw her coming up
the street, propelling herself with efficient, confident strokes of the
wheels.

I cut the engine, hopped out, and went to meet her. She looked
good—her hair was back as usual, doubtless a concession to the
heat and humidity, and she was wearing a sleeveless blouse that gave
me my first really good look at some of her skin and her body. And
a good look it was.

"Is that your car?" she said, looking past me.

"Yeah. You look great. Can I give you a hand?"

"Thanks. You can't park there, you know."

"I know, I don't want to leave it there, I was hoping we could
go somewhere." I was aware I was talking a little fast. I needed to
slow it down.

"Go somewhere? What do you mean?" She didn't sound happy.

"Look, I know what you said, but—"

"No, Jun. I don't want to drive anywhere."

"Can I just—"

"No. I told you around here."

I reached into my pocket and handed her the flyer. "This is
what gave me the idea. Do you know him? I know you like jazz."

She unfolded it and her mouth dropped open slightly. "Do I know Terumasa Hino? Are you joking?"

"I don't know. He's . . . good?"

"He's amazing. I have all his records."

I was glad I hadn't lied to Kyoko when I told her Sayaka was a fan. "I saw the flyer, that's where I got the idea. I know I probably shouldn't have, but it just seemed like something that could be fun. Because I know you like jazz. So I went out to the club and checked it out. I met the owner and she said she'd help—"

"What do you mean, 'help'?"

I realized I was brushing up against sensitivities I had barely even considered, much less understood. "Well, I told her I had a friend who was a big Terumasa Hino fan—"

"You told her what? You didn't even know I knew him."

"I know, I guess I was going out on a limb a little, but I figured you might like him."

She was looking exasperated. "And?"

"And I told her—Kyoko's her name, by the way—that you were in a wheelchair, and she said that was no problem, all we had to do was get there early, by eight-thirty, and if I could carry you down the steps, she would follow with the wheelchair. If it folds. Does it? Fold, I mean. She asked and I didn't know."

Her expression was transitioning from exasperated to pissed. Shit. I didn't even know what I'd done, exactly, but I'd blown it.

"You think I want to go someplace, and be carried around?"

"No, I didn't think it would be like that—"

"Have you carry me around like a broken fucking doll, while some woman I don't even know follows us with my wheelchair? That's your idea?"

"No, that wasn't—"

"I'm going to go, okay? This was a bad idea. I'm sorry."

"No, wait. Wait. Can I say something?"

She pursed her lips and nodded.

I tried to collect my thoughts. "Look, I don't know why you're in a wheelchair. I know it's not your fault. I mean, what I mean is, if you were blind and I wanted to go out with you, I'd offer you my arm. If you were deaf, I'd bring along a notepad so we could talk by writing. You're in a wheelchair, so I can just push you or whatever, okay? Or carry you, if there are stairs. Or, I know there's more to it than that and I haven't really thought about it, but I feel like, it's just a practical problem. I can walk, and you can't. So let me help you. It's like, you know jazz and I don't. I mean, I know a little—Bill Evans—but that's about it. So you can teach me. You can help me, too."

She bowed her head for a moment, then looked up. "But don't you see? I could teach you jazz, and then you'd know jazz. You can carry me, but I'm never going to be able to walk."

"I know. And I'm sorry. I feel like I keep saying stupid things. But if you don't let me help you, or someone help you, you're never going to get to see Terumasa Hino. And I hear he's amazing."

She sighed.

"You sure you don't want to just give it a try?" I said. "I think there's plenty of room in the van. I'll drive really slowly and carefully. Whatever you want."

There was a long pause. Twice she started to say something and didn't. I waited, hoping and trying not to. Finally, she said, "Did you see their bathroom?"

"What? No, I didn't."

"Well, welcome to just one small example of the dozens of things you haven't considered about my life, Jun. I'm not blaming you. Why would you think about these things? But a club like that . . . my wheelchair won't even fit in the bathroom. Do you see how . . . do you see what this is like for me? I don't like going to new places. With new people. It doesn't work out well."

"It hasn't, you mean?"

"Yeah. It hasn't."

"But . . . are you going to stop trying?"

She shook her head. "I don't know."

"I didn't see the bathroom. It's probably pretty small."

"I'm sure it is."

"Can I say something?"

She gave a little laugh. "Could I stop you?"

"I've been in some . . . difficult situations. I don't want to talk about them. I don't even want to think about them, not now, anyway. But what I learned in those situations is to not be sentimental. To just be practical. People need to go to the bathroom, just like they need to eat and drink and sleep. So when you need to go, I'll push your chair for you, or you can do it, and you put your arms around my neck, and I'll get you seated, and I'll back out and close the door and you call me when you're ready. I know you have to go to the bathroom sometimes. I mean, you're beautiful, but you're human. Humans need to go to the bathroom. At least that's what I hear."

She laughed, but other than that didn't respond.

"Will you trust me?" I said.

She looked away. After a moment, she started nodding, almost imperceptibly. "All right," she said. "Okay."

I couldn't stop myself from grinning. "Okay. Okay, great. On the way over, I want you to tell me all about this guy Terumasa Hino, okay? Teach me about jazz."

She smiled, a little uncertainly. "Okay."

She pushed herself over to the van. I walked alongside her. "Now listen, if I do anything wrong, or anything that makes you uncomfortable, you just tell me, okay?"

"Yeah, I've got that covered."

I opened the cargo doors and slid out the two-by-sixes. "I can just push you up, is that all right?"

"I can do it." She took hold of the wheels and propelled herself up with a quick series of long, smooth strokes. She was stronger than she looked. Well, of course—her upper body was constantly getting exercised. From behind, I was able to take a close look at her legs. She was wearing jeans, but I could see the limbs inside were withered. I wondered again what had happened to her. Well, if she wanted to tell me, she would. Otherwise, not. I slid the two-by-sixes back in, closed the doors, went around front, and drove off. I went slowly and carefully—I didn't want to take any chances on Sayaka getting bounced around in back. These days, you'd probably be arrested for putting someone in a wheelchair unsecured in the back of a cargo van, but it was a different world then. No child seats, no shoulder belts, no bicycle helmets, no safety warnings or polarized plugs . . . it's a wonder anyone even survived to reproduce.

On the way to Shinjuku, she told me about Hino: jazz trumpeter; led his own quartet; his instruments, his influences, his significance. She said he was on the cusp of fame and she thought one day he would be a legend. I realized I'd gotten really lucky seeing that flyer. If it had been anything else, I didn't think she would have come with me. We'd be having sushi or something in Uguisudani. Not that it would have been bad, but this was different. I liked how engaged she was, how enthusiastic. I liked how out of the ordinary this was for her. How special. I liked that it showed she trusted me.

"So what is it about jazz?" I asked as we drove.

"You said you like Bill Evans, right?"

"Right."

"Well, what is it about Bill Evans?"

I had to think about that. I'd never tried to articulate it before. "I don't know. Listening to him . . . if always feels like a haven. Does that make sense?"

She laughed. "It makes perfect sense. You listen to Hino tonight
and then tell me more, okay?"

I managed to find us a spot on the street not too far from Taro.
I was feeling confident, optimistic. A part of my mind lingered on
the late unpleasantness—the pooling blood, the smell of gun smoke,
the animal shriek of a man stabbed in the guts—but for the most
part it felt compartmentalized. Walled off. Safe. That was another
part of my life, another part of who I was, but it had nothing to do
with tonight. I was someone else now. Maybe I shared his memories, but that other person wasn't here.

I actually believed I could maintain that. I was too young to
know that some memories don't fade, or age, or die. That the weight
of some of what we do accumulates, expands, coheres, solidifies.
That life means coming to grips with that ever-present weight,
learning how to carry it with you wherever you go, understanding
and accepting that it'll be with you and on you and in you for all
your days, until you reach a point where all the energy you ever had
is devoted just to shouldering its mass. And when you're finally able
to set down that burden, it'll only be because it was time to set
down everything else, too, everything you had, or have, or were ever
going to have. And you better hope that's really the end of it,
because no one knows what happens after.

I pushed Sayaka along in the wheelchair, mindful of our surroundings, on the lookout for anyone in a punch perm and cheap
suit swaggering in our direction. But I saw no yakuza, only streets
crowded with every kind of pleasure-seeker: groups of students
going for a cheap dinner or a movie; businessmen entertaining
clients; salarymen sneaking off for some sexual recreation before
heading home and lying to their wives. There were people laughing
and talking and horns honking and touts calling from storefronts
and the sounds of motorcycle engines and the rumble of trains. A
weird kind of harmony amid the chaos, a melodious cacophony.

When we got to the entrance to Taro, I said, "So here's the tricky part. What do you want to do? I can help you down, get you seated, and send someone up for your chair. Will that work?"

She nodded. She looked a little scared.

I thought the easiest thing would be to just scoop her up in my arms, but I imagined she wouldn't like that. I knew I wouldn't—it would make me feel too much like a baby, an invalid. "What's comfortable for you?" I said. "I'm thinking if I squat down next to you, you can put your arm around my neck, I can put mine around your waist, and away we'll go. Sound okay?"

She nodded again. "Yeah."

I got down next to her, and we did it the way I suggested. It was more awkward than I'd anticipated, and I realized I'd been stupid—I'd helped drunks walk, and wounded men walk, and I was expecting something similar here. But she couldn't put any weight on her legs at all. They were useless, just dangling from her body. God, no wonder she must have hated being out of her chair, relying on other people.

"Wait a second, I don't think this is going to work," I said. "Here, I have a better idea."

I shifted around until I was facing her, my back to the stairs. "Put both arms around my neck. Tighter. That's it. Now just . . . lean against me. Don't worry, I won't drop you, I've got the bannister." I put my free arm around her waist and arched back a little so I could take some of her weight onto my torso, then started down the stairs backward. She was surprisingly light. But of course—her legs would weigh almost nothing. I moved slowly and carefully. I tried not to notice how her breasts felt pressed against my chest, or how her arms felt around my neck, or what her back felt like through her blouse. Or how good she smelled. I wasn't notably successful.

We made it without incident, if "without incident" can be said to include our unspoken agreement to not mention the hard-on that arose to accompany our passage. What can I say, I was only twenty. I was horrified when I felt it start to happen, but there was nothing I could do. And my embarrassment was made worse by the smile she seemed to be trying to suppress. I didn't know what kind of feeling she had down there, but somehow she seemed to be aware of my condition.

We went inside the club. Kyoko was issuing instructions to a thirtyish guy behind the bar and to two college-age girls I assumed were waitresses. When she saw us, she immediately sent a bartender to retrieve the wheelchair, and made sure he placed it front center. In fact, there wasn't a bad seat in the place—it was too small for anyone to be more than a few paces from the stage. Kyoko chatted with Sayaka for a few minutes—how Kyoko had opened this place, who she booked here, the musicians they both liked. Apparently, Kyoko was personal friends with Hino, and promised we would have a chance to meet him. Sayaka was ecstatic. People started drifting in, and within a half hour, the place was packed.

"Everything okay?" I asked as we waited for Hino and his quartet to come on.

She nodded. "Yeah. Kyoko's really nice. Natural. A lot of people think if you're in a wheelchair, you must be stupid, and they talk to you like a spinal injury is the same as brain damage. She's not like that." She paused, then added, "Neither are you."

A minute later, the lights dimmed, and Hino and three other guys came walking briskly up the side of the room, the only place where there was any kind of free passage. The room broke out in wild applause. Hino raised his trumpet above his head and gave it a shake in greeting, and the applause and shouting redoubled.

They took their positions on the stage—Hino, the pianist, the bassist, the drummer. Then, without any fanfare, they started playing. I didn't know the piece—I knew very little jazz at all back then—but it was beautiful. Starting softly and building slowly, it was elegiac and full of longing and it made me happy and sad, sometimes alternately, sometimes at the same time. It made me feel like I was missing something and I didn't even know what it was. It was alluring, but frustrating, too, to be able to sense something so profound and not be able to grasp it.

I realized I was nodding along to the music and stopped myself, embarrassed. I saw Sayaka glance at me and smile. I looked around. Everyone was nodding their heads, or tapping their toes, or swaying slightly. It was hard not to. These people didn't know each other, none of us did, and yet we were all responding the same way. It was like a community of strangers, united by . . . what? I didn't know. Whatever we felt in the music.

When the song was over, the room erupted in fresh shouts and applause. Hino introduced his quartet, and explained that the song was called "Alone, Alone and Alone." I must have been the only one there who didn't already know.

While they played, Sayaka and I snacked on a variety of small plates. Sayaka didn't drink—I thought maybe because she didn't want to have to be taken to the bathroom more than absolutely necessary, but I wasn't sure—but I ordered a whisky. I didn't know what the hell I was doing, but I figured whisky was a sophisticated drink and it seemed like it would go with jazz. Of course, when the waitress asked what brand I wanted, I was stymied, and covered by asking her what they had. Hibiki and Yamazaki, she told me. Mentally flipping a coin, I told her I'd have a Yamazaki. Twelve-year-old or eighteen? Feeling like the mask of sophistication I'd tried to don was being peeled right off me, I told her the eighteen. Straight or rocks? Was she fucking with me? Straight, please. At which point, the q-and-a game mercifully ended. As it happened, the Yamazaki was so good I ordered another, and would have gotten a third if Sayaka had been drinking with me, and if I hadn't needed to drive later.

I was surprised at how much I enjoyed the performance—not just the music, but the experience of sharing it with a roomful of strangers. I had expected any pleasure I might take in it to be mostly vicarious, but it turned out to be much more than that. Occasionally, I would be struck by something discordant—an image or a sensation of what I had done in the last few days. But I was able to push those intrusions away. If I could continue to be mindful of the moment and not of my memories, I thought, I'd be all right. That was one life. This was another. They were separate, and I would keep them so.

When the show was over, the applause finally done, and the patrons beginning to file out the door, Kyoko introduced us to the band as promised. Hino gripped Sayaka's hand in both of his and bowed simultaneously. It was a nice gesture, a combination of the western and the eastern, with a lot of warmth in it. Kyoko brought over one of Hino's albums and he signed it for Sayaka. She couldn't stop smiling, and I was glad to see her shedding some of the detached cool that had so characterized her when we'd first met.

Sayaka needed the bathroom before we left, and it went fine. If she felt any embarrassment about having to be helped in and out, she didn't show it. I followed suit when she was done, and paid the bill at the door.

"Well?" I said. "You ready?"

She nodded, and we got her up the stairs pretty much the same way we'd gotten her down. With pretty much the same embarrassing impediment on my part. The bartender followed us up with the wheelchair. I helped Sayaka get seated, we said goodnight, and headed back to the van.

"Was it okay?" I asked, pushing her along through Kabukichō's neon-lit alleys, maneuvering around revelers, Sayaka's head swiveling as she took in the sights and the noise and the crowds. I knew

I was being paranoid, but still I was careful to keep my head down, just on the remote chance I might be recognized.

She glanced back at me. "It was amazing. Thank you."

That made me really happy. Without thinking, I said, "Hey, do you feel like taking a walk? I mean—"

She laughed. "I know what you mean. Where?"

"I don't know. Ueno Park, maybe? It's right next to Uguisudani, so . . ."

There was a pause, then she said, "No, let's do something different. I want to see something new."

That was encouraging. I thought for a moment. "Do you know Kitazawa-gawa?"

"The *hanami* place?"

"Yeah, in Setagaya. It's crowded when the blossoms are blooming, but otherwise it's just a nice place for a stroll." I realized as I said it that "stroll" wasn't the right word. But she'd already told me she understood what I meant.

She smiled. "Well? What are we waiting for?"

chapter
twenty-two

We drove the short distance southwest, parked, and got out. Setagaya was an upscale suburban part of Tokyo, outside the Yamanote, where people with money might move if they wanted a little less urban density and a little more green. It was quiet most of the time, and at night could be remarkably serene. And Kitazawa-gawa, a kind of nature walk to the extent such a thing could be said to exist in Tokyo, was particularly charming in the evening, with a little creek burbling along beside it, lots of grass and trees, and evocative shadows cast by tall iron streetlights. I pushed Sayaka along, enjoying her company, liking that she trusted me enough to take her somewhere new. I was beginning to appreciate how difficult it must have been for her to get around. The world was nowhere near as handicapped-accessible then as it's since become, and every grassy or other soft surface, every narrow space, every curb represented an obstacle. And that's with someone there to help. Alone, just a few short stairs would have been for her what a twenty-foot wall would be to me.

"It's another universe out here," she said, looking around us and up at the trees.

"I know. Tokyo's like the blind men and the elephant. Every part you touch fools you into thinking you know the whole thing. But I don't think anyone can really know Tokyo. It's too big, and too . . . I don't know. Mysterious."

She glanced back at me. "You really like it, don't you?"

I didn't answer right away. The wheels of her chair crunched softly along the pavement. Somewhere, a dog barked. Other than that, the city was silent and still.

"It's kind of a love-hate relationship, I guess."

"Why? Because you're half?"

Haafu is a neutral Japanese word for people of mixed parentage, words borrowed from abroad carrying less emotional content.

"Yeah, you know. I never really felt accepted here. I loved it, but it didn't love me. I guess it's kind of pathetic that I'm back. Like showing up on the doorstep of a girl who kicked me out. But . . . shit, it's a long story."

"You have someplace to go?"

Apparently, I did not. I told her a little about my childhood in Tokyo. The taunts, the bullies, my father's conflicted shame. "It's not a great place to grow up if you're not really Japanese," I said. "I mean, if you're a hundred percent something else, they don't care. They might even admire you. But if you're half . . . if you look Japanese but you're really not . . . they hate that."

She laughed. "You think I don't know?"

"You mean the wheelchair? Do you get discriminated against? I'm sorry, I admit I've never really thought about it."

"Not the wheelchair. Being Korean."

I stopped pushing and looked at her from the side. "You're Korean?"

"Second-generation *zainichi*. And it's just like you said. Japanese hate us because they can't tell us apart. I mean, all prejudice is crazy, but it's even crazier when you have to hire a private detective to track down a person's lineage so you can know whether to discriminate against him!"

We both laughed. I said, "So you're Korean. I didn't realize."

"Yeah. Sayaka Kimura. My parents chose Sayaka because they didn't want people to know, but Kimura's kind of a giveaway."

Kimura was a typical *zainichi* surname, though not exclusively so, an easy variant on the native Kim.

"Well, I wouldn't have known."

"Does it bother you?"

"No. I like it. It's nice to know another outsider. Is that part of why you want to go to America?"

"I just want to get out of here. I told you, it's not really love-hate for me. It's just hate. I want to go someplace that's not so big, that's not growing so fast, that's not so overwhelming and impersonal. Someplace where they don't care where you're from, or where your parents are from."

I didn't know that America was really that. It hadn't been for me. But maybe it would be for her. I started pushing again. "What will you do there?"

"I haven't figured that out yet. College, to start with, if I can save enough money."

So she hadn't been to college. I wondered if that embarrassed her, if it was why she hadn't answered at the hotel when I first asked.

"And after that?"

She shrugged. "Whatever I want. I want to get a good job. And be free, really free. I feel like I've been living such a stultified life here. I need to take more risks. And I don't know why, but I'm afraid to take them here."

"You think America will make you braver?"

She looked back at me, maybe trying to see if I was teasing her. I wasn't.

"You think that's silly?"

I thought about Cambodia. "No. Most people think bravery comes entirely from within, but it doesn't. It depends on a lot of things. Maybe one of them is just . . . where you live. Your culture, your surroundings."

She nodded. "I swear, this city is killing me. I just feel so inhibited here. I imagine America, and I see myself doing anything, doing everything. Maybe I can drive there, if someone invents a car with hand controls. And I want to scuba dive. Why not? You don't need legs for that. And skydive . . . why shouldn't you be able to skydive in a wheelchair? You think falling is any harder for me? It's easier." She paused and looked around. "I just have to get out of here first."

I didn't know about scuba diving and skydiving, let alone all the rest. But why disabuse someone of her dreams?

I saw a park bench next to an old, gnarled tree, bathed in the shadows cast by one of the lights set out along the path. "Do you want to sit? I mean . . . shit, I'm sorry, I keep doing that."

She shook her head. "Don't be sorry. I like it. That you see I can go for a walk in the chair. And that sitting next to a park bench isn't the same as being in the chair."

"Thanks for that. I've been feeling a little stupid at times."

She looked at me in a way I couldn't interpret. "You're not stupid."

I positioned the wheelchair next to the bench and sat close to her.

"All right," she said. "So now you have to answer your own question. What is it about jazz? I saw you tapping your feet and nodding your head. Did you like it?"

"A lot, yeah."

"Why?"

I told her about how it had made me feel . . . that feeling of longing for something I didn't even know I lacked. And how I was struck by the way the music had created this sense of kinship and commonality in a room full of strangers, all of us feeling the same thing.

"Yes," she said, when I was done. "That's it, exactly."

"Was this your first concert?"

"Yes. And it's exactly what I imagined it would be like. No, better. It was really special. Thanks for taking me. Thanks for . . . encouraging me."

I felt myself blushing and looked down for a moment. I didn't want to look like an awkward kid with her.

But she spotted it anyway and laughed. "Are you blushing?"

Shit. "I didn't think you could see it, in the shadows."

"I couldn't. But then you looked down."

"Oh, great," I said. We both laughed, then were quiet for a moment.

I looked at her. "Can I ask you something personal?"

She brushed a hair back from her face. "Sure. If I don't want to answer, I won't."

"How . . . were you born that way? Or did something happen? You said 'injury' before, so . . ."

There was a long pause. Then she said, "I was sixteen. On my way home from school. A car hit me from behind."

A strange, clear sympathy opened up inside me. But I didn't know how to express it. I only said, "I'm sorry."

She shrugged. "I don't even remember it. I woke up in the hospital."

"Did they catch the guy who did it?"

"Oh, yeah. He totaled his car trying to get away afterward. Drove it into a wall. I got this, and he didn't have a scratch on him."

I didn't say anything.

"He was drunk. But it turned out he was also a big-shot politician. A lot of connections. His people offered my parents some money as an apology. But really to keep their mouths shut and not make trouble."

"Damn."

"My parents wouldn't take it. They wanted to see the guy in jail. But then some other people came to the house and recommended my parents take the money."

"Yakuza?"

She nodded. "So what could my parents do? They took the money and signed some papers. It wasn't even enough to cover the operations I needed."

I thought about the four yakuza I'd killed earlier that day. I suddenly wished I could do it again. Well, I'd be going after Mad Dog soon enough. And Mori, another big-shot politician. The thought was both grim and glad.

"Where are your parents now?"

"They're gone. They were old. They had me late—they thought they couldn't have children, and then after all those years they wound up with me."

"I'm sorry."

"Don't keep saying that, or I won't tell you any more sad stories."

I smiled a little, for her benefit. "Do you remember the name of the guy who hit you?"

She nodded. "Nobuo Kamioka. I'll never forget it."

"Do you . . . I would want to kill him." I didn't mean to say it. It just bled through somehow.

She was quiet for a moment. "My father felt like that, I know. And I guess I did for a while, too."

"Not anymore?"

"I don't know. At some point, I learned not to think of it that way. I believe in karma."

"Do you?"

"Yeah. I believe in the end we get paid back what we deal out."

I hoped that wasn't true. "Has Kamioka been paid back?"

"I don't know. I don't really think about it. I'm not responsible for someone else's karma. I just want to live my life, be grateful for what I have and not be bitter about what I don't, you know? Focus on the future, not the past."

I nodded. "I think that's a good attitude."

"But you don't share it?"

"I'd like to."

There was a pause, then she said, "You know, you were pretty intimidating with that drunk guy the first time I saw you. You were so calm. Like hurting him or not hurting him was just a kind of . . . equation. But then with me, you're awkward and sweet. I can't figure you out."

I shifted on the bench. "There's nothing to figure out."

"Yes, there is. I can tell you're hiding something."

"I don't think so."

"What do you do for a living here, anyway? You've never mentioned it."

"Well, that's part of this jam I'm in."

"The one you've nearly sorted out."

"Is there another one I don't know about?"

"I don't know—is there?"

"I'm pretty sure it's just the one."

"You're not going to tell me?"

I realized this was always going to be a problem if I tried to keep one foot in the dark and the other in the light. I'd been naïve in not facing it earlier, and I should have been prepared for it, because now Sayaka was asking me the most ordinary of questions and I had no answers.

"I . . . was in the military for three years."

"What military?"

I was reluctant to say more. America's war in Vietnam was hugely unpopular among young people in Japan. I didn't want her not to like me. And I didn't want to have to explain myself, either. But I didn't see how to avoid the subject anymore.

"The American military. Army."

"You mean Vietnam?"

There it was. I nodded.

"You were in Vietnam?"

I nodded again.

"What did you do there?"

How do you answer something like that? I said, "I did all the horrible things people do in wars and that they're uncomfortable talking about afterward."

"Did you kill anyone?"

It was weird. I was so used to feeling younger than she was. Now I felt older.

"It was a war, Sayaka. Killing people is what you do in a war. Unless you're in the rear, which I definitely wasn't."

"I'm sorry. You said you didn't want to talk about it."

"It's okay."

"But you did bring it up."

And suddenly I felt like the younger one again. "Just to point out that what I've been doing here is a kind of . . . holdover from contacts I made there."

"You mean spy stuff?"

I looked at her. She was just curious, she wasn't judging me. "I don't want to lie to you," I said, "and I don't want to get you in any trouble by telling you things you shouldn't know. I don't know how I got mixed up in it all exactly. I mean, outside what I learned in the military, I don't have a lot of skills. I don't have anything to fall back on. And this opportunity came along, and I just took it. And one of the things I like about you is that you're not connected to any of it. And I . . . and I don't know what I'm trying to say, and I'm going to stop."

"Are you sure? You're cute when you babble."

I laughed.

She added, "And now you're blushing."

"Okay, I'm not going to talk anymore."

"Bet you will."

"Bet you're wrong."

"See? I win."

I laughed again. "All right. So . . . you live in Uguisudani?"

"About half a kilometer from the hotel. Why?"

"I was just wondering. I mean, do you really never go far from there?"

She sighed. "No, not really. Sometimes I tell myself I should. But it's scary not to know what I'm going to find. I've gotten in trouble a few times and it's just . . . it's unpleasant. To be helpless and to have to rely on the kindness of strangers. It can be . . . humiliating. So over time, I've gotten in the habit of staying where I know the layout. Where I'm comfortable."

"So you really must have trusted me to come out with me tonight." It was just a neutral statement, but I think there was a little wonderment in my tone.

She looked at me. "You want to know what did it?"

I nodded. "Sure."

"It's when you told me you thought of me as the girl at the hotel."

I tried to puzzle that out, and couldn't. "I don't get it."

She laughed. "You see? You're doing it now, stupid. The girl at the hotel. Not the girl in the wheelchair. It's like you don't even notice it."

I leaned over as though to get a better view. "You're in a wheel-chair?"

She laughed and punched my shoulder. I caught her fingers in mine. Without thinking, I brought her hand to my mouth and kissed it.

She looked down. "I don't know, Jun."

"You don't want me to kiss you?"

"I don't know."

"Well, we could just try, and if it's not good, we could stop."
She laughed again, softly.

I kissed her hand again and leaned closer. She was still looking
down. I let go of her hand and touched her chin. Very gently, I
raised her face toward mine. She looked in my eyes.

"You really are beautiful," I said.

She shook her head and said nothing. I liked being so near to
her. I leaned closer and kissed her as softly as I could. She didn't
exactly kiss me back, but she didn't pull away, either.

I pulled back a fraction, feeling happy and dopey. "Was it horrible?"

She shook her head again. "No, not too horrible."

"Okay, then I'm going to do it again." Her mouth was slightly
open, and this time I kissed just her bottom lip, lingering there for
a moment before I eased away.

"Still okay?" I said.

"I just . . . I don't know what you want with me."

"What do you mean?"

"I mean, look at me. What do you want with me?"

Maybe she didn't mean it literally, but I took a long look. I liked
what I saw. Her breasts were small and beautifully shaped, her neck
was long and slender, and her shoulders and arms, her whole upper
body looked strong and fit and graceful. Her skin was pale and
smooth. And her lips . . . God, it had been nice to kiss her, even
though it had been so soft it barely qualified.

"I'd answer that, but I think you'd slap me."

She laughed softly. "I just don't get it."

"You mean, because of the wheelchair?"

"Yeah."

I took her hand again. "I don't know. I just like being with you.
I liked kissing you just now. I wouldn't mind doing it again."

She laughed again. "I really don't get you."

"I'm sorry."

"I don't think it's your fault, exactly. You know, I don't even . . . I don't even know if I can . . . you know. I don't know if I would feel anything."

"You mean, you never . . ."

She shook her head. "No, never. Not even before the accident."

"Oh. Well, maybe we're getting a little ahead of ourselves, right? I mean, I haven't even thought about that. Well not *not* thought about it. But I haven't thought a lot about it. Not constantly, anyway. Sometimes I find myself thinking about something else for a few minutes before it comes back, that's what I mean."

She laughed. I realized I really liked making her laugh. I'd never been the funniest guy in the world, and I was envious of people who had a talent for that kind of thing, but there was something about her that brought it out in me.

"It's not just that," she said. "I haven't even kissed someone since I was a teenager."

"Why? Did you not want to?"

"I don't know. Most guys who want to date a girl in a wheel-chair . . . either they pity me, or they think they're doing something noble, or they think they can get whatever they want because I must be desperate, or some combination of those things. It's just never made me feel good about myself. So after a while, I stopped trying."

"I don't know why anyone would think any of that about you. Desperate is about the last thing you seem to me."

She nodded. "Thanks."

"Don't thank me. I'm just trying to think of something that'll make you want to kiss me again."

She smiled, and then her eyes welled up. It caught me by surprise, and apparently it did her, too, because she gave a startled little laugh and turned away to hide it.

"I'm sorry," I said. "I was just trying to make a joke."

She shook her head and wiped her eyes, her face still averted.

I felt bad. I realized I'd been treating her more or less the way I would have treated any girl I liked, and while on the one hand she clearly responded to that, on the other hand she had wounds inside her I knew nothing about, no more than she knew about mine.

"You know," I said, "if it makes you feel any better, I've only been with one girl myself."

She laughed and wiped her eyes. "Liar. With those little ears, they must be throwing themselves at you."

I laughed too. "No, it's true, there's only been one." This wasn't technically true, as I couldn't claim to have eschewed all professional companionship during the war, but other than that, Deirdre Calhoun had been my first, and to that point my only. "She was my high school girlfriend," I went on, "and I told her I was going to marry her when I got back from the war. But the marriage part never happened."

"Why?"

I blew out a long breath. "I was gone for longer than I'd first been thinking. And war changes you. We were both different people when I got back. Everything was different."

"I'm sorry."

"It's okay. It just didn't work out. But I'm here now."

She looked down. "It's just hard for me."

"I think I understand. At least some of it."

"I mean, if I wanted to go home right now—and I don't, but if I wanted to—I couldn't just leave. I have to rely on you. I hate being helpless like that. I hate it."

"I get it. I'd hate it, too. What do you think we should do?"

"I don't know."

"Well, while you try to figure it out, I'm going to kiss you again, okay?"

She looked in my eyes. Then she whispered, "Okay."

So we kissed again. And this time, I didn't pull back. I reached out and brushed her cheek with the backs of my fingers, and she opened her mouth and I touched her teeth with my tongue a little, just to let her know I wanted more, was ready for more if she was, and then I felt her tongue and we were really kissing, and I cupped her face in my hands and she leaned forward and did the same to me and she opened her mouth wider and put her tongue inside mine, and she made the most beautiful sound, I can't even describe it but it was a sound of pure pleasure, the sound someone would make if she tasted something unexpectedly delicious and was nearly shocked by it. We kissed and kissed and touched each other's faces and hair and she ran her fingers along my ears and we were laughing and holding each other and it went on and on and on. And it was the best kiss I'd ever had.

And then we were just holding each other and laughing and my back hurt because it was awkward leaning into her from the bench but I didn't care, in a weird way it felt good. And then, all of a sudden, she stiffened and pulled back and said, "Oh, no, oh shit oh no."

I'd been in such a reverie, I felt like I'd been slapped. "What? What is it?"

She glanced down at her lap and tried to cover it with her hands, but couldn't. She'd peed. Not just peed, she was still peeing, and couldn't stop it. She shook her head in helpless humiliation.

I jumped up. "Oh, let me get you someplace!"

"Just get me home."

"Shouldn't we—"

"Just get me home."

"But I told you, it doesn't—"

"Just get me home!"

I wanted to say something, to tell her it didn't matter, I didn't care, but I couldn't think what to say. I felt awful. I realized I needed to piss, too—we'd been sitting out there for a long time.

And then I got a crazy idea. I started to rethink it, then thought, *Fuck it, what do you have to lose?*

I took a deep breath and just let my bladder go.

"Take me home, okay?" she said. "Now."

"Okay, just one second, I'm having a little problem myself."

She looked at my crotch, at the darkening pool of liquid running down my leg.

She shook her head incredulously. "What are you fucking doing?"

"You think I've never pissed my pants before? The first time I got dropped in Indian country I did. Hell, I know guys who shit themselves. Tough guys, guys it would be death to mess with. It's just nobody likes to talk about it."

Her mouth was agape. "I don't believe you're doing this."

"What, you think you're the only one who can? Why shouldn't I get some relief, too?"

She put her head in her hands and started shaking. I thought she was crying, but then I realized she was laughing. She looked up at me and shook her head. "You're crazy. You are really crazy."

I looked at the dark spot on my pants and we both started cracking up. It was medium intensity at first, but then it just built and built. At one point, she took two quick breaths and got it under control just long enough to say, "That was . . . the most romantic thing anyone's ever done for me," and we were both hit with another paroxysm.

When the laughter finally started to ebb, I said, "Maybe I should get us back to the van. We'll roll down the windows."

We laughed again and I pushed her back along the path. I can't say it felt good to walk with urine sloshing in my shoes, but on the other hand at least I didn't still need to take a leak.

Back in the van and heading east, she said, "Thank you, Jun. Really, thank you."

"I told you, it's nothing. It doesn't bother me."

"I'm lucky, actually. The injury to my spinal cord isn't complete. A lot of people need a catheter, but I don't. But I have to be careful not to wait too long. I haven't had a problem in a long time, but it's still something I'm always afraid of. And tonight, I think getting excited . . . I'm sorry."

I glanced in the rearview mirror, but it was dark in back and I couldn't see her. "You don't have one thing to apologize for," I said. "Not one." Then I added, "Wait, did you say you were excited?" And we both cracked up again.

Once we were in Uguisudani, she gave me directions to her apartment. I parked and opened the back of the van, and she rolled down to the pavement.

"So this is the place?" I asked. It was a soulless five-story ferroconcrete building, pretty new looking. Drab, but no more so than the one I lived in. Or used to live in. I wasn't exactly sure of my status.

"Yeah. No stairs, see? Straight shot between here and the elevator."

"You want me to come up?"

She paused. "I don't know, we both need to clean up . . ."

"Oh, listen, if I come in, cleaning up is a requirement. Is there a bath?"

"Yeah, that's half the reason I chose it, it's new and the units all have their own baths. Back and forth to the *sentō* everyday would be a nightmare."

"Well, what do you think?"

"What are you going to change into?"

I patted my bag. "I have a change of clothes right here."

"I wondered why you're always carrying it."

"I just don't have anywhere to leave it. No fixed address at the moment and all that. So . . . can I come up?"

I could tell she was nervous. But she said, "Okay."

She lived on the second floor, a neat, functional 1K apartment—what in America would be known as a studio. A single bed on a platform, unlike the usual Japanese futon on the floor. Obviously easier to get in and out of. A kitchen table with no chairs. A tiny television. A nice stereo. That was about it.

We took our shoes and socks off in the *genkan*, but my feet were still moist with piss. "I should wipe my feet before I come in," I said. "Do you have any towels?"

"Yeah. Hold on." She wheeled herself in, pulled a towel out from a cabinet, and set it down on the floor. I stepped onto it. Fortunately, my pants had stopped dripping, but a bath and a change of clothes would be a welcome development.

Without thinking, I said, "Take a bath with me."

"What? Jun, no."

"Hey, it's just to get clean. I have nothing but good intentions."

She laughed a little nervously. "No, I don't think so."

"Why?"

"I . . . I don't know you."

"Yes, you do. You know me better than a lot of people."

She looked down. There was a long pause. She said, "I don't want you seeing my body. My legs."

"We can turn off the light."

"You don't understand. They're like . . . little rubber sticks. They just hang off my body."

"You think if I see your legs, I won't be attracted to you?"

She nodded. Christ, she looked so honest, and so ashamed . . . it made my heart ache.

I knelt in front of her and took her hands in mine. "Sayaka. That's not going to happen."

She didn't say anything.

"Come with me," I said. "It'll be dark. We'll soap up and rinse off and then we'll sit in a warm tub and I'll kiss you and hold you like we were doing at Kitazawa-gawa. And we won't do anything else if you don't want to. Okay?"

"Oh, God, I don't know."

"Okay?"

There was a long pause. Finally, she said, "Let me get in first."

She disappeared into the bathroom. I heard the water come on, and then the light went off. A few minutes later, she called out softly, "Okay."

I walked over to the bathroom door. I could see her in profile. She was leaning forward, her arms across her breasts. Japanese baths are typically part of an integrated shower room—an enclosed space with a tub on one side and an equally large area for showering alongside it. This makes it easier to shower and get clean before getting in the tub, which is a requirement in Japan and, in my opinion, in all other civilized places, as well. I've never understood the idea of soaking in a tub full of the grime floating off your body. On the other hand, a half hour earlier, I had deliberately pissed my own pants, so maybe my opinion on these things shouldn't be taken too seriously. Anyway, Sayaka had left the chair in the shower area alongside the tub, her clothes piled under it. I realized she would do her showering in the tub—it would be easier sitting in the tub itself, and also left the shower area for the wheelchair. And indeed, there were handles installed in the walls and a rope pulley dangling from the ceiling, all obviously designed to make her passage to and from the tub easier. To make it possible at all.

"Can you turn the light out in the living room?" she said. "It's still too light here."

"Do you have a candle?"

"Just an emergency candle, under the sink in the kitchen."

"I'll be right back." I found the candle, lit it on the stove, and set it down in the sink outside the shower/bath room. Then I turned out the light in the living room and came back in. The light was nice like this. I pulled off my wet pants, then my shirt, then my underwear, and pushed it all under the wheelchair. I was as hard as any twenty-year-old about to get in a bath with a girl can be, which is to say, painfully hard. She glanced at me, then looked away. I felt as embarrassed as I thought she must be.

"What's easier?" I said. "Should I get behind you?"

She nodded, her arms still crossed over her breasts.

I eased in behind her, doing my best not to stab her in the back. She handed me the shower wand. The water was running, but she hadn't yet put in the drain plug. I wet my body, soaped up as best as I could under the circumstances, and rinsed off. I put the wand down and gently soaped her back. "Is it okay?" I said.

"Yes," she whispered. I rinsed her back, then lathered up my hands again and did her shoulders. I pulled her against me and slowly leaned back. I kissed her neck, her ear, and she turned her head and we stayed like that for a few minutes, just kissing. She was still covering her breasts. I soaped her arms, and then, very gently, eased them away from her body. She resisted for just a second, then let me. I started soaping her breasts, and if I thought I'd been painfully hard earlier, this made it nearly unbearable. Every time my fingers glided over her nipples she would moan into my mouth and it was making me so crazy my balls started to ache. I soaped her throat and her belly and she started rubbing against me, using her arms on my legs to move herself back and forth in a way I was afraid would make me come if she didn't stop. Yeah, what can I say, twenty years old. It's a trade-off.

My hand went lower and I started touching her, rubbing and stroking, my fingers sliding back and forth along her soapy hair. "Is it okay?" I said, breathing hard.

"I can't . . . I can't feel you down there. But everything feels good. Everything."

"Are you sure? Because . . . you're really wet."

"I am?"

"Yeah. Here." I rinsed our hands and the front of her body. She touched herself and looked at me. "I . . . but I can't feel it."

"Come here," I said. I pulled her back into me. We kissed and I started touching her again. She was so wet my fingers slid easily inside. "Can you feel that?"

"I'm not . . . I don't think so."

"My finger's inside you. I'm moving it. In and out." Jesus, saying it out loud was such a turn-on I couldn't believe it. With my free hand, I started rubbing her breasts again.

"Are you serious?" She reached down and felt alongside my hand, her fingers intertwining with mine. "Oh. Oh. I don't know, I can't feel it, but it's making me feel good. I don't understand. But . . . God, you're making me feel good."

She started rubbing against me the way she had been, panting, pressing into me, kissing me. I put my free hand on her throat and kissed her harder. Her soapy back sliding up and down my cock felt insanely good, like a mild, undulating electric shock. I was embarrassed I was going to come like that. I whispered, "Sayaka, if you keep moving like that, I'm . . . I'm going to . . . you're going to make me come."

"Really?" she said, turning a bit and looking at me and continuing to slide slowly up and down. "I can make you come like this?"

"Yes," I whispered, looking into her eyes.

"Oh, I want you to. I want to feel you coming. Come for me. Come from me doing this."

At that point, it didn't matter what she said—I couldn't have stopped myself if I'd tried. I felt my balls contract and my cock jump and there was an explosion of molten pleasure, and I cried out and gripped her throat and looked into her eyes, and my hips started moving involuntarily as though we were fucking and the look on her face was beyond beautiful, and she said, "Oh, you're coming, oh, oh, oh," and she reached across and cupped my face while my orgasm went on and on. I was embarrassed I was coming on her back like that but she kept sliding up and down and she was so excited she was panting, and I just thought *Fuck it* and stopped caring whether I should be embarrassed, it felt too good and if she wasn't why should I be?

When it was finally done, I sagged against the back of the tub, spent and bewildered. I didn't know what I'd been imagining when I proposed the bath—something, I guess—but not that. Sayaka turned to her side and snuggled into me. I stroked her hair and slowly caught my breath. She rubbed my chest and said, "Was that good?"

"Are you kidding? Could you not tell?"

She laughed. "I want to hear you say it."

"It was incredible. The way you were moving . . . it was making me crazy. I'm sorry."

"Sorry? For what?"

"Well . . . I think I got it all over you."

She laughed. "I want you to do it again."

My head spun. "Oh, man. If you say so."

We rinsed off, then filled the tub and lay there talking and laughing until the water started to cool. She told me where to get a fresh pad for her wheelchair, and I threw the dirty one and all our clothes in the washing machine. When I was done, she was in bed, under a light quilt. She said, "You're staying, right?"

"Unless you're kicking me out. But you know I don't have anywhere else to go, so that would be cruel."

She laughed. "It's a small bed, but . . ."

"I think we'll manage." I got in next to her. We lay on our sides kissing. I was hard in about zero-point-two seconds. Yeah, twenty years old.

She said, "Is it okay . . . I want to touch it."

I kissed her and stroked her cheek. "You can do anything you want."

She reached down and her fingers curled around me. "Oh. That's what it feels like. It's nice. I like it."

"Oh, man, I do, too."

She laughed. Her other arm disappeared beneath the quilt. A moment later, she held up a glistening finger and looked at it in wonder. "I'm wet," she said.

I licked her finger and she gasped. She said, "Can you . . . can you be inside me? I want to see if I can feel it."

I nodded. "Here. Let's get you on your back." I moved her legs and got between them. They were as limp and shrunken as she had said, but I didn't care. I barely noticed. I put my weight on my elbows and looked in her eyes. "You do it," I said. "Guide me."

And she did. I held very still while she got the feel of things and moved at her own pace. After a minute with me maybe an inch inside, she said, "I can't feel it, but it feels good. I can't explain. Can you push a little?"

I laughed a little breathlessly. "I've been trying not to. Here, is that okay?"

The feeling of her fingers wrapped around me even as I slid deeper into her was glorious, intoxicating. "It's good," she said. "Push more."

I did. She said, "I don't understand. I can't feel it there, but I can feel it everywhere. God, it's lovely."

"Oh, good. It's lovely for me, too." I moved a little faster, deeper. I was starting to breathe hard.

She pulled the quilt off us and turned her head to the side to watch. "Oh, that's so good," she said. "Seeing you do that. God, that's so beautiful."

Having her watch like that, experience me moving inside her with her hand and her eyes, was insanely erotic. Panting, I said, "I think . . . I think I have to stop."

"Yes, stop. Don't come inside me. Even if I can't feel it, I can still get pregnant."

With difficulty, I slowed down.

"But I want you to," she went on. "Next time, with a condom, I want to feel that, okay?"

"Oh, God, yes. Ask me anything."

She laughed and I managed to pull out just in time. She said, "Did you come?"

I shook my head. "No. Almost, but no."

She reached down and started moving her hand up and down my shaft. "Oh, God," I said. "God."

She was looking right into my eyes. "I want to make you come again."

"Oh, fuck . . . you are . . ." I groaned, and came on her belly to the firm rhythm of her hand.

When I was done, I collapsed onto my side next to her. She reached down to her belly, then brought her finger to her lips. For an instant, she seemed to remember herself, and looked suddenly self-conscious. "I wanted . . . to see what you taste like," she said.

I shook my head slowly, watching her in wonder, absolutely speechless.

She slid her finger into her mouth and smiled. "It's good."

"Oh, I can't tell you how glad that makes me."

She laughed. "When you were inside me, I couldn't feel it . . . but at the same time, I could. And now I feel . . . I can't explain it. So relaxed. Like something really good happened to me. Like I had a wonderful dream I can't quite remember. It's so strange. So . . . God, it's so lovely."

I looked at her, saying nothing, just spent and happy and feeling I was halfway in love. She said, "Tell me what you're thinking?"

"No, it's stupid."

"Tell me."

"That . . . the way you trusted me tonight. With everything. And this was your first time. I'm just . . . blown away."

She nodded. "Me, too."

"I don't want you to be embarrassed with me, okay? Your legs, or whatever. None of it bothers me."

"I'll try."

"Well, you've been doing pretty well so far."

"Have I? I guess you'll have to get me into bed more often. I want to try everything with you, okay? Everything."

And for the rest of the night, we did. To this day, it was the best night of my life.

chapter
twenty-three

We slept late the next morning, having been up and active pretty much the entire night before, and also as sleeping in was Sayaka's habit. When we woke, she had to get to class and I needed to go meet McGraw. But I told her I'd see her at the hotel that night.

"You know," she said, "if you really need a place to stay, you could stay here."

I couldn't very well tell her that right then, money was the least of my problems. "I don't know," I said. "I feel like I'd be imposing."

"You wouldn't. Not if you'd be willing to stay up with me for a while when I get home from work."

I laughed. "How about if tonight, I stay at the hotel, and I go home with you after? And then we'll see."

She smiled. "That sounds good."

I stopped at a shoe store and bought new shoes and socks. The proprietor, a grizzled *oyaji* who looked liked he'd seen just about everything in his time, was either too polite or too jaded or both to ask why the ones I had on smelled like a urinal. I told him I'd just wear the new pair out of the store. He nodded and didn't offer to dispose of the ones I was replacing, and I did him the courtesy of not asking, instead finding a trash can outside.

After I'd returned the van, I headed out to Inokashira, a heavily forested park in the west of the city and the place where McGraw had said he wanted to meet. Inokashira was a huge cherry blossom attraction in the spring, when people liked to take paddleboats up and down the eponymous pond at its center, to better delight in the blossoms extending on either shore all the way down to the waterline. The shrine, located in the northwest of the pond, was dedicated to Saraswati, the Hindu goddess of everything that flows—water, music, words, knowledge. For whatever reason, Saraswati was known as Benzaiten in Japanese, where she was revered as a Shinto deity, as well.

I crossed the bridge to the bright red shrine—a fusion of Chinese, Indian, and Japanese styles. A few tourists milled about, and I saw a couple of Japanese families enjoying a morning outing. McGraw was there already, predictably enough, taking pictures, dressed in slacks and a polo shirt, looking like a birdwatcher or amateur photographer. He was carrying the usual shoulder bag—looked like it was time for another delivery to Miyamoto. He saw me and walked over.

"Son, you are a goddamn one-man slaughterhouse, did anyone ever tell you that?"

Seeing McGraw right after leaving Sayaka was surreal. Like two parallel dimensions suddenly brushing into contact with each other. "Not in those words, no."

"Well, what words did they use?"

"Something about my having a temper."

He laughed. "Is that what you call it? Four yakuza, shot to death in Fukumoto's house. One of them one of his captains."

"What do the police think?"

"From what I hear, the working theory is a Vietnamese gang and a dispute over drug trafficking. The Vietnamese gangs have a reputation for violence, and Christ almighty, whoever did this is about as violent as you could ask for."

For whatever reason, I had the feeling he was baiting me. Surprisingly, I didn't care. He had something I wanted. Beyond that, at the moment he didn't matter.

"Say, I meant to ask you something," he said, mopping his brow. "How did you know about Benzaiten? I make it my business to know these places, because they're out of the way and good for meetings, but this is hardly Kaminarimon in Asakusa."

"My mother was American."

"Meaning?"

"Meaning a lot of what the natives take for granted, a visitor treasures."

"So it was your American mother who made you aware of your Japanese heritage?"

"I guess you could say that."

"Odd."

I shrugged. "Didn't you say we're sometimes defined by our paradoxes?"

He nodded. "I did say that, didn't I? Didn't realize it was true."

I didn't care whether it was true or not. I just wanted to get down to business and get this thing finished and behind me. "So? Where's the file?"

He set the bag on the ground. I would pick it up when we were done. "We'll get to that," he said. "First, Miyamoto will be waiting for you tomorrow at noon in the lobby of the New Otani Hotel."

"Okay."

He glanced at the shoulder bag I was carrying and frowned. "Two bags . . . looks a little odd."

"It's temporary."

"So is life."

There was an odd pause. I thought it was strange he wasn't going on to micromanage me about how to do the exchange—follow Miyamoto into a restroom, slide the bags under the stalls, whatever. Or saying anything snide about my tradecraft or lack thereof. I'd gotten so used to his bullshit, its absence was mildly disconcerting.

After a moment, he said, "Can't you see you're too good to be just a goddamn bagman?"

I was surprised. "It's honest work," I said, not knowing where he was going.

He chuckled. "Look, I know I ride you hard—"

"Yeah. You do."

"Well, why shouldn't I? What are you? A glorified errand boy. You want me to respect the guy who shines my shoes, too?"

I said nothing.

"You want respect? Do something worthy of respect. Look, I'll admit it, I was wrong about you. I didn't think you could step up. But Jesus Christ almighty, was I wrong. I was a bad manager, I put you in the wrong role. Now I see where you belong, see what you were made for, and it's impressing the hell out of me. In the right role, you're exceptional. You move fast, you show good judgment, and damn but you're fucking deadly. I could use a man like you, I really could. Talent like yours is rare."

I didn't like the *I*, and I didn't like the *use*. "Maybe I just got lucky."

He snorted. "Luck is a skill, son. Don't let anyone tell you otherwise."

"Don't call me son."

"Don't be just a bagman."

I don't know why I was so reluctant. Maybe some part of me sensed I was being manipulated. Maybe some part of me recognized that any further, and the water would be over my head. Maybe I just wanted time to think.

Or maybe it was the promise of what I might be able to have with Sayaka, if only I could get clear of this shit.

"Let me just say this," he said. "This program you've been involved in. What you think you know is just the tip of the iceberg. It needs to be managed and I need good people to manage it."

Again, that *I*. "I'll think about it."

"You should."

"In the meantime, you owe me a file."

"Look, forget about Mad Dog. I'll find another way to take care of him. Maybe he can be bought off, let me look into it."

"You're saying a guy named Mad Dog can be bought off? You told me this is about honor."

"Yeah, and some people's honor is more expensive than others'. I don't know Mad Dog's price—do you?"

"No."

"Besides, if the Gokumatsu-gumi thinks it's under attack by some ultraviolent Vietnamese gang, Junior's apt to be careful for a while."

"You said he was a fuck-up."

"Jesus, you're worse than my ex-wife. Do you have any idea how much of a pain in the ass it is to have to argue with things I've actually said?"

"Well, is he a fuck-up or not?"

"He's a fuck-up. That doesn't mean you're going to find him sitting undefended in all the usual places at all the usual times."

That sounded promising. I said, "Are there usual places and usual times?"

He sighed. "A few."

"Where's the file?"

He nodded for a long moment, as though confirming a thought. "You're good," he said. "No question. But you've got one obvious limitation, and I'll tell you what it is."

I said nothing.

"You're a hammer. Or maybe a buzz saw would be the better analogy. Well, regardless. It's what you do, it's what you are. And if all you are is a hammer, you're going to spend all your time trying to make things into nails."

"Where's the file?"

"Christ. Kabaya Coffee in Ueno. Sit at the counter—"

"I'll know where to find it."

"You will, huh?"

"Unless you've done something fundamentally different this time."

He shook his head disgustedly. "I told you, not ineducable. More's the pity."

I left McGraw and rode Thanatos to Kabaya. It was in Yanaka, near Ueno, the northeast of the city, part of Shitamachi, all narrow streets and tiny wooden buildings. Kabaya turned out to be one of these: a two-story corner structure, once clearly a dwelling, with a traditional tile roof and wood walls so antique they had blackened from decades of storm and sun.

The inside was as tiny as that of Café de l'Ambre, and equally unpretentious. Wood floors, wood walls, wood ceiling; three tables and twelve chairs; a counter that could seat eight. A matronly woman standing behind a cash register greeted me with a bow and an *irasshaimase* when I came in. I returned the bow, then spent a moment scoping the room. It was half full, mostly neighborhood-looking people: housewives enjoying a coffee klatch, retirees doing something to offer a little structure to their days. The counter was empty. I sat in the seat second farthest from the door. The counter-man, who I guessed was the hostess's husband, presented me with a small menu. I told him I would try a cup of the house blend and a portion of buttered toast. While he prepared my order, I glanced around and, seeing that no one was paying me any attention, felt under the stool for the file. There it was, taped dead center, where it was least likely to be accidentally discovered. I pulled it free and pocketed it.

Someone had left a copy of the *Asahi Shinbun* newspaper on the counter. I glanced over. The front page had news about pollu-

tion-borne illnesses afflicting thousands of Japanese. Horrific neu-
rological disease and birth defects in Minamata and Niigata, where
Chisso Chemicals and Showa Electrical had released untreated
mercury into the local waters. Asthma in Yokkaichi, caused by vast
amounts of sulfurous oil burned at the Daiichi Petrochemical Complex. *Itai-itai-byō*—it hurts–it hurts disease, so named because of
the agonies of its victims—caused by the cadmium Mitsui Mining
had released into the rivers of Toyama Prefecture. The corporations
were fighting the victims in court; their flunkies had attacked a
photographer who had documented the horrors of Minamata; the
government was helping cover things up. The same types who
forced Sayaka's parents to take the money and keep their mouths
shut. I asked myself if there was a reason I should ever refrain from
killing these people. I couldn't think of one.

When I had finished my coffee, I rode over to Sumida Park,
a narrow strip of green along the river of the same name alongside
Asakusa. Among mothers pushing babies in strollers and toddlers
playing on the swing sets, I went through the file. Its contents
weren't encouraging. The photos were redundant—I already knew
what he looked like, from Ueno, and then from when I'd seen
him staring down at me at the Kodokan while Pig Eyes tried to
choke me to death. As for whereabouts, Junior kept two condo-
miniums, one in Roppongi, the other in Aoyama. There were
several nightclubs he was said to manage, but between the two
residences and the three nightclubs, if not more, I was facing a
shell-game dynamic. Absent some specific actionable intel or a
very lucky break, finding Junior could take a while. And all that
time, I'd be living like a fugitive, with a yakuza contract hanging
over my head.

I thought about Sayaka. I wondered what she was doing right
then. Studying English? Reading a book? I knew so little about her.
But at the same time, I felt like I did know her. She'd let me in,

literally and figuratively, and I was still awestruck by that, by everything that had happened. I had to force myself to stop thinking
about it and get back to the file.

When I'd memorized the information, I burned the pages in a
public ashtray overflowing with cigarette butts, then headed over
to a payphone and called McGraw. "Look," I told him, "that file
you gave me, it's not enough. I need something more specific. I held
up my end, now it's time for you to hold up yours."

There was a pause. I thought he was going to push back, so I
was pleasantly surprised when he said, "I know, it wasn't nearly as
complete I was hoping. I have to tell you again, you work a lot faster
than I'd been expecting. The kind of information you need takes
time to put together. I'll keep working on it. And if something
comes up, if we catch a break, I'll let you know right away."

I didn't like it, but didn't see how I could ask for much more.
I hung up.

I spent the rest of the day reconning Junior's various haunts. If
I had known for sure which one and at what time, there would have
been a number of approaches. But five possibilities? The two residences were as close to a choke point as it looked like I was going
to get. But I could wait all night outside either one of them, and
I'd never know if he was just out late or if he'd turned in early at the
other one. Or if he was spending the night shacked up with one of
the girls from his clubs.

As evening deepened into night, I decided I was wasting my
time. Maybe I'd have better luck with Mori. Miyamoto's hit hadn't
been as important to me because Mori wasn't a threat, just a job.
And maybe I had some vestigial concerns about the ethics of that.
But I reminded myself that the guy was in the life. I thought of
Kamioka, another big-shot politician, the one who'd crippled Sayaka. And of the corporate officers and corrupt politicians who had

poisoned thousands of people and then conspired to deny them justice. I realized I didn't have any pity for any of them. Was I rationalizing again? Maybe. But did that make my analysis inaccurate? Mori had made his own choices. Now he had to live with the consequences.

Or not.

chapter
twenty-four

I stopped at a discount store and bought a suit, shirt, and tie; some hair gel; and a pair of reading glasses. Back at the hotel in Ueno, I showered, changed into the suit and tie, and slicked my hair. I popped the lenses out of the glasses and put them on. I looked in the mirror—nothing likely to fool anyone who knew me, but enough to throw off any witness descriptions. The suit alone made me look like someone else. I couldn't remember the last time I'd worn one. My father's funeral, maybe. At my mother's, I'd been in my military dress uniform.

Not only did the outfit look strange, it also felt uncomfortable. When I'd tried it on in the store, beyond "a suit" I didn't know what I was looking for, and I realized I was probably making a dozen mistakes in the way I was wearing it now. Was the tie knotted correctly? Should I button the jacket? For anyone with an eye for such things, subtle mistakes could be remembered or otherwise draw attention. It wasn't good that I was only just realizing this. I was in trouble now, Mad Dog still out there, gunning for me, and I shouldn't have been playing catch-up with my preparations. I'd been stupid and complacent, like a homeowner who never bothered to buy insurance because nothing bad had ever happened before.

I resolved to never again be unprepared for the shit hitting the fan. I would pay attention to small things—the way people dressed and spoke and walked. The things that made them part of a background environment, or made them stand out against it. I would watch them, try to consciously identify the signs and behaviors that made them who they were, and then imitate and adopt those things as my own. It would be like performing a role, with the preparation a kind of acting school. I'd make it a game, and play it every day.

But that was for later. Assuming I made it to later. For now, I had to work with what I had.

I thought about how I might get close to Mori, how I would do it, how I would get away, how I would try to create distractions. A plan cohered. It was crude, it was ugly, and it was improvised, but given the parameters, I thought it would work. This one didn't have to look natural, after all. This one could look like anything.

I stopped at another discount store and bought a plain *furoshiki*—basically, a large bandana. You don't often see them in Japan these days, as they've been largely replaced by plastic shopping bags, but at the time they were widely used to wrap and carry everything—groceries, packages, boxed lunches.

Or, in my case, just a rock.

I rode around until I spotted a road crew doing construction—not something that has ever taken long to find in Tokyo, where make-work collusion between the yakuza and the Construction Ministry has long been a national disease. I parked and hunted around at the edges of the site, away from the workmen, outside the range of the floodlights, until I found what I was looking for. Not a chunk of asphalt or concrete, which might crack under pressure, but a fist-sized stone. This one was just right—maybe twice the size of a billiard ball and considerably heavier. I wrapped it in the *furoshiki* and drove off to Akasaka.

I parked Thanatos in a crowded lot off Roppongi-dōri, then walked into Akasaka. The air was dense with humidity and the smells of fried soba and beer and yakitori, the hum of conversation and laughter and madcap beeping of *pachinko* machines and the horns of taxis fighting their way through knots of pedestrians. The buildings on either side were low, many of them still of wood, but I could see how rapidly the area was changing, with five-story structures replacing two-story, and ferroconcrete replacing wood. Each building had an illuminated sign running up its side, advertising clubs and bars and restaurants. The sidewalks were crowded with salarymen out for an evening's entertainment, couples walking arm in arm on their way to dinner, a few foreign tourists gawking at the spectacle. Hostesses in kimonos and cocktail dresses hurried to work. Touts stood in front of entrances, handing out flyers, calling to passersby. Here and there, the sidewalk was blocked by an illegally parked sedan, the driver waiting for his designated passenger, yakuza or politician or some other VIP, and the crowd would flow around it.

After a few minutes of letting the crowd carry me along, I saw the sign for Higashi West. It was in one of the newer buildings, and on its fifth floor, the highest. The name was spelled out in English, no kanji, no kana—a nod, I supposed, to the cosmopolitan flavor it promised. There was a car at the curb, driver in front, curtained windows in back. Not necessarily Mori's, of course, but it made me hopeful. If he was here, though, and if this was his car, there would be a very short window between when he left the building and when he entered the vehicle. Not a lot of time to get to him.

I dropped the *furoshiki* and the rock wrapped inside it in a garbage container, then headed into the building's vestibule. Three inebriated salarymen got on the elevator with me. I kept my head down and my eyes averted until they exited on the third floor and left me to continue alone to the fifth.

The doors opened to reveal a somewhat gaudy interior—a lot of red velvet and curtains and lace, a caricatured Japanese take on European luxury. The air was heavy with tobacco and Scotch, and someone was crooning Don McLean's "American Pie," top of the charts that year, from somewhere within. The decor might not have been to my taste, but this was clearly a high-end club, the women certain to be attractive, charming, educated, and intelligent—and not at all for sale. Though westerners who find entirely natural the idea of paying for sex are simultaneously mystified at the notion of paying for conversation, is the divide really all that wide? It's not as though a woman in the former circumstance actually wants to sleep with you, or enjoys doing it, any more than a woman in the latter situation relishes your conversation. If one is unnatural, then isn't the other, as well? Which isn't to say that sex with a hostess is an impossibility. It just isn't something that can be purchased for cash. Instead, much as was the case in the geisha houses from which the modern hostess club is descended, a sexual relationship might develop over time, with the right customer, after much extracurricular wooing, and only if the girl wants it.

A Japanese hostess stepped forward to greet me. "*Irasshaimase,*" she said with a bow. Welcome. She produced an ice-cold *oshibori*, a damp washcloth, and I wiped my hands and face gratefully.

Before she could lead me to a table, I said, "I'm embarrassed to inform you, but I'm not here to stay. My boss has told me to find him a suitable place to entertain in Akasaka. I've heard favorable things about your establishment, but would it be all right if I just took a look for myself? He won't be satisfied if I don't."

The hostess smiled. "Of course. Are you sure we can't get you anything to drink?"

I smiled back, thinking she was wise to try to earn my gratitude with such a small investment. "No, no, I really don't want to put you to any trouble. Already from what I can see, I think your club looks most appropriate. Would it be all right though if I were to just . . ."

She bowed. "By all means, please, feel free."

I thanked her and walked inside. If Mori wasn't here, I didn't know what I would do next time—the "I'm just here for my boss" routine would last only so long.

The place was shaped like an L, with the long end going left from the entrance. I turned into it. There was a short bar and four tables, all occupied. At one of the tables stood the guy who was singing, the microphone partly obscuring his face. Mori? I thought so. Two western hostesses and three Japanese tablemates were laughing and applauding. I moved to the side and looked more closely, matching the face to what I had seen in the file photographs. No question now, it was him. His English was as impressive as his voice, and I was struck by a moment of private irony, the notion that he was singing a song about the plane crash that had killed Buddy Holly, Ritchie Valens, and the Big Bopper—"the day the music died."

There was a bottle of Suntory whisky on their table, mostly empty. That might have meant they'd been there for a while. On the other hand, a guy like Mori would almost certainly have a bottle-keep—his own paid-for bottle, which the club would store and take out for him. No way to know. I'd just have to wait for as long as it took. The main thing was, he was here. I was never going to get a better chance.

I used the bathroom and headed out, thanking the hostess on the way. She escorted me to the landing and pressed the button for the elevator, waiting for it to arrive and then bowing low until the doors had closed.

I headed back out to the street, searching for the right venue. I had initially assumed I'd just ride the elevator up and down until Mori emerged, but the way the hostess had waited with me suggested this would be a no-go. Weird behavior, and therefore both suspicious and memorable. Not to mention the many opportunities it would give multiple people to see my face.

I looked around. Most of the buildings had exterior stairwells that were used primarily for storage in violation of local fire ordinances, and the Higashi West building was no exception. I supposed I could hang back inside the entrance to the stairwell and maintain a good view of the elevator. But then his back would be to me. I'd have to do something to confirm it was him. Well, I didn't see a better way.

I retrieved the rock and the *furoshiki*, rewrapping the cloth so that it only covered half the rock—the half I was holding. I didn't think the porous stone would take a fingerprint, but I didn't want to take a chance, either. I ghosted back to the stairway and waited in the shadows. I felt nervous and out of control. Was I really doing this again, so soon after Ozawa and Fukumoto and the other three? But what difference did proximity make? The opportunity was what mattered, and the opportunity was now. I'd lain more ambushes in the jungle than I could count, and reminded myself the only meaningful difference between then and now was the venue. And why shouldn't I do it? Mori meant nothing to me. Would I pay ten thousand dollars to save his life? Because that's what I'd be doing, if I walked away now.

Several dozen people came and went while I waited, and each time a group emerged from the elevator, I'd get a pointless adrenaline dump while I tried to assess from behind whether one of them was Mori. I stretched and did light calisthenics to stay limber, switching the cloth-covered rock from one hand to the other, breathing deeply in and out. I reminded myself repeatedly of who I was supposed to be tonight, how I would act, how I wanted this to look to any witnesses and to the police. I was starting to feel exhausted, and had endured so many false alarms, that when a group of three men in identical dark suits emerged from the elevator, it took me a moment to realize from the build and posture of the one in the middle that this was probably him. *Shit.*

I eased out from the stairwell, getting closer, afraid to commit in case I was mistaken. What light there was came in a pall of yellow from a few inadequate sodium vapor lamps, and the men were mostly in shadow. Good concealment for me, but it made positive ID a bitch, too.

The men had paused in front of the sedan. They were chuckling about something—what, I couldn't make out. I wanted to circle around the car and come at them from the front so I could get a clear look at his face before I committed. But I was afraid if the timing were bad, he might get into the car before I could close with him.

I was already in character. My heart was pounding and I was juiced with adrenaline. *Fuck it.* I paused and said in Japanese, "Mori-san? Is that you?"

All three turned, the one in the center slightly more quickly. I saw his face. It was him.

"Yes, I'm Mori," he said, annoyance in his tone. "Who's that?"

My heart was slamming harder. I tightened my hand around the cloth-covered rock. I was only three meters away.

I thought I was going to be able to get closer before he would react. But something in my demeanor cued him. He flinched and turned to the rear car door. Grabbed the handle. Started to open it. Everything happening now in slow motion through my adrenalized vision.

"You like fucking my wife?" I shouted. "You like fucking my wife?"

He yanked the door open and started to pull himself inside. I grabbed him by the collar with my free hand, hauled him back, and straight-armed the rock into the back of his head. It connected with a satisfying crunch and I felt the rigidity flow out of his body. His companions jumped back, one of them crying out, "*Oi!*" I barely heard him.

Mori slumped over the trunk. I still had my hold on his collar and used it to drag him face down to the pavement. "You like fucking my wife?" I screamed again, sounding as hysterical as I felt. I reared up and smashed the rock into the back of his head again. This time, there was nowhere for him to float with the blow, and I heard the crack of his skull opening. I hit him a third time, still screaming. And then again.

I let the rock fall from the *furoshiki* and took off in the direction I had come from. The whole thing had taken maybe ten seconds. I'd given no one time to react. Maybe the driver would think to try to chase me, but it was a one-way street and he was pointed in the wrong direction. And I thought it would be some time before his companions recovered from their shock, and even then I doubted they'd have the stomach to come after someone who had just done what they'd witnessed. Still, I cut through the first alley I came to, and then a parking lot, and a minute later I was out of Akasaka proper, on quiet, deserted neighborhood streets. I stopped running and made myself walk at a normal pace, my breath heaving in and out of my chest. *Relax,* I told myself. *Relax. You're a civilian again. Just a normal salaryman. Relax.*

I ducked into an alley and let the shakes pass through me. Killing with electricity was better than killing with a gun, and killing with a gun was better than killing with a rock. It was a matter of proximity, and therefore of intimacy. It wasn't logical—dead was dead, whether brained with a rock or bombed from thirty thousand feet—but it was true. I'd killed at close range in Vietnam and Cambodia, and I reminded myself this was no different—ethically, morally, whatever. I reminded myself that Mori was in the life and knew he was taking his chances, or should have known. But even so, the shakes were bad this time.

The way Mori had reacted had spooked me. He'd seen the violence in my demeanor, the intent. Some of that had been deliberate: I wanted it to look like a brutal crime of passion, barely planned and hastily executed, the antithesis of a detached, professional hit. To bolster that impression, I had played a role, that of enraged, jealous husband, which is what I wanted the witnesses to report and the police to investigate, and playing that role involved making myself *feel* like the role. But that wasn't all of it. Some of what Mori had sensed, I thought, was simply a part of who I was. Or, to put it another way, my very presence had warned him of what I was going to do. If he'd been a little faster, or I a little slower, that warning might have made the difference. And it was the same with those *chinpira* in Ueno. Whether it was overt posturing or subliminal messaging, either way I was inadvertently warning people of what I was about to do, and therefore giving them time to prepare. Was there any upside to that? No, there wasn't. In the field, if something represents only a cost and no offsetting benefit, you jettison it. I had to find a way to jettison this, too—to control those unconscious, nonverbal signals, retract them, conceal them. There had to be a way to be able to do great violence, ultimate violence, without any outward manifestation ahead of the violence itself. I thought something like that would be rare. Certainly I'd never seen anything like it myself. But if there were a way to acquire it, it would offer significant tactical advantages.

I realized I was distracting myself from the nature of what I had just done by focusing on the tactics. I'd done so many after-action reports after missions that the reflex was now ingrained. I found myself grateful for that.

I left the alley and ditched the glasses in a garbage bin. The *furoshiki* went into a sewer drain. I scrubbed the slickness out of my hair, loosened the tie, and kept walking. Five minutes later, I was riding Thanatos north on Uchibori-dōri. It was only when I was under the bright lights of the main road that I noticed my sleeve was flecked with blood and gore. It didn't show up too badly on the dark jacket, but on the white sleeve it was impossible to miss.

Shit. I should have stashed a change of clothes somewhere. How could I have been so stupid?

I pulled over and rolled up my shirtsleeves, just enough so they didn't show beyond the edges of the jacket. Then I found a public restroom, where I examined myself in a mirror and scrubbed the gore off my hands. At a discount store, I bought a tee shirt and a pair of jeans. None of the costume changes was particularly expensive, but I was far from rich, and between the various props, the nightly hotel rooms, and gas for Thanatos, I was glad I had a load of cash waiting for me back at the hotel, with more on the way.

I stopped in a park and changed into my new clothes, using the tie to wrap the shirt and suit around a rock and sink the whole package into a pond. Doubtful anyone would ever find it; if they did, it would offer no connection to me. Routine forensic DNA analysis was still far in the future.

Back on Thanatos, clean and in my new clothes, I started to feel calmer, more detached. But I was still horrified to consider how much I'd just relied on luck. How well did I really know the areas in which I was operating? Kita Senju might have been another city. And even Akasaka . . . I knew the main streets, sure, but the alleyways? The hidden passages between and through buildings? And what kind of shape was I in? For the mat, top shape, sure, and if I ever had to use judo to save my life, maybe I'd manage, as I had when Pig Eyes had attacked me at the Kodokan. But what if I had to run, *really* run? The half a kilometer out of Akasaka had gassed me. What if I'd needed to go farther? Could I have outlasted whoever was chasing me? Probably not. And that wasn't good.

I needed to game things out better in my head. I needed to take what I'd learned about combat—the mentality, the preparation, the focus—and apply it in life generally. I needed to stop pretending there was some clear dividing line between the military and the civilian, the jungle and the city, war and peace. There wasn't. Not before, and certainly not now.

I called Miyamoto from a payphone. "It's done," I told him in my disguised voice.

"Already?"

For some reason, the comment annoyed me. "How long did you want to wait?"

"I didn't. I'm just . . . surprised. That you were able to do it so quickly."

"I want you to get me the balance of what you owe me tomorrow. Same place, same rules. Place it there at eleven in the morning. Do you understand?"

"Of course. The money will be there. But listen. I'd like to have a way of contacting you. You seem . . . very professional. I'm sure the people I represent would like to do business with you again."

I almost said no. But then I thought, *What's the downside?*

"I'll leave you a number where you can reach me," I said. "In the same place you leave the money, after I retrieve it. Now, repeat back to me how, where, and when you're going to leave me the balance."

He did. When he was done, I said, "I know we have a mutual friend. But you should know, if I see anyone trying to make me when I go to retrieve that payment, I will hold you personally accountable."

"I'm going to place the envelope there myself. As I did last time. No one else will even know where to look."

I hung up. I didn't feel great. But I reminded myself that sometimes there's just what you can do, and what you can't.

I'd done it. Now I had to live with it.

chapter
twenty-five

I headed back to the hotel in Uguisudani. The closer I got, the more nervous I felt. The night before had been magical, but then Sayaka and I had both gone back to our separate lives. Did she feel the same way I did? What was she thinking? Would it be awkward? And she was probably wondering all the same about me. Or wasn't she? That would be worse, much worse.

But at the same time, worrying about Sayaka was a relief. I felt like I was riding away from someone else, some other part of myself, and leaving him behind. Thinking of Sayaka made me feel like . . . like what she imagined me to be. Wanted me to be. I was different with her. She'd said as much, and I felt it, too. I wanted to make it so that one world would have nothing to do with the other. And that by stepping into that world, I'd close the door on the other. It felt possible. It felt good.

She was at the desk when I walked in. She smiled when she saw me, but there was tension in her expression, too.

"Hey," I said, walking over. "You look good."

That seemed to relax her a little. "Yeah? So do you."

I had to push back an image of Mori, but I managed. "Hey, no flirting with the customers."

She laughed a little at that. There was an awkward pause.

I ran my fingers through my hair. "Last night—"

"I know."

I felt myself flush. "You don't even know what I was going to say!" Actually, neither did I.

She laughed. "You're right. I'm sorry."

"I was just going to say . . . it was amazing. I kept thinking about it today." It sure as hell beat everything else I was thinking about, but I kept that part to myself.

She smiled. "Yeah, me too. I couldn't wait for tonight. Well, for tomorrow morning. When I get off here."

"Sure you can't slip away for a special, really loyal customer?"

"This place? Even if I could, and I can't, no. This is just to pay the bills. I don't want to have any other associations with it."

"All right, I guess I can wait. Can I kiss you goodnight?"

She looked around nervously. "Okay, but make it quick—I really don't need some drunken salaryman seeing us making out and getting the idea that's what I'm here for."

She unlocked the door and I ducked inside. I really just meant to give her a simple goodnight kiss, but it pretty instantly turned into more than that. She broke it off, breathing hard. "Get out of here, you. You're too tempting."

"Oh man, so are you."

I went back around. "I have to charge you," she said. "They know when a room's been used because of the maid service. Otherwise, I wouldn't."

"Don't worry about it. I don't want to get you in trouble." I gave her the money and took the key. "What time should I come down?"

"I get off at seven. But don't meet me here. I don't want people to see us together. Just come to my apartment, anytime after seven-thirty. Okay?"

"I can't wait."

She smiled. "Neither can I."

chapter
twenty-six

I spent the following morning at Sayaka's. It was amazing—as good as the first time, and maybe even better, because now the ice was broken and we were getting a little more used to each other.

Several hours in, she was lying on her back, drifting in and out of sleep. I was turned on my side, my head propped on my fist, watching her. I didn't want to get too comfortable—it would have felt great to nod off, but I had to meet Miyamoto at noon. And retrieve the money beforehand. I didn't want it exposed for longer than necessary.

She glanced at me, her lids heavy. "What?"

"What, what?"

"Why are you looking at me?"

"I like looking at you."

She smiled and touched my cheek. "You're sweet."

I kissed her fingers. "You really think so?"

"Yeah. Really."

"Some people think I have a temper."

"Not with me."

I kissed her softly on the lips. "I like how I am with you."

She didn't say anything. She just smiled, tracing my ear, my jaw, my lips.

I glanced at the clock by the bed. "I have to go."

"Work?"

"Yeah."

"Still don't want to tell me?"

"I can't."

"Jun, you're not married, are you? I mean, you said you'd only been with one girl, but . . ."

The question caught me so off guard it made me laugh. But of course I could instantly see why she'd be concerned. "No."

"I didn't think so, but then . . . I wondered. It's weird knowing so little about you."

"I told you. You know me better than most."

"Do I?"

"Yes."

"It feels like that. But then I feel like . . . maybe I'm being naïve."

I stroked her cheek. "You're not naïve."

"I've never thought so, anyway."

"You're not. Let me just get out of this jam—a work jam, it's not marriage or a relationship or anything like that. And then we'll see, okay?"

I looked at her for a long moment. I guess my expression must have been kind of dopey. She said, "What?"

I smiled. "I just feel lucky."

There was a pause. She said, "Do you want to stay here tonight? You can if you want."

"I kind of like seeing you at the hotel. I think I'd miss you if you weren't here."

She laughed. "You really are sweet. Okay, then, see you tonight?"

I kissed her. "See you tonight."

I rode Thanatos to Ginza. On the way, that phrase, *I feel lucky*, kept echoing in my mind. It was bugging me, and I didn't know why. I pushed it aside. There was one small thing I needed to take care of, and then I'd retrieve the money. I had to focus.

I found a guy delivering bento lunches on a motor scooter—an ordinary guy, doubtless unimaginative but responsible, and also doubtless in need of cash given the likely wages of the bento delivery industry. I asked him if he'd like to make a quick ten thousand yen. All he had to do was open a bank account for me, Taro Yamada, the Japanese equivalent of John Smith, right here at the local branch of the Taiyō Bank. I'd give him the cash, he'd sign the paperwork, ten thousand yen for fifteen minutes' labor. He didn't hesitate. It was done and he was back on his scooter before those bento lunches even had a chance to cool. Next, I called a telephone answering service and established an account for someone named John Smith, setting up payment through the new bank account.

The necessary infrastructure established, I rode Thanatos to Aoyama-itchōme and got on the Ginza line from there. I pulled on my little disguise as the train left the station, and when I got out at Gaienmae, I saw no one lingering after the train had departed. I picked up the envelope as I had last time, and taped my alter ego's new phone number to the bottom of the seat. Now if Miyamoto needed to reach the contract killer I'd put him in touch with, he could. Ten minutes later, I was back on Thanatos, with ten thousand dollars in a bag around my shoulder. Not bad.

I headed over to Akasaka-mitsuke, parked near the New Otani, and walked the rest of the way. Miyamoto wasn't there yet. Rather than wait for him in the lobby, I strolled around the hotel, imagining how I would get to me if I were the opposition. It was a good game and I knew I needed to practice, to get as fluent in the city as I had become in the jungle.

I knew that in McGraw's imagination, or at least in his hopes, my meetings with Miyamoto were always super cloak-and-dagger. And initially they had been, at least to some extent. But over time, it had become increasingly relaxed. So I wasn't at all perturbed when Miyamoto came in and waved as soon he saw me.

He came over and bowed low. "Thank you again for the great service you have done me."

Of course, I played dumb. "What do you mean?"

"The . . . friend you introduced me to. He proved most helpful. Professional and discreet."

"Really? He didn't say anything to me. Well, discreet, as you say. But I'm glad it worked out. Your people were . . . pleased?"

"Very pleased. It seems I'm now worthy of a whole new level of respect, and I owe it all to you. It has been my good fortune to know you."

Good fortune . . . luck again. Why was that notion bothering me? Again, I pushed it aside. "You don't owe me anything," I said. "I just hope you don't get a promotion out of this—I'd miss our meetings."

He laughed. "Do you have a little time? The hotel's garden is wonderful—over four hundred years old. A beautiful sight to contemplate while drinking tea."

So we spent an hour or so enjoying tea in the lounge overlooking the garden. Miyamoto commented on my new apparent mindfulness in the way I sipped and savored, saying he was honored I had listened to his silliness. I told him it was my honor that he would so patiently instruct someone so unworthy. It was easy to switch bags naturally when we stood to go. As I headed toward the back exit, Miyamoto said, "I won't forget what you did for me, or that I owe you a service in return."

"Really, you are much too kind. All I did was offer an introduction."

"And you are much too modest. I am in your debt."

"Okay, you can pay for the tea again next time."

He laughed. "That will hardly suffice. But yes. Until we meet again."

A number of things had been roiling my mind, including that weirdly disturbing notion of luck and fortune, and though I'd suppressed it all while chatting with Miyamoto, I wanted to think carefully about what was bothering me now. So I rode Thanatos the short distance to Zenpuku-ji, a small temple constructed in 824, making it Tokyo's oldest after Sensō-ji in Asakusa. Zenpuku-ji was a quiet space with a giant ginkgo tree said to be as old as the temple itself, with both the tree and the temple surrounded by graves, many of them ancient. It would be a good place to work things through. In my experience, nothing fosters more sober, careful thought, more honest reflection, than finding oneself the sole living trespasser in a sanctum of the dead.

I parked, walked up the stone path, and began pacing among the trees and ancient markers. It was cooler in the cemetery, the leaves providing some shade and the lack of asphalt offering less material to radiate the sun's heat. It was quiet, too, the surrounding neighborhood genteel and the traffic distant. A little ways off stood a monk, head shaven, robes black, chanting and lighting incense before one of the graves. The breeze carried the smoke to where I walked, and the pungent smell brought me back to my childhood in this city, as it always did, as I suspected it always would. I thought of my father, buried in another Tokyo cemetery not far from here, the memory of whom was becoming increasingly remote for me, detached, improbable. I would think of him, and wonder whether I was remembering the man, or instead remembering mere memories, my recollections themselves simulacra. And of my mother, a much fresher wound, interred in a faraway continent as her grief-stricken parents had pleaded and as I, reluctantly, had acceded, believing—perhaps foolishly—that our first duty is to the living and that the dead, infinitely patient, will always understand.

One thing that was on my mind was Sayaka, wondering if I was married. It was almost funny on one level, but on another it made me feel deeply uneasy. Because there were things about me I knew I could never tell her, things she would never understand or accept, things I would never want her to know regardless. Things I had done not only in war, but in this very city, just days earlier . . . some of them on the very afternoon of the night we'd first made love.

But you told her there were things you couldn't talk about, right?

Yes, I had, and I had told myself that was a kind of honesty. But was it really? On the surface, yes, but one level deeper it seemed like the worst kind of lie—the kind shaped like the truth for the benefit of one person, and in order to more effectively deceive another.

I didn't know what to do. Just run off with her? I had the ten thousand dollars from what I'd done for Miyamoto . . . would that be enough to get us established in America? And even if it were, what would I do then? I'd still be the same cast-aside former soldier with no education, no prospects, and no skills useful for anything I could ever explain to Sayaka or anyone else.

I shook my head. What would she think, if I told her I was contemplating running away with her? Would she even want that? She'd probably think I was a love-struck kid with a crush.

Or maybe she wouldn't. I didn't know. I felt like we'd already passed the point where it might have been possible to just slow things down or make them go backward. I hadn't seen it coming and didn't see it when it went by, either, but it felt like we were falling in love. Which meant Sayaka was falling in love with some-one who, if she knew what he really was . . . I didn't know what she'd think. I didn't want to consider what that knowledge would do to her, after the way she had trusted me and opened up to me.

Maybe the best thing, the only thing, was to just finish the situation with the yakuza and then find a way out. Never tell her any of it, or anyone else, either. And as months became years and years became decades, the things I had done here this week, and in the war before that, would lose more and more of their potency and feel farther and farther away, until finally they would be just distant memories, like stars in a faraway galaxy whose light took millennia to reach earth, and even then could be seen only dimly, if at all. I could do that. I could keep it all separate. I'd been lucky so far, hadn't I?

Luck again. Why was my good luck bothering me? I mean, if the timing hadn't been so good outside Fukumoto's house . . .

I stopped and thought about that. The timing had been good, hadn't it? I mean, almost miraculously good. I thought getting in would be hard, but in the end, it had been easy.

On the one hand, of course, the whole thing hadn't been easy at all. It had turned out there were four people in that room, two of them armed and who nearly got the drop on me. And the wife coming home just as I was leaving, that certainly didn't feel like good luck. No, I suddenly realized, what had been rubbing me the wrong way was how perfectly *timed* my arrival felt. The very moment I showed up to recon the house was the very moment the mistress happened to be leaving it. The mistress, who was driving a convertible, who had an automatic garage door opener, who drove a short distance and then parked her car with the garage door opener accessible inside it.

And what about that interior garage door? The house was obviously designed, and presumably purchased, with security in mind. Leaving an interior door unlocked like that seemed awfully sloppy under the circumstances. And the wife . . . when she'd gone in, I'd heard her turn the key and then grunt under her breath, then turn the key again. Now I thought I understood what had happened: she expected the door to be locked, and thought she was unlocking it. She was perplexed when she realized she was mistaken. And why would she have been perplexed, unless that door was typically locked? And if it was typically locked, why had it been left unlocked at the exact moment of my arrival?

Yes, I'd been lucky in various ways since this whole thing had started. Ozawa in the *sentō*, and Mori outside his club . . . the recon required to get the timing of that sort of thing right could take days, even weeks. But still, most people are creatures of habit. Ozawa had to bathe more or less every evening, especially during Japan's hot and humid summer. Mori liked to party at his club. Those felt like things that, one way or the other, were going to be mostly a matter of time, and it didn't take all that much luck for the necessary time to be minimal. And even if those first two hadn't gone as smoothly as they did, it was mostly just a question of waiting and assessing a little longer. It wouldn't have been that hard. But Fukumoto . . . that timing had been *perfect*. If I hadn't seen the mistress leaving the house right then, I had no idea when or how another opportunity would have presented itself.

I blew out a long breath and kept pacing. I hadn't wanted to face it; that's why I hadn't thought it through. But my unconscious had been trying to tell me anyway. I'd been an idiot to try to ignore that feeling in my gut. Another thing I knew not to do in the jungle, and had to relearn in the city.

All right. Assume it was staged. How?

Well, let's say . . . someone cued the mistress that I was coming and it was time for her to pull out. Maybe someone parked on the street, communicating with a radio. I couldn't really know—there had been a number of parked cars, and I hadn't checked them at all closely. Another lesson, I realized: I'd approached Fukumoto's house oblivious to how I would defend the terrain if *I* were the one waiting for me. I'd done it differently to some degree at the New Otani just a little while earlier, and I wondered now whether that hadn't been my unconscious, trying to signal me that I needed to sharpen up. Regardless, I hadn't adequately placed myself in the enemy's shoes in Fukumoto's neighborhood, hadn't examined myself through the eyes of potential opposition. I'd been lucky to live to enjoy that lesson, and I would make damn sure to apply it going forward.

All right, how *wouldn't be all that hard. But then* who?

McGraw was the obvious answer. Who else could it be? He was the one who'd given me the file. I'd shown him I was impatient, hadn't I? I'd wanted those yakuza files first. And he'd noticed the bag I was carrying, too, first at the Chinese restaurant where we'd met, and then at other places as well. He was sharp—he'd know the bag meant I was on the run, and therefore feeling pressed, and therefore eager to resolve this as quickly as I could. He'd know I would head to Fukumoto's house as soon as I had the file with the location.

But . . . why?

Had he wanted me to walk into Fukumoto's house to be ambushed? But that didn't make sense. If they'd had a spotter outside alerting the mistress, they could as easily have alerted the yakuza security inside. They could have been waiting on the far side of the garage and gunned me down the instant the door closed. They wouldn't even have gotten my blood on Fukumoto's nice carpeting. Instead, I was the one who had surprised them.

It felt like someone had greased the skids for me. Whoever it was had wanted Fukumoto dead. But that didn't make sense. *I* was the one who wanted Fukumoto dead. I'd proposed the hit to McGraw as a solution to my problem with the yakuza. It was my idea, not his. There had been the thing in Ueno with the *chinpira*, which had been a total coincidence, and then . . .

I shook my head. It was crazy. Once I started questioning one thing, it called into question everything.

Then maybe you're just being paranoid. A few coincidences, that's all it was. It happens.

No. That felt like denial to me, like a narcotic. Of course I didn't want to question everything—it was too much effort, too disorienting, too frightening. But dying would be worse, wouldn't it? It wasn't a question of how it all made me feel. I had to set that aside. What mattered was the truth.

All right. What do you know? Not what you think you know, but what you know for sure. Start with that.

Really just one thing: that McGraw had wanted Ozawa dead. That file had been pretty complete, and it had gotten me to the house and then to the *sentō*. And McGraw had proposed the whole thing as a quid pro quo for helping me out with Fukumoto. I looked at it from every angle I could imagine, and I couldn't find a way around it: the one fact I had so far was that McGraw wanted Ozawa dead.

But someone had wanted Fukumoto dead, too. Someone who'd made sure I was able to get inside his house. Who else could it have been but McGraw? But if he *had* wanted Fukumoto dead, what was it, just a crazy coincidence that I had proposed it to him?

No. Coincidences like that don't happen.

I paced among the markers, frustrated, sweat trickling down my back. I could sense the shape, the contours, but I couldn't see the details.

Okay, how about this. McGraw knew where you'd be meeting Miyamoto to hand off the cash that morning in Ueno. He sent those chinpira *to provoke you. How many times has he told you he knows about your temper? He knew you'd do what you did, that you'd have a problem with the yakuza as a result, that you'd propose killing them as a solution. He'd let you think it was your idea, but that would be just a manipulation.*

It didn't feel quite right. Almost, but not quite. Knowing I would kill one of the *chinpira* . . . it was just too uncertain. McGraw was good, I'd seen that, but he wasn't psychic. It had to be some-thing else.

All right, what if they had just robbed you? What if the plan had been to get to you before the exchange, beat you up, take the bag, and run? You'd be fifty grand in hock to the CIA. You'd be desperate, trying to get McGraw to believe you hadn't just stolen the money yourself. At which point, he would have proposed a way for you to pay off your debt: kill these people for me.

Jesus. What happened instead . . . he'd just been improvising. Things hadn't turned out the way he'd been expecting, so he adapted, created a plan B, achieved the same result.

But what about Pig Eyes, at the Kodokan? He was trying to kill you, no question. If he'd succeeded, how would you have carried out McGraw's hits?

I kept pacing, examining the pieces from different angles, weighing them, rearranging them, seeing which I could get to cohere.

Pig Eyes . . . that would have been part of the original fuck-up. I wasn't supposed to kill anyone in Ueno; it was supposed to be an easy ambush and robbery. But I *did* kill someone. And then Mad Dog, who doesn't know McGraw's full plans or whose pride is so wounded he doesn't care, gets his crew and tracks me down on his own. McGraw doesn't know about it . . . doesn't even want it, because it would mess up his plans. Yes, that's why he had looked surprised when I'd first told him about what happened at the Kodokan. The thing about the yakuza putting a contract out on me had been bullshit, intended to manipulate me, and then I responded, "Yeah, I know, they just tried to kill me." It had thrown him, albeit only for a moment. And then he was back on his game. Christ, he was good.

All right, but what about the Fukumoto file? It wasn't very

complete. If McGraw had really wanted Fukumoto dead, why didn't he give me an actionable file, like the one he gave me for Ozawa?

Because from McGraw's perspective, Fukumoto was supposed to be random. Not something he'd been preparing for. If he'd handed you a detailed, actionable file, you might have been suspicious. All he needed was to get you to the house, and the girl would get you inside. You followed those cues like a pigeon pecking a lever.

Why, though? What was McGraw up to? What was the game? I didn't know. But whatever it was, it involved taking out Ozawa, the head of the LDP Executive Council; Fukumoto, the head of the Gokumatsu-gumi, Tokyo's biggest yakuza family; and Fukumoto's son Mad Dog, presumably the father's heir.

I paused. Why was I assuming McGraw wanted Mad Dog dead? If Mad Dog were in fact the heir, might it not be the case that killing the father was intended to pave the way for the son?

But then why manipulate me into proposing to kill Mad Dog, too?

Remember, he was improvising. Maybe that wasn't part of the original plan. McGraw was controlling the order of the files he gave you, remember? First Ozawa. Then Fukumoto Senior. Then Fukumoto Junior. He was saving Junior for last because unlike the first two, he doesn't want Mad Dog killed at all. Remember, at Inokashira he tried to talk you out of going after the son.

I still didn't quite see it. Because, in the end, McGraw did get me the file. I'd just retrieved and memorized it the day before. Was it filled with bullshit? A wild goose chase, intended just to placate and distract me?

Or maybe it's intended to fix you in time and place. Then they can easily clip the guy who did Ozawa and Fukumoto. No loose ends.

But the problem with Mad Dog's file was that it wasn't specific enough. The same generality, the same surfeit of nexuses that would prevent me from fixing Mad Dog would prevent anyone from prop-

erly fixing me. Plus, if the idea was to get me to go after Mad Dog
so I would fix myself in time and place for an ambush, why had
McGraw tried to talk me out of going after Mad Dog entirely?

I chewed that one over. I decided it was just as McGraw said:
he'd been looking at me as nothing more than a bagman, a useful
idiot, someone expendable. That is: manipulate me into taking out
Ozawa and Fukumoto Senior. If there's a problem, I take a fall; if
it goes smoothly, McGraw takes me out. In the first instance, he
denies the connection; in the second, he severs it. And then he had
second thoughts. Why? Because I'd done better than he'd been
expecting. Much better. He'd realized maybe I could be more useful
to him and his program, whatever it was, alive than dead. And when
I'd resisted, he'd decided, *Okay, so be it, we'll stick with plan A.*

Which was?

*Manipulate you into clipping Ozawa and Fukumoto Senior. After
which, the one who gets clipped is you.*

But if that was the case, why not do me himself? We'd met just
the day before, at Inokashira. He knew I was coming. For that matter, he knew I was going to be at the New Otani just an hour ago.
Neither would have been that hard.

*Maybe he was going to at Inokashira, and then he'd changed his
mind because he thought you'd be more useful alive, like you said. Or,
more likely, he just doesn't want to do it himself. That's not his style. He
manipulates other people into getting their hands dirty on his behalf.
He doesn't take those kinds of risks himself.*

Not unless he absolutely has to, anyway.

One thing was clear. I had to up my game. I'd been looking at
the world as though down deep it was no more than what its surface
indicated. But there were levels I hadn't sensed, connections I hadn't
considered. There was a world beneath the world—the real world.
And I needed to start living in it, or I was going to die there.

All right. What's your next move?

My next move was that every time McGraw wanted to meet me, or otherwise did something that could fix me in time and place, I had to assume it was an ambush, and adopt appropriate counter-measures. I'd been hellishly lucky he hadn't dropped me already. What was that Churchill saying? "Nothing in life is so exhilarating as to be shot at without result." That's what this felt like. Now the trick was to stop making myself an easy target.

I asked myself if I wasn't being paranoid. In the last several days, I'd killed six people. What I was feeling now . . . could it be just the product of a stunted conscience, disturbed in its slumber?

All right, look at it this way: any downside to approaching McGraw as if your concerns are legitimate?

I couldn't think of any.

And any downside to approaching McGraw as though he's been telling you nothing but the truth?

Hmm. Just an ambush and my own violent death, I supposed.

Good. Not such a hard decision, then.

If I was right, McGraw was going to make some kind of move soon. I'd done what he wanted. From here on out, all I would represent to him was a liability. How had he put it at Taihō, the night I'd first proposed—or he'd manipulated me into proposing—that I kill Fukumoto Senior and his Mad Dog son? *This is a business relationship. You provide some benefit, and you represent a cost.* Well, the benefit was done; now would be the time for cost-cutting. I'd have to be careful as hell, but I realized that for the moment I had an advantage: he thought I was dumb. And maybe I had been, but I was getting smarter now. I'd seen something and he didn't know I'd seen it.

You know, the thing about ambushes is, they can work both ways.

That was true. McGraw could propose a meeting, think he was laying a trap . . . and I could walk up behind him and blow his face off through the back of his head. I didn't need a rock for this one. I had that yakuza's Hi Power.

The problem was, I wasn't *sure*. Was I sure enough to completely revise my view of what was going on, and take appropriate security measures? Hell yes. But was I sure enough to drop my CIA case officer without even knowing what he'd been up to or what he'd mixed me up in?

No. I wasn't. That one sounded like out of the frying pan, into the fire. If the frying pan got unbearable, I'd jump wherever I had to. But I wasn't there yet. I needed to keep cool. Be smart. And remain patient. McGraw was going to make a move. I could feel it. I just didn't know what it was going to be. But I would soon enough.

chapter
twenty-seven

As it happened, I didn't have to wait long for my break.
I'd pulled back from scouting the locations where I was
supposed to have a shot at nailing Mad Dog. Too much risk the
person getting nailed would be me. I checked in with my answering
service regularly, but no word from McGraw. I had time on my
hands and would start to get antsy, then remind myself the smart
play was just to wait.

I was spending every morning and day with Sayaka. The only
times we were apart were when she had to go to class or work. In
bed, it seemed like every time was better than the one before it. I
didn't know why, exactly. Probably because we were getting more
comfortable with each other. But also, I thought, because we were
getting more comfortable with ourselves. I loved how unselfconscious she was. She still didn't like my seeing her legs, but even that,
I felt, was going to fade over time, and on everything else she was
amazingly unaffected. She wanted to try everything—sex was like
a giant experiment for her, a limitless, undiscovered country, and
her lack of inhibition in bed was a giant turn-on for me. A few
times she would do something and then catch herself, as though
realizing maybe she was going too far, and then she would see how
much I loved it and she would just plunge ahead. I realized I'd gone
into this thing unconsciously assuming I'd be teaching and guiding
her. Well, whatever I had to teach, she'd learned it in about a day.
Since then, she'd been teaching me. Occasionally, I'd catch a flash

of the toughness, the guardedness she'd displayed when I'd first met her and on the subsequent nights I'd come to see her at the hotel, but those moments only served to remind me of how much she was trusting me, how far she was letting me in, and moved me tremendously. Sometimes I'd worry I sounded sappy, and think maybe I should be a little more self-censored, but whatever I said or did, she always seemed to respond in kind. It was overwhelming, certainly more than I'd been expecting and more than I could really grasp. Underneath it all, I still felt guilty for what I knew in my heart was a horrible deceit. But I couldn't tell her, and I also couldn't stop what was happening between us. Once I had sorted out McGraw and everything else, maybe Sayaka and I would talk about where all this was going and what it meant. But there was no rush on that. As long as we kept getting those precious morning hours in her bed, I didn't want to think about the future, and I don't think Sayaka cared.

On the fourth of these wonderful mornings, while Sayaka was in class, I got the message I'd been waiting for. McGraw. I called him.

"You making any progress on that problem you were trying to solve?" he said.

"No," I said, my heart beating hard. "No luck so far."

He grunted. "You didn't seem to need luck before. You sure you're really trying?"

Son of a bitch, I thought. *You have people watching and waiting—at some of the nexuses, maybe all of them. And they've been reporting to you that I'm nowhere to be seen.*

"Are you crazy? Why wouldn't I be trying?"

"Forget it, I'm just being disagreeable. Anyway, it doesn't matter. I think we just caught that break we were hoping for."

Oh, we is it, *now?*

"Tell me."

"You might have seen on the news . . . a certain someone was laid to rest yesterday in Yanaka Cemetery."

I had seen it, in fact. Fukumoto's funeral had practically been a state affair. I hadn't even considered trying to get close to Mad Dog there. I doubted there was a gangster in Japan not in attendance.

"Yeah?"

"There was a lot of pomp and circumstance. Not exactly an intimate gathering. I have it on reliable authority someone close to the deceased will be paying his private respects tomorrow afternoon."

"What time?" I wanted to sound eager. And in fact, I was. Just not for what McGraw was thinking.

"Jesus, you want to know what he ate for breakfast, too? I'm not that far up his ass. That's as much as I know. But it's reliable."

"How'd you hear?"

"That would come under the heading of sources and methods, son. And need to know. If you want to say thank you, though, I'll say you're welcome."

"Thank you."

"You're welcome. Now listen. These guys have a family plot. Right in the center of the cemetery. Land as expensive as the Imperial Palace grounds. Apparently in section nine, right next to where the Tokugawa shoguns are buried. Does that mean anything to you?"

I smiled. He still thought he was dealing with someone blind. He didn't know I'd been figuring out how to see. "Well, I don't know what section nine is, but I know where to find the Tokugawa burial plot."

"Another spot your mother took you?"

"Yeah," I said, feigning irritation, being the hothead he was accustomed to underestimating. "Is there a problem with that?"

"Relax, son. I'm just impressed again, that's all."

No, you want to know if I'm familiar with the terrain so you can predict my approach. If I'm unfamiliar, I might wander at random. If I know where I'm going, I'll do something sensible. Random isn't predictable. Sensible is.

"All right. This sounds promising."

"Go get him, tiger."

He hung up.

Tiger? I thought. *You have no idea.*

I bombed on Thanatos straight to the cemetery. I didn't think McGraw would be expecting this; more likely, the plan was to hit me when I arrived for Mad Dog's private visit tomorrow. Still, it wasn't impossible McGraw would assume I'd recon the area first. I had to be ready for that.

Yanaka was an old cemetery in an old ward of the same name, part of Shitamachi. Numerous important personages were laid to rest among the thousands of plots there, including, as McGraw had noted, the Tokugawa clan. It was also known for a glorious five-story pagoda that two mad lovers had set ablaze with themselves inside some years before, and for cherry trees so densely packed and spectacular that the cemetery's central street was known as Cherry Blossom Avenue. Though I knew all this from childhood visits during *hanami* season, I was hardly an expert on the terrain. But I was about to become one.

I circled the cemetery on Thanatos, then cut through it in all directions, my head sweeping left and right, searching for problems. Seeing none, I dismounted and started scouting on foot. My bag was unzipped, the Hi Power within easy reach.

It didn't take me long to find Fukumoto's plot. It was on a raised square of land surrounded by an old stone wall—a kind of cemetery within a cemetery, within which sat symmetrical rows of markers, some of simple granite, others multilevel, polished pagodas.

Fukumoto's grave was at the northwest end: a massive gray obelisk, the earth before it freshly turned and barely visible beneath scores of enormous bouquets. Each wall was about twenty-five meters long and about two meters high. There was only one entrance—a gate on the south wall. I immediately understood why this was the spot: Yanaka was enormous, and I might approach from any direction. But at some point, if I wanted to get to someone inside the plot, I was going to go through or wait at this gate. Where they would position people would flow from that.

What would you do if you wanted to get to you? That's what they'll do. And then you can do it to them.

It would depend on manpower. If they had only one or two, they'd be at the gate or just inside it. But if they had a spotter, someone whose job was to note my approach and radio the others . . .

I walked the circumference of the wall, examining the various possibilities. The ground outside the north wall was higher, and from here I could see over it. It occurred to me that they might know or suspect I had the dead yakuza's Hi Power. If so, they couldn't count on my entering through the gate. It wasn't impossible I'd walk right up to this wall and start shooting. Of course, they wouldn't be worried about my hitting Mad Dog—his "visit" was almost certainly a ruse, and I doubted he would even be present—but they'd need to know where to get to me regardless. If they really wanted things covered, my guess was a minimum of four people: two inside, two out.

Ten meters out from the north wall was another plot, on higher ground. I walked over, went up the stone steps, and immediately liked what I saw. This was another enclosed plot, but unlike Fukumoto's, this one owed its privacy not to a stone wall, but to a perimeter of thick bushes about four feet high. I walked inside, squeezed into the gap in the bushes on the south side, and was rewarded with a panoramic view of the wall surrounding Fukumoto's plot. Anyone approaching Fukumoto's plot from any direction other than due south would be visible long before ever getting close. If I were doing it, I'd have a man right here, plus two more near the southeast and southwest corners of Fukumoto's plot, plus one inside. The one inside would be someone who superficially resembled Mad Dog, maybe in dark glasses to obscure any discrepancies. If I had the manpower, I'd put one more man inside Fukumoto's plot, who'd be playing a bodyguard or a friend, or perhaps another bereaved relative. It wouldn't matter; the point would be just to make it two against one if for whatever reason I managed to get inside the wall.

I considered for a moment. Could I really be sure Mad Dog wouldn't be there? It was possible McGraw had set this thing up using only his own people and had never said a word to Mad Dog, but I doubted it. I didn't think McGraw had the necessary manpower, for one thing. If I saw anything other than an authentic-looking Japanese cast of characters, I might easily spot the setup and abort. No, I didn't think McGraw could have arranged this without Mad Dog knowing, and helping. And even if McGraw had told him to stay the hell away—that just the promise of Mad Dog's presence was sufficient and that the reality would be unnecessary—Mad Dog didn't strike me as the type who would listen. He'd come to the Kodokan to watch Pig Eyes try to kill me, after all. Wouldn't he want the chance to watch me die here, as well? He wouldn't think the danger was excessive. Not with all the additional men, and the element of surprise.

The strange thing was, I didn't think the underlying dynamics had changed so much from when McGraw had first told me I had run afoul of the Fukumotos. Mad Dog still wanted to kill me—whether out of honor or some other mix of motives, I couldn't know. But his reasons were secondary to his intent. He wanted me dead, and it could only be to my benefit if the one who wound up dead were him.

And not just Mad Dog. The reasoning was equally applicable to McGraw. I didn't expect him to be at the cemetery tomorrow—his style seemed to be to work through cutouts and dupes—but maybe I'd get lucky.

I spent the rest of the afternoon getting intimate with the terrain—the angles of approach, the cover and concealment. Tomorrow would be a kind of experiment, a proof of concept. If it worked out the way I was expecting, Mad Dog would be just an appetizer. McGraw would be the main course.

chapter
twenty-eight

I spent the night at the hotel and then, as had become our habit, the drowsy morning hours at Sayaka's. We would wind up in bed within minutes of our arrival and make love for an hour or two, sometimes getting up to eat a small breakfast, sometimes too exhausted and spent to move.

This time, she had pushed me on my back and straddled me, a position I knew she had come to like. Her arms were amazingly strong and she supported herself with one hand on my chest, reaching down with the other to guide me in. She kept her hand there, holding me, feeling through her fingers what her injury denied her from feeling elsewhere. I caressed her face, her breasts, her hips, loving the way she looked like that, moving, swaying, her face partly hidden by her hair. Periodically, she looked down to take in with her eyes what she was feeling through her hand. I loved when she did that, loved how unselfconscious she was about it, how it seemed to fill her with awe and wonder. She looked back at me and rode me harder, more urgently, her mouth open, her breathing hard, confusion and frustration playing out alternately across her face.

"Jun," she said, and moved faster, almost angrily. She had so much weight on my chest it was getting hard to breathe, and she was grinding herself into me so hard it hurt my pelvis, albeit in a wonderful way. "Jun," she said again, looking into my eyes, and then again, more loudly, and then her mouth opened in a perfect

O and her eyelids fluttered and her voice dissolved into a long, startled cry.

I kept moving with her, confused, surprised, afraid to hope. Was she coming? God, it was so beautiful, she was so beautiful.

It went on for a long time, and then suddenly she was sagging against me, panting. I held her and stroked her hair and whispered her name over and over. She settled against me, her face to my shoulder, and I could feel tears against my skin.

"Are you okay?" I said softly, still stroking her hair, trying to see her face.

She pushed herself up and looked at me, her eyes watery, her cheeks streaked with tears. She shook her head. "That felt so good. I never felt anything like that."

"Sayaka . . . did you, do you think you just came?"

She smiled and fresh tears spilled down her cheeks. "I don't know. It just . . . it felt so good. Like an explosion. But did I? I didn't know I could." She cried harder. "I didn't know."

I felt my own eyes fill up, and I pulled her into me, embarrassed she would see. But I was too late. She pushed herself up again and laughed. "Jun," she said. "My tough guy."

I laughed, too, but the tears were still coming.

She stroked my cheek. "Why are you crying?"

I cleared my throat and tried to blink away the tears. "I'm not."

She laughed again. "Liar."

I wanted so much to tell her I loved her. To just blurt it out. But I was afraid to. I was afraid she'd think it was just a crush, that I was too young for her, that I was being silly.

But I did. God, I loved her.

"I'm just happy," I said. "You make me happy."

Sometimes I wonder now whether it would have made any difference if I'd told her right then. Probably not. And I try to convince myself that she knew anyway. But I'll never really know. I wish I'd told her. Wish it as much as I wish anything. But I didn't.

I headed out not long after that. I felt bad I couldn't tell her why beyond that it was work, and it made me feel worse when she didn't press. I wanted to get this all behind me. But to do it, I couldn't just walk away, not unless I wanted to spend the rest of my life in rooms at shabby love hotels, constantly looking over my shoulder. If I wanted to win, first I had to double down. Then I could leave behind everything I'd been mixed up in. Dead, buried, and gone. Over time, maybe even forgotten.

I stopped at a discount store and bought a pair of green pants, a green long-sleeve tee shirt, and a green baseball hat. Not exactly top-level camouflage, but enough to confer an advantage. I also picked up some face paint, the kind children use to turn themselves into cats and turtles and God knows what. I left my bag in a coin locker in Ueno Station—keeping only the Hi Power—parked Thanatos, and walked to Yanaka. I used a public restroom on the way. I'd deliberately drunk nothing that morning and I didn't really need to go, but still I knew it was probably my last safe piss for a while.

I was several hours early, but had to approach carefully in case they might anticipate that. I didn't think they would—I'd never shown up early to meet McGraw, and he would have noted this laxness on my part, likely assumed he could count on it, and then briefed Mad Dog's people accordingly. But no sense taking chances.

I came in over the northeast wall rather than through one of the entrances. I doubted they had the manpower to post someone at every gate, but on the other hand I didn't know what kind of influence Mad Dog might command following his father's death. Maybe there were dozens of soldiers trying to curry favor with him.

I made my way to the elevated plot by cutting between the grave sites, avoiding the main roads traversing the cemetery. Again, probably unnecessary, but also again no downside to being careful. There were only a few people about, mostly pensioners walking dogs; a few devoted friends or family members laying flowers or lighting incense; mothers with toddlers in the attached children's park. Nothing rubbed me the wrong way.

Approaching from the north, I avoided the stone steps, instead pulling myself up the side and into the row of bushes there. I waited, watching and listening. Crows cawed; summer insects buzzed; a Yamanote train chimed in the distance. Other than that, it was as quiet as . . . well, you know.

I opened the little jar of face paint and wiped diagonal streaks across my face, my fingers tracing the lines from combat memory. Then I pocketed the paint, flipped the baseball cap around backward, flattened out on the earth, and waited. It was hot and humid and the mosquitoes were a pain in the ass, and I realized I'd probably been excessive in wondering whether Mad Dog and his people would put themselves through this kind of discomfort. You'd have to be crazy. Or at least accustomed to much worse after humping a sixty-pound ruck in the Southeast Asian boonies. The sick thing was, it was comfortable for me. Yes, I was holding a pistol rather than a CAR-15, and Yanaka smelled like city rather than jungle, but overall it felt familiar, natural, like something I'd been honed for and maybe even was meant for. I felt compact and mean and deadly. And God help the team that was coming here to take me out.

I'd been in place for two hours when I heard footfalls on the stone steps to my right. I kept perfectly still, glancing over without moving my head. A burly, thirty-something, punch-permed Japanese guy in a double-breasted suit with lapels as wide as the wings on a 747 was approaching. A nice little adrenaline flush spread through my gut. Okay, looked like they'd sent the yakuza A-team this time, not a threesome of incompetent *chinpira*. He walked with a swagger, I noted, and I liked that, liked the over-confidence it suggested. He didn't even examine his surroundings. He just walked over to the south side, found a relatively sparse spot in the bushes, and pushed the branches aside. He pulled out a radio, keyed it up, and said, "I'm here. Yes, I can see you both."

So there were three of them. Okay. Was one of them Mad Dog? I got the feeling no. Three would be the bare minimum to cover points of ingress. These guys were the assault team. If Mad Dog was here, it would be as a spectator, maybe at some remove. No way to know except to go through these three, and then see if anyone was still around when I was done.

He squatted, keeping the radio in one hand and holding the branches aside with the other. It didn't look comfortable. But I supposed he wasn't expecting to be there long. Well, it would be rude to keep him waiting.

I pulled myself forward on my elbows, the Hi Power at the ready. If he turned, I'd drop him, but if it came to that I had to assume his comrades would hear the gunshot and I would lose the element of surprise. Better to get close and do it quietly. I spent ten minutes creeping out of the bushes and onto the grass. Once the potentially noisy branches were behind me, I was able to move more quickly. I covered the twenty feet from my line of bushes to his in under thirty seconds, keeping to a low crouch. He never heard me, never had a clue, not even when I was directly behind him.

I raised the Hi Power with the butt end protruding past my wrist and hammer-fisted it into the base of his skull like I was trying to bury it there. There was a satisfying crack, and he shuddered and then began to pitch soundlessly forward. I hauled him back by the collar, smashing the butt into his face on the way down. He landed on his back, the grass muffling the sound of the impact. His eyes were unfocused but his mouth was twitching—he wasn't dead yet. I dragged his head back by his punch-permed hair and something came off in my hand—Christ, it was a toupee. I tossed it aside, sunk my fingers into his eye sockets, pulled his head back, and blasted the butt of the Hi Power into his exposed throat. I felt cartilage breaking and knew he was done.

The radio screeched. *Shit.* A voice said, "You all right?"

I picked it up and keyed the mic. "Yeah. Just taking a leak." The reception was sufficiently shitty that I didn't think he'd notice any difference between my voice and the dead yakuza's.

"Make it fast. You're supposed to be watching."

"Okay."

I dropped the radio and patted him down. He was unarmed—okay, this one was just the spotter. I propped him up, sat behind him, put my feet against his lower back, and shoved him into the bushes, his pants sliding up his legs as he went. When he was far enough forward so they could see him again, I pulled some branches behind his back to keep him in position. Not exactly lifelike, but the other two were far enough away and there was enough foliage concealing him to make me confident they wouldn't notice anything was wrong.

I proned out and looked out at Fukumoto's plot, making sure there was plenty of green concealing my camouflaged face. I could see his two buddies, one at the southwest corner of the wall, the other at the southeast, just as I had figured they would be. They were hanging back under the trees, partly for concealment, I imagined, and partly to get out of the sun. Hanging back like that had certain advantages, but it entailed a critical disadvantage, too: though they had line of sight to the now-dead spotter's position, they couldn't see each other.

I picked up the radio and checked the controls. Tempting to take it with me, but I didn't see any way to mute it short of turning it off entirely. Even if I cranked the squelch, it might not be enough to prevent it from coming on in the face of a strong signal, and if one of the other yakuza decided to get on the radio when I was coming up behind them, it would blow my position. So I turned it off, wiped it down, and left it in the grass alongside its late owner. Then I slid down from the elevated plot the same way I had come in and began circling wide clockwise, using the trees and thick stands of darkened markers for concealment. I didn't need to move quietly this time, and was able to come up behind the southeast guy's position in a matter of minutes. I crept soundlessly through the trees, the Hi Power out now, my heart racing. There he was, leaning against a tree trunk, dressed like the first guy, smoking a cigarette. These guys weren't much on cover for action, but on the other hand I supposed not too many people were going to give an obvious yakuza a hard time for loitering in a cemetery.

Five meters away, I angled out so I could see him in profile. The way he was leaning against the tree, I wasn't going to have complete blind-spot access to his back the way I had with the first guy. I had just worked out that my best chance would be to rabbit-punch him with the muzzle of the Hi Power when, whether out of dumb luck, or animal instinct, or for no reason at all, he turned and looked right at me.

His mouth dropped open and his hand went for the inside of his jacket. But I already had the Hi Power out, and before he could even grab what he was reaching for it was pointing at his face. I looked in his eyes and shook my head twice, and he got the meaning: *Don't do that, you won't make it.* His hand slowly came out and he started to put both arms in the air.

"Take it out with your left hand," I said quietly. "Slowly and carefully. Place it on the ground. I've got all the slack on this trigger taken up already. One twitch and you die. You don't want to make me twitch."

He complied. When the gun was on the ground, he said, "You have no idea who you're fucking with, do you?"

"Why don't you tell me?"

He laughed.

Well, he was tough, I'd give him that.

"Face down," I said. "On the ground."

He laughed again. "You want to live? Turn and run. And you better run fast. And far."

"I might do that. But I'll get a better head start with you face down. Or dead. Which is it going to be?"

Again, he complied.

"Arms above your head," I said. "All the way. Fingers splayed. And spread your legs."

I didn't know it at the time, but the psychology of compliance is interesting. Getting the initial yes is the hard part. Once the subject starts complying, each subsequent step seems like just a minor addition to what's already been done, and you can get a remarkable amount of cooperation. At this point, he was so obedient we might as well having been playing Simon Says.

Of course, it didn't hurt that in his yakuza arrogance, he assumed I was just going to hightail it. If he'd known what I'd done to his friend five minutes earlier, I doubted he would have been nearly as sanguine.

Once his arms were above his head and his legs were spread, there was no way he could effectively react to anything I did. Which is why he didn't have a chance when I stepped up alongside him, raised my leg, and stomped the back of his neck. His arms flapped and his body jerked. He was probably dead already, his spinal cord severed, but I stomped him twice more to be sure. I rolled him over and took his gun—another Hi Power. Standard issue with the Gokumatsu-gumi, apparently. I shoved it in the back of my pants, took a deep breath, and started circling clockwise again.

It took me less than a minute to reach the third guy. I eased up behind him and saw I was just in time—he had the radio out. "Hey, are you there?" he said. "Somebody answer me."

I stepped out so I was ninety degrees from him, the Hi Power leveled at his head. "Of course they're not answering," I said. "They're dead."

He jumped and turned toward me, his right arm reflexively going for his jacket but stopping when he saw the muzzle of the Hi Power.

Son of a bitch. It was Pig Eyes. The guy who'd tried to strangle me at the Kodokan, who had almost lost a testicle for his troubles.

"You want to live or you want to die?" I said.

He spat. "Put down the gun. We'll see how it goes then."

"Sure, I'll put it down. Right after I shoot you in the face with it. Like you said, we'll see how it goes."

His arms drifted upward, his nostrils flaring with anger.

"Now slowly take out your gun with your left hand. And slowly put it on the ground."

He did.

"Now turn and put your palms on that tree, spread your legs, and lean forward so the tree is taking all your weight."

He did so, but not to my satisfaction.

"No, that's not enough. Spread your feet further. And move them farther back from the tree."

He did.

When I was satisfied he could do nothing defensive without spending at least a full second getting his legs under him and his hands off the tree, I approached and picked up his gun. Another Hi Power. I jammed it in my waistband, my pants getting tight under the belt with the bulk of the two pistols. "Who sent you?"

He glanced behind so he could see me. "What do you mean?"

"Don't look at me. Look at the tree. I mean, who do you work for? Who wants me dead?"

He didn't answer.

"Your friends are dead. That could be bad news for you, or good. Bad because I can easily make you dead, too. Good because, if I don't, there's no one to contradict your story about what happened here. You could tell them I surprised the guy at the other end of this wall, you chased me, I jumped on a motorcycle and fled. Yeah, maybe you'd have to cut off a pinkie digit to show how contrite you were, but you could tell them your honor would never be fully restored until you had tracked me down and killed me. They'd let you live. I won't. Now, who wants me dead?"

There was a pause while he did the math. He said, "Mad Dog."

"Why?"

"You killed his cousin."

"What about his father? Who killed his father?"

"We don't know. But we'll find out."

Interesting. It sounded like either Mad Dog didn't know it was me, or he didn't want people to know he knew.

"Where is he?"

"I don't know."

"I don't believe you. You know him well. He came with you to the Kodokan. So he could watch. Is he here?"

"I don't know."

"Bullshit."

"I'm telling the truth."

"After you killed me here, how were you supposed to report to him?"

"We're supposed to call him."

"What number?"

"I don't have it here. It's written down."

I knew he was lying, but I had no way to make him tell the truth. I could try scaring him, beating him. And eventually he'd cough up a number or an address, and I'd call or go there, and find out he'd given up his favorite bento delivery service, or his dry cleaner, or masseuse, or whatever.

No. This was a dead end. I stepped in close and raised the Hi Power to hammer-fist his head the way I had the first guy.

But I'd miscalculated. Pig Eyes understood I had no reason to let him live. I'd killed the other two; why would I let him go? He'd know I wouldn't, and he'd know I'd do it from close, not wanting to risk attracting attention with the sound of a gunshot. And while the average person will deploy a dozen forms of denial to avoid accepting the truth of his imminent demise, this wasn't an average person. He was a tough career criminal, smart enough to be in some sort of leadership position. An expert judoka. And during the time I'd spent fruitlessly questioning him, I'd given him precious moments to build his resolve and his readiness.

So the instant I stepped in to finish him, he did the only thing he could. He snapped his arms out and let gravity take over. If I'd been thinking properly, I would have jumped back and just shot him, the hell with the noise. But I'd already committed to the hammer-fist, so I followed him down with the butt of the gun, catching him with a weak blow that lost whatever energy it might otherwise have had because his body was moving through space ahead of it. The side of his head smacked into the tree, he twisted, threw a leg past my knees, and scissored, taking my legs out. I went down on my back, getting the wind knocked out of me, the two guns cutting painfully into my spine. He was on the gun and strad-dling my torso amazingly fast, gripping the barrel in both hands, twisting the muzzle away from him. My finger wasn't in the trigger guard—good because if it had been, the way he was twisting the gun would have snapped it off; bad because it meant I couldn't shoot him. But my hands and wrists were strong from hundreds of hours of gripping the heavy cotton *judōgi*. No matter how frantically he tugged and twisted, he couldn't get the gun away from me. But nor could I get it from him. He changed tactics and smashed my hand into the ground, once, twice, again. I felt the impact up my arm and knew I was going to lose the gun. I reached behind my back with my left hand, felt the grip of one of the other pistols, pulled it free with a yell. He let go with one hand and grabbed the second gun in it just as I thumbed the safety down. Now we were both holding two guns, each of my hands around the grips, his hands around the barrels. His judo technique might have been better than mine, but one hand against one hand, I was stronger. I slid my finger into the trigger guard of the pistol in my right hand and, staring into his eyes, started turning the muzzle implacably toward his head. His pig eyes were bulging and his teeth were clenched, but his shaking arms weren't enough to stop me. At the last instant, he tried to leap back, but too late. I put a round into the side of his face. Brain matter and skull fragments blew out the opposite side, and he slumped to the ground next to me.

I scrambled out from under him, scared about the noise of the shot. My hand felt numb from the way he had pounded it against the ground. Did I have blood on me? I couldn't have avoided it entirely, though from what I had seen I thought most of it had exited to my side. I glanced around. I saw no one in the immediate vicinity, and maybe whatever visitors were in the area, saying their prayers and laying their wreaths, would listen for a moment, and then tell themselves it must have been something else. It didn't matter. I had to get the hell away. I thumbed the safety up on the unfired gun and shoved it back into my pants, held the other under my tee shirt, and started walking fast on shaking legs.

I'd gone maybe twenty feet when I heard a car to my left. I turned just in time to see a black sedan screech to a halt on the access road I was crossing. The driver was pure yakuza—scarred face, punch perm, dark glasses. And in the backseat—

Mad Dog.

I brought out the Hi Power and took aim with a two-handed grip. The driver floored it. There was the sound of burning rubber and wheels spraying pebbles and then he was rocketing straight at me. I pressed the trigger. I'd been aiming at the driver, but the shot went through the windshield dead center—that numbness in my hand was screwing up my aim. I tried to recalibrate and then he was on me. I dove out of the way, breaking into a judo roll and yelling involuntarily as the two pistols bit into my back. I didn't care—I was just glad the damn things hadn't seen fit to fire and shoot my ass off.

I came to my feet and had just enough time to fire once more. It hit the trunk, and then the car went around the corner and was gone. If I was lucky, the bullet went through the backseat and drilled Mad Dog. But I didn't think so—it had hit too far to the other side. And I didn't think the first shot had hit him, either.

I made my way quickly back toward where I'd originally come in, the baseball cap pulled low, wiping the face paint off with spit and a handkerchief. I kept my head down and stayed on the narrow dirt paths between plots, avoiding the main roads and pedestrian arteries. I couldn't avoid passing a few people, but between the cap and my averted face, I wasn't unduly concerned about anyone identifying me for the police.

So Mad Dog had been here—as a spectator, naturally, not a player, the same as at the Kodokan. They'd heard the shot and thought someone had dropped me. Maybe they'd radioed and hadn't gotten an answer. Regardless, they'd come racing around so Mad Dog could see his trophy, recently stuffed and mounted.

Well, slight miscalculation, asshole.

I kept moving, my back singing where the pistols had bitten into it. Yanaka Cemetery was large enough to have its own *kōban*, police box, and though I imagined the officers there were more accustomed to helping the newly bereaved locate the plots of loved ones and instructing *hanami* revelers to clean up the garbage disgorged by their picnics, I didn't want a confrontation. I didn't want anything at all to get in the way of my finishing Mad Dog. And that lying piece of shit, McGraw. I thought again of what he'd said. *This is a business relationship. You provide some benefit, and you represent a cost.*

You got that right, I thought. *I do represent a cost. And I'm going to cost you everything.*

chapter
twenty-nine

Cutting through Ueno Park on my way back to the station, I ducked into a public restroom and examined myself in the mirror. I'd done an okay job getting the face paint off, but there was enough residue on my skin to make me look noticeably green around the gills. I scrubbed it off in the sink and wet my hair back. There had been some blood on the green tee shirt, but I'd pulled it off and balled it up, and the navy polo shirt I'd been wearing under didn't show any blood at all. My back and hand ached but were functional. I got my bag from the locker, dumped the guns in it, tossed the tee shirt in a refuse container in the park, got back on Thanatos, and took off. The gun I'd used to kill the third yakuza I tossed in the river. It was okay—now I had two spares.

After riding west for ten minutes, I realized I was all right, I'd made it. I promptly got the shakes, and had to pull over in a park and wait while they subsided.

Christ, that had been a near thing with Pig Eyes. And with the car after it. I'd been careful, but I'd also been lucky.

And damn, I'd been so close to nailing Mad Dog. If my hand hadn't been messed up, if I'd had just another second to prepare, if I'd been a little cooler . . .

It didn't matter. I was alive. I'd have another chance. I'd *make* another chance.

I went to a payphone and called McGraw. It wasn't something I'd do now, with the benefit of experience and the understanding that warnings put you at a disadvantage when afterward you have to act. But back then, I was still young. With a temper, as McGraw had been keen to point out. I wanted my hands around his throat, and for the moment, this was the closest I could get.

They put the call through to him. "Surprised to hear from me?" I said.

"Why would I be surprised?"

Christ, he was cool, I had to give him that.

"I didn't think you'd expect me to walk away from Yanaka."

"What are you talking about?"

"There was a whole fucking yakuza team. They knew exactly where I'd be and when I'd be there."

There was a pause. "What happened?"

"Who told you Mad Dog was going to be there today?"

"I told you, son, sources and—"

"Don't call me son. And don't give me any more bullshit about sources and methods. I'm not just going to take you down, McGraw. I'm going to take you out."

Another pause. "You want to watch what you say. Son."

"This was a setup, asshole. If you weren't behind it, your source was. Now who fucking told you Mad Dog was going to be there?"

"I don't like your tone."

"Yeah, well I don't like your face, but I don't waste time whining about it. Now I'm going to ask you one more time. You don't want to answer, it's fine, I'll know exactly what it means. Who. Was your fucking. Source."

Another pause. For the first time since I'd met him, I felt McGraw was flailing. He was stalling for time. Trying to come up with the right lie. It would have to be persuasive. Consistent. Intriguing enough for me to follow . . . maybe to yet another setup.

"It was Mad Dog."

"Mad Dog?"

"Yeah. He must have known I'd tell you. I guess he's got a bug up his ass. You did kill his cousin. I should have seen it coming. My fault. I'm sorry."

"You know Mad Dog well enough for him to share his daily calendar with you, but the best you could do with that file was, 'Here, I think you can find him in Tokyo'?"

I knew I had him with that. I'd put him off balance and then swept his legs out from under him.

I thought he was going to come up with some increasingly desperate bullshit to try to explain. Instead, he laughed. "Like I said. Not ineducable. Christ, what a waste. You, a bagman. You should have considered my offer."

"Why? Why'd you do it?"

"I've said too much over the phone as it is. You want to hear more, let's sit down over a drink and discuss this like civilized men."

"That's the problem, McGraw. I'm not civilized."

"You name the place. It can be anywhere you want."

"I'll tell you where the place is going to be, asshole. Your fuck-ing blind side. Get used to checking it."

"What are you going to do, hotshot, kill me? It's not enough you have the yakuza on your ass, you want the CIA, too? What are you, superman? Use your fucking head."

"I'll see you soon, McGraw. You better try to see me first."

I hung up, breathing deeply. I was seething, and not just at McGraw. As the conversation had gone on, I'd wondered what benefit I'd achieved in calling him. None that I could think of, other than whatever short-term rush you get from adolescent posturing. And what cost? I'd warned him I was coming. Well, not that he wouldn't have known it anyway, but still, what was the upside?

And his offer of a get-together. Why had I rejected that? I could have used it. I'd been more invested in saying *Fuck you* today than in killing him tomorrow. What sense did that make?

Relax. No harm done. You can call him back, tell him you were just angry, you've thought it over and you want to meet. Sure, he'll think it's a setup, but he'd think that anyway.

That made me feel a little better. And besides, maybe it would be useful to hear him out. If there were a way it could be done safely, I could learn something, even if it was just by reading between the lines of his lies. I was in a bad spot, and more than anything I needed intel. But I had no good way of getting it. I considered Miyamoto, but didn't know if I could trust him, or whether he would have a clue anyway. He was just another bagman; why would anyone have ever told him anything? And Mad Dog was inaccessible, and everyone else I'd touched had turned to dead. I was flying blind. And there was no one who could help me see.

I thought of the girl, Fukumoto's mistress. She would know something. She'd been close enough with Fukumoto to be in his house, but was also working for the opposition to have him killed. But I had no way to get to her. She might as well have been on the dark side of the moon. What was I going to do, drive around the city, hoping to spot her in her pretty yellow Porsche?

But you know the plate—that jikōshiki *green. Shinagawa, 1972.*

Yeah, but what the hell could I do with that? I had no way of tracking it down.

You don't. But Tatsu does. For the National Police Force, looking up a license plate number would be about the easiest thing in the world.

Son of a bitch. I thought I'd been nearly out, but maybe I had a way back into the game.

chapter
thirty

I called Tatsu from another payphone. He picked up with a typically
brusk, "*Hai.*"

"It's me, Rain."

There was a pause. "Rain-san. I was beginning to think something happened to you."

"I'm sorry. I've just been a little . . . overwhelmed."

"Everything all right?"

"More or less. I have a favor to ask, though."

"Name it."

"If I gave you a license plate number, could you tell me who
owns the car and where I can find her?"

There was a pause. "That would be illegal."

Coming from Tatsu, it wasn't a protest. More an aside.

"Tell you what," I said. "Get me the information, and I'll buy
the beer."

"That sounds like a good deal for at least one of us."

I laughed. It really was good to hear his voice. I gave him the
number, then said, "Where would you like to go? I'm treating, so
pick something good."

"How about Shinsuke, in Yushima? I haven't had good *izakaya*
food in a while. Do you know it?"

"No, but I'm sure I can find it."

"I'll meet you there at five o'clock tonight. This way, I can get
home at a reasonable hour. My wife is very strict."

I couldn't help smiling at this, knowing it was nothing but bluster from a guy who damn well *wanted* to get home to his wife, and to the two young daughters his face lit up over anytime he talked about them. It just would have been unseemly for a Japanese cop to admit he would rather have been home with his family than out drinking with his *nakama*, his buddies.

I picked up a change of shirt, pants, and underwear, bought a rest at a random love hotel to shower, then spent an hour at a coin-operated laundry washing my clothes. When I was done, I headed over to Yushima.

I had no reason to distrust Tatsu, and in fact I trusted him as much as I trusted anyone. Still, I thought I should discontinue my practice of punctuality, and be in the habit of showing up at places early. So I got to the restaurant at four o'clock. It didn't open until five—but that was okay. I strolled the neighborhood, a salt-of-the-earth part of Shitamachi with a relaxed, low-key atmosphere and a surfeit of old-fashioned eateries and watering holes. Along the way, I stopped at Yushima Tenmangu, a sizeable Shinto shrine famous for its plum trees and dedicated to Tenjin, the *kami* of learning. It was a popular place for students from nearby Tokyo University to pray before exams, and it seemed fitting that I did so now myself, given how much I was trying to learn and how little time I had to do it. And given what it would mean if I failed to pass the final.

I returned to Shinsuke at five o'clock. Tatsu was just getting there, too, his shoulders rolling, his head jutting forward the way it did when he walked, as though someone had him on a leash and he was fighting it. From the white shirt and tie, he might have been a salaryman, but there was a toughness to Tatsu, and a tenacity, that read like something else. We bowed and shook hands, and I clapped him on the shoulder. There was something so Japanese about Tatsu it made me feel American by comparison.

Shinsuke turned out to be an old-school *akachōchin izakaya*, a classic place, not a chain. It looked like it had been there for a while—a long wooden counter, the men behind it in traditional cotton *yukata* robes; nothing but locals talking, reading, laughing, creating a nice, low hubbub of conversation you didn't have to shout over; a great selection of classic pub food. We ordered small plates of sashimi and *karaage* chicken and *agedashi* tofu; tomato and asparagus salads; a couple large bottles of beer, enough to get us started but probably insufficient to accompany the entire meal.

We each filled the other's glass, toasted, and drank deeply. "The information we talked about," Tatsu said. "Will you tell me why you need it?"

Small talk was never going to be Tatsu's forte. I made a face of exaggerated hurt. "I haven't seen you in months, and that's it? No 'How are you?' No 'How've you been?'"

He nodded as though accepting a rebuke he had heard many times before. "How are you?"

"Fine, thanks for asking. You?"

"Busy. What are you doing these days? Have you found work?"

For a moment, I wondered if maybe I would have been better off without the small talk. Was his question innocent? Or was he suggesting he might have suspicions about my activities that he would prefer, for the sake of our friendship, to avoid? Tatsu was more subtle than I—though I supposed that wasn't saying much—and I sometimes had trouble reading him.

"No, nothing really. I'm dating someone, though."

He raised his eyebrows. "It sounds serious."

"I barely mentioned it."

"You wouldn't have mentioned it at all otherwise."

I laughed. Tatsu couldn't stop being a cop, even when it was just reflex.

"Yeah, it is kind of serious, I guess. She's . . . pretty special. We'll see. How about you? How's your wife, your daughters . . . ?"

He beamed. "Very fine, very fine. I'm fortunate they put up with me."

Though it's slackening a bit in more modern times, the custom in Japan is to say something mildly disparaging about one's spouse or children, even in response to a compliment, lest one seem unduly proud. But the closest Tatsu could come to adhering to the niceties was to say something disparaging about himself. It was touching.

"I think they're very lucky to have you."

He shook his head and turned away to take a sip of his beer. I smiled. Had I managed to embarrass him?

The food arrived and we dug in. It was delicious, and I had no trouble understanding why Tatsu liked the place.

"Anyway," he said, around a mouthful of chicken, "I was asking if you might tell me why you need the information you asked for."

He could have given me the information before asking the question. That he hadn't suggested there might be a quid pro quo.

I took a swallow of beer. "Are you asking as a friend, or as a cop?"

"As long as I don't hear about anything illegal, we're just two friends, enjoying an evening at an *izakaya*."

I smiled. This was about as obvious as Tatsu ever got. He was telling me to feel free, short of any outright confessions.

"I'm in a bit of a jam. I think the girl knows who's behind it, and why."

"Did you . . . do something to hurt someone's feelings?"

I laughed. Tatsu had seen me get up in a few faces back in the day. "It wouldn't be the first time, right?"

"This jam . . . how serious is it?"

"I've faced worse."

"What you've faced has left many better men dead. How serious?"

"Pretty serious."

"Can I help?"

"The information on the girl is all I need."

He nodded as though considering that, then dipped a slice of *maguro* in soy sauce, chewed and swallowed it, and washed it down with beer. "If you're mixed up with the yakuza, I don't think a little information from the motor vehicles department is going to be enough."

I looked at him, appalled by his instincts. "Why do think it's yakuza?"

"Surely you've heard? Hideki Fukumoto, the head of the Gokumatsu-gumi, was gunned down at his home in Denenchofu the other day, along with three associates. And today three Gokumatsu-gumi soldiers were killed while visiting his grave."

That "surely you've heard" felt uncomfortably dry to me. "Yeah. The papers were speculating about some kind of turf war, Vietnamese gangs or something like that."

He enjoyed some of the tomato salad and drank a bit more beer. Was he trying to make me sweat? Finally he said, "This doesn't feel like Vietnamese to me. Those gangs are fearsome, but impulsive. And fundamentally small-time. This feels like a decapitation strike. Regardless, whoever is involved, I believe they're no more than a cat's paw for someone more intelligent and ambitious. I expect they're being duped, and, when they're no longer useful, will themselves be eliminated."

Well, it wasn't particularly flattering from my perspective, but he had the broad outlines right.

"Decapitation strike . . . you mean the son is in charge now that Fukumoto is dead?"

"That is my understanding."

"But why would you think I was mixed up in any of that?"

He shrugged. "The woman whose license plate number you gave me. She is a known associate of Fukumoto Junior. A girlfriend."

My throat went dry. Here I'd been thinking I was being so smooth, yet I'd handed Tatsu everything he needed to put the pieces together. I took a sip of beer, realizing as I did so that Tatsu would probably read it as nervousness. Christ, no wonder I'd been avoiding him. The life I was in and friendship with a cop was too dangerous a combination.

But he told you how he knew of the yakuza connection, right? A cop wouldn't do that. A cop would have held back, seen what else he might elicit, what lies he could trap you in.

That was true, and somewhat reassuring. Though still, he *had* held back, to some extent. He could have told me earlier in the conversation. Instead, he'd waited to see if I would talk more, say something incriminating, before showing his hand. A classic interrogation technique. I had to be careful.

"That is a hell of a coincidence," I managed.

"Indeed. So much so, I feel no need to inquire into your whereabouts at the times of these killings."

I took another swallow of beer and let out a long breath. He was telling me he wasn't going to press it further, that we were all right. But . . . Jesus.

I cleared my throat. "So . . . you think the dupes who did it will find a way to survive what they've gotten themselves mixed up in?"

He looked grave. "I wouldn't bet on it. If they would listen, I would advise them to run."

"Run from the yakuza?"

"They would have to run far."

"They probably would, if they thought they could. If they thought it would work. But maybe they feel they need to finish what's been started."

He sipped his beer. He knew I would tell more if I wanted to. And maybe he hoped I would another time, if not tonight. Was that the quid pro quo? We were friends; he would prefer not to ask directly. And it would be rude for me to make him.

"So that thing at Fukumoto's grave today," I said. "You think that was what, someone trying to finish the Fukumotos' control over the Gokumatsu-gumi?"

"I'd be more interested in your theories."

I'm sure you would. "The truth is, I'm flying blind. If I had a theory worth a damn, I'd tell you, but so far I don't know more than what's been reported in the news. Of course, if I learn more, I'll tell you."

He looked at me and nodded once as though to say, *Deal.* "I think this is about control, yes, though control over what or by whom I don't know. And I think whoever killed Fukumoto Senior knew or anticipated that his son would be at Yanaka today. Either the information was faulty, or the son got away. The son denies having been there, but I don't believe him."

I'd been hoping he would know more, but it seemed he was going on even less than I had. "What do your superiors think?"

He laughed. "A turf war with the Vietnamese. Always the most comforting, conservative, conventional view."

I could have mentioned the CIA payments, my role as a bagman, McGraw—those were important pieces, and maybe if Tatsu had them, he could combine them with whatever other information he held and provide me with some actionable intel. But I couldn't do it. Telling a Keisatsucho cop about CIA payments to the LDP . . . it was too big, too explosive. I wasn't going to put myself in the middle of something like that. I did consider asking him about Ozawa. Something like, *Hey, hypothetically, what if that guy who died at the* sentō *in Kita-Senju weren't accidental?* But it felt too risky. A bunch of dead gangsters was one thing, but if Tatsu suspected I had killed the *sōmukaicho* of the LDP, that would probably be a bridge too far. It wasn't just my concern about my own skin, though of course that was part of it. I also didn't want to put him in a position where he would so starkly have to choose between *giri* and *ninjō*—duty, and human feeling. And besides, it seemed he didn't know that much anyway. I decided to hold questions about a possible Ozawa-Fukumoto connection in reserve, for an emergency. First I'd see what I might get from Mad Dog's girlfriend.

Although he hadn't handed that information over yet, had he? I wondered what he was waiting for, what I was missing.

We spent a while commiserating about his frustrations at having to kowtow to a bunch of cerebrally challenged higher-ups, and finished the meal with *ochazuke* rice and plum sherbet for dessert. When we were done, I paid, and we headed out.

The sun was down, but the air was still radiant with the residual heat of the buildings, streets, and sidewalks. I smelled skewered chicken and onion roasting over briquettes at a street stall *yakitoriya* on the corner next to us, dripping fat sizzling on the fire. From somewhere down the street, a man was karaoke-crooning to accompanying cries of approval and delight—the signature sounds of a *sunaku*, a tiny neighborhood bar. From the second floor of the tiny wooden house across from us came the distinctive *crack!* of a dozen *shinai*, the bamboo practice swords used in kendo, accompanied by as many war cries, the house practically shaking with the simultaneous violence of the *kendōka's* distinctive stomping attack. An old man in a blue *yukata* shuffled past us, probably on his way to the neighborhood *sentō*, his wooden *geta* clop-clopping on the pavement. The Yamanote train's arrival bells pealed from nearby Ueno Station, like an aria underpinning it all. *Tokyo nocturnes*, I thought, and couldn't help but smile at this city I loved no matter how I tried not to.

Tatsu stretched, then patted his belly. "Thank you for dinner. It was delicious."

"My pleasure." He still hadn't given me the information about the girl. What was he waiting for? Had I missed some cue?

There was a pause. He cleared his throat. "May I say something I'm sure is unnecessary?"

So I had missed something. "It would be unlike you, but sure."

"The girl. I hope your plan is simply to follow her, or at worst to brace her."

"What else would it be?"

He sighed. "As I said, I'm sure that's all it could be. Still, so many people have died violently in the last few days. And while I wouldn't be so foolish as to suggest that violence solves nothing, it has also been my observation that violence can also be a kind of . . . contagion. Often it begins with difficulty, but then gets progressively easier. It starts with limits, and those limits then begin to dissolve."

"Yeah. I know what you mean."

"Whoever killed those yakuza is likely guilty of manslaughter, if not murder, yes? Legally speaking."

I looked at him, wary. He was warning me. But of what?

"I'd say that's true."

"And yet, morally, guilty of little if anything. After all, legalities aside, is the world not a better place with fewer gangsters in it?"

"I think you could make that case, sure."

"But a woman . . . or a child . . . that would be different. There would be nothing moral about that. Nothing redeeming."

I nodded, trying with only partial success to push away memories from the war. "I agree."

"I knew you would. Among people who use violence, there's only one real dividing line. Either you have limits. Or you don't."

"Well, the reasons are important, too."

"Up to a point. But everyone believes his own reasons are good ones. In the end, it's the limits that separate men from monsters."

Finally, I saw it. As always, he was being courteous enough to express his concern exclusively in terms of what would be best for me. But unspoken was an admonition: *If I give you the information about that girl and you hurt her, her blood would be on my hands. And I would make you pay for that.*

"You have nothing to worry about," I said. "Regardless of what might have happened to those other people, I'm sure the girl will be fine."

He nodded, reached into his jacket pocket, and handed me a folded piece of paper. "If you need help with anything else, I hope you'll ask. I'm concerned this won't be enough."

Coming from Tatsu, that was practically sentimental. "Nothing I can't handle," I said, and instantly remembered Sayaka's response: *How many people do you think have been in over their heads, and said that right before they drowned?*

Tatsu headed to the train station; I went back to the shrine. It would be a good place to read whatever he'd gotten me about the girl. And I thought another prayer for success in the test I was about to face couldn't hurt, either.

chapter thirty-one

Tatsu's information on the girl was a spymaster's fantasy—home address; work address; employment records; bank records; names and addresses of relatives; detailed information about known associates based on phone records. Either McGraw was incompetent in the files he'd put together on Mad Dog, or he'd been sandbagging, as I'd suspected. And I knew McGraw was anything but incompetent.

Her name was Rei Takizawa. She worked as a hostess in a club in Roppongi, one of the ones managed by Mad Dog. Based on phone records and street scuttlebutt, she'd been involved with him personally for the last three years. So what had she been doing at Fukumoto's house that day?

Maybe . . . three years is long enough for her to know the father well, maybe even to have privileges about entering the house. Maybe Mad Dog took her there that morning on a pretext, a business discussion with the old man, whatever, then went out while she cooled her heels in the kitchen. The old man doesn't mind . . . she's gorgeous, maybe he enjoys her company. Maybe she flirts with him a little. Maybe he even has hopes. Whatever. The point is, she sticks around. Mad Dog hasn't really left; he's parked on the street, waiting to spot me. When he does, he tells her to leave, reminds her to make sure I get a good look at her pressing the button on that garage door opener.

It felt plausible. It felt right. I doubted she would know everything. But she would know something. Maybe even a lot.

I stowed my bag in a locker at Tokyo Station—holding on to one of the Hi Powers and to the ten thousand I'd earned from Miyamoto's job, feeling superstitious about both—and checked in with my answering service from a payphone. There was a message from Miyamoto, saying it was urgent. That was odd. And another from McGraw, telling me to call him, there was more he wanted to tell me that I needed to consider. *Right*, I thought. But it was good he was still trying. I knew I hadn't handled it well earlier, popping my cork, threatening him, and maybe now I'd have the opportunity to lull him into thinking I was willing to cooperate rather than intent on taking his life.

Before calling Miyamoto, I also checked with the service I'd established for my John Smith alter ego—the person Miyamoto had thought he was hiring to take out Mori. Miyamoto had already contacted me at my own service, so I wasn't expecting to hear from him at the other number, too. So I wasn't really sure why I was checking in. Maybe because it just felt thorough. Regardless, I was stunned when the person on the other end told me a Sean McGraw had called. McGraw, calling Miyamoto's contract killer?

It could only mean one thing: McGraw was trying to take out a contract on me. I almost laughed at the thought of it. The idiot was trying to hire me to kill myself. And I was glad at the thought that he was so low on resources that he had to resort to this kind of desperate outsourcing. It could only be good news for me.

Was Miyamoto in on it, though? Well, there was one way to find out. I called him.

"I got your message," I said.

"Ah, I'm so glad you called me, my friend. I've been terribly worried. Are you free to meet?"

Alarm bells went off in my mind. "I'm not, actually. Can you tell me over the phone?"

There was a pause. "Well, I suppose I'll have to. I feel awful about this, but . . . my superiors insisted I provide them with the contact information for the gentleman you introduced me to recently, who helped me out with my problem. And . . . the problem they want his help with now is you."

I had a lot of shit going on, and maybe I wasn't going to survive it. But damn if it didn't feel good to know I could trust this guy.

"Did you give them the information?"

"Yes. Under duress. But I didn't tell them who had provided the introduction. And I want you to know, I wouldn't have told them anything at all if I weren't reasonably sure of one thing."

"Which is?"

"Let us just say . . . I don't believe the man you introduced me to could ever hurt you. My sense is that you are too close."

For the second time in the last five minutes, I was stunned. Miyamoto . . . he knew? Or at least suspected?

"You needn't say anything," he went on. "And of course I'm not sure. If I were, I wouldn't be so concerned to warn you. But . . . when you said to me, 'Don't tell them it was you,' it made me wonder after."

I was silent for a moment. Then I said, "You're a good friend, Miyamoto-san."

"You did me a great service," he said. "You've always treated me well."

I thought of an expression my father had once told me: *Be good to people on your way up. You may meet them again on your way down.*

"No more so than you've treated me."

"But how have I repaid you?"

"You warned me, at considerable risk to yourself. If you were ever in my debt, it is I who am now in yours."

"Don't be ridiculous. I'm just grateful you called. I must confess, I've been a bit of a wreck."

"You have nothing to worry about. I'll handle it. And I'll find a way to repay you."

"You owe me nothing. I'm the one who remains in your debt. But regardless, if you continue to properly enjoy tea, that will be repayment enough."

I took this to mean two things. First, that he appreciated the way I responded to his tutelage. Second, that he wanted me to live a long and uneventful life.

I promised him I would keep him posted, then rode off, still chuckling about McGraw. Maybe I'd even call him back, use my disguised voice, tell him I'd do it for some outrageous sum, and bilk him. It would make killing him afterward feel even better.

I rolled into Hirō and found Takizawa's apartment. It was a new building, five stories, with a gated underground parking garage. I parked Thanatos nearby, and didn't have to lurk in the dark for long before a car went out. I rolled under the door. Tatsu's file included the number of her assigned parking spot. It was empty. To make sure, I walked the perimeter of the garage. Lots of high-end cars, but no yellow Porsche.

Okay, maybe she's at work.

I headed to Roppongi, and this time, I hit pay dirt. The club was called Prelude. It was on a quiet spiderweb of backstreets off Roppongi-dōri, a part of the district whose establishments relied on long-term relationships rather than deploying touts to suck in street traffic, whose patrons valued discretion over neon and conversation over kinks. There was a parking lot across from the club. Lots of fancy foreign cars—Mercedes, Alfa Romeos, a Maserati. And one yellow Porsche 911 Targa, license plate Shinagawa 1972.

Hello, Takizawa-san. So good to make your acquaintance again.

The lot was surrounded on three sides by a cinderblock wall about five feet high. On the other side of the far wall was an old wooden house, the lights all off. I parked Thanatos in an alley next to the house, then stood behind the wall, pooled in darkness. I could see both the entrance to the club and Takizawa's car. I doubted anyone would notice me. If they did, I'd just mumble something about having had too much to drink, feeling I might vomit, needing a quiet place to do it, and play the rest by ear.

I thought of McGraw. He would have supported the story by gargling with gin and probably spilling some on his shirt and hair so he would reek of it. He probably would have pissed himself, too, the better to disgust anyone who engaged him, and motivate them to realize they had better things to do than question a drunk.

Well, maybe next time. I didn't have any booze with me, and having pissed myself once recently, I had no desire to repeat the experience. Anyway, it was sufficiently dark behind the wall that I didn't think there would be a need.

It occurred to me that I might have a shot at Mad Dog. I'd been focused on Takizawa, but there was as good a chance Mad Dog might show up here as anywhere. And maybe better than most, if this was where his girlfriend worked. With the Hi Power, I wouldn't need a lot of time. My biggest problem would be taking out whatever security contingent I expected he'd be traveling with.

But probably the opportunity wouldn't present itself. I'd be happy if I could just get a few moments alone with Takizawa.

Several patrons came and went. I realized I should have brought something to eat—these clubs could sometimes go until three or four in the morning.

A sedan pulled up and a man got out. It took me a second to recognize him.

Kawasaki. The guy I'd seen on TV—Ozawa's replacement after the *sentō* hit, the LDP's new *sōmukaicho*.

What the hell?

I was so surprised to see him that I was slow to react. But then I realized, if there was some connection between Kawasaki and Mad Dog, Kawasaki was the one I needed to be talking to more than Mad Dog's girlfriend. But how? Killing him was one thing. Controlling the environment long enough to interrogate him was another matter. And it was already too late. A hostess opened the door, and Kawasaki went into the club. The door closed and he was gone.

I eased back into the shadows, my head spinning.

A coincidence?

No. I was beginning to believe in coincidences the way I believed in unicorns. What was obvious, what mattered, was that there was some kind of connection between the new LDP *sōmukaicho* and the new head of the Gokumatsu-gumi. And between each of them and McGraw, who had wanted both their predecessors eliminated.

And . . . Jesus. If there was a connection between the two new guys—and how could there not be?—then Kawasaki's presence here indicated Mad Dog was probably here, too, or soon would be. Gaining sufficient control of Kawasaki, or even of Takizawa, for an interrogation would be difficult. But popping out of the shadows and dropping Mad Dog and a couple of guards with the Hi Power struck me as eminently doable.

Are you sure about the connection? Think about it. Whatever it is, it's got to be sub rosa. Why would they do something as open and notorious as meeting at Mad Dog's own club?

Who could say? Maybe they were celebrating, toasting their respective elevations and the glorious future they would usher in now that the old guard was gone. And why not meet openly? Yes, Mad Dog's father had died violently, but at the hands of some Vietnamese gangsters. And Kawasaki's predecessor hadn't died violently at all. He'd suffered some sort of cardiac event, and slipped peacefully beneath the waters at Daikoku-yu. Just a coincidence. All the hostess clubs in Tokyo were mobbed up, and prominent politicians were some of their best customers. No one was going to look askance if Kawasaki were seen at Mad Dog's place.

I tried to fit the pieces together. McGraw wanted both Ozawa and Fukumoto dead. He manipulated me into killing them. Why? *So Kawasaki and Mad Dog could take over their respective operations. Something to do with the CIA's financial assistance program, presumably.*

Yes, that seemed reasonably clear. But again: why? McGraw had told me Ozawa had been keeping too much of Uncle Sam's money for himself, that his failure to spread the wealth was causing resentment and risking the program overall. Was he running a similar program through the yakuza, with a similar problem to be solved in a similar fashion? Maybe. But if he'd leveled with me about the LDP side of the program, why not level with me about the yakuza side of it, as well?

Because he wasn't leveling with you at all.

All right. I unscrewed the license plate from Thanatos, then screwed it on again backward. I could have hidden it as I had earlier, but if I had to move quickly, I might not have time to retrieve it. In the dark, I doubted anyone would notice. After that, there was nothing to do but wait. It could have been worse—the night was warm; my position was comfortable; I was even able to move around and stretch to stay limber.

The hours went by. More people came and went. At midnight, a sedan pulled up. I saw the driver—Kawasaki's. I didn't have a good move. Shoot the driver, and make Kawasaki drive away with me at gunpoint? Maybe, but there were a dozen problems with that scenario, including getting Kawasaki in the car, keeping him in the car, hoping police didn't respond to the sound of gunfire and that no one from the club would see or hear what was going on. Worse, focusing on Kawasaki might blow my chance of getting to Mad Dog. Between satisfying my curiosity by questioning Kawasaki on the one hand, and ending the threat to myself by killing Mad Dog on the other, the correct course was obvious.

Are you even sure Mad Dog is a real threat?

I chewed on that. I had to remember to discount anything McGraw had told me. Still, I'd seen Mad Dog leaning over the railing at the Kodokan while Pig Eyes tried to strangle me. And he'd been at Yanaka Cemetery, too. Yeah, I didn't need McGraw's say-so to know Mad Dog was really after me.

The door to the club opened. Kawasaki, with one of the hostesses. Not saying goodnight—leaving together.

Okay, looks like your "they're celebrating their success" hypothesis was largely accurate.

Did this mean Mad Dog was inside? My guess was yes.

Kawasaki and the hostess got into the sedan. I had no way to get to him cleanly even if I wanted to. And I didn't want to. Not if I had a shot at Mad Dog instead.

I waited. At one point, I considered going into the club, but then rejected it. Too many witnesses. No way to know the layout or the level of opposition. No way even to be sure Mad Dog was inside.

I stretched, staying limber, ready to leap the wall and charge in with the Hi Power the moment I saw any sign of him. I could have shot from behind the wall, but if I missed I didn't want him to have a chance to get to cover or drive off. I wanted to drop him point-blank.

At close to two-thirty, another sedan pulled up. It remained there, engine idling. A burly yakuza in a tracksuit got out of the back. He left the door open and scanned the area for a moment. He looked like security, there to usher someone safely into the back of the car. Mad Dog's men? This could be my chance. My heart started beating faster, and I breathed slowly in and out, relaxing myself. The bodyguard turned his attention to the entrance and I eased over the wall, crouching in the shadows.

I waited like that for ten minutes. The door of the club opened.

I tensed to spring forward, but it wasn't Mad Dog. It was Takizawa, the girlfriend. Okay, maybe this meant Mad Dog was coming shortly, too. I kept perfectly still, breathing slowly in and out, watching.

Takizawa looked at the yakuza without recognition, and started to go around the car. "Hey," the yakuza said in Japanese. "You're supposed to come with us."

Takizawa looked at him, plainly discomfited. "What?"

The driver, another tough-looking guy in a tracksuit, got out. The engine was still idling. "Yeah," he said. "Come with us. Too dangerous to be alone."

It felt all wrong. It felt like a hit. And she sensed it, too, even if she couldn't articulate it. Her gut was sounding a klaxon like, *Why wouldn't Mad Dog have told me I was going to have an escort? Why is the driver getting out, as though to intimidate or encircle me? Why do these men feel like a threat rather than protection?*

She took a step back. The closer yakuza grabbed her by the arm. She tried to pull away and opened her mouth to scream. He popped an uppercut into her belly. She doubled over with a muted cry, and he picked her up and threw her in the backseat. He got in and pulled the door closed. The driver glanced around, got in, and they drove off. No one else had seen anything. I was the only one.

My gut told me Mad Dog was in there. He was the primary. I might never get a better chance.

I thought of Tatsu, about what separates men from monsters.

For one second, I was paralyzed between competing imperatives. Then, *Fuck!* I jumped back over the wall and onto Thanatos, and roared off after them.

They'd been heading toward Roppongi-dōri, where, because of the divider in the road under the overhead Metropolitan Highway, they'd have to turn left. But once they were on Roppongi-dōri, they could go anywhere, and if I weren't close I'd almost certainly lose them. I didn't think they would kill her in the car—it was risky enough to drive someplace with a kidnapped girl in back, but a body would be worse. Probably the plan was to take her someplace quiet and do it there. Still, I couldn't be sure. Maybe she would try to scream again. Maybe someone would miscalculate. Maybe they didn't give a shit about risks and just wanted to silence her as soon as they had the chance.

I turned onto the street just in time to see them making the left onto Roppongi-dōri. I hit the throttle and Thanatos rocketed forward. I slowed just enough to make sure I wasn't going to be mowed down by an oncoming vehicle, then turned left behind them onto the street. It was late enough that there wasn't much traffic. With a little luck, the light at the Akasaka intersection would be red. When they stopped, I'd pull up alongside them and start shooting. They'd never know what hit them. I hung back, two lanes to the right, waiting for my chance.

But someone must have checked the rearview and recognized me. I was looking ahead to see if luck was going to be with me at the traffic light, then glanced over barely in time to see the yakuza in back climbing halfway out the passenger-side window and training a pistol at me over the roof. *Shit!* I swerved just as the gun kicked and I heard the report of the bullet. He shot again and missed again. He was firing backward from the opposite side of a moving vehicle, and probably had scant training in any kind of marksmanship, let alone combat shooting, but somehow I didn't find any of that particularly comforting. He fired again. The elevated Metropolitan Highway ran parallel to Roppongi-dōri here, right up the center of the multilane street. I cut through a break in the metal guardrail and roared up along the median, feeling naked on Thanatos, praying the concrete pillars and the guardrail would offer at least a little protection from a lucky shot.

He kept shooting. I counted six shots, seven, eight. An automatic, then, not a revolver. But how many rounds in the magazine? I swerved, barely avoiding a pylon, watching for obstructions, glancing at the car, looking for an opportunity, my throat tight, my heart hammering. The Akasaka intersection was just ahead, the median enclosed there in a metal fence. I was running out of room. A ninth shot. I heard it ricochet off the metal divider, and then the sound was behind me. A tenth shot tore a chunk of concrete out of one of the giant pillars just to my left. I waited. Was he reloading? Did he even have a reload?

I glanced over and didn't see him—he'd disappeared back into the car. The end of the median was just ahead. The light at the intersection was red. I saw another break in the guardrail and cut left through it. I leaned forward, twisted back the accelerator, and rocketed up alongside them, the Hi Power out and ready. We blew through the red light. The driver cut right and tried to force me into the divider but I was ready for the move and had room to maneuver in the intersection. I cut in the same direction he had, firing into the driver-side window. The glass blew out. He swerved hard left. I didn't think I'd hit him; he had just panicked from being shot at from close range. *Yeah, see how you like it, motherfucker.*

The other yakuza popped out the back passenger side again, probably with a fresh load or his partner's pistol. I pulled up alongside the driver. He glanced at me, panic in his eyes. I held the Hi Power steady and pressed the trigger. His head exploded and the car swerved into me. I hauled the handlebars right and nearly lost control of the bike, but held on. The car swerved the other way, out of control now. I hit the brakes so it would go past me. I saw the guy poking out the back window trying to pull himself in, his face a mask of pure terror. The car jumped the curb and sideswiped a riser of metal stairs leading to a pedestrian overpass, took out a row of parked bicycles, and stopped. I cut left, pulled up onto the sidewalk, and rolled forward cautiously from behind, the Hi Power at the ready.

There was no need for the gun. The yakuza who'd been shooting was dead, no more than a mass of mangled meat hanging from the back passenger-side window. I circled onto the street, dismounted, and leaned Thanatos against a pedestrian guardrail. I shoved the Hi Power into my pants and tried the back driver-side door. It was locked. Takizawa was inside, huddled and shaking—alive.

"Takizawa-san!" I shouted. "Open the door!"

She glanced at me and recoiled, plainly terrified.

I looked around. There weren't many cars out, but the few I saw were slowing for a better look. One of them pulled over ahead of us.

"I'm trying to help you!" I shouted.

All she did was cringe.

The driver who had pulled over got out and started running toward us. "Can I help?"

"Yes," I said. "Get to a phone, call an ambulance. I'll stay here. There's someone hurt in the backseat—I'll stay with them."

Nothing like giving someone firm, clear instructions in an emergency to get action. The guy took off. Thank God for Good Samaritans.

I reached around through the broken front driver-side window, popped the back door lock, and opened the door.

"Takizawa-san," I said, "are you hurt?" I was trying to create the right first impression. She was terrified, confused, possibly hurt. I had to establish myself as someone who cared about her before I could hope to get any compliance.

"I . . . I don't know."

"Those men were going to kill you. Mad Dog sent them. More are going to come. If you want to live, we have to get you out of here. Right now."

She glanced left. If the yakuza's mangled body hadn't been in the way, I thought she might have tried escaping out the passenger-side door. As it was, she was trapped. "Who . . . who are you?"

She didn't recognize me from the brief look outside Fukumoto's house in Denenchofu. I would have handled it if she had, but this way was better. "I'm the guy who can tell you what's been going on. And keep you safe. But we have to go right now, before more of those men get here. Come on. Give me your hand. Let's get you out of that car."

There was an instant of hesitation, then she reached out with a shaking hand and took mine. I pulled her toward me, gently grasped her elbow, and started leading her to Thanatos. Then I realized—Christ, I'd been so focused on so many other things, I'd almost forgotten.

"Wait," I said. I pulled out a handkerchief and wiped down the door lock and handle. Then I took her by the arm again, and helped her onto the back of Thanatos. I jumped in front of her and revved the engine. "Put your arms around my waist," I said. "Come on, do it. We'll get you someplace safe."

She did. I pulled slowly away from the curb. There were more cars slowing down and probably some of them would report seeing a man and woman leaving on a motorcycle. But it wouldn't be much for anyone to go on. The license plate was reversed and I doubted anyone would be able to describe either of us with much accuracy.

I drove to Shiba Kōen, a park in the incongruous dual shadow of the ancient Zōjō-ji Temple and the considerably less ancient Tokyo Tower. I parked Thanatos amid some dark trees, and we sat on a park bench. The trains had stopped running for the night; there were no sounds of traffic; even the insects were silent. The center of the park was completely still.

"Are you all right?" I asked again, trying to show some empathy. And though I was aware of the tactical uses, I wasn't faking it. Her makeup was smeared and she was confused and terrified, but she was as stunningly beautiful as I remembered from outside Fukumoto's house—more so, even, without the sunglasses and the hauteur I'd sensed that day. Whoever she was, she clearly was out of her element and in a mild state of shock.

"I just . . . don't know what's going on. Who are you? Why are we here? I want to go home."

"I'll take you home if that's what you want. But I'm afraid that for now, that's the first place Mad Dog would look for you." Again, I was hoping that an expression of concern plus my willingness to do whatever she wanted would get her to relax, to trust me.

"I just don't understand. There must have been some mistake. Why would he . . . how could he . . ." She covered her mouth and started crying.

I handed her my handkerchief. "I think it's because you know he had his father killed. That's not something he wants anyone else ever to know. You helped him, didn't you?"

"No!" she said, still crying. "I didn't know about any of that. He told me he needed me to stay at the house. He gave me a walkie-talkie. He told me to wait in my car in the garage and leave when he told me to. And to make sure whoever was outside the house right then saw me pressing the garage door opener. I asked him why, and he told me to just trust him, it was important. I thought it was just some kind of game, so I did it. And he told me to drive somewhere close by and leave the car afterward. I didn't understand why, but I did it, I did it for him. And then . . . on the news that night . . ." Her voice cracked and she sobbed.

Was it the truth? My gut told me yes. Certainly it tracked with everything I suspected. But maybe she was just a good liar. I had no way to know.

"He had his father killed," I said. "I think so he could take over the business, but I'm not sure. Do you know any more than that?"

She shook her head. "I don't even know him anymore. He's crazy. He snorts *shabu* all the time. He's been hitting me. Why didn't I just run away? I've been so afraid. I don't know what to do."

Shabu was Japanese slang for amphetamines, a popular drug in Japan since pretty much the Meiji Restoration. As a yakuza prince—and now as king, I supposed—Mad Dog would have plenty of access.

"All right. You're safe now. You're going to be okay. I have a friend who can help you. A cop."

"A cop? No! I don't want to talk to the police. Don't you know, Mad Dog owns half of them?"

"Not this one. Nobody owns this one."

"They're all corrupt."

"Not this one. He'll protect you."

"Nobody can protect me from him. He's evil, he's lost his mind. He's high all the time, he rants about all these things that don't make any sense, oh my God, why didn't I just run when I could?"

"What? What does he say that doesn't make sense?"

"I don't know. Since . . . since his father, he's paranoid. Why wouldn't he be, can you imagine his conscience? His father was such a kind man, the newspapers have it all wrong, when I read it I want to scream—"

"But what is Mad Dog saying? Why do you say he's paranoid?"

"It's always something about an assassin. An assassin stalking him, he has to be careful. I think it's just his guilty conscience. He's losing his mind from what he did, and the drugs—"

"What else about the assassin? How's he protecting himself?"

"I don't know. He says . . . he says he knows how to get to him. A girl in a wheelchair, something like that."

My heart stopped. The world grayed out. An adrenaline bomb mushroomed inside me.

"What? What about a girl in a wheelchair?"

"Just that. The assassin . . . Mad Dog knows how to get to him. The girl in the wheelchair. I don't know, I'm telling you, he's insane!"

"How? How could he know about that?"

"Know about what?"

"The girl in the wheelchair!"

"He says . . . the girls tell him. The streetwalkers. He has all these informants."

God, I'd been stupid. So stupid. The same place, night after night, the same collection of prostitutes, seeing my face, seeing the license plate on Thanatos, seeing Sayaka and me getting into the van in front of the station, coming back late together, leaving her apartment together. Maybe correlating sightings in Uguisudani with other reports, maybe even reports from Kabukichō, where I'd known there would be yakuza and stupidly told myself that even if someone saw me, I wouldn't be recognized. So stupid. No, they hadn't recognized me at the time, but how hard would it be to put the pieces together after the fact, in response to *Anyone seen a guy pushing a girl in a wheelchair . . . ?*

I pulled out a pen. "Call this guy," I said, writing Tatsu's number on her palm. I had to draw huge numerals, my hands were shaking so badly. "Ishikura Tatsuhiko. He'll help you. He'll protect you. Call him."

I sprang from the bench and leaped onto Thanatos.

She ran to me. "Wait! I don't know what to do—"

"Call Ishikura!" I shouted over the whine of the engine. "And don't go back to your apartment!"

I roared off, my mouth desert-dry, my heart pounding like a war drum, my eyes brimming with tears. *Please,* was all I could think. *Please, please, please.*

chapter
thirty-two

I rocketed to Uguisudani on the elevated Tokyo Metropolitan Expressway, the wind buffeting my body and whipping back my hair, my eyes streaming. I tried to concentrate along the way, to not let fear and rage and my temper dictate the approach.

Think. Think. Think.

I breathed steadily in and out, getting my mind clear. Then:

It could be a setup. They could be there now.

Yes. But . . .

If they knew about Sayaka, why haven't they already tried to get to you at the hotel?

I considered. Focusing on the tactical problem helped keep the fear in check.

Maybe they only just found out. And they decided that after Yanaka, trying to ambush you without insurance was a losing proposition. So they came and collected their policy, and now they'll just demand that you surrender yourself as the payout.

It didn't matter. I could figure all that out later. For now, I just had to get to her.

If she's still there.

I tried to push the thought away. I couldn't.

I parked Thanatos a quarter mile from the hotel and pulled out the Hi Power, folding a discarded page of newspaper over it for concealment.

Slowly. Slowly, goddamn it. Where would you set up if you were on the other end of this? That's where you need to look.

I moved as carefully as I could. The streetwalkers were still out. I couldn't know which one had given me up. I wanted to kill them all.

Outside the hotel's privacy wall, I paused and dropped the newspaper, the Hi Power at high-ready, breathing quietly, *listening.* Nothing. Just the normal sounds of nocturnal Uguisudani: a few cars in the distance, a barking dog, music from a pub. I popped my head past the side of the wall and back. Nothing. I eased around and pulled up to the side of the entrance door, my heart pounding like a war drum.

One. Two. Three.

I burst inside, the Hi Power out, sweeping the room, moving, getting off the X the way I'd learned in the jungle. The reception area was deserted and morgue-silent. Sayaka was behind the desk, looking at me.

I swept the room one last time, then moved up alongside the window, the Hi Power still in hand. "Are you all right?" I said.

She looked both angry and afraid. "What the hell is going on?"

"I don't want to explain here. We need to go. Right now."

"Two men were here an hour ago. They said, 'Tell your friend to get in touch. If he doesn't, we'll come back.'"

I was so relieved I could have cried. She was all right. They hadn't hurt her. They hadn't taken her. I supposed they figured, *Why bother? She's in a wheelchair, she's not going anywhere.* And she worked the night shift in a crappy love hotel—it was obvious she had no money and no means of flight. They could get to her anytime they wanted. If they wanted to motivate me, it was better to maintain the threat than it would be to fulfill it. To point the gun rather than pull the trigger.

This time. Next time, I couldn't say.

"I'm just glad you're okay. But we need to go."

"You know what else they said? 'The good news is, you won't feel it when we dump you from that wheelchair and fuck you on the floor. The bad news is, you won't be able to run away.'"

I thought of the *chinpira* in Ueno. They were trying to bait me again, get me reactive, make me lose my temper, make me lose control. I wouldn't let them.

But that didn't mean they weren't going to pay.

"Sayaka, I'm sorry. I'm so sorry. I never thought—"

"You never thought what?"

"That any of this would affect you. I thought I could keep it all separate. But they tracked me here. They want to get to me through you."

"I knew it was something like this. Your 'jam.' I knew it."

I wanted to scream. I wanted to kill someone, kill all of them. I fought to keep a lid on it. "I'm sorry. I was so stupid. I'm sorry."

"What are you going to do?"

"I can't even think about that now. First I need to get you safe."

"Where? Where am I going to be safe?"

"I don't know, a hotel—"

"I'm in a hotel."

"A different hotel. Where they wouldn't know where to find you."

"Look at me, Jun. I'm pretty easy to describe. Pretty easy to find. Where are you going to hide me?"

I had no answer to that. I was so desperate to protect her, and I didn't know how. I'd thought because I could keep it all separate in my mind, I could keep it all separate in the external world, too. Stupid. Fatally fucking stupid.

"We'll get you out of town," I said, flailing. "Even out of the country. And then—"

"With what? Do you know what that nice apartment with its

bath costs me every month? What I have left over, I spend on English lessons. I barely have anything saved."

I reached into my pocket and pulled out the money from Miyamoto's job. I put it on the counter under the window. "Here. This is ten thousand dollars. It'll get you to America. It's what you want, isn't it? To get out of this shithole and go to America? Well, here it is."

She looked at the money. "I don't want this."

"I don't care if you don't want it, you need it!"

"Where did it come from?"

"Do you really care where it came from? Would you rather take this money and make yourself safe, or get gang-raped and killed by a bunch of fucking yakuza?"

She looked at me balefully for a moment. But she took the money. Thank God.

"I'm going to call them," I said. "They're not going to do anything before I do that. You'll be able to get away. They're not expecting you to leave the country. They don't think you can."

"What are they going to make you do?"

"They're going to insist I meet them somewhere."

"Why? So they can kill you?"

"That'll be the idea."

"Then you can't do it."

And all at once, I realized how I could. It was a long shot, it was insane . . . but it also had the smooth, ineluctable symmetry of fate.

"I have to," I said, and felt an enormous weight settle onto me. It was the weight of conscience, of history, of kismet. It was the weight of everything I'd done, all the choices I'd made, all my foolish hopes and ongoing rationalizations. It was the weight of a man who'd dreamt he might be a butterfly, and knew in his soul upon waking that he was no butterfly dreaming he was a man. This was my life. My reality. My sad, doomed destiny.

"Have to what?" she said. "Meet them? That's insane. Don't do that. Tell me you won't do that."

I shook my head. I wanted to tell her everything. To make her understand. More than anything, to tell her I loved her.

"What?" she said again. "Why won't you tell me? Wait, I'll come out, we can talk."

She spun the wheelchair around. But without that glass between us, I knew my resolve would crumble.

"I have to," I said again, and was gone before she'd even made it to the door.

chapter
thirty-three

I rode west, practicing the disguised voice I'd used with Miyamoto, making sure I had it down because unlike Miyamoto, McGraw was used to me in English. I found a payphone and called him. It was late, but they put me through. "You left me a message," I said.

There was a pause. "That's right. I appreciate you getting back to me. I understand you're a problem solver. And you come highly recommended."

"Who recommended me?"

"A fellow named Miyamoto. And some other mutual friends of ours."

"What kind of problem do you need solved?"

"I'd prefer if we could discuss it in person."

"I don't meet people in person. Not unless they're the problem I was hired to solve."

He laughed—a little nervously, I thought. "Well, let's just see if we can establish the general parameters. First, I have to ask this. If the problem you were hired to solve were . . . an acquaintance of yours, would you still be interested?"

"That would depend on the price."

"Well, that's a sensible answer. It's good to hear. And what would be the price if the problem were named . . . John Rain?"

I paused as though surprised. "That's a bit more than an acquaintance you're talking about. An old friend, in fact."

"Is that a problem of principle, or price?"

"The price would be fifty thousand U.S."

"Fifty thousand? That's five times what you charged Miyamoto."

"Miyamoto's problem was a stranger. For this one, I'll need extra. For my conscience."

McGraw laughed. "Tell you what. Twenty-five. For your conscience."

"The fifty is nonnegotiable. If you want it done, I'll get it done. But the price is fifty thousand."

There was a pause. "All right. Agreed. Payment upon delivery."

"No. Half upon delivery. The other half up front."

"I can't do that. I don't know you. I'm not going to leave twenty-five thousand dollars someplace and then have you tell me it wasn't there."

"We would face the same difficulty upon completion."

"Upon completion, at least I'll have completion. Before that, all I have is risk."

I paused as though torn between the promise of the big payday, on the one hand, and bending my rules, on the other.

"All right," I said. "But you know what the collateral will be in the event of default."

"Yes, I do."

I thought of Mad Dog. Was I going to have to worry about someone else at the ambush beyond my alter ego?

"One other matter," I said. "Have you hired anyone else for this?"

"What? No, why would I do that?"

"I wouldn't know your reasons. Redundancy, perhaps. A plan B. That's not what matters. What matters is, you need to know my rules. When you hire me, it's an exclusive. I won't tolerate someone else tripping up the smooth running of my operation. That is also nonnegotiable, and also subject to collection of collateral upon default."

"I understand. You don't have to worry, there's no one else. Hell, how many people do you think I could staff this with, anyway, at fifty grand a pop?"

"Again, I wouldn't know."

"Well, I'll tell you, then. You're it, and that's it. Now, how soon can you do this?"

"Impossible to say right now. It depends on too many factors."

"I might have something that could fix him in time and place for you. Would that be worth a discount?"

"No."

"Yeah, I didn't think so. All right, I'll give it to you anyway. I need this done."

"How will you get it to me?"

"Check in with me again tomorrow. With a little luck, I'll have something then."

"Regardless, we have a contract?"

"If you can guarantee success within a week, we do."

"I can't guarantee it. But I can tell you it's likely. With good information from you, very likely."

"Well, if you want the money, get it done. And hopefully I'll have more intel for you tomorrow."

I hung up. I should have felt relieved, excited, triumphant.

Instead, all I could feel was that weight. I wondered if I would ever get used to it.

chapter
thirty-four

Ipicked up my bag from the locker at Tokyo Station, tossed the
gun I'd used to kill the driver into the Sumida River, then spent
the night at a love hotel in Shinjuku, wanting to be far away from
the scene of the latest crime. I made sure there were no streetwalkers in the neighborhood, and parked Thanatos far away. I barely
slept. I couldn't stop thinking about Sayaka. She didn't know the
first thing about protecting herself, not from something like this,
and even if she did, what could she have done? Yes, I was pretty sure
they would bide their time with her, waiting to see whether the
threat they'd established would be sufficient to get me to walk right
into whatever ambush they had in store. But still, I couldn't know
any of that. I couldn't be certain. So I was gambling, gambling with
Sayaka's life. But I didn't know what else I could do. I told myself
again and again that this was the least worst option. And tried not
to imagine anything beyond that.

I went out early the next morning, and took a walk around
Shinobazu Pond in Ueno Park. The pond, with a circumference of
about two kilometers, had three sections, one of which—called the
Lotus Pond for reasons impossible to miss upon even a casual
glance—was in the summer almost completely covered with giant
lotus plants. Here and there, in those areas where the lotuses were
less thick, ducks and other migratory birds swam and fed, and enormous, listless carp glided along, nudging at the mud, searching for
whatever carp subsist on. I was glad to see the area was fairly empty

in the early morning hours—on summer evenings, it could be crowded. There were a few dog walkers; some pensioners doing Tai Chi; an apparent nature photographer with a camera on a tripod. I examined the area carefully, trying to imagine everything, anticipate everything. If I could make it work, I decided, this was the spot.

When I was satisfied with my preparations, I went to a payphone and called McGraw, this time as myself. I told him I'd gotten his message.

"I'm glad you called," he said. "Look, you know me. You know my values. Maybe they're not good values, but they're consistent. And like I've been telling you, for me, this is business. I made a bad business call, and now I'm trying to make it right."

"Business? That's what you call threatening a girl in a wheelchair?"

"What are you talking about?"

Was he playing dumb? Or had that been Mad Dog, acting on his own? No way to know, at least for now. I decided to drop it. "What do you want?"

"Look, I know you're pissed and that's understandable. But if you act on that, you'll be doing something dangerous, probably suicidal. I'm not threatening you, just telling you the facts. Whereas, if you can set that temper aside and look at the situation dispassionately, you'll see that what I'm offering you has a huge upside. More flexibility than what you've been doing, and ten times the money, maybe more. We each have something the other could use. I don't understand why you would just walk away from that."

I noticed he wasn't calling me son anymore. Yeah, well, now he was trying to flatter and lull me, not keep me in my place. He might not have thought I was ineducable, but he must have still thought I was dumb.

"What are you proposing?" I said, playing along.

"Just meet me. I'll tell you all about the program, and how you fit into it. You name the place. I'd suggest someplace public, where we'll both feel comfortable, but other than that, your call."

Sure, something public. As though that would make a difference. As though the assassin you think you just hired to take me out would find a few patrons in a restaurant a meaningful impediment.

What McGraw didn't realize was that I *wanted* something public. But for my reasons, not his.

"How about Shinobazu Pond?"

"Sure, that would be fine. Where specifically?"

"You know the Benten Shrine, on Benten Island? Right in the center."

"Of course I do."

"I'll meet you there tomorrow morning. Eight o'clock."

"That would be fine. I'll look forward to it."

"If I see any yakuza, they better finish me this time."

"There won't be any yakuza, or anyone else. This is just you and me."

I hung up. So far, so good.

My next call was to Tatsu. He'd offered to help me beyond just getting me Kei Takizawa's information, and I was going to have to take him up on it. "Hey," I said, when he picked up. "It's me again."

There was a pause that made me decidedly uncomfortable. "Why are you calling me?"

I went from decidedly uncomfortable to distinctly on edge. "What do you mean?"

"Kei Takizawa was murdered in her apartment early this morning."

I felt gut-punched. "Oh, fuck."

"This time, I'm going to need you to explain your whereabouts." His voice was cold.

"Damn it, Tatsu. I told her to call you. I told her not to go back to her apartment."

"What are you talking about?"

"Can you meet right now? I'll tell you everything."

Twenty minutes later, we were walking around the pond. I told him what had happened the night before. I told him where I'd stayed, and that the clerk would probably remember me.

"That's not necessary," he said. "Forgive me for doubting you. I should have known . . . you wouldn't do something like this."

I wasn't as certain as he was. But weirdly, I wanted to deserve his confidence.

"I wouldn't and I didn't. But I should have known she wouldn't listen to me. She was out of her mind and told me she didn't want to go to the cops because most of them are in bed with the yakuza. I should have called you myself and told you to pick her up."

He sighed. "Well, she was scared, but she wasn't stupid. Remind me, why do you think Fukumoto Junior had her killed?"

This part was delicate. "She told me Mad Dog is the one who had his old man killed, and that he used her to help make it happen. It sounds like this was just a case of tying up loose ends."

We walked in silence for a moment. "I don't think you're lying to me, Rain-san. But your truth is like the lotuses on this pond. Captivating, certainly, but more than anything they conceal what lies beneath."

I glanced out at the lotuses, then at him. "That was unusually poetic of you."

He nodded. "An early morning flight of fancy. Was it inaccurate?"

"All right. I'll tell you what I know. And then I'm going to ask you another favor. A slightly larger one than last time."

So I told him. I elided what needed eliding, but he got the drift. Miyamoto I left out entirely, claiming I knew nothing about my bagman counterpart, which would have been expected in any event.

Not many bagmen would be stupid enough—or, as it had turned out, fortunate enough—to have struck up the kind of friendship and trust I had with Miyamoto. Naturally, I told him nothing about the service I had performed for Miyamoto, or about my involvement in any of the other killings. He would intuit and suspect much of it, of course, but he'd already told me that as long as I confessed to no crimes, we had an understanding.

"This is potentially explosive," he said when I was finished. "The CIA, bribing Japanese politicians?"

"I think they conceive of it more as 'political assistance' or whatever than as bribes."

"I'm sure they do. What kind of proof do you have of any of this?"

I had a feeling he would ask. "Virtually none. It's all done with cash and through cutouts. And before you ask me to go in undercover, number one, the answer is no, and number two is, I'm blown anyway. They're all after me."

"All because of the incident at Ueno? Those *chinpira* who jumped you?"

He knew it was bullshit. And he could sense the rest. But I wasn't going to confirm anything.

"As far as I know."

We walked in silence again. The sun was up now, and it was beginning to get hot. There were more people around, more sounds of traffic and trains in the distance. The city was stirring itself from slumber.

"What will you do?" he said. "This time, you've really pissed off the wrong people."

"That's . . . the favor I need to ask."

"Yes?"

"Those two yakuza killed on Roppongi-dōri last night—or actually, early this morning. What's the procedure with the bodies?"

He shrugged. "The bodies were taken to the Jikei Hospital morgue. They'll be pronounced dead, a forensic pathologist will examine them and file his report, and they'll be cremated. Why?"

"I need one of them."

He stopped and looked at me, and for once, his unflappable calm, which always seemed the product of his ability to think faster and see farther ahead, seemed to desert him. He shook his head as though bewildered and said, "For what?"

I told him my plan. "All I need from you," I said, "is a little help . . . shaping the way it looks after."

"You mean a cover-up."

"That seems like a strong phrase. No one's going to get hurt. And it seems like a fair trade in exchange for the kind of information I just gave you on CIA payoffs to the LDP."

"You have no proof of those payoffs."

"Maybe not, but now that you know about them, and everything else, you'll know where to find proof. If you want to look for it. I'm not sure it's a good idea. These people don't like exposure, I've discovered."

He nodded, watching me.

"What?" I said.

He sighed. "I feel unaccountably sad."

"Imagine how I feel."

He offered a small smile. "Do you need money?"

I squeezed his shoulder, touched. "No. I've got enough."

"A passport?"

"That . . . I could use a little help with. Wouldn't be a good idea to travel under my own." I realized I should have thought of a new passport sooner, before it counted. So much had been happening, I hadn't gamed things out all the way through. I promised I would never let that happen again.

"I can help you with the travel papers. But how long will you stay away?"

"How long do you think I'll need to?"

"At least a year," he said, nodding resignedly and sounding like a doctor delivering the diagnosis for a fatal disease. "Probably longer."

I looked out over the lotuses. The sun was fully visible above them now.

"Well. I've always wanted to see the world."

"Haven't you seen enough?"

I tried to smile, but it faltered. "Yeah. But I guess I'm going to see a little more."

chapter
thirty-five

I spent the day getting to know Jikei Hospital. The *reianshitsu*, the hospital morgue, was in the basement of the sprawling facility. Unlike the bright, windowed, carpeted areas above, obviously intended for public consumption, the basement felt dim and dreary, an afterthought, a relic. Dusty cardboard boxes lined the peeling walls; the tile floor was chipped and cracked; an old wheelchair sat in a corner, a stack of paper folders moldering in its seat. I thought of Sayaka, then shoved the thought away. The overhead florescent lights, cold, inert, and faintly buzzing, seemed only to enhance the gloom rather than dispel it. Hardly an Elysian Fields kind of a sendoff for anyone who wound up here, though I supposed there weren't many complaints.

I passed several hospital employees while I wandered in the area, and while I was prepared to deal with any inquiries by responding in English as though I were a lost, illiterate, visiting Nisei, no one took any notice of me, much less challenged my presence. Not only did the Jikei morgue lack security, it also plainly lacked security consciousness. Which suited me perfectly.

When I was satisfied I was sufficiently familiar with the layout of the hospital and its grounds, I picked up a few items I thought I would need: lubricant, from a bicycle store; a surgical mask, surgical scrubs, and a white lab coat from a medical supply store; a blanket, hat, spare shoes, and a new shoulder bag, from a discount store. Then I rented a car from a company in Ueno. I told them I needed it for only twenty-four hours, paid a cash deposit, and left Thanatos parked right around the corner. Then I checked the John Smith answering service. Unsurprisingly, there was a message from McGraw. I called him.

"Okay," he said. "We managed to catch a break."

It was weird, hearing him use the same phrase with his new go-to guy that he'd used not so long ago with me. "Yes?"

"I'm supposed to meet him at eight o'clock tomorrow morning at Benten Island. Shinobazu Pond, in Ueno Park. Do you know it?"

"I know Ueno Park."

"The pond's at the south end, and the island's in the center of it. You won't have any trouble finding it. Now, here's the thing. Rain's probably expecting this to be a setup. Hell, for all I know, he's using it to set me up. He's gotten pretty wise tactically, and I'm expecting him to show up very early. If you want to get to him, I'd advise that you get there at sunup. I imagine he'll be there not long after to reconnoiter. But he's going to recognize you, right? Is that a problem? Will it make him suspicious?"

"No. The opposite."

I could almost hear him smiling. "Good. Well, good hunting. Call me when it's done."

Oh, don't worry about that, I thought.

I bought a couple of bento lunches, and found a love hotel in Shinbashi. I ate, showered, and tried to get some sleep. It wouldn't come. The gulf between what had been my hopes, and the reality that had exposed those hopes as daydream and delusion, was too vast, the contrast too stark, the outcome I was hoping for too bleak. Assuming I could even achieve that outcome. The stakes I was playing for were at once so high, and also so dispiriting. I felt like a man whose alternative to death in the electric chair was life in prison. Life in solitary. Life without possibility of parole.

At three in the morning, I changed into the scrubs and lab coat and drove back to Jikei. It wasn't much of a disguise, but in case

someone saw me, at least it was something. There was an alley leading to a set of concrete stairs that themselves descended to the corridor to the morgue. The idea, I supposed, was to provide a discreet
loading area for the delivery and removal of corpses, the sight of
which might be troubling for visitors coming to offer well wishes
to their convalescing relatives. The alley was dark and empty now,
just some refuse containers and sagging cardboard boxes lining the
brick walls. A single incandescent bulb hung from a corrugated
awning over the stairs, casting deep shadows over the pipes and
metal ducts on the walls all around. I backed the car in, cut the
engine, eased the door shut, and waited, listening. Nothing. Just
the quiet hum of the building's air-conditioning.

At the bottom of the stairs, there were two rusted metal doors,
each with a frosted glass insert, secured only by a trivial knob lock.
I'd considered jamming the lock when I'd been here earlier in the
day, but had rejected the idea as too likely to be noticed. Besides, I
was confident I could handle it. If I was wrong, my backup plan
was the emergency room entrance, but if possible I didn't want to
be seen at all. I crept down the stairs and glanced through the
frosted glass. Nothing, just the vague, florescent-lit contours of the
corridor. I pulled out the tube of lubricant I'd bought earlier, after
seeing how rusty the hinges looked, and applied it now. The lock
took me less than a minute to defeat and I made a mental note to
thank the *nandemoya* in Shin Ōkubo, assuming of course I survived
what I was planning. I opened the door a fraction, moved it back,
opened it a fraction more, and so on, letting the lubricant work its
way into the hinges. Finally, when I'd confirmed it was moving
noiselessly, I moved inside.

The corridor looked exactly as it had earlier in the day—the
boxes, the dust, the abandoned wheelchair—though if possible it
felt even more still and silent. I crept up to the morgue door. It was
wood with a frosted glass insert. I could see the light was off inside.

Almost certainly no one was in there, but best to be careful. I pushed the door open, grimacing at the squeak, and said, "Shimura-san, are you in there?" In the unlikely event of an answer, I would apologize for my mistake and purport to go looking for "Shimura-san" elsewhere, and the intrusion would be disguised as something other than surreptitious. But unsurprisingly, there was no response. The room was empty.

I closed the door behind me and quickly oiled the hinges—no sense making any unnecessary noise on my way out. There was a decent amount of light spilling in through the glass from the corridor outside, and I had no trouble seeing. The walls to either side were lined with refrigerated drawers, three high, five across. On the far wall was a long metal cabinet, drawers closed, top covered with instruments. In the middle of the room was a large metal table with a drain in the center and a light fixture hanging over it—the spot where the pathologist would conduct exams. The air was heavy with antiseptic and bleach—not pleasant, but it beat what it must have been concealing.

I paused to game out how I would react if someone showed up while I was in here. This was a version of the when/then thinking that had been drilled into me in counter-ambush training, and I was pleased to see how, with sufficient motivation and practice, it applied also in more urban settings. I decided if I had time to hide, my best move would be to go under the metal cabinet. It had high legs, presumably to make it easier to get a mop under in case of spillage from the examination table. If there was no time for that, I'd say something about being overwhelmed and needing a quiet place to collect myself. Thin, but better than just standing there stammering.

I hit the refrigerated drawers methodically, starting top left and moving down right. Most of them were empty—maybe it had been a slow week for the hospital. One of them contained a startlingly voluptuous young woman, who I assumed from her unblemished condition was a drug overdose. Several were of ordinary-looking old people who I assumed had died naturally at the hospital. The next was of a bloody, mangled corpse—the yakuza who'd been crushed when the car crashed on Roppongi-dōri. I was getting warmer. The next was the prize I'd been looking for: the car's driver, who I'd shot in the head. His height, weight, and build were similar to mine. That was good. And the point-blank shot from the Hi Power had rendered his face unrecognizable. That was better.

I realized I should have brought the wheelchair in. Now I would have to go back out to get it. I went to the door and paused to listen. From somewhere down the corridor I heard a door close. Then footsteps approaching. *Shit.* A maintenance man on the graveyard shift? Who else would come down here in the dead of night? I doubted whoever it was would come in, but I couldn't take the chance—I had no reasonable explanation for being here, and if someone saw me, it would make taking the corpse that much more problematic.

I dashed to the bank of refrigerated drawers, slid the yakuza in, and closed the door. Then I dropped down and rolled under the metal cabinet. I lay face-up, my head turned to the side, breathing silently through my mouth. The footsteps stopped. Had someone heard me somehow, and come down to investigate? I heard the door open and close. Whoever it was didn't turn on the light. *What the hell?*

I saw a man's shoes and the lower half of a pair of surgical scrubs. There was something stealthy about his approach, surreptitious. Again, I thought, *What the hell?*

I heard one of the refrigerated drawer doors open, the tray inside sliding out. The sound of cloth moving. Silence for a few moments. Then the unmistakable rhythmic beat of a man masturbating. *Jesus,* I thought. *The dead girl. I almost got caught stealing a corpse by a guy jerking off to one*. And in the crazy tension of the moment, I had to stifle a fit of hysterical laughter. Then I thought, *Well, everyone needs a hobby*, and it got worse. All I could do was lie there under the cabinet, choking back laughter, and listen to this guy—a resident, probably, a physician-in-training, a fine, upstanding practitioner of the healing arts and pillar of the community—panting and abusing himself to a corpse. Was it Bismarck who said no one should have to see how laws or sausages are made? It occurred to me the Iron Chancellor had omitted an important third item, and the thought almost did me in again. I clamped my jaw shut and waited, and presently the skin-against-skin sounds of Mr. Hippocratic Oath's strange self-pleasure quickened, his panting became a moan, the moan itself dissolved into a satisfied groan, and then there was silence again. I heard the sound of cloth moving over cloth, the tray sliding back into the refrigerated drawer, the door closing after it. Then footsteps, the door to the room opening and closing, and footsteps outside, fading and then gone entirely.

I waited about a minute, just in case the guy might have forgotten something and come back for it. When nothing happened, I rolled out, came to my feet, and checked the door again. All clear. I went out, moved the boxes off the wheelchair, pushed it inside, and slid out the yakuza again. He'd been dead for about twenty-four hours, and in cold storage for much of that time, so his rigor mortis was pretty advanced. I spent several minutes flexing the joints until I was able to get the body off the tray and into the wheelchair. As I moved him, for the first time I noticed his back. Shit, he was covered in tattoos. Well, not covered—he was a young yakuza, and apparently only getting started—but still, there was a fair amount of ink. Clearly a yakuza body, not civilian. Okay, nothing I could do about it now. And I supposed the skin ink would be no more problematic than the rigor mortis and lividity and other incongruities that would similarly give up the game if Tatsu weren't able to hold up his end. I put it out of my mind and focused on the simple if unpleasant job at hand, and within five minutes, I had the body and the wheelchair in the trunk of the rental car. Once I had pulled out and was safely away, the surrealism of the whole tableau hit me again, and I started laughing so hard I almost had to pull over.

I thought about the young doctor in love, a mental description that produced another laughing fit. I was glad I'd only had to overhear the episode; I thought if I'd been forced to witness it, I would have to find a way to bleach my eyes. But on reflection, I was glad to know such things could occur. After all, the hospital morgue had just lost a body, and I wouldn't have wanted a facility where everything was carefully checked and monitored and confirmed to be the one trying to explain the body's absence. No, I thought it would be better for the incident to have occurred in a place where at least some of the employees might prefer to disappear a little paperwork rather than report that a body had been misplaced. I imagined recollections might become suitably vague, records difficult to find, chains of custody confused and contradictory. The one constant would be that no one would want to own up to losing a corpse. And why would they have to? After all, who would want to steal one?

As I got closer to Ueno Park, light was creeping into the sky. The improbable craziness of what had just happened faded, and the reality of what was coming next began to weigh increasingly on my mind. Compared to getting and moving the corpse, I didn't think the next part would be hard. But luck was always a factor. Of course, luck could be managed, but what happened after this would be almost entirely out of my hands. It would all come down to how tightly Tatsu could control the investigation and steer it where it needed to go.

chapter
thirty-six

I parked in a deserted lot near Shinobazu Pond. It was five in the morning, and though the summer sun hadn't yet made it over the horizon, the sky was now completely light. The area was quiet and empty.

I got the yakuza's body out of the trunk and situated in the wheelchair, slipped the hat and a surgical mask on him to conceal the mangled mess that had once been his face, and covered him with the blanket I had bought the day before. I closed the trunk and wheeled him into the park. For anyone who happened to be up and about at this hour, I'd look like an attendant from a nearby hospital or convalescent home, kindly taking out an old and rather arthritic ward to watch the sun rise over the lotuses.

At the south end of the pond was a public restroom. I wheeled the yakuza in, dragged him into a stall, locked the door, pulled myself over the top, and wiped down the spots I had touched. Doubtful anyone would be here in the next fifteen minutes or so, and even if someone did come in, there were two open stalls.

I pushed the empty wheelchair back to the car and drove it to a medical clinic near the station, wiping the handgrips before walking away. No one would know who it belonged to or how it got there, but nor would anyone pay it any mind. Eventually, someone would bring it inside and the clinic would appropriate it, or it would be discarded, or stolen, or whatever. Regardless, it wouldn't be connected with me. The scrubs and lab coat went into a nearby trash bin. Then I returned the car to the rental agency. They were closed, and it was a little unusual for someone to return a vehicle outside business hours, but there was enough space under the door to slide the keys. I got on Thanatos, rode back to the pond, and parked right across from it. I cut the engine, dismounted, and stood there for a moment, just gazing at that beautiful machine. Roman Red and Egret White. I sighed. I patted the gas tank, the seat. I smiled a little, knowing I was being stupid. It was just a motorcycle. I supposed I was turning it into some kind of surrogate, a microcosm of the life I was leaving, a receptacle for all my sorrow and regret. But I couldn't help it. "Going to miss you," I said, and turned and walked away.

I headed back to the bathroom and climbed over the stall where I'd left the yakuza, pausing to wipe down the spots I touched. The body was getting warmer, which was good. A non-refrigerated victim would mean one less discrepancy for Tatsu to have to manage. I opened my bag, pulled out some clothes, and dressed him. Underwear, socks, everything. I took off the shoes I was wearing and put those on him, too, taking the new pair for myself. Soles without any scuff marks would have looked strange, and again, the fewer discrepancies Tatsu had to manage, the better. There were going to be enough as it was.

I put my wallet in his pocket, and, smiling grimly now, a folded piece of paper with McGraw's number on it. I even put my watch on his wrist. I slipped my bag around his shoulder. Everything I owned was inside it. Even the letters from my parents, the fading photographs, everything. All I kept were the gun and some cash. Probably there was some symbolism in that. If so, I was too young at the time to be dissuaded by it.

I stood and looked down at the yakuza, at myself. My heart was beating hard. There was no coming back from this. In a weird way, I felt I really was about to die, that Ueno Park had become a giant gallows and I was ascending the steps.

I unlatched the stall door with a knuckle, eased it shut behind me, and went to the restroom entrance. The path around the pond formed a C from here, with the restroom at its center. I could see far in both directions. No one was around. I dashed back to the stall, got the yakuza's arm around my neck and my arm around his waist, and hauled him up. If someone saw us now, I was just helping my stumbling-drunk drinking buddy back to his apartment after an all-night bender. Weak, but probably enough to get me by. But there was still no one around. I heard a Yamanote train pull out of Ueno Station, traffic in the street. Tokyo was waking. I wouldn't have long to wait.

There was a waist-high metal fence separating the path from the pond. I propped the yakuza against it, his ass on its edge, the balance of his body tipped toward the lotuses, the only thing preventing him from going over my grip on one of his wrists. I took the hat off his head and pulled it low over mine. The surgical mask went into one of my pockets. Then I pulled the last of the Hi Powers from the back of my pants, and waited.

A few minutes later, I saw two old women in track suits walking toward me on the path to my right, apparently out for a little early morning exercise around the pond. I checked left, and was pleased to see an old man with a small dog. I wondered absently what it was about old people that got them up so early. Well, it didn't matter. The main thing was, they looked like sober, reliable, socially conscious citizens, who no doubt would make good witnesses. Their eyesight might be somewhat in doubt, but I wasn't worried about them getting too close. They didn't look like they'd be able to mount much of a chase.

I monitored them with peripheral vision until they were each about twenty-five meters away. Then I raised the gun, pointed it just past the yakuza's unrecognizable head and out into the lotuses, and held it there for a long, theatrical moment. I fired. The sound was huge and unmistakable in the early morning quiet surrounding the pond. I let go of the yakuza's wrist and the body tumbled backward into the water with a splash. Several ducks took off from around him, quacking. I kept the gun out for just a moment longer, making sure everyone had time to confirm what they thought they had just heard and seen. Then I glanced furtively left and right, tucked the gun back into my pants, and walked off the path through the bushes and trees, keeping my head down as I moved, trying to look like a criminal.

I had no doubt the pensioners who had been walking toward me, stunned and in disbelief, would hurry over and check the water. They would see a body in it. They would call the police and describe what they had just witnessed: a man, shooting another man point-blank in the face and then fleeing on foot. Tatsu was waiting for that call, and knew roughly when to expect it. He would be the first to arrive. The water and muck would somewhat conceal the discrepancies I was worried about, at least to any casual observers, and Tatsu would have to handle the rest. The victim, he would discover, had no next of kin, and even if he did, the injuries to his face would make identification difficult. His identity would have to be confirmed by what was found in his pockets, and in the bag around his shoulder, and by the motorcycle key he was carrying and the motorcycle itself, registered in Tokyo, parked close by. The dead man was named John Rain, and the only clue to what happened to him would be a phone number in his pocket. A phone number Tatsu, as lead investigator, would naturally call, so that he could question the person on the other end of it. Did you know the victim? What was your relationship? Why was he carrying your phone number? Where were you when he was gunned down?

Of course, McGraw would claim to have no knowledge of me, and insist he had no idea why I would be carrying his phone number. No one would be able to prove otherwise, or even be much inclined to try, given his diplomatic immunity and likely connections. On top of which, I knew he'd have an alibi. After all, he had known there was going to be a murder in Ueno early this morning, and he was a careful man, a thorough man. Still, the pucker factor he would feel under Tatsu's penetrating cop gaze and pointed questioning would help blind him to the real reason he was being interviewed: to provide unimpeachable, official police confirmation that I was dead. After which, he could rest easy. He would have no way of knowing news of my death had been greatly exaggerated.

Not until I told him myself.

chapter
thirty-seven

I called McGraw and told him it was done.

"You're sure?"

"Entirely sure."

"Well, that's wonderful. I'll just need independent confirmation. I'm sure you understand."

"Confirmation wasn't part of our bargain."

He cleared his throat. "It was an implicit part. Look, I'm talking about just a few hours, I don't think it'll take me longer than that. And then we can meet and I'll pay you what you're owed."

I smiled. I knew he would come back to insisting we meet. Wanting his own killer for hire was the motivation. The leverage he had as the party holding the money was the opportunity.

"A meeting was also not part of our bargain."

There was a pause. It was fascinating to see a slightly different aspect of his persona in play. He'd always treated me like a punk. This new guy, he respected. Maybe even feared.

"Then we'll change our bargain, all right? Listen, I could use someone like you. You have nothing to worry about from me. It sounds like you did a good job and I've got others like it if you're interested. This could be a lucrative relationship. But I'm not going to do that with someone who's no more than a faceless voice on the other end of a telephone."

I waited a long moment, as though struggling with my doubts. Then I said, "Where?"

"Zōshigaya Cemetery. Do you know it?"

I smiled again. "Can you spell that?"

He did. And told me to meet him there in the northwest corner at four o'clock that afternoon. It was enough to give me déjà vu.

"Let me say this," I told him. "I don't like the way you have modified our agreement but I have acceded to your wishes. If after my accommodation, you fail to show up with my money at the appointed place and at the appointed time, you won't hear from me again. Do you understand what that means?"

There was a pause. "I understand fully."

I hung up, smiling grimly. I thought of the monk I had seen at Zenpuku-ji Temple. It had never occurred to me before, but I wondered where they bought their robes. Well, a logical place would be Nakamise-dōri, the dense shopping arcade leading to Sensō-ji, Tokyo's largest Buddhist temple.

I rode the subway to Asakusa, feeling hobbled, trying not to miss Thanatos. I had no trouble finding what I needed—in fact, there were dozens of stores selling more than I reasonably could have hoped for. I thought I could probably get away with no more than the *kesa* robe, which would conceal whatever I was wearing underneath. But I sensed that if I did so, I wouldn't feel the part, I would still carry myself as a civilian. So I bought everything—not just the outer garments, but the special underclothes, too, and the slippers and split-toe socks. I would have preferred footwear better suited to pursuit and evasion, but reasoned that part of what made Buddhist monks move like Buddhist monks was what they were wearing on their feet.

I stopped at an electronics shop and bought a barber's electric clipper. Then I went to a love hotel, shaved my head, changed into my Buddhist garb, and looked at myself in the mirror. I was pleased—it looked pretty genuine. The shaved head and the robe were so associated with monks, I thought the combination would work almost as a trigger, temporarily overriding any discrepancies. When I left, I sensed a few raised eyebrows at my monkish passage from such a den of earthly pleasures, but Japan is nothing if not a polite society, and no one said a word.

I took the Ginza line back to Ueno, changed to the Yamanote, then rode to Ikebukuro, where I stashed my bag in a coin locker, keeping only the Hi Power. If Buddhist monks had designed their *kesa* robes specifically for concealed carry, they couldn't have done any better. I could have been hiding a bazooka under the excess material, and I doubted anyone would have noticed so much as a bulge.

I didn't think McGraw was going to arrive quite as early as usual, knowing as I did that he would first be spending a few uncomfortable hours being interviewed by some of Tokyo's finest. Still, I wanted to be there first. I walked from Ikebukuro, came in at the northwest entrance, and headed southeast, insects buzzing, crows calling raucously from the trees, the sun beating down on my freshly shaved scalp. I was surprised at how much the genuine clothes made me feel like a monk. I would remember that—that the details mattered, not just in how you looked, but in how you *felt*, in the kind of unconscious vibe you emanated and that people might key on one way or the other. The only reminder that I was here for something other than the lighting of incense and prayers for the dead was the Hi Power tucked into my waistband and concealed beneath the robes. There was another monk in the cemetery, along with a few other visitors, but thankfully he seemed as happy to avoid me as I was him. It was one thing to look like a monk to a casual observer. It would be quite another to sound like one to someone who knew better.

McGraw didn't show until nearly three-thirty, and I had to suppress a smile when I saw him—Tatsu must have been grilling him pretty hard. He came in through the southeast exit, just as I had expected. And why not? It wouldn't be good tradecraft to show up exactly at the designated meeting point without first reconning the area from another direction. He walked right by me, not twenty feet away, carrying one of the bags we had used for our exchanges, and looked right at me—but utterly failed to make the connection. The shaved head, the clothes, the context, his conviction that I was dead—it all served to obscure his ordinarily acute powers of perception. That, and maybe he was feeling stressed about not getting here as early as he would have liked for a meeting with a demonstrably dangerous person he knew almost nothing about, a person who made him nervous.

"McGraw," I said, as he passed my position.

He stopped and turned. Maybe he thought he'd heard wrong. Maybe he thought, *Clever, my new assassin disguised himself as a monk.* Whatever it was, it occupied enough of his brain's processing power to keep him standing there, looking confused, while I walked toward him. When I was ten feet away, he realized. His mouth dropped open and his ruddy face went white. His body tensed as though in preparation for flight. I shook my head, showed him the Hi Power, then slipped it back beneath my robe.

"What is it, McGraw? You look like you've seen a ghost." A little corny, but it was so perfect.

"I . . . How . . ."

"No. I'll ask all the questions. You'll provide all the answers. Tell me now if you have a problem with that. I'll put a bullet in your head right here and save myself some time."

He swallowed. "There's no problem. I just—"

"Open the bag and show me what's inside. Slowly."

He did. The bag was stuffed with hundreds, just like it was when I used to pick it up from him for delivery to Miyamoto, a thousand years earlier.

"Now set it down. Slowly. Good. Step away from it. Good. Now lift your shirt. Keep it up. Good. Now turn all the way around. Slowly. Good. Now lift your pants legs. Good."

When I was satisfied he was unarmed, I picked up the bag. "Now walk. I'll be right behind you. Be forthcoming in your responses to my questions. I'm not going to make any big speeches. If I get bored, I'll shoot you and leave you here among all the famous people whose graves you used to photograph. Are we clear?"

He nodded and started walking.

"I have to tell you," he said over his shoulder. "This was a beautiful play. Christ, but I underestimated you. You realize this makes you even more valuable to me, don't you? You're a ghost now, you can go anywhere, do anything. Invisible. Deniable. Name your price, you're obviously worth it and I'm not going to haggle with you."

"You set me up, didn't you? Those *chinpira* in Ueno. That was you. To dupe me into killing Ozawa and Fukumoto Senior."

"Yes, that's true. I won't deny it. At the time, I didn't realize how capable you are. How valuable. They were supposed to rob you and put you in the Agency's debt. They were incompetent, though. I should have expected that, with Mad Dog running the show."

"Then why did Mad Dog try to have me killed right afterward, at the Kodokan?"

"Because you killed his cousin. I told you, he's a fuck-up. Like the cousin you killed. A hothead, like you used to be, before you started to wise up."

"If Mad Dog is so lame, why are you working with him? Why would you want him in charge of the Gokumatsu-gumi?"

"That's exactly what I've been wanting to tell you about. If you'd just listened to me earlier when I tried to call you off Mad Dog, we could have done business. I never wanted any of this to happen."

I didn't respond, and he went on. "All right, the program. It's not that complicated, really. It's just a way of channeling money from American corporations to Japanese decision makers—the people who can ensure the American corporations get the contracts they want, and that the U.S. government gets the policies it needs."

I smiled, liking the way silence seemed to draw him out. I might have thanked him for teaching me the technique.

"Decision makers . . ."

"That's right. You know Japan. The government, the corporations, the yakuza . . . they're all just different limbs attached to the same body."

"And you wanted to cut off some of the limbs?"

"Not cut off. Replace, with something better."

"You told me Ozawa was charging too much. And Fukumoto, too?"

"No, that was just a convenient story because you insisted on knowing why I wanted Ozawa killed. What you need to understand now is that the opposite is true. They were taking too little. Do you understand?"

I didn't, so I said nothing. After a moment, he went on. "The problem was, the old guard was too conservative. They felt they were making enough and didn't want to rock the boat by demanding more. Even though I encouraged them."

"Why would you encourage them to demand more?"

"Because if there's more for them, there's more for the Agency—and we need the goddamn money. Look around you. Communist China's next door. So is Communist North Korea. That was my war, son, and we lost thirty-four thousand men just for a goddamn stalemate. And Vietnam is going to fall, too, now that Nixon's pulling out the last combat troops. Fifty-eight thousand American lives, and we're outright going to lose this time, it won't even be a draw. Do you understand? Communism is more dangerous than ever, and the politicians who left you high and dry in Vietnam are pretending that just because we got a bloody nose or a couple of barked shins we don't have to fight it anymore, they can just cut all our funding so they can build rural electrification plants in Appalachia or whatever it is they do to buy votes these days. So yeah, we need this funding, the politicians aren't giving it to us, and the taxpayer doesn't want to cough it up either, because they're misinformed and they don't trust the clusterfuck politicians who lost in Vietnam. Can't really blame them for that, but that's the state of play."

"So you want to be able to skim off the corporate bribes the CIA is funneling to Japanese politicians. To create . . . a slush fund."

"If you want to call it that, yes."

"With you in charge."

"That's right."

"Just here in Japan?"

He glanced over his shoulder and smiled. "I wasn't kidding when I said you were smarter than I thought. Of course not just Japan. This thing can be taken global. Hell, it already is global, but small time. It can be expanded. I want you to help me expand it."

"By killing people who don't get what you're trying to do?"

"What would you prefer? That we invade another country and lose another fifty or sixty thousand men?"

"Are those really our only alternatives?"

"Apparently so. Look, there's a lot of money out there, if we can work with people with the imagination to ask for it and divide it equitably."

"You mean kickbacks to you."

"Not kickbacks, partnerships. I'm offering a way to grow the pie. The recipients keep more, and I keep more."

"Embezzling from graft, is that it?"

"Jesus, are you just trying to insult me? I'm creating a covert action fund, all right? The fund is necessary, and on balance, my means are pretty benign. I know some operators who are trying to make ends meet by smuggling heroin into the United States. You probably knew some of them, too, in Vietnam. This is better."

"Even if I agreed to be part of this, how would you call off Mad Dog?"

He glanced back at me, his eyes bright with hope. "Leave Mad Dog to me. He depends on me. I can manage him. Anyway, he thinks you're dead, remember?"

"What about the girl in the wheelchair?"

"She'll be fine. She only mattered as a conduit to you."

"So you did know about her. And you were okay with it." I brought out the Hi Power.

He realized he'd slipped. "Look, I didn't want to. It was Mad Dog's idea."

"I thought you said you could manage him."

"I can. I'm sorry for what happened. Let's wipe the slate clean, all right? This is a different set of circumstances than before. I know how valuable you are now. And you know how important the program is."

"Did you know about Takizawa, too? Mad Dog's girlfriend?"

"Don't get all sanctimonious on me now, Rain, all right? You're no different than me. You got yourself in a jam and were more than willing to kill your way out of it, remember?"

I thought of Tatsu. "It's about having limits. I have them. You don't."

"Limits? Please. Killing Mad Dog and his father was your goddamn idea, even if I did lead you to it. And you didn't hesitate when I told you you'd have to take out another guy who didn't even have anything to do with it."

"They were principals. Not bystanders."

"That was a happy coincidence. You're making a virtue of a necessity."

"So you did know about the girlfriend."

"Respectfully, son, I think you're focusing on the wrong things here."

"Am I?"

He must have felt it in my tone. He stopped and turned to me.

He saw the Hi Power and went white. "Now listen to me. Don't revert to being a hothead now, okay? You don't think I'm protected? You don't think I share the wealth with people back home?"

"You think that means they have your back? They won't stick their necks out once you're gone. They'll just find a new business partner. Costs and benefits and all that."

"Yes, they do, they do have my back."

He was flailing now. I found it deeply satisfying.

"Besides," I said. "I'm dead now, remember? You said it yourself. I can do anything."

He licked his lips. "Is this about the girl in the wheelchair? Look, I'm sorry for that. I didn't realize you were that close."

"Then why did you and Mad Dog threaten her? She wouldn't have seemed any use to you if you didn't know I cared for her."

He held out his hands, beseeching. "Look, son, you've got it all wrong. If you'll just listen to me, we can—"

"I told you. Don't call me son."

His hands started to come up in an instinctive and futile flinch. I raised the Hi Power and pressed the trigger. The pistol jumped in my hand. The crack of the shot was loud among the gravestones. A small hole appeared in McGraw's forehead. His mouth dropped open and his eyes turned in, then his body crumbled to the ground.

I put the Hi Power back beneath the robe, and walked away at a dignified, monkish pace. I glanced around. A few visitors were looking about, wondering what they had just heard. But when all they saw was a harmless monk, they went back to setting out flowers, and lighting incense, and saying their prayers for the dead.

chapter
thirty-eight

I spent the next few days in a torment about whether to contact Sayaka. I was reasonably confident that, with Mad Dog believing I was dead, she would be safe. And that probably no one was watching her. Probably. But if I was wrong, I could get her killed. I kept morbidly imagining what it would have been like to tear back to the hotel on Thanatos that night and find her not alive and angry, but raped and beaten and dead. The thought was unbearable. I'd been lucky the first time had been just a threat. I doubted I'd get so lucky again.

When I was ready, I called Tatsu. We met at Meiji Shrine. He looked long and hard at my shaved head when we saw each other, but said nothing. As we strolled beneath the shrine's towering trees, he told me how things had gone at Ueno and with McGraw. He'd handled everything just as I had hoped, and no one suspected anything. I briefed him on what I'd learned from McGraw. It was the least I could do.

"You're lucky you were able to speak to him," he told me. "It must have been just afterward that someone executed him at Zōshigaya Cemetery."

"I know, I saw something on the news. Maybe someone in his organization learned he was flapping his gums."

"Indeed," he said dryly. It wasn't always easy for me to know what Tatsu was thinking. But one thing was becoming clear about his general philosophy: being a cop was more about the ends than it was about the means.

"Will you be able to use any of what I've told you?" I asked.

"I think so, though it will take some time, and some maneuvering. I understand the corruption goes to the very top—Finance Minister Satō, Air Force Chief of Staff Genda, even Prime Minister Tanaka. But with the information you've given me, I can make at least some of it come out."

"What about the States? McGraw suggested he was spreading the skim to American politicians, too."

"It would be naïve to believe otherwise. Whether anyone will care is another story. But supposedly there's a senator named Frank Church who's forming a committee on intelligence and other abuses. This might interest him, too. I'll get him what I can."

We walked. It was pleasant under the trees, cool for a summer morning, quiet. The shrine itself was an oasis of stillness within the swirling city around it. It was the kind of place I loved in Tokyo. The kind of place I would miss.

"It's been relatively quiet for the Keisatsucho since you died," he said. "Other than McGraw, no more bodies turning up."

"Well, that's good. I'm sure you guys need a break from time to time."

"Yes. Though I keep expecting to hear about Fukumoto Junior's untimely demise. But for the moment, he seems to be all right."

Mad Dog. Punting on him wasn't easy for me. I reminded myself for probably the hundredth time it was the right call, the only call. McGraw's death could be attributed to a dispute with the guy he had hired to kill me. Mad Dog dying right afterward would be too much of a coincidence. Tatsu had handled the discrepancies with the yakuza's body, but if anyone started looking too closely, the story would unravel. And if the story unraveled, Sayaka would be at risk again. So Mad Dog got to live. I took some small comfort in knowing my decision was a sign of greater maturity and self-control. But still, it was killing me.

"As long as Mad Dog thinks I'm dead," I said, "he has nothing to fear from me."

"But while he's alive, you won't be safe in Japan."

Christ. Was Tatsu encouraging me to go after Mad Dog? I would have loved to, but I didn't want to tell him why I couldn't.

"Of course," he went on, "Fukumoto Junior is weak, and not widely respected. He is seen in certain quarters as illegitimate, the product of nepotism. His enemies might even learn of his role in his own father's death. I wouldn't want to be him if that information were to emerge."

I looked at him. Was he telling me he was going to make that happen?

"Anyway," he continued, "perhaps you'll be able to return sooner than you imagine."

"I don't know what will be here for me when I do."

"I'll be here. Perhaps we can work together again."

I laughed. "Oh, have we been working together?"

He shrugged. "Not always intentionally, but our activities often seem to dovetail, do they not? Would it be a bad thing if that were to . . . continue?"

"I don't know. I'd have to think about it." I doubted I would, though. I had no desire to ever again be part of anyone else's larger strategy. I might be a contractor, but I was never going to be an employee.

"You know," he said, "there's just one thing I don't understand."

"Yes?"

"I said there had been no more bodies as such, but there was another shooting. Just last night."

"Really?"

"Yes. A quite prominent LDP politician. Nobuo Kamioka. You might know the name."

"No, it doesn't ring a bell."

"Indeed. What's strange is that he was shot in the spine. He'll never walk again, but his assailant didn't kill him."

"Maybe the assailant missed."

"Kamioka claims the assailant was a Buddhist monk. And that before pulling the trigger, the monk told him, 'Karma is a bitch.' Does that mean anything to you?"

"Only that, if karma's a bitch, I hate to think of what it's got in store for me."

"A coincidence, then, that you called me only this morning, not before?"

"What, do you think I had something to take care of first?"

He shrugged. "I was expecting you to call sooner. The very morning you were 'killed' in Ueno Park, in fact."

"Sorry. I got hung up."

"I have the strangest feeling ballistics will match the bullet that killed McGraw with the one that paralyzed Kamioka."

"Think you'll find the gun?"

"No, I'm quite certain we won't."

"Well, that's a shame."

He glanced at my scalp. "I also wondered about your new hairstyle."

"Just a summer look. I'll probably grow it out again."

He gave up and we walked in silence again. At the exit at Harajuku, he handed me a passport. "You can go anywhere now," he said. "But where?"

Tokyoites surged past us in all directions, going to work, going for coffee, going shopping, going home. The scene was madcap, frenetic, like something played back on film at just slightly faster than normal speed. The sun moved behind a dark cloud, and for a moment the city looked lit in sepia.

"I don't know," I said. "But when I open a newspaper and read about a scandal involving American payoffs to Japanese politicians? I'll think of you."

He smiled. "I don't think Fukumoto Junior will last."

"We'll see."

"But other than that, I hope Tokyo will be peaceful for a while."

I thought of Sayaka. "I'm sure it will be."

chapter
thirty-nine

A s it turned out, Mad Dog lasted only about two years. I don't
know whether Tatsu had anything to do with it, but apparently a cabal of Gokumatsu-gumi lieutenants had him killed, and
proceeded to govern as a council, instead.

Not long after that, Senator Church's committee convened in
America. Lockheed was accused of paying tens of millions of dollars
in bribes to foreign officials—not just in Japan, but all over the world.
None of it was traced to American politicians. The focus was all on
Lockheed and its rogue board of directors. Still, in Japan the scandal
took down the finance minister, the air force chief of staff, and even
the prime minister, as Tatsu had hoped. So that was something.

With America's attention diverted to Lockheed, did McGraw's
program reconstitute? Probably. Trying to stamp out payoffs to politicians is like trying to outlaw prostitution. Hell, it's the *same* as trying to outlaw prostitution. Corruption, I'd learned, isn't discrete, and
what appears to be a series of floating structures is in fact an archi-
pelago, its islands continuous, connected, coalescing below the waterline. But I didn't care. It wasn't my problem, and I wasn't going to let
it be. When I'd killed Ozawa at the *sentō*, I'd briefly wondered whether
I was now one of the bad guys. By the time I did McGraw, I'd figured
out there are no bad guys, any more than there are good guys. There
are only smart people, and stupid ones; puppets, and puppet masters.
Better a wise *rōnin*, I decided, than a naïve samurai.

Still, I thought maybe Tatsu had a point with his notion of limits. I'd told McGraw he'd been wrong to go after Sayaka because she was a girl, because she was a non-principal. And his response was that I was making a virtue of a necessity, that he and I were just the same. Was he right? I recognized that would depend on me. I decided to live with limits. Or at least try to.

Miyamoto kept my secret, and we wound up working together when I returned to Japan. And Tatsu and I wound up working together, too—quite a lot, in fact. But that's all another story, and none of it happened until many years later. Because, even though Mad Dog didn't last, my self-imposed exile did. I spent a decade fighting in various mercenary conflicts, and while those, too, are other stories, perhaps for another occasion, for now I'll just say that, at the time, I told myself those conflicts were the reason I stayed away. But in retrospect, I realize they were more of an excuse. The real reason was Sayaka.

I wanted to contact her before I left Japan. Of course I did. But I was afraid Mad Dog would learn I was still alive and might come after her again. It was torture to hold back. I had no way of knowing what she knew or what she believed after the last time I saw her at the hotel. Maybe she saw something on the news about what happened at Ueno, and believed I was dead. Maybe she hadn't heard anything, and didn't know why I'd walked away or what had become of me. Maybe she heard about Kamioka, shot in the back, his spine severed, and thought of karma, and wondered whether karma was me. But if I contacted her, what would happen? If I saw her, I didn't think I could bear not to be with her. And if I was with her, she would become a target again.

So I went back to war, in unlikely places, far from Japan, far from everything that had happened, far from Sayaka. To protect her.

No. That isn't true. It's not a lie, but it isn't the truth.

Because even after Mad Dog was killed, still I stayed away. I told myself that surely, one way or the other, she would have forgotten me? Moved on? Built a new life? But over time, I realized my reluctance was because of more than that. It was because . . . of what she would think of me if she knew what I had done. What I had become. What I *was*.

How could she understand? The money I had given her—she would want to know where it came from. Maybe she would be horrified she had taken it, and hate me for having persuaded her. She would ask questions, incessant, probing questions, and no matter what I told her, she would believe the truth was even more appalling. And probably it would be. I would implore her, explain my limits, and she would hear nothing but the rationalizations of a monster.

I was paralyzed by longing and fear. And as the years went by, somehow, no matter how close I came to trying to find her, I always held back. I told myself that if I really cared about her, I should just leave her alone.

But in the end, I couldn't.

She wasn't easy to track down. You have to remember, this was long before Google, and Facebook, and all the other tools that make it easy for people you'd prefer to keep in your past to occupy your present. But eventually, I found her. She had made it to America, her dream. San Francisco. She had gone to college, and then started a foundation for teaching disabled people skills. She'd received awards from various Asian American organizations. She'd even gone scuba diving and skydiving in her wheelchair, just as she'd said she would. *Life* magazine wrote an article about her exploits, praising her as "an inspiration, an example of the limitlessness of the human spirit and of the opportunities afforded by the American Dream."

And she was married. A Korean American. A lawyer. Probably a good guy. They had a son, the first time I checked. Eventually, when I checked again, they had a second.

So no, I never contacted her. I watched, but only from a distance. I listened, but didn't speak.

Instead, I tried to make myself forget. To forget that first time, when I'd intervened with the drunken asshole at the hotel and she had wheeled out to the street to reluctantly thank me, and the way her face had glowed while Terumasa Hino played at Taro, and later that night, when we had kissed at Kitazawa-gawa, and I'd pissed myself so she wouldn't feel embarrassed, and the way she'd let me move her arms in the bath so I could touch her breasts, and how she liked to turn her head and watch as she guided me inside her, and how she'd cried when she learned she could come, and those glorious mornings we would exhaust ourselves in her small bed, and how beautiful she was to me, how she was so, so beautiful.

Sometimes I go to her Facebook page. It's silly, I know. Pathetic. And every time I do, I promise myself next time I'll be stronger. I don't even know what impels me. Why are the most painful memories also the sweetest; why does the sweetness always draw us back no matter how long the pain might have kept us away beforehand? I don't know, any more than I know why sometimes I have to sit in the dark and listen to Terumasa Hino playing "Alone, Alone and Alone." I just do. I can't seem to help periodically disinterring that little box of memories, no matter how lachrymose its contents. I try to stop. But sometimes there's just what you can do, and what you can't.

The years have been kind to her, very kind. She's graying now, but her hair is still long and her smile still radiant, and that guardedness, that toughness that had so characterized her when we first met, is gone now, replaced by an easy comfort and confidence. She doesn't need anyone to think she's tough. She knows she is. And maybe her family has softened her. She has grandchildren now. Toddlers, but still. Where do the decades go.

I look at her photographs, and the photographs of her family, and I imagine a life that might have been but that wasn't, a life I naïvely thought I could achieve and might even deserve, but that circumstances and my own actions precluded.

I wish I'd told her I loved her. It bothers me that I didn't. I'd been so close, and then I'd held back. I tell myself it would have made no difference, and I believe that's true. But at least then she would have known.

I miss her. God, I do. It's beyond missing; it's a kind of mourning. And not just for everything we had, but for everything we might have had, could have had, if only I had made other choices, if only I had been someone else, or something else.

But who, or what, would that be? I try to imagine it and I can't. It feels like a delusion, a deception, a dream.

All the world's a stage, isn't that what Shakespeare said? *And all the men and women merely players.*

And so they are. So we all are. But that's poetry. The prose is simpler. Sometimes there's just what you can do. And what you can't.

Acknowledgments

Once again, my friends Koichiro Fukasawa and Yukie Kito were invaluable in answering all my questions about Tokyo: new and old; native and foreign; cultured and *gehin*. They also introduced me to Taihō Chinese Restaurant in Minami Azabu, which I used in the book and which for the food alone would have deserved a grateful acknowledgment. And they were great occasional company while I was otherwise living like a hermit in Tokyo, researching and writing the book.

I'm sure I got any number of things wrong about life for paraplegics, and I look forward to people sharing their thoughts so I can update the "Mistakes" page on my website. Whatever errors I might have made, they were in spite of the excellent information I found on various websites. A few that were particularly helpful were:

10 Correct Ways to Interact with People with Disabilities
http://www.themobilityresource.com/10-correct-ways-to-interact-with-people-with-disabilities/

10 Things to Never Say to a Person in a Wheelchair
http://www.themobilityresource.com/10-things-to-never-say-to-a-person-in-a-wheelchair/

Dating Paraplegics: The Ultimate Guide
http://www.streetsie.com/dating-paraplegics-guide/

Deep Sea Diving in a Wheelchair (Sue Austin)
http://www.youtube.com/watch?v=PCWIGN3181U&feature
=endscreen&NR=1

How to Push a Wheelchair
http://cripwheels.blogspot.jp/2006/07/how-to-push-wheel-
chair_31.html

Sex and Paraplegia
http://www.youtube.com/watch?v=4TaLQiiFUUY

Cameron Hughes is the guy who urged me to stop acting like the
world was made only of walkies and to create a character with disabilities, and Sayaka wouldn't have come to be without his encour-
agement. He was also generous in sharing his insights, experiences,
and suggestions for further reading. And I'm sure he'll be the first
person to point out my mistakes. ☺

Once again, I'm indebted to Michael Kleindl of Tokyo Food
Life, who's been ferreting out the most offbeat, delicious, out-of-
the-way restaurants, bars, and coffeehouses in Tokyo for over twenty
years. Mike was kind enough to point me in the direction of a few
places that have been around since 1972 or earlier (you can find
links on the "Places" page of my website, linked below), and as
always his recommendations were a pleasure to research and hugely
enriched the book:

http://www.tokyofoodlife.com
http://www.barryeisler.com/photo_places.php

Nobuo Kamioka, Professor of English Language and Cultures,
Gakushuin University, kindly recommended several books of

photographs of 1960s and 1970s Tokyo that were especially helpful as I tried to imagine the city of forty years ago. More on these in the Author's Note.

If you want to see your humble author using the kind of circle drag Rain deploys in Ueno, here's your video. That's uber-martial artist, teacher, and writer Wim Demeere showing me how to make the drag nastier. If you recognize Wim's name, it might be because I named a character after him who appeared in several of the Rain books. Rain finally took him out when they met face-to-face, but if it had been the real Demeere, I think Rain might have been in trouble. Check out Wim's Rain fan fiction on his great self-defense blog:

http://www.wimsblog.com
http://www.youtube.com/watch?v=ODCfOWTy8po#at=225

While we're on the subject of combat techniques, as with everything else that appears in the book I've tried to convey Rain's chapter 1 suplay as vividly as possible. But if you want to see the move in the real world as well as in your imagination, here are two nice examples—the first executed by a seven-year-old!

http://www.youtube.com/watch?v=QLkUbYTSexs
http://www.flowrestling.org/coverage/249282-Journeymen-
    Freestyle-Duals/video/632901-Araoz-5pt-Throw-SUPLAY

Also: for more on the Tueller Drill "21 feet" rule, here are two videos. I practiced this kind of drill with Simunition at Peyton Quinn's Rocky Mountain Combat Applications Training institute, and it is eye-opening. Twenty-one feet is a lot closer than you might think:

http://www.youtube.com/watch?v=jwHYRBNc9r8

http://www.youtube.com/watch?v=FL1zX-SrBH0

To the extent I get violence right in my fiction, I have many great instructors to thank, including Massad Ayoob, Tony Blauer, and Rory Miller. Their courses and other materials are superb and I highly recommend them for anyone who wants to be safer in the world, or just to create more realistic violence on the page:

http://www.massadayoobgroup.com
http://www.tonyblauer.com
http://www.chirontraining.com

Rain's notion of "Don't insult him, don't challenge him, don't threaten him, don't deny it's happening, give him a face-saving exit" is courtesy of Peyton Quinn of the Rocky Mountain Combat Applications Training institute. Another great course:

http://www.rmcat.com

The flying triangle strangle in chapter 3 is courtesy of Dave Camarillo's excellent book *Guerilla Jiu-Jitsu: Revolutionizing Brazilian Jiu-Jitsu*, a must for any serious grappler:

http://www.amazon.com/Guerrilla-Jiu-Jitsu-Revolutionizing-Brazilian/dp/0977731588/ref=sr_1_2?s=books&ie=UTF8&qid=1374452406&sr=1-2

I don't know much about electricity, but learned a lot from this website on fatal electric shocks:

http://engineering.dartmouth.edu/safety/electrical/TheFatal-Current.html

MythBusters was hugely helpful in helping me understand that yes, a dropped appliance really can electrocute you in the bathtub. Note, though, that the *MythBusters* didn't get everything quite right. In fact, electricity in fresh water can be more dangerous than electricity in salt:

> http://dsc.discovery.com/tv-shows/mythbusters/videos/appliances-in-the-bath-minimyth.htm
> http://www.boatus.com/seaworthy/magazine/2013/july/electric-shock-drowning-explained.asp

Tom Hayses and Dan Levin were generous in sharing their expertise on all matters electrical and helping me tune up the electrocution sequence. I'm not particularly technical and might have gotten something wrong anyway, but not for lack of trying on their part.

For Rain's thoughts on the effects of proximity in killing, I'm again indebted to Lt. Col. Dave Grossman for his disturbing, original book, *On Killing: The Psychological Cost of Learning to Kill in War and Society*:

> http://www.amazon.com/On-Killing-Psychological-Learning-ebook/dp/B003XREUV2/ref=tmm_kin_title_0?ie=UTF8&qid=1375672344&sr=1-1

Dr. Yoshikatsu Eto and Dr. Hiroyuki Ida, both of Tokyo's Jikei University School of Medicine, were generous in providing a tour of the institution's facilities and in answering my unusual questions about the disposition of the dead at and through the hospital. Obviously, the shenanigans that occur in the hospital's morgue in the story are the product only of my (twisted, yes, I know) imagination, and in any event reflect a security posture from an era much more innocent than the current one.

Once again, Jeroen ten Berge and Rob Siders provided terrific cover design and formatting services:

http://jeroentenberge.com
https://52novels.com

Thanks as always to the extraordinarily eclectic group of "foodies with a violence problem" who hang out at Marc "Animal" MacYoung's and Dianna Gordon's No Nonsense Self-Defense, for good humor, good fellowship, and a ton of insights, particularly regarding the real costs of violence:

http://www.nononsenseselfdefense.com

Thanks to Naomi Andrews, Jeroen ten Berge, Alan Eisler, Koichiro Fukasawa, Dan Gillmor, Montie Guthrie, Tom Hayse, Charlotte Herscher, Mike Killman, Lori Kupfer, Dan Levin, Lara Perkins, Ken Rosenberg, Johanna Rosenbohm, Ted Schlein, and Alan Turkus for helpful comments on the manuscript.

Most of all, thanks to my wife, Laura, for damn near a quarter century of unwavering support, belief, and confidence, in every kind of weather. And awesome editorial, too. Thanks, babe, for everything.

Author's Note

Part of my writing method has always involved extensive on-site research for all the locales I use, but obviously *Graveyard of Memories*, set in 1972, presented a challenge in this regard. The challenge was multiplied by my desire to use real places—bars and jazz clubs and coffeehouses—that readers could visit if they wished.

I decided on a threefold solution: use existing places that have been around since at least 1972; concentrate the action in the older parts of Tokyo, chiefly in the east of the city, which have changed less over the decades than those in the more cosmopolitan west; and peruse photo books of 1960s and 1970s Tokyo to get a better feel for what's different and what is largely unchanged. For lovers of the city, I recommend these books (the translations, doubtless inelegant or worse, are mine):

東京のちょっと昔—30年前の下町風景, 若目田 幸平
　　(*A Little in the Past of Tokyo: Images of the Downtown 30 Years
　　Ago*, Kouhei Wakameda)
東京—写真集・都市の変貌の物語1948~2000, 石井 実
　　(*Tokyo Photo Book: The Story of a Changing City, 1948–2000*,
　　Minoru Ishii)
1960年代の東京・路面電車が走る水の都の記憶, 池田 信
　　(*1960s Tokyo: Memories of a City of Trams That Ran Like Water*,
　　Akira Ikeda)

The result, as always, is a series of locations that are described as I found them—but also as best as I could imagine they looked and felt when Rain was only twenty.

That said, here and there I had to cheat a little, and this is the place to come clean. So: although Taro, the jazz club to which Rain takes Sayaka in Shinjuku's Kabukichō, is long gone, its successor, Body & Soul, also opened by Kyoko Seki, is alive and well in Minami Aoyama. It's one of Tokyo's best and worth the trip:

http://www.bodyandsoul.co.jp

Also, as far as I know, the exterior of Kabaya Coffee in Yanaka is unchanged from at least 1938, when the shop opened in the tiny building it still occupies. The interior, however, has been updated. Accordingly, Rain's description of the inside of the shop is a product only of my imagination. But I recommend the shop, the kind of *kissaten*—old-style coffeehouse—found only in Japan, and also recommend the entire Yanesen (Yanaka, Nezu, Sendagi) area where you'll find it:

http://www.toothpicnations.co.uk/my-blog/?p=6778

And here's some more information on the places that appear in the book . . .

Kamiya in Asakusa, where Rain meets with his case officer Sean McGraw after getting jumped in Ueno, is Tokyo's oldest western-style bar. Big, boisterous, and unpretentious, with communal tables. If you're a foreigner, you might be a bit of a novelty. Try the *denki buran*—electric brandy—or stick with the draft beer:

http://travel.cnn.com/tokyo/drink/kamiya-bar-849180
http://www.kamiya-bar.com

A nice photo tour of contemporary Uguisudani, where Rain first meets Sayaka at one of the area's numerous love hotels:

http://pingmag.jp/2013/03/25/welcome-to-uguisudani/

Taihō Chuuka Ryōri (Chinese Cuisine), the second place Rain meets McGraw:

http://tabelog.com/tokyo/A1316/A131602/13001670/

Lion Coffee in Shibuya, where Rain retrieves a critical file:

http://blog.uchujin.co.uk/2010/09/lion-cafe---tokyo's-worst-"best-kept"-secret/
http://www.tokyofoodlife.com/?p=1829

A wonderful photo tour of the Arakawa line, Tokyo's last surviving public tram:

http://ldersot.smugmug.com/photos/swfpopup.mg?AlbumID=25699252&AlbumKey=mLnMtm

And another:

http://lifetoreset.wordpress.com/2012/09/01/aboard-toden-arakawa-one-of-tokyos-remaining-street-car/

An article on some of Tokyo's best *sentō*. This is where I learned of Daikoku-yu, site of the electrocution hit (and a great place to visit for an afternoon soak):

http://travel.cnn.com/tokyo/visit/sento-spectacular-tokyos-
amazing-public-baths-199776

A nice article about a walk through Kita-Senju, home of Daikoku-
yu *sentō*:

http://www.japantimes.co.jp/life/2011/01/09/environment/
the-narrow-roads-of-senju/#.UdAtQhaHoUw

Café de l'Ambre, a classic Tokyo *kissaten*, and a good place for a
dead drop, too:

http://www.tokyofoodlife.com/?p=323

Kabaya Coffee—another classic McGraw favors for dead-drop com-
munications:

http://www.timeout.jp/en/tokyo/venue/8951/Kabaya-Coffee

A very cool photo blog of the Nakagin Capsule Tower:

http://www.ignant.de/2013/09/05/1972-by-noritaka-minami/

And a report from two western architects who managed to secure
and live in one of the apartments there:

http://www.domusweb.it/content/domusweb/en/architec-
ture/2013/05/29/the_metabolist_routine.html

Here are some amazing photos of student demonstrations in Tokyo,
1968–1971:

http://www.magnumphotos.com/C.aspx?VP3=SearchResult&
ALID=2TYRYDMD2HVR

For inspiration about the vibe of Tokyo's 1972 jazz scene, I loved this photograph of a young Terumasa Hino, along with a few other legends of jazz—Shinjuku Dug, 1968:

http://openers.jp/culture/tips_event/artdish0617.html

And Hino's "Alone, Alone and Alone," the piece he and his quartet perform at Taro in the book, was wonderful to write to. Gorgeous, haunting music:

http://www.youtube.com/watch?v=Nn-LQpFhGIY

Politics

More on the CIA's long-standing financial role in Japanese politics:

http://www.nytimes.com/1994/10/09/world/cia-spent-millions-to-support-japanese-right-in-50-s-and-60-s.html

The CIA underwriting foreign politicians is nothing new. Here's a recent revelation, this one from Afghanistan:

http://www.nytimes.com/2013/04/29/world/asia/cia-delivers-cash-to-afghan-leaders-office.html

A brief history of the Lockheed bribery scandal in Japan:

http://en.wikipedia.org/wiki/Lockheed_bribery_scandals#Japan

A brief history of the Church Committee. Senator Church said in 1975, "I know the capacity that is there to make tyranny total in America, and we must see to it that [the National Security Agency] and all agencies that possess this technology operate within the law and under proper supervision, so that we never cross over that abyss. That is the abyss from which there is no return."

http://en.wikipedia.org/wiki/Church_Committee

Today, for any overseas behavior the U.S. government might want import to America, it has only to cite Senator Lindsey Graham, scholar, savior of the Constitution, and inventor of the profoundly Jeffersonian slogan "The homeland is the battlefield":

http://www.washingtonpost.com/blogs/right-turn/wp/2013/
04/19/sen-lindsey-graham-boston-bombing-is-exhibit-a-of-
why-the-homeland-is-the-battlefield/

About the Author

PHOTOGRAPH BY NAOMI BOOKER, 2007

Barry Eisler spent three years in a covert position with the CIA's Directorate of Operations, then worked as a technology lawyer and start-up executive in Silicon Valley and Japan, earning his black belt at the Kodokan International Judo Center along the way. Eisler's bestselling thrillers have won the Barry Award and the Gumshoe Award for Best Thriller of the Year, have been included in numerous "Best Of" lists, have been translated into nearly twenty languages, and include the #1 bestseller *The Detachment*. Eisler lives in the San Francisco Bay Area and, when he's not writing novels, blogs about torture, civil liberties, and the rule of law. http://www.barryeisler.com